Katie's Journey

Havoc in Wyoming

Part 2: Katie's Journey

Millie Copper

Written by Millie Copper

Edited by Ameryn Tucker

Proofread by Light Hand Proofreading

Cover design by Dauntless Cover Design

Original cover design by Kesandra Adams

Also by Millie Copper

Now Available

Havoc in Wyoming: Part 1, Caldwell's Homestead

Havoc in Wyoming: Part 2, Katie's Journey

Havoc in Wyoming: Part 3, Mollie's Quest

Havoc Begins: A Havoc in Wyoming Story

Havoc in Wyoming: Part 4, Shields and Ramparts

Havoc in Wyoming: Part 5, Fowler's Snare

Havoc Rises: A Havoc in Wyoming Story

Havoc in Wyoming: Part 6, Pestilence in the Darkness

Christmas on the Mountain: A Havoc in Wyoming Novella

Havoc Peaks: A Havoc in Wyoming Story

Havoc in Wyoming: Part 7, My Refuge and Fortress

Stretchy Beans: Nutritious, Economic Meals the Easy Way

Stock the Real Food Pantry: A Handbook for Making the Most of Your Pantry

Design a Dish: Save Your Food Dollars

Real Food Hits the Road: Budget Friendly Tips, Ideas, and Recipes for Enjoying Real Food Away from Home

Join My Reader's Club!

Receive a complimentary copy of *Wyoming Refuge: A Havoc in Wyoming Prequel*. As part of my reader's club, you'll be the first to know about new releases and specials. I also share info on books I'm reading, preparedness tips, and more. Please sign up on my website:

MillieCopper.com

Who's Who

Katrina "Katie" Andrews: Twenty-one-year-old college student working toward a bachelor's degree in graphic design. She's living on her own in Manhattan, Kansas—at least, that's what her parents think. Not wanting to disappoint them, she hasn't mentioned her boyfriend moved in several months ago.

Leo Burnett: Katie's boyfriend. A business major at K-State, construction worker, and Marine. Leo has been studying to become an EMT but isn't sure if that's the route he wants to go.

Mollie Caldwell: Wife to Jake and mom to daughters Sarah, Angela, Calley, and Katie plus a ten-year-old son, Malcolm. With a full-time work-from-home job, homeschooling Malcolm, and their small farm, she keeps busy.

Jake Caldwell: Single until age thirty-seven, he married Mollie and suddenly became a dad to four girls. A couple years later they added their son. Jake juggles work, a farm, and family life—sometimes it's a struggle.

Angela Carpenter: Katie's older sister, wife to Tim, and mom to two-year-old Gavin, living in Casper, Wyoming. Angela and Katie are very close.

Calley Curtis: Two year's older than Katie, the sisters have had a rocky relationship. Things seem to be better now. Calley and her husband, Mike, make their home in Casper. Mike's parents, Roy and Deanne, live next door. Mike's recently single sister, Sheila Stapleton, also lives in Casper. They're a tight-knit family, at least it seems so on the surface.

Sarah Garrett: Katie's oldest sister and wife to Tate. They recently moved less than two hours away from Katie's parents—neighbors by

Wyoming standards. Tate's parents, Keith and Lois, along with his older sister, Karen, are visiting from Oklahoma.

Alvin and Dodie Caldwell: Jake's parents, Katie's adopted grandparents. They're both in their seventies and fiercely independent. They live in Prospect, Wyoming, near Jake. As things progress, they worry about Jake's brother, Robert, and his wife and children living in California. Have they been severely affected by these tragedies?

Doris and Evan Snyder: Neighbor and good friends of Katie's folks. Evan is a retired deputy sheriff, having been part of the Specialized Services Division. Doris is retired from both the Navy and a government job. She insists she wasn't a spy or anything, but she doesn't talk about the work she used to do.

Dan Morse: The community bully. He tends to make a show of knowing it all. Evan calls Dan "an imbecile who lacks a shred of common sense."

Terry, Belinda, and TJ Bosco: Community members. Terry stands up to Dan at the community meetings. Belinda, a nurse practitioner, is fourth generation Bakerville and related to the founders of the community. TJ is friends with Malcolm. Belinda's mom, Tammy, a retired labor and delivery nurse, and dad, Tom, retired hunting and fishing guide, also live in the community.

Phil and Kelley Hudson: Community members. Katie's mom, Mollie, considers Kelley one of her closest friends. Phil, retired Coast Guard, is a leader of the community. Kelley is a psychiatric nurse practitioner, retired from the Commissioned Corps.

David, Betty, Noah, and Andrew Hammer: Neighbors and friends of the Caldwells. The Hammers are Texas natives recently transplanted to Wyoming. They love the cooler weather and wide-open spaces. David and Betty are both retired. Noah is sixteen and Andrew is in his early twenties. Two more adult children live in Texas with their spouses and a grandbaby. Their oldest son lives back east.

Olivia Hatch: Nearby neighbor of Mollie and Jake. Katie and Olivia become fast friends. Olivia's son, Tony, is friends with Malcolm, and her young daughter, Lily, loves everyone. Olivia's husband, Jason, is away for work.

Chapter 1

Thursday, Day 1

The punch comes in hard and fast, straight for my nose. I block with my right forearm while raising my foot to catch him below the belt. Bullseye. He folds into my kick. I grab him by the head and raise my knee to his chin. One, two, three, four times. While he's bent over, I quickly step around him and grab him by the neck.

"Wait, wait, wait, did you feel the tap to your stomach? He just shoved a knife in your gut."

I wipe the sweat from my eyebrow.

"Katie? You okay?"

"Sure, Master. Just catching my breath. I didn't feel the tap to my stomach. Thought I had him this time." I gesture toward Leo, my sparring partner and boyfriend.

"It was definitely close," Leo says with a smile, while Master Lewis nods.

"You're doing really well. It's hard to believe you've only been at this a few months," Master says. "Of course, staying after for the private class when you can is a help, plus practicing on your own. I think that's good for tonight. See you guys on Tuesday."

We attend Krav Maga class, the fighting system of the Israeli Defense Forces, on Tuesdays and Thursdays, provided I don't have a shift at work. It's both an amazing defense mechanism and a serious workout. I never thought I could push my body so hard. When Leo and I first started talking about preparedness, thanks to my mom and stepdad, self-defense was a topic that came up. I knew I wanted to be able to protect myself if the need arose.

Years ago—after my dad died and before my mom married Jake—my mom, three sisters, and I took a mom and daughter self-defense course. We went to a place used for Girl Scout and church camps, with the classes starting on Friday evening and ending late Saturday. We even stayed overnight in dorm rooms, sleeping on bunk beds.

I was very young then, only seven, and one of the youngest people at the retreat. I still had a great time and learned some good stuff. After that weekend, we'd practice at home. Logically, I should've always practiced with Calley since we were close to the same age, but we'd have different partners and rotate, so sometimes Mom was my partner.

We'd pair up, with the fifth person acting as commentary to give a different perspective. From something we'd learned in the class, yelling "*Fire!*" became our call to action. The fifth person would yell it out, and we'd go at it—trying to be careful not to hurt each other by going at half speed and not really connecting. Of course, once in a while, the connections did happen.

Soon, other interests took over and we stopped sparring as a group, but sometimes Mom and I'd still practice together. It was kind of a fun thing we did on our own.

Several times over the years, Mom has encouraged me to take another self-defense class. She and Calley took a class together a year or two ago, and it refreshed some of the stuff they learned in the past. Last fall Mom; my stepdad, Jake; and my little brother, Malcolm, started taking a martial arts class. They love it.

Mom suggested I look into Krav Maga since it's considered to be a very effective form of self-defense. It's also very trendy right now, and many places teach it. There are three gyms and a college group teaching it here in Manhattan, Kansas.

A little research led me to believe only one gym was legit; the others were not teaching true Krav Maga. Not necessarily a bad thing, but I wanted the real McCoy. Leo agrees we made the right choice in our gym.

The primary goal in Krav Maga is to neutralize your threat as quickly as possible, doing whatever is needed to preserve your life, but never doing more than is necessary. I had a hard time with the aggressiveness and simultaneous offensive and defensive maneuvers. I was afraid I'd hurt someone. Not in the class—we don't aim to hurt in training drills—but in real life.

How funny is that? I'd only use Krav Maga if *my* life were in danger, and I was afraid of hurting my attacker? I worked through that pretty quickly. Now, if someone comes after me, they'll get exactly what they deserve. I won't go down without a big fight. A BIG. HUGE. FIGHT.

In addition to the classes and private lessons, Leo and I spar together several times a week. While I'm new to this, Leo is a Marine and learned similar fighting techniques. Even though I'm much smaller than him and he's better trained, the moves I've learned can still hurt. I discovered this rather quickly when, in the heat of battle, I forgot to pull my punch and gave Leo a bloody nose. Oops.

It's about ten o'clock. I'm chilling on the sofa, exhausted and a little sore after tonight's practice. Leo and I are both on our tablets. I'm looking at information about Billings, Montana, since my sister Sarah and her husband, Tate, moved there last month to be closer to our mom and Jake. I like the idea of being around family, so Leo and I are talking about checking it out.

We live in Manhattan, Kansas, while attending K-State. Well, I'm still attending; he graduated a few weeks ago. I'll graduate in December with a degree in graphic design. At that point, we plan to move . . . somewhere.

I do somewhat have my hopes set on moving to a warmer environment without snow, perhaps Las Vegas, but we're keeping our options open. Over the Fourth of July, we're going to visit my folks and Sarah. It'll be the first time they meet Leo. And when we come clean on the depth of our relationship.

A Facebook notification pop ups. What's this about?

I turn to Leo. "Have there been terrorist attacks?"

"What?"

"My supervisor just canceled the Sip and Paint I was supposed to facilitate Saturday because of terrorist attacks. Here it is. *'Planes crash while landing at LAX, JFK, and ORD. Terrorists suspected.'* Oh no, Leo. It looks bad."

"I see it here." Leo pulls up a news channel online and turns on the live streaming.

"What we know at the moment: at 10:22 eastern time, American Airlines flight 2245 from Miami to JFK crashed while attempting to land. At 10:34, United flight UA343 from Phoenix crashed at Chicago O'Hare while attempting to land. An unidentified flight into LAX crashed at 10:42 eastern. An unidentified flight into DFW crashed at 10:48 eastern. At 10:52 eastern, all flights were ordered to be grounded. Those in the air have been diverted to the nearest airport. At this point, we believe these events to all be related."

Four crashes? The alert only mentioned three. The news guy looks away from the camera for a moment. He touches his ear and shakes his head.

"Friends, we're receiving reports of a fifth crash moments ago in Miami. We don't have any details. With five crashes within just over half an hour, we fully believe these to be related."

Leo and I look at each other. Leo speaks first, "An event like this, it's going to be as hard on our country as 9/11 was. I hope we'll see people pulling together the same way they did then."

"I was only five when 9/11 happened," I tell Leo. "I remember seeing it on the news, but my mom didn't let us watch much. She was upset for days. And I remember the first time we drove into Portland after it, and I saw the tall skyscrapers and asked if a plane would crash into them. Mom said, 'No, of course not,' and that she hoped nothing like that would ever happen again."

Leo pulls me close. He says nothing, simply holds me quietly. We remain this way for many minutes. The news report is still playing on the tablet. The announcer says the president will be addressing the nation soon. I think of Mom. She's away from home this week, in Oregon for work. She flew out and is now stuck there. If this is an attack, how could they stop it from happening again?

The newscaster makes what sounds like a choking sound or a sob. He starts speaking, barely controlling his emotions. *"We are receiving reports of multiple explosions going off near JFK. These are separate from the plane crashes and are possibly large car bombs. Again, what is believed to be multiple car bombs have been detonated near the John F. Kennedy Airport. JFK was the site of an airline crash less than an hour ago. It's hard to believe these are unrelated events. We're expecting an address from the president any moment."*

Leo holds me tighter. I'm crying now. I don't know much about car bombs. I don't know how big of an area could be affected. I ask Leo if he knows.

"I really think it depends on the size and how it's constructed. The truck bomb set off at the Federal Building in Oklahoma did a considerable amount of damage, and something like 170 people were killed."

My text indicator sounds, causing me to jump. It has to be either Mom or Jake. I'm right. It's Mom. She sent a group text to my siblings—Sarah, Angela, Calley—and me. I read it aloud.

"Jake and I are enacting Plan A. You should think about doing this also. We don't know what tomorrow will bring. We included information on Plan A in your backpack on the sheet: Smart Practices. I love you."

A few months ago, Mom and Jake sent me a very large backpack filled with items they thought I'd need in order to get to their home in Northern Wyoming—they made me a bug-out bag. Besides for physical items, they included maps and notes they thought would be helpful.

"Should I grab it, Katie?"

"What, Leo?"

"Did you want me to grab the paper? It's in the outside pocket of the backpack?" Leo asks as he's walking to the coat closet.

"Yes," I gulp out between sobs.

"Oh, hey, it looks like the president's coming on. I'll read this after he's done."

He repeats some of what we already know about the first two crashes. We hadn't heard the details of the final three. He briefs us on those and the car bomb at JFK, then continues briefly about our great nation and how we *will* overcome this. His speech lasts only a few minutes total.

Leo turns down the sound on the tablet. He leaves the streaming report running and angles it so we can see it as he reads Mom and Jake's *Plan A* aloud.

"Sometimes you may need to do a little extra. If you notice a local or national situation that could turn concerning, you should immediately do a few extra things, as long as doing these things will be safe. Jake and I call this Plan A.

"If we're enacting Plan A for a nationwide event, we'll let you know. You can enact Plan A on your own at any time. You may find yourself in a Plan A situation we don't know about.

"One example could be a protest in your town. You live in a college town and could have student protests. I'd encourage you not to participate in these. Even though they'll likely be nonviolent and

you're within your constitutional rights to civilly protest, these nonviolent protests can turn violent in the blink of an eye."

Leo drops the sheet and gives me a nod. "I guess I never thought about that."

I lift a shoulder in response and motion back to the paper.

He gives me another nod before continuing.

"Plus, it's possible not everyone will have the same agenda. Some people attend protests with the sole desire of violence starting so they can loot. And, of course, the Aggieville riots happened right there in Manhattan and could happen again. Here is what our Plan A looks like:

- *We drive into town, taking our gas cans with us.*
- *We take out as much money from our bank's ATM as they allow. You know we keep quite a bit of cash at home, but if there's a Plan A event, we want as much cash on hand as possible. There may be a run on banks, banks may declare a "holiday," they may limit transaction amounts, etc. We're at the mercy of the bank, and they have our money. If we're wrong and nothing happens— no biggie. We still have cash to use or we can put it back in the bank when things have calmed down.*
- *Next stop is the grocery store. We keep a list of things we think of and will shop from this list, adding other things that seem appropriate. For you, we'd suggest more food. Easy-to-cook or no-cook things and shelf-stable with some nutrition. You can always pick up the standard milk, bread, and eggs too. People tend to buy up these things and the shelves may be bare. Just remember, if the power goes out, eat the fridge items first. It may be smart to turn the eggs into hard-boiled eggs as soon as you return home. What else do you need? Toothpaste, a toothbrush, Advil, a small blanket? Pick them up. You can always use these things, so buying them now causes no financial loss. Do you need a propane canister for your one-burner stove, included in your bug-out bag? Most likely you do. Even*

if you have one on hand, a second is only a couple bucks. Warm chili tastes better than cold chili.

- *Depending on the time of day, we may decide to stop at a sporting goods store, hardware store, or lumber yard. Think long and hard about additional stops. Get in and get out of these places so you can return to the safety of your home.*

- *Finally, fill your gas tank and your gas cans."*

When Leo finishes reading, he looks at me and asks if I have any questions.

"I don't, but I think we should do it. We'd best get going." I'm pretty sure SuperMart is open all night but briefly wonder if they might close because of tonight's attacks.

"Uh-oh," Leo says, gazing at his tablet. He turns it in my direction.

BREAKING NEWS:
BOMBS HAVE NOW BEEN DETONATED NEAR
ALL AIRPORTS AFFECTED BY TONIGHT'S CRASHES

Leo turns up the sound.

"We now have reports of bombs going off near all of the airports with earlier plane crashes. About fifteen minutes ago, we confirmed several bombs detonated in or near JFK. About seven minutes ago, bombs went off almost simultaneously near LAX, DFW, Chicago O'Hare, and Miami International Airports.

"We're not yet receiving reports of casualties but expect the numbers to be quite high. The bombs appear to have targeted first responders and the multitudes of people still at the airports after all flights were canceled due to the crashes."

I'm crying again, and Leo takes a moment to console me. "We gotta go, Katie. Your folks' *Plan A* sounds like it may be necessary instead of just a good idea."

We take Leo's truck. The streets are quiet, most likely with everyone glued to their TVs.

I have to admit, when my bug-out bag first arrived, I was disappointed. It was February, and I thought maybe it was a belated Valentine's gift. The package was huge, so I had visions of a giant box of chocolates, even though I haven't received any sort of Valentine's gift since I was in elementary school. A girl could hope.

Mom started getting interested in what she calls "planning for an unknown future" while I was still in junior high school. I now know the popular term is prepping, which I suppose makes my mom and stepdad preppers.

It started after a storm left us, and the rest of our county and surrounding area, without power for several days. I was in sixth grade then and thought it was a fine time. The electricity went out on Sunday and didn't come back until Saturday morning. We had the entire week off from school.

Mom and Jake made sure we used everything in the fridge and the few things we had in the freezer those first days. Mom had frozen a lot of wild blackberries, and while she did try to get those used up, within a couple of days the bottom of the freezer looked like blackberry soup.

Jake said we were very fortunate the water never shut off. It was some kind of gravity-fed system and worked even without power. Another community nearby had a similar system, but they did lose water when a tree fell on something important. That was the first time I heard Jake use what has become one of his favorite phrases: water is life.

The storm produced hurricane-force winds, and there were fallen trees everywhere. We couldn't even get out of our rural neighborhood the first couple days because of the downed trees. Once the winds stopped, people started clearing the roads.

We took a drive into the town of Alto—our nearest metropolis, about fifteen miles away—and were surprised at how terrible the town looked. Many of the store windows had blown out and were either boarded up or in the process of being boarded up. Pretty much every store in town was closed because of the damage and/or lack of electricity. Jake said it was good we had filled up both the cars on Friday, before the storm hit, since none of the gas stations were open.

One of the best things about the power outage was Mom reading to us each night. As an avid reader, she had a large collection of books. She read some mystery story to us, which I can't even remember now, but it was so wonderful just to sit in the living room and listen to her read. She had a battery-operated lantern by her, giving out just enough light to read, and we had candles around the room so the rest of us could somewhat see.

While it was a fun and easy week for me and my sisters, I know Mom and Jake breathed a sigh of relief when the power came back on. The next week, things were mostly back to normal for us, but many people in the area had lots of damage to their houses or businesses, and their normal didn't return for some time.

After the storm, Mom said she wanted us to have some things in place in case something similar happened. She started doing internet research, and what she learned was the beginning of her interest in being prepared. At first, she didn't share much of what she discovered with me and my sisters, but we learned enough to see Mom was really worried about the things that could happen.

I don't think she ever really thought anything terribly bad could happen. Even as they became more serious with prepping, she and Jake would still laugh sometimes about how silly they were. A few years ago, they started a thirty-acre homestead, setting the entire place up to be a retreat for our family and close friends.

After that, Mom and Jake both made several jokes about their tinfoil hats. Now I wonder if they might not have been the smart ones. What did Heller say? *Just because you're paranoid, it doesn't mean they're not out to get you.*

We stop at my bank first. I balanced my account earlier today and know I have $162 in my checking and $578 in savings. I take $300 out of savings and do a transfer of $270 to my checking. I don't think the transfer will reflect until tomorrow, but I think having it in checking will make it easier to get to than in savings—in case I need to use my debit card at a store or gas station. I leave the money in my checking to use at the store.

I also have cash on me from my server tips last night. I serve at an upscale restaurant four nights a week. While cash tips aren't super common, they still happen on occasion. Tips left on credit cards are added to my paycheck, but I try to stash the cash, calling it my discretionary fund.

At home, I have a few hundred I've collected, mostly in singles, and a large amount of change. I tend to use my tips for my everyday needs like groceries and gas. The larger bills get used first, and I put the change and singles in a coffee can. I'd banded the singles together a few days ago, so I have an idea how much I have of those, but I haven't counted the change for a while.

In addition to my server job, I'm doing a paid internship, twenty hours a week, at a graphic design firm. This is my second summer working for the firm, and while it's very educational, it's also extremely challenging. Translating what's in a client's head to the final product isn't always easy. One of the big things I'm learning is how to work with people to turn a rough idea into something that translates well and can sell.

We go to Leo's bank next. While Leo and I are both very careful with our money, it's for different reasons. I'm careful because I have to be. I pretty much live paycheck to paycheck as the epitome of a starving college student. Leo, on the other hand, is just cheap—or, as he insists, *frugal.*

Leo's twenty-seven and just graduated from K-State a few weeks ago with a degree in business. Now that he has the degree, he's kind of regretting it. He wishes he would've followed his heart and done something different. In high school he played football and planned to go on to college. He even had a scholarship offer.

A few weeks after his high school graduation, his parents died in a car accident. He forfeited his scholarship and decided against college. He says he didn't do much of anything for a couple of months, and then one day, he walked into the Marine recruiter's office and became a Marine.

The first year after he finished active duty, he did construction. Then he started college at K-State. Leo grew up in a small town in Southern Kansas near the Oklahoma and Missouri state lines and knew all about K-State from a young age. It was even the school he was accepted at when his parents died.

Selling his folks' assets and using the life insurance policies they had, plus the money he'd stashed while in the Marines, left him able to pay his way through college.

He isn't rolling in money, but he's comfortable. He still watches his funds very carefully. We moved in together a few months ago. Before, he lived with three other guys to save money.

Leo is amazingly handsome, with light brown hair cropped short on the sides but with a little length on top, and the most amazing green eyes. He's a full foot taller than me, at six foot four, and muscular. He's very athletic, and in addition to the martial arts classes, he jogs, lifts weights, plays basketball with friends, and enjoys long bike rides— which is something we have in common.

Our next stop is SuperMart. We've brought Mom's list along and use it as a guide to fill two carts. We add a few extra things: a tarp, a few emergency blankets, big packages of toilet paper and paper towels, and several cans of fruit. I barely pay attention to what Leo's putting in the cart he's pushing. One of his sporting goods purchases catches my eye.

"What's that for, Leo?"

"What? The fanny pack?"

"Yeah. After my bug-out bag arrived and we started getting things ready, you bought a decent backpack. Do you really need a fanny pack too?"

"Maybe. I thought it might be handy for carrying ammo, which is where we're heading next. It's not quite what I had in mind, but I don't see what I'm looking for here. In fact, let's grab a fanny pack for you too." I'm not sure why he's buying me a bag for carrying ammo since I don't even have a gun, but I say nothing.

Next, Leo buys several boxes and varieties of ammo. I hate to admit that, other than a .22 handgun and .22 rifle, I have no idea what else he may have in the way of guns. While we're there, he buys a large knife in a sheath to go on his belt. I'm pretty sure he already has one of these in his backpack since we somewhat modeled his after the pack Mom and Jake made for me, and I have a giant knife.

When we finally get to the checkout, both carts are very full. I'm wondering if my checking account has enough to pay for my cart. I'll use my tip money and the money I pulled out of my savings if needed.

As Leo's unloading his cart, he tells me to start adding my stuff. He's going to pay using his credit card. I nod in agreement but ask if I should buy something to get a little more cash. I'd planned to use my money for these purchases, and more cash might be good.

"That's a good idea," he says. "I'll do the same thing." We finish loading the checkout belt, then put the divider out so he can do his second transaction and I can do mine.

The cashier asks if we're stocking up after the terrorist attacks. Leo said it seemed like it might be a good idea to get here tonight since tomorrow people might be on edge. She nods and says she's off in fifteen minutes and plans to buy things before she leaves.

When it's all said and done, we have three carts' worth to put in his truck and we each have another hundred in cash. As we head to the parking lot, I notice there are quite a few more cars than were here before. I'm glad we got here when we did.

Next stop: the gas station. Leo fills his tank, which takes very little, then tops off the sixty-gallon fuel tank in the bed of the pickup. This was another purchase made after Mom and Jake sent my bug-out bag. They suggested I buy a couple gas cans so I'd have an option for more fuel in case I had to drive home in a hurry. While I did buy two five-gallon cans, Leo bought a ginormous tank for his truck.

He's added stabilizer to this but uses a siphon thing to pull gas out once a week, adds that to his truck, and adds fresh gas to the tank. He told me, since it's diesel, it should stay fresh longer than gas would. He has a two-gallon fuel can he uses when transferring gas from the sixty-gallon tank to the truck. He fills this also.

The convenience store is open, so he goes in and buys two gas cans, filling them for my SUV. All of the sudden, I wish I would've brought my car, too, so I could fill it fully. Leo must be able to read my mind.

"I'll get you home, we'll get all this stuff inside, then I'll take your car and fill it tonight."

"Thank you, Leo. I'd like that very much."

It's a few minutes before 1:00 a.m. In some ways, I feel this started days ago instead of just a few hours ago. Leo and I get everything in the apartment, and I start putting things away as best I can while he takes my SUV to the gas station.

I'm in a second-floor walk-up—meaning there's no elevator. Normally this isn't an issue, but with our magnitude of purchases, we made many trips up and down tonight. We tried to be very quiet so as not to wake everyone else. There are still many lights on, and some windows showed the blue of a television screen. I quickly discover, with the food stores we've been working on recently and tonight's stuff, we're out of room.

Now I'm kicking myself, wondering why I didn't think of buying totes. Totes would be great to put these things in. I consider calling Leo to see if he can grab some but decide he's likely almost back. About twenty seconds later, the slight scraping of his key in the lock confirms my thought.

He agrees totes would be good and says we can get them in the morning. He also says he'd like to go to the sporting goods store for a few things, then cryptically adds, *"As long as it seems like a safe thing to do."*

12

Chapter 2

Friday, Day 2

I roll over and look at the clock. 9:00 a.m. I'm still exhausted and wonder why. Then, last night comes back to me—the plane crashes and the explosions. How many people were killed? We didn't hear any firm numbers last night, but there were estimates of several thousand between the planes and the ground explosions.

What's that noise? Leo? He's at work. My heart's pounding as I quietly get out of bed and tiptoe to the door. It's slightly ajar, allowing me to slip through and into the hallway. There's the noise again. Humming? I think about grabbing the zapper stick—a walking stick shocker thing included in my bug-out bag—from the closet.

Darn it, though. The closet door squeaks, and I'd lose the element of surprise. I'm starting to think a handgun by my bed would be a good idea. My cell phone? Jeez, I should've at least picked it up off the nightstand. I'll take a quick peek.

Keeping my body hidden, I stay against the wall. I bend slightly, then ease my head out so I can look toward the living room and kitchen.

Leo! What's he doing here?

"You scared the daylights out of me. What are you doing here?"

"Oh, hey, babe. Sorry about that. I was trying to let you sleep. It didn't occur to me to tell you I was home."

"Well, next time, tell me. I thought you were a robber or something. Man, my heart's still pounding. How come you aren't at work?"

"I went to the job site, but the foreman said we're taking today off on account of the attacks. We'll work again on Monday."

"Oh? Why's that? I mean, why are you taking it off?"

"I think he thought people would be too upset to work, and he didn't want to risk anyone getting injured because they weren't paying attention."

"Huh. Interesting. I'm pretty sure I still need to go into the ad agency and the restaurant. You think I should call them?"

"You could, but I think they'd call you. He said he tried to call me. I don't know why I didn't get the call."

"Okay. I'll just go into work like normal."

"You hungry?"

"Yes. Very. And something smells good."

"I made French toast and sausage. I was going to make bacon, but then I remembered you don't really care for it, so . . . "

"Thank you, Leo. That was very sweet, even if you did take several years off my life by scaring me half to death."

"Sorry, babe."

"Look at this mess. We have stuff everywhere."

"How about I buy those totes? We could keep things organized a little better."

"Good idea."

After breakfast, my phone rings. It's the receptionist from the ad agency telling me not to come in. No one really wants to be there, so they're going home. She'll see me on Monday at my usual time.

"Well, I guess you were right about them calling me."

"Yep. I'm not surprised. I imagine many places shut down fully today or tried to work and decided to go home. But the restaurant's likely to stay open. People will be looking for companionship this evening, and going out for a meal might make them feel better—more normal."

"As much as I'd like to take a Friday night off, I don't want to miss out on the tips. Friday nights are usually pretty good."

"Since you don't have the ad job, want to go for a run?"

"Yeah, let's do it. A run sounds good."

And it is. As usual, we start off together, talking and running. As we become too winded, the conversation stops. Then Leo picks up his pace, leaving me to stay at my comfortable stride.

I started jogging years ago. When Mom and Jake were first married, I'd sometimes go with him. Jake's a very slow jogger, so it was a perfect introduction to the sport.

During high school, I used jogging and bicycling to stay in shape for cheerleading. Mom also introduced me to healthy movement— something like yoga but without some of the spiritual aspect—which I loved then and now.

After my run, I'm on the lawn of our apartment building stretching when I see Leo down the block. I hurry and finish so I can get in the shower first.

My hair's still wet and I'm not wearing makeup. Leo's in the kitchen drinking orange juice.

"Shower's all yours."

"Great. Thanks, Katie. I'll be quick so you can finish getting ready."

"No hurry. I have plenty of time. My shift's not until 5:30."

When Leo comes out, he's fully dressed and looks ready to leave.

"You going somewhere?"

"I thought I'd go look for totes and go by the sporting goods store. You want to come along?"

"Can you wait while I fix my face and hair?"

"Sure, I can wait. But I think you look pretty good already."

I put my long, highlighted-brown hair in a tight bun. It's easy to do when it's still wet, but not so easy when it's dry. With the natural curl bordering on frizzy ringlets, it tries to get away from me. Makeup doesn't take too long, and then I put on jeans and a blouse.

Leo is on his tablet when I go back to the living room.

"Any news?"

"Nothing new on last night's attacks. There is new news, though I'm not sure what to make of it."

"Oh, what's that?"

"The second story today, with the first being last night's attacks, of course, is multiple cases of foodborne illnesses, both E. coli and typhoid."

"Typhoid? That doesn't happen here. When I was looking into mission trips, I found many places where typhoid is common, but my food handler's class pretty much said we didn't need to worry about it unless we had dirty water or something."

"Yeah. It's common in Asia, Africa, and Latin America, but not here—at least, not until recently. There have been some outbreaks in homeless camps lately, but nothing widespread. Today there are almost three hundred cases of typhoid reported, and in several areas of the US, E. coli has over one hundred cases, with some deaths. A few typhoid deaths, too, but I think it's easier to treat than E. coli if it's found in time."

"What's causing them?"

"Still unknown. The cases are too widespread to be a localized event. They're trying to find the common thread. A few prepper sites are connecting this to the terrorists, but you know how that goes. They connect everything to conspiracies. Remember the shooting in Wyoming last month? Lots of conspiracy stuff."

"I'm not sure they're wrong on that one. It sounds way too fishy with the dead teen who had his ID on him and other shooters with no ID, then the deaths of the teacher and secretary, and the family who stopped the shooting disappearing. Definitely fishy. But back to the food poisoning. Is it happening here?"

"I don't think so. I can't find any reports from here. I think we should be careful, just in case. Maybe, until they know where it came from, let's think about what and where we eat. E. coli is most common in, what?"

"Ground beef not cooked enough and fresh produce. Washing the produce helps."

"Okay. So we cook our meat well and wash our produce. Maybe we should plan to only eat at home until we have more information on where this is coming from. What do you think?"

"I guess. I was looking forward to my staff dinner tonight, but I don't want to get sick. What if people at my restaurant get sick? That'd be terrible."

"Honey, you continue to do what you need to do. I'm sure your management has been made aware of this, and they'll do what's needed."

"You think so?"

"Probably."

I wonder if he does really think so or if he's just trying to make me feel better. I'd really hate it if an outbreak were traced back to the restaurant where I work. But Leo did say there haven't been any reports here, so that's good.

"I'm ready to go if you are."

"I am. Let's go."

We take my SUV today. Transporting totes seems like a better idea in an enclosed space than the bed of a pickup.

The store is plenty busy. Besides for regular-style totes, we also buy some that slide under the bed. We get little riser things to make the bed a little higher, since we're not sure the made-for-under-the-bed totes will actually fit under the bed.

I joke about how I might need a step stool to get in bed now, so Leo finds a folding one and adds it to the cart. I insist it was only a joke, but he says we're getting it anyway. He's noticed I climb on the counters or a chair to reach things in the kitchen, and this is a safer option. He's probably right.

We talk about buying more staples but decide our apartment is overflowing, and we'd need more totes if we bought more stuff. Then the totes would have to sit out. It's smarter to send another shipment of things to Mom and Jake instead.

We started sending shipments of food to them after the backpack arrived. In one of the notes included with my pack, Mom said to bring all the food I had if I had to bug out for home because I may need it on the trip, and if not, it'd be a welcome addition to their food stores.

At that time, my folks didn't know anything about the secret I was keeping—*Leo.*

I know it was silly to keep Leo a secret. After all, I'm twenty-one and living on my own. I think about telling Mom every time I talk to her, but it just never seems like the right time. Besides for the fact my three sisters have all recently been married and those were rather stressful, Mom and Jake have been having a hard time lately since their friends Sharri and Kenny died. Luckily, things seem to be getting better between them.

Mom and Jake both credit a renewed faith in God for improving their marriage. They say once they started putting God at the center of their lives, things changed.

When my dad was alive, we went to church weekly. After he died, Mom stopped going. I'm sure she was still a believer and probably still read her Bible, but she simply didn't feel comfortable attending the same church, and finding a new one wasn't comfortable for her either.

After my Grandpa Sam, my mom's dad, died, she and Jake started attending church. Calley and I usually went along. During that time, I felt I had a true purpose. I knew God loved me and had great plans for me. I thought he might even be calling me to the mission field.

I found a great church here in Manhattan and was very involved. But a few months ago, I stopped going—shortly before Leo moved in with me.

I know the life I'm leading, living with Leo when we aren't married, isn't right. I never intended it to go down the path it did, and

I feel terribly guilty we started . . . uh, *relations* and moved in together before we married.

I still believe in God and know Jesus died for me, but I guess I'm not following Him very well. Leo and I talk about our faith a lot. He grew up in a Christian family. He still attends church most weeks, choosing to go to the first service on Sunday morning while I'm still sleeping. I've considered going with him but haven't. I'd feel like a phony at his church, as much as I started feeling at my own church.

While Leo's no longer a complete secret, I still haven't told anyone in my family about us living together.

It's not really that I'm ashamed or think they'll be disappointed in me. Mom's told me many times how she wants nothing but happiness for me. I'm just not ready to drop a bomb on them. I want them to have a little more time to heal from their grief and troubles without thinking they need to start planning another wedding.

Mom and Jake do know we're dating; they just don't know we're serious. Very serious. I love Leo, and I know he loves me. Shortly after my bug-out bag arrived, we built him a similar one, and I told him he could come home with me if it was ever warranted.

Leo felt, if he'd be joining our family, he wanted to contribute. We decided on storing a thirty-day supply of foods we usually eat in our apartment. These would be the normal canned and packaged items we're both comfortable preparing. Food we can pack and take back to Wyoming if the need arises.

"What do you think about sending food to your folks?" Leo asked a few months ago, after we'd finished stocking the apartment.

"What do you mean?"

"Well, I don't want to be too presumptuous, but I'd like to think if you had to use your fancy backpack and head to their place, you'd want me to go along."

"Well, duh."

Leo gave me a big smile and a kiss on the nose, then said, "So we should send supplies to them so I'm not a burden."

"Yeah, it's probably smart. Though, I know they'd never think of you as a burden. They'd realize how much of a help a big, strong guy like you would be. Believe me—you'd work for your keep." I gave him a playful jab on the bicep.

"Mm-hmm. I'd work for my keep, but I'm also going to contribute. You've told me they've made a point of not just having a producing farm, but storing food also. What'd you say their goal is? One year of food per person?"

"Uh, right. At least, I assume so. That was always the goal when we lived in Casper. When they moved to Bakerville, they set up the house to accommodate for storing food and supplies. In passing, Mom mentioned they increase the stock every time there's a wedding."

"So, if we were married, they'd be planning on me joining you?"

A look of horror must have crossed my face because he immediately said, "Calm down, babe. I'm not saying let's rush out and get married so your parents will buy food for me to have in case of the apocalypse."

"Oh, yeah, right. I know that's not what you meant. It's just . . . "

"It's just you still haven't told them about me, so they wouldn't even know to store food for me."

"I'm sorry, Leo. I'm trying," I said quietly.

He didn't say anything for a good minute, then said, "So since we aren't to the point of announcing our relationship, how about we go ahead and send things to them. We can keep me out of it. You can present it as you wanting to help. You think they'd be good with that?"

"Yes, probably so. But they do know my money is pretty tight, so they might wonder."

"You okay with them wondering? It might give you a good opportunity to . . . I don't know, bring up our relationship maybe."

"Yeah, I suppose it would."

We both sat quietly until I asked, "What'd you have in mind?"

"I've looked at several packaged, long-term storage collections. They're two to six serving pouches packed in buckets and allot minimal calories to cover a person for a designated amount of time."

"Okay, sounds confusing."

"Slightly. And the reviews are mixed. The calories are iffy, the taste is iffy, and the price is high. Another option is buying bulk goods like rice, beans, and grains. That tends to be less expensive but lacks the convenience of the pouches. Where the pouches are prepared with just hot water, the bulk items have to be cooked."

"Yep. My folks mainly do the bulk items. They have dehydrated foods they use for backpacking and to add a little convenience to the food storage, but those are more like extras."

"I understand. It'd be pretty expensive to buy a year's supply of dehydrated meals for . . . what? Over a dozen people?"

"More than that. I think closer to twenty, figuring my grandma and grandpa and Mike's family. Mom told Calley to bring them too. That's the only way she'd ever get Calley and Mike there."

"Hmm. So, definitely too expensive. But I think for you and me, it might make sense to send some dehydrated things. Plus, the convenience of those might be a welcome addition to their storage."

"Oh . . . so you aren't just thinking we'd send food to eat?"

"What?"

"You know, whatever we send is what we'd eat."

"No, I can't imagine it'd work that way. I'd suspect, in an emergency situation, everyone would band together. There'd be a central kitchen, and everything would be prepared for the masses. Wouldn't you think it'd be that way?"

"I don't know . . . I guess I didn't really think about it. Mom and Jake have guest quarters and each one has a small kitchen, so I guess I figured we'd cook in the separate kitchens."

"Maybe so. At least in the beginning that might make sense, but as time went on, I would think you'd want to conserve fuel and cook together. I think we should make it clear to your folks we're . . . *you're* . . . sending things to add to the general supplies. Not to hold separate for your personal needs."

"Okay, yeah. Makes sense. So we'll send some dehydrated things?"

"Yes, some freeze-dried meals. I wanna send an assortment. Let me show you what I've found."

He pulled out his iPad and opened several bookmarked tabs.

"I think we should send this bucket collection. It's supposed to be three-months' worth of food for two people—720 servings. I did the math and, assuming the calorie count is accurate, it's about nineteen hundred calories a day. A little light, especially for me, but it's not bad. The reviews are good, and people seem to like the taste for the most part. They have the price marked down, and I found a 10 percent off coupon. Plus, right now, they're doing free shipping."

"Leo, it's crazy expensive."

"It's about $430 a month. How much do you usually spend each month on groceries? Before I moved in, I mean."

"Oh . . . well. Fifty bucks a week. I guess that's about right for two people for a month."

"Right. And you eat several meals a week at the restaurant. So it's really not too bad. But we can do much better on bulk foods, so we'll concentrate on those. We'll also throw in some #10 cans of freeze-dried foods. And I want to include some MREs, strictly for convenience."

"Aren't those the same as the meals we're looking at?"

"No, they're different. Freeze-dried and dehydrated foods need water to rehydrate. Except a few things, like freeze-dried strawberries, which can be eaten as is. MRE stands for *Meal Ready-to-Eat*. They're nothing to write home about—their purpose is sustenance, plain and simple. I've eaten more than my share in the short time I was active."

"When you were a Marine?"

"I'm still a Marine," Leo said with a wink. "But, yes, when I was in. It's a total setup with the main dish, sides, dessert, condiments, chewing gum . . . the whole deal. They even have a little heater for the main dish and sides."

"Oh, sure, I've heard about those. I think I also heard they taste pretty bad."

"The chili mac isn't terrible, and I like the ravioli too. The main problem with the MRE option is they don't have near the shelf life the freeze-dried meals have. Something like only five years. And they're not readily available—at least, not for civilians and not ones with a full shelf life left. We could probably find them at a military surplus store, but they'd probably be close to expired."

"I don't think that'd be a good idea. I mean, I don't want to eat expired food. Plus, we're buying things for something that could maybe, possibly, perhaps, someday happen. Seems a longer shelf life would be smarter."

"I completely agree. So I've been looking at civilian MREs. They're considerably different than the military version, but I think they'll be okay. The convenience factor is increased over the meal packages. They'd really come in handy if we had any . . . uh, incidences of needing to be out on patrol."

"Out on patrol? You think we'd have to do that?"

"Maybe. I've been looking at a lot of information and . . . well, who knows? I mean we're talking about something that hasn't happened yet, at least not in the US, so we don't know what would be needed. We can look at things that happened in other countries when there was some sort of civil unrest. And . . . gosh, Katie. It's a little overwhelming. I just don't know."

21

Leo was scaring me a little bit. I thought about a fictional book series I read, when an asteroid hit the moon and knocked everything out of whack. In that scenario, I guess I could see how something like an easy-to-eat MRE would be helpful.

"I guess I can understand what you're saying."

"Okay, good. Then let's add a spattering of the MREs, three months of the packaged meals, and finish off with the grains and beans. Maybe throw in some ration bars also."

"I think I've had those. They taste a little bit like lemon flavored pie pastry?"

"Maybe. I don't think I've ever had them. I just found them when I was researching. Here's a picture."

"Yep. Mom and Jake have some of them. They opened a package, and we did a taste test. I didn't mind them. What do you think of adding a few things like cans of tuna and chicken? I could order those online and have them shipped directly to my mom."

"Sure, good idea. Canned meat isn't very economical but would be good to have. Canned salmon too. I like those salmon patty things you make."

"My mom's recipe," I beamed.

"Well, they're good."

I called Mom about this before we started any of the shipments of storage foods. She was, understandably, surprised.

I thought she was going to start crying at one point when I told her I'd been thinking a lot about things since the backpack arrived, and how I wanted to do my part to provide for myself and the rest of the family.

Mom finished the conversation with the same statement she always makes when we talk about the possibility of the end of the world as we know it: *"I hope we never have a real need for these things, but I feel better knowing they'll be there if we do need them."*

Chapter 3

At the sporting goods store, Leo heads for the gun counter. He asks me if I want a gun. While I've shot his .22 handgun and rifle, plus Jake's .22 rifle, I don't really want my own and tell him so. He says he's decided to get another pistol and a larger hunting rifle than the .243. He has a concealed carry permit, so the purchase goes quickly.

We also buy more gear for our bags. Leo wants to add a second water filter for each of us, a couple of emergency blankets, and some more dehydrated meals. I'm wondering how I could carry a pack any heavier than it already is, but Leo assures me it won't add much weight.

"Katie, I think we should get more cash out of the bank. We can put it back in after this is all over if we don't need it. I'm going to go in at my bank and pull out quite a bit. We can do the same at yours."

Last night I took three hundred out of my savings, then moved all but eight dollars to my checking. Then I took a hundred out when we shopped. "You can just take me through the ATM. I only have a little over three hundred in checking, so it's no trouble to pull it out through there."

We stop by his bank, and I wait in the car. Then we go through my bank's ATM. With last night's money, my tips on hand, and this money, I feel practically rich. I need to add it up, but it should be somewhere close to eight hundred bucks, not counting my coins. Of course, it's all the money I have.

I should make tips tonight, and I get both my intern stipend and my restaurant paycheck on Monday. Like Leo said, I can always put this money back in the bank for bills if I don't need it. If I do need it, I'll be happy I took it out.

Once we're back at the apartment, the risers go under the bed. It's not too terribly high, and I tell Leo I won't be needing the step stool. He laughs and says we'll keep it in the kitchen since I do need it there.

We try to organize things into the bins, and for the most part, it goes well. Toward the end, there's a bin of miscellaneous stuff. We add the second water filters and emergency blankets, and divide up the meals for our backpacks.

"Oh, hey, Leo. I wanted to ask you something."

"Uh-huh. What's up?"

"How come you bought a hunting rifle instead of an assault rifle?"

"Assault rifle?"

"Yeah, you know, the black one. Well, the different black one. I noticed your hunting rifle was black and not wood, but my mom has a black hunting rifle, so . . . I mean the *assault* ones."

"You mean, like an AR-15?"

"Yes, exactly. An AR . . . assault rifle."

"AR stands for ArmaLite rifle, after the company who developed it in the 1950s. The 'AR' doesn't stand for *assault rifle* or *automatic rifle*. It's just a name, like BMW stands for Bavarian Motor Works."

"Really? How'd I not know this?"

"Many people don't. And really, why would you? The media portrays those scary black guns as assault rifles, forgetting assault is an action not an object. A gun is an object not an action."

"Okay." I shrug. "So why didn't you buy one?"

"I don't need to. I have one—well, two, actually."

"What do you mean you have two? Where are they?"

"On the top shelf of the closet."

"On the top shelf of the closet? In the bedroom?"

"Yes."

"I've never seen them there."

"Do you get many things from the shelf?"

"Well, no. I put stuff up there when I moved in. Stuff I don't need to use often. And . . . I'm trying to think of the last thing I took from there. I can't remember. I can't really reach the shelf without a chair, so it's kind of a pain."

"Exactly. I think we were talking about your use of chairs to reach high places earlier today."

"Hardy, har, har. You're a funny man. So you have a gun—two guns—just sitting on the shelf?"

"No. I have two guns secured in their cases sitting on the shelf."

"Oh. Well, okay. I was just wondering why you didn't buy one of those instead of the hunting rifle. I'm kind of surprised you never told me about the *non*-assault rifles in the closet."

"I never thought about it," Leo says with a shrug. "They're there alongside my .243. One of my handguns is right next to it, one is in the drawer of my nightstand, and the other is in the hall closet, top shelf."

"The nightstand and hall closet? I guess it's good I didn't know about those this morning. I was so scared thinking you were a burglar . . . I was wishing for a gun."

"Really? That surprises me."

"Yeah, it surprised me too."

He nods. "Well, I put the new purchases on the bedroom shelf."

"So you have how many guns?"

"With today's, I guess four handguns—but one is only a .22—and the four rifles. Eight. A nice even number." He gives me an exaggerated wink.

I half-reluctantly nod in agreement. "Yeah, I guess it's a nice even number."

"The cases each lock. Only the sidearm in my nightstand isn't in a locking case. Someday I should buy a safe, but for now, the individual locking cases make sense. I bought the hunting rifle because, if we did end up going to your parents' place, I want to be able to help with our food supply. The .243 is okay for antelope and whitetail deer. And it'll work for mule deer with a well-placed shot, but the .30-06 will be perfect for both mule deer and elk. Didn't you tell me Jake elk hunts? What does he shoot?"

"I'm pretty sure he shoots something like what you just bought. I don't really know, though. Calley is the one who went hunting—not me."

"The gun I got is a good gun for big game, and with a bolt action and decent scope, it can be very accurate. I think it'll be a good hunting rifle. If you wanted to hunt deer and antelope, you could use the .243. Is that what your mom shoots?"

"I don't think so. I don't really know what it is. Maybe a 300-something, it's not the same as Jake's. I don't know."

"Maybe a .308?"

I shrug. "I really don't know. She used to have a different one but got a new one last year. I haven't seen it and wasn't really listening when she told me about it."

"Has your mom been hunting long?"

"Last couple of years. Well, sort of. She took Hunter's Safety when she was real young, the seventh grade. Her dad always said he'd take her but never did."

"That's too bad."

"Yeah . . . she didn't have the best childhood."

"I remember you telling me about her sister dying when they were young and her parents divorcing after she finished high school. But I didn't realize it wasn't good growing up."

"No, not too good. She doesn't talk about it, but after her sister died, her mom shut down and didn't pay much attention to her. Mom doesn't even know where her mom is. She thinks Spain. My grandpa died when Malcolm was a baby. He and my mom did make up before he died, which I know meant a lot to her."

"That's hard."

"It is. Anyway, we all went with Jake when he'd go on his hunting trips. We'd camp for the week, and Calley and I would take turns going out with him on his hunts. Just hiking. We weren't actually hunting. It was fun. Then, when we moved to Wyoming, Calley started hunting with Jake. Malcolm was just a baby then, so Mom didn't want to leave him to hunt. Calley was nineteen, I think, when she decided she didn't want to hunt anymore. Mom decided Malcolm was old enough, so she started going.

"I know Mom really likes the hiking part of hunting. And she likes the filling-the-freezer part. I asked her if she likes the killing part. She told me no, but she decided a long time ago, if she was going to eat meat, she'd know exactly where it came from and would be willing to look it in the eye. That explains a lot with them raising chickens and buying beef from a friend of hers. She'd go to their ranch, see the cows, and pick up the meat. Now Mom and Jake even raise sheep and pigs for food. She says they could eat the goats also, but I don't think they ever have." I grimace.

"I guess your mom's right. So many people think, if they buy their meat in a grocery store and it comes in a plastic package, an animal didn't give its life to feed them. It's kind of amazing to me people think that." Leo chuckles.

"Really? People are very strange. What time is it, Leo? My shift starts at 5:30."

"Eight after four. You still have some time."

He's right—I do. It won't take me long to change into my work uniform. The restaurant's only a few blocks away, so I'll walk. Leo doesn't like me walking home, so he'll pick me up. He says it's way too late for me to be out walking when I have a closing shift. He's probably right, but I never thought anything about it before he made a fuss.

I did suggest I could take the fancy zapper stick, but he said he'd rather just come get me. I could drive my SUV, but parking is so terrible there, I'd end up parking almost by my apartment anyway.

The restaurant's considered upscale American cuisine. We have wonderful steaks, lamb, duck, and seafood, along with fancy side dishes like roasted garlic chèvre smashed potatoes and truffle french fries. It's really quite nice.

We close the dining room at 10:00 p.m., but it's often between 11:00 and midnight before I'm done. The cocktail area stays open with a bar menu until midnight, but I rarely work the bar side.

I only work the late closing shift on Fridays and the occasional Saturday. If I have a Monday through Thursday shift, I'm off by eight o'clock. We're closed on Sunday. It's wonderful having Sundays off.

"Katie, you mind if I turn on the news? See if there's anything new?"

"Sure, no problem. I'm going to go in the bedroom. I want to do laundry tomorrow, so I'm going to start getting it together. I suspect yours is already in your basket and ready to go?"

"Yeah, but you don't have to do it. I can do it or I can go with you to the laundromat and help you with it all."

"We'll see."

Before I start on organizing my laundry, I pull out my tablet and check the school message boards. There's lots of talk about the attacks, and several people—especially the professors—are comparing it to 9/11 and encouraging us all to come together. The general consensus is we're a nation divided, and most people expect riots instead of togetherness. Sad, but likely true. I've read enough.

I'm sorting the pile of clothes I have in the closet. I'm always amazed Leo's able to keep his stuff so organized. Maybe I need to take tips from him. I jump when he says my name.

"Jeez, Leo. You scared me."

"Katie, come on out to the living room. There's been more attacks. They've taken out bridges."

"What?" My question comes out more like a screech. The newscaster looks very grim.

" . . . the Brooklyn Bridge, connecting Manhattan and Brooklyn; the Golden Gate Bridge in San Francisco; Mackinac Bridge, which *connects the Lower and Upper Peninsulas of Michigan; Seattle's Lacey V. Murrow Memorial Bridge; and Portland's Marquam Bridge. We believe these are just a few of the bridges that have been attacked. Even as I speak, I'm receiving more information and occasional explosions are being reported throughout the US. We expect more information shortly.*

"Again, there appear to be widespread incidents of explosions on or near bridges throughout the United States. At this time, we can confirm explosions on the Brooklyn Bridge, Golden Gate Bridge, Mackinac Bridge, Lacey V. Murrow Memorial Bridge, and Marquam Bridge. We're working on getting more information and details on the extent of the damage. We have unconfirmed reports of explosions on other bridges and will provide additional details once these reports have been confirmed."

I'm not sure what to think. Last night, airplanes were crashed and airports blown up. Today bridges are exploding, and one of those bridges is in Portland. There are so many bridges in Portland crossing over the Willamette. I don't know which is which, but I know when we went from the east side to the west side, we had to take at least one bridge and sometimes more.

If we wanted to go to Vancouver, Washington, we had to go over a bridge since the Columbia River separates Portland and Vancouver. I'm trying to think which one the Marquam is. Whichever, I have no doubt there were plenty of cars on it. There are always plenty of cars on all of the Portland bridges.

"Katie, honey. Are you okay?"

"No. I'm pretty sure I'm not. I used to live in Portland. They attacked Portland. What about our bridge? The one not too far from us on Pillsbury?" Each word I say comes out as more of a shriek than the last.

"I don't know, babe. I'd like to think our little town isn't large enough to be on these guys' radar."

The announcer comes back on and says forty-five bridges across the US were attacked by suicide bombers. A list of the bridges scrolls across the screen. Three of the bridges connect the island of Manhattan to other New York City boroughs. A bridge over the Potomac in DC was hit. The Seven Mile Bridge, connecting the Florida Keys; The Lewis and Clark Viaduct, connecting Kansas City, KS, and Kansas

City, MO; and the Speer Blvd Bridge in Denver were all hit, and so many other places—I can't keep them straight.

Not just the one bridge in Portland but five, including both of the bridges over the Columbia connecting to Vancouver. I can't imagine how anyone will get anywhere in the Portland area. I know, if I was there, I'd be wanting to leave, but it might be a challenge.

I go to the bathroom to blow my nose and wipe my eyes. When I come out, Leo hands me a glass of water. We settle back on the couch as the president comes on the screen. I barely listen as he goes through what has happened. It all sounds so terribly bad. So, so bad.

One thing that caught my attention during the president's address was that other bridges, not attacked today but deemed likely targets, will be closed. He didn't say how long they'd be closed. Is this going to make things even harder for Mom to get home?

Leo and I sit in silence for a few minutes. Then the newscaster comes back on.

"We have confirmation of the forty-eight bridges attacked today and the towns affected by this act of terrorism. If you are in these towns, please follow the instructions of your local officials. Staying at your home is safest, but please do heed calls to donate blood and requests for any trained first responders or medical personnel."

The announcer goes on to read off each bridge and city. We already heard about most of them, but nonetheless, we listen intently.

After he finishes reading, the channel breaks to a commercial and Leo cuts the sound.

"Katie, this a big deal."

"Yes, I know."

"You may want to think about going to your parents' house now."

"We."

"What?"

"*We,* Leo. You're going with me, right?"

"Yes, of course I'm going with you. We may want to think about going."

"How do we know now is the time? What if this is just another isolated event and everything's fine tomorrow?"

"I don't think these are isolated. These are planned attacks. And if the foodborne illnesses are also intentional, then they're attacking us in multiple ways. We can't travel with flights grounded and bridges exploding. We can't eat with food being poisoned. What's next?"

I sigh. "You may be right. But it doesn't seem like this is the type of event Mom and Jake would want to have us there for."

"Didn't they say to come home if you feel unsafe? Better to be there and not need to be than to not get there."

"Yeah. But I don't feel unsafe. I feel perfectly fine here. I don't really need to cross any bridges or take any airplanes. I won't eat at the restaurant and will only eat food here. We'll avoid the things likely to be contaminated. How can we not be safe?"

"What if they're contaminating the water?"

"We'll only drink bottled. Or use our filters."

"If that's the case, I'd better go buy a whole lot more bottled. We don't have enough to last any length of time. Maybe a week, which may not be enough. Plus, if other people are having this same discussion . . . We should save our filters in case we need to leave."

"Do you mind going and buying more water?"

"I'll do it, babe. But we need to really stay on top of what's happening. Are you going to work your restaurant shift?"

"Yes. In fact, I'd better get myself together."

"I'll drop you off on the way to get water and maybe a few other things. While you're at work, I'm going to get things ready in case we need to leave in a hurry. I was thinking, maybe, if we do need to leave, we should take both vehicles. How do you feel about that?"

"I don't mind driving, but how can we stay together? What if we get into trouble along the way?"

"We'll be okay. And if things seem really dangerous, we'll dump your SUV and continue in my truck."

"Dump my SUV? I'd kind of like to have it. At least to sell. Not dump it."

"Katie, if things were so bad we needed to dump it, we'd be to the point where selling it wouldn't be an option. At least, not right away. And we'd do our best to put it somewhere we could go back for it later. Okay?"

"I guess." I shrug, even though I don't like the idea at all. "Taking both would make sense so we could haul as much stuff as possible. Everything we have could be helpful. Jeez. I can't believe I'm even saying this. I can't believe we're discussing this like it's a real thing."

"I know. It doesn't seem possible. And there's a good chance nothing will come of it and we're planning for something that doesn't happen. That said, having a plan is a good thing."

"I'm going to try calling my mom before I get ready. I want to see where she is. I know she isn't anywhere near Portland or Seattle, so that's good."

Voicemail again. So annoying. I really wish my mom had a carrier who provided better coverage in Oregon. It works fine in Wyoming, but it totally sucks trying to get ahold of her when she's in Oregon. I've started a text when my phone rings. Jake.

"Hello?"

"Katie. You have a minute to talk?" Jake sounds absolutely exhausted.

"Of course. Have you talked to Mom? Is she okay?"

"I just hung up with her. She's outside of Redmond, Oregon. She's fine. I guess you've heard about the bridges?"

"I have, Jake. They attacked the bridge connecting Kansas City, Kansas, to Kansas City, Missouri. Can you believe that? And a bridge in Denver. Attacking the bridges is going to make transportation difficult. It makes me not even want to drive for fear of having to go over a bridge."

"I suspect you're not the only one feeling that way. Your mom and I were wondering if you feel like you should stay there or try to make your way here?"

I don't want to tell him Leo and I were just discussing this. I cover the mouthpiece and whisper to Leo, "Jake wants to know if I'm coming home."

Leo whispers back, "I'm not opposed to it. Have you changed your mind?" I shake my head no. Leo gives me a slight frown. I uncover the mouthpiece and return my attention to Jake.

"I'm not sure, Jake. While these latest attacks are terrible, it still seems like attacks and not a widespread event, you know what I mean?"

"I do. While these are terrible attacks, they're still not near you— "

"Exactly, Jake."

"—and you're feeling safe in your home, so it's normal to want to stay. The hard thing is knowing when the right time to leave is. I'd prefer you err on the side of caution and leave sooner rather than waiting until the last minute. I know your mom would prefer that too."

"I know. And if I ever feel unsafe, I'll for sure leave."

31

"Does your friend plan on coming with you? Leo? Will you bring him if you come home?"

I let out an involuntary sigh. I know I shouldn't be so secretive about Leo. I decide to come clean . . . well, mostly.

"Yeah. I'd like to bring him. The things we've been sending were so he wouldn't be a burden if it hit the fan and we needed to come home."

"Your mom thought that might be the case. We appreciate it. What are your plans with Leo?"

"What do you mean? I'd like to bring him home with me if I have to bug out."

Jake laughs a little. "I mean, in general. Are you two serious?"

I decide to tell Jake more. I quietly say, "I love him. He loves me. We're serious."

"And were you planning on bringing him up here to meet us under normal circumstances?"

Jake sounds irritated. I didn't want to upset him.

"I am, Jake. We were waiting for school to get done and Mom to come back from her trip. You know, we're planning on coming up over the Fourth of July, to cheer on you and Mom in your 5K. I know I've been kind of quiet about him, and I didn't really mean to be. It was just . . . awkward. I know you and Mom aren't wanting any weddings right now, so I was trying to keep things quiet so you wouldn't start freaking out about another wedding. Well, not *you* freaking out but Mom. And we're not to that point, so . . . You'll like him. I promise. Don't be mad. I wasn't trying to be sneaky. Not really, anyway."

"I'm not mad, Katie. I just want what's best for you. And it's pretty hard to imagine any guy being good enough for you."

I laugh a little. I'm glad he's not mad. "Well, Leo's pretty amazing. I told Mom some about him. Did she tell you?"

"She said he went to school with you and graduated last month. She said he's a few years older than you."

"Yes. He's a good guy. You'll like him. He majored in business but works construction during the summer. Before college he was a Marine. We bike and run together and have lots of things in common. He likes to hunt and fish, so you'll have things in common with him too." We talk a few more minutes about Leo and me not being able to reach Mom.

32

When I hang up, Leo hugs me and says, "Thanks, Katie."

"For what?"

"For telling Jake you love me and I love you. It's true. I do love you. And it is serious."

Leo and I just stare at each other for a moment. You know, one of those mushy, full of love stares.

"I know I should've told them a long time ago. I should tell them you live with me. But it's so easy not to when I'm so far away from them. And I know they'll think we should get married."

"You don't?"

"What?"

"You don't think we should get married?"

"Uh . . . I don't think we should have this conversation when the world might be collapsing."

"If the world is collapsing, Katie, then I'd want to be with you during the collapse, and I think being married would be very nice."

"Very nice, huh?"

"You know what I mean. I just know I love you and can't imagine not being with you—plus, I think it's the right thing to do."

I nod. I can't argue with it being the right thing to do. We shouldn't have moved in together. "Okay. I need to text my mom and then get ready for work. Can we talk about this later?"

He kisses me on the nose. "Yes, we'll talk about this later."

Leo goes into the bedroom, and I send my mom a quick text. I try to lay out everything I'm feeling, without sounding too scared. I let her know I'm staying put for now and I should be fine. I finish with *call me if you can.*

Chapter 4

Leo drops me off at the restaurant. I'm surprised at how terribly quiet the place is.

We start serving dinner at 4:00 p.m., and by now, especially on a Friday, we usually have many tables filled. But right now, there's only a two-top and a four-top. Crazy. After I put my stuff in my locker, the manager, Ms. Jacobson, thanks me for coming in. She says we'll have a quick meeting at six since everyone should be there by then. In the meantime, I can start on side work but don't do any filling.

The motto at most restaurants is, *"If you have time to lean, you have time to clean,"* so clean is what I do.

As the meeting starts, Ms. Jacobson clears her throat. Not to get our attention, since we're all silent, but maybe out of slight nervousness, which is unusual for her. She's a very capable person and decidedly shows this in how she acts and looks. Her blazing red hair is done almost in a bouffant, and combined with her classic, form-fitting dresses and pointed-toe heels, she could be a twin to the lady in the show about a sixties' ad agency. She's a terrific manager and is always very fair.

"Thank you all for coming in tonight. You probably noticed it's a little quiet in the dining room. With the attacks of last night and this afternoon, I'm not sure many people feel like dining out tonight. As is our standard on slow nights, we'll be asking you to clock out early in accordance with our service needs."

After a few minutes, it's decided we'll keep one busser, very light kitchen staff, the bartender, one bar server, our hostess, and two wait staff. I'm one of the ones who's staying.

By 8:15 I've had one table, and they're cashed out but lingering over coffee, so I get them a warm-up. Clark, the other server tonight, has had two tables. He takes a break while I do some cleaning. Our menu is slightly altered: no salads due to the food problems, and no rare steaks. We can still do medium-rare and anything cooked further.

When he returns, I take my break. I check my phone to see if Mom responded to my text. She did. She tells me she understands me staying where I am. She's on the road again after Jake told her about the traffic. She loves me and hopes to talk to me soon.

I wonder what traffic she's talking about. I text back, saying I love her and to stay safe. Internet on my phone is iffy from the break room. I can't connect to find out anything about the traffic Mom mentioned. I decide to ask Ms. Jacobson if she knows anything about it. I suspect she's been either on her computer or listening to a radio in her office and is keeping up to date on things.

Her door is slightly open, so I knock softly.

"Come in, Katie. Is everything all right?"

"Yes. I'm on a quick break and checked my phone to see if my mom called. She's in Oregon on a business trip."

"Oh my! She's not in Portland?"

"No. She works in a small town on the coast. When the planes crashed last night, she drove down the coast instead of going through Portland or Seattle to get home. She's somewhere in Central Oregon, I think."

"That's good, but I imagine you're worried. She doesn't live near here, correct?"

"Correct, ma'am. She and the rest of my family live in Wyoming. Except my sister Sarah. She's in Billings, Montana, not far from my mom. I was wondering something . . . my mom mentioned a traffic problem in her text. I'm not sure what she's referring to. Do you know?"

"Yes, I believe so. Many roads are at a standstill with people trying to leave the cities with bridges attacked. Some can't really get out, like those on Manhattan Island, New York. The other bridges have been closed. The tunnels are clogged. They're using the ferries to help people leave who want to leave, but FEMA and the governor are encouraging people to stay and shelter in place. Same thing is happening in most places. What road's your mom on?"

"I don't know. I'm not sure exactly where she is, but do you know if the Portland area roads are clogged?"

"How about I see what I can find out for you? I'll come out to the floor and let you know when I have more info. As slow as it is, I should probably send you or Clark home. I hope you don't mind me singling you out tonight to stay."

"No, not at all. I don't mind staying. It's easier to be here than to be at home worrying."

"Thank you, Katie. I'll let you know what I find out."

When I return to the floor, Clark goes to the service area to do some side work. While he's off the floor, a new table comes in. This is a five-person table—a mom, dad, and three preteen to teenage children. They all look very sad. I wonder if I look this sad.

As I deliver their waters, the hostess is seating another table, plus it looks like someone else is waiting to be seated. Maybe Clark and I will both be staying.

Clark returns from the service station. I catch his eye, and he raises an eyebrow in response. Several more tables have been seated, giving us each four tables. Four to six tables at a time is what I like to think of as my "sweet spot," as long as none of them are large tables. The four I have are two- to five-tops, so I'm good. I let the kitchen know to expect to get busy.

Clark and I get all our new tables situated with drinks—water from a bottled water service, which Ms. Jacobson says assured her will be fine for serving. We make sure to point this out as we pour. As we do this, we see several more people at the podium. I'm wondering if my sweet spot might be turning sour.

I go to my family of five table, and they immediately tell me they need a few more minutes. The two-top nearby is nearly ready. I'm entering their order into the computer when Ms. Jacobson walks over.

"Katie, I checked on the roads out of Portland, and they're a mess. So full of traffic they're like parking lots. After checking those, it occurred to me to check I-70 from Kansas City. I don't know why I didn't think to do this before. They're also very busy. While not as bad as the Portland roads since it's such a higher population, they're still quite full. We've seriously picked up, but I wonder if we might be seeing people who have fled Kansas City. Let me check in with the kitchen, then I'll be available to help as needed. I'm glad I didn't send anyone else home. I was very close to doing so."

Now there are several new tables in my section. Clark has more new ones also. We're hopping, and my adrenaline is pumping.

Catching snippets of conversation, it's clear this rush is of people who have escaped Kansas City—the Kansas side, I suspect, since the bridge was taken out and the Missouri people would likely head east or maybe south. I know there are other bridges they could use, but would they? I sure wouldn't. Which makes me wonder, why are people leaving? Do they think the bridge attack was the first wave like the airplane crashes were last night? I guess it makes sense.

I start thinking of my customers as refugees. I guess, in a way, they are. Of course, they're dining at a pretty fancy restaurant for refugees. I do notice all are ordering the more economical dishes. Not that anything is cheap on the menu, but none are big spenders.

The cocktail area is pretty quiet, so Bree, the cocktail waitress who stayed on, is helping us as she can. I suspect Ms. Jacobson is in the kitchen. The busser's doing an excellent job, so we're mostly staying afloat.

Thankfully, everyone's very understanding. Since so many came in at once, they seem to recognize we've been overwhelmed.

The steady stream of customers continues—from no business at all at 8:15 to a full house less than an hour later. The cocktail area has picked up also.

As my original family of five finishes, the dad says, "It sure is good to finally be off the road. What should've been a two-hour trip was more than double. As soon as we hit I-70, we knew we weren't the only ones leaving town. You know, our home is so close to the Viaduct, we felt the explosion."

"Yeah, that was so scary," one of the daughters says. "The windows rattled, and stuff fell out of Mom's china cabinet. Even broke her favorite figurine and a few plates."

The mom sighs. "It's just stuff, honey. I'm glad we left. Who knows what else these terrorists have planned for our city. At least Manhattan should be nice and quiet. We'll stay here a few days until things calm down." She turns to me. "Works out well since our oldest is interested in going to K-State anyway, so it's nice to see the town."

When ten o'clock is getting near, we have several more tables fill. The new people look like they need a good meal and, possibly, a stiff drink to ease their nerves.

Ms. Jacobson is walking around the tables, making sure everyone's doing fine. She even greets the new people who've just been seated and have nothing more than water.

Ms. Jacobson walks over to me. "Katie, we're going to have a quick meeting in the kitchen. Join me?"

"Of course, Ms. Jacobson." I stand along the edge where I can look in the mirror and see most of the dining room, plus the hostess at her podium.

"I know this has been a strange night. From no one here to being extremely busy—you all are doing wonderfully. The kitchen has done amazing at keeping up. I've just walked around, and those who've been served are very pleased," Ms. Jacobson says.

"I believe all the people we've seen since shortly after eight have been people leaving KC. Under normal circumstances, KC to here isn't but a couple hours. Less, even, for most people. But tonight is not normal. The interstate is moving very slowly. The people who just came in indicated they'd been on the interstate almost five hours.

"As you all know, we usually close the dining room at 10:00 p.m. and leave the cocktail area open with our bar menu until midnight. I've already spoken with Mr. Lowery about this but wanted to ask the rest of you if you would mind staying, and we can leave the dining room open a bit longer and offer the bar menu."

Mr. Lowery is the owner of the restaurant. He's a good guy, as far as I know. Very pleasant and kind. He and his wife come in sometimes. I've served them, and they even left me a nice tip. Not embarrassingly nice but definitely respectable. The bar menu is limited to deep fried foods and foods that are easily prepared, like bread plates and finger foods.

Ms. Jacobson continues, "Mr. and Mrs. Lowery will be here shortly to help. Bree is scheduled until closing and staying." She turns to our chef. "Can your staff stay?"

"Yes, we have all spoken about it and will stay."

Several more tables have filled in the few minutes we've been having our meeting. I need to get back out there. At least the hostess is taking water around.

"Ms. Jacobson, I'll stay," I say. "But I need to take orders, and several more tables have already been seated."

"I'm staying, and ditto what Katie said," Clark adds.

"Thank you. Yes, please go. We'll seat people throughout and start handing out the bar menu."

Clark and I hustle to get our tables taken care of. It's now a few minutes after ten. Ms. Jacobson is working in the bar, and there are a few people waiting for tables. The bartender is also hopping from person to person.

Mr. and Mrs. Lowery have arrived and are at the serving station, helping Clark.

I ask Ms. Jacobson if I can take a quick minute to call Leo and let him know I'll be late. Leo says he'll be here shortly before midnight and can wait as needed.

The night continues, with more people coming in. Our usual clientele, on a normal night, is primarily adults enjoying an evening out, but tonight we're seeing many children. I half expect tensions to rise since we're so busy, and while we're doing our best, I'm sure we're not quite as quick as people would like. The bar menu does help, and people seem to be pleased with the lower prices, so it's not bad at all.

Right before midnight, Leo slips in. He's sitting at the bar nursing a Perrier, and I briefly wonder why he isn't having a beer. Neither of us are big drinkers, but he'll have an occasional beer or glass of wine. I don't care for beer and about half a glass of wine is enough for me.

With the Lowerys, Ms. Jacobson, and all of us running right up until we lock the door at midnight, we're exhausted.

It's a full hour before the restaurant is cleared out, cleaned, and looking like it should. I'm very thankful I'm off tomorrow. Ms. Jacobson and the Lowerys thank us all as we escape out the door.

"You look exhausted, babe," Leo tells me.

"My feet hurt. I'm okay otherwise."

"After you called, I wondered how busy our town was. I took a little drive before coming to get you. It looks like all of the hotels are filled. Pillsbury Drive, coming off I-70, was still pretty busy. I ran a few errands, then took the truck back home and walked here. I brought your running shoes if you want to change into them." Leo motions to a small backpack hanging off one shoulder.

I'm amazed he'd think to bring my running shoes. My heart swells a little.

"I was kind of wondering if we might have parking troubles. If the hotels are full, people might just park on the street or near any greenspaces."

"I'm okay to walk. Parking's always a challenge by the restaurant anyway."

The downtown area is still quite busy, even though it's after one in the morning. We suspect these are people from the interstate, almost ten miles south of us, and are looking for a place to spend the night. I think Leo's right, they'll be parking on the curbs soon.

Things are still quiet in our little neighborhood. For this, I'm very grateful.

We're safely inside our apartment. There are even more totes in the living room than when I left.

"They're still mostly empty," Leo tells me. "I thought the food could go in them, so I bought enough to pack it all. It'll make it much easier to transport. I do have to say, I didn't think about the roads jamming up like they are. Things could be difficult if we decide to leave. We'll want to look for alternate routes. I topped off our gas tanks too. I think gas may become an issue."

"What do you mean?"

"The news is saying towns are running out of fuel, towns in the evacuation areas—that's what they're calling them. Some places are just nuts. The roads are at a standstill. The little towns have had all their services exhausted. No motel rooms, no fuel, and restaurants and even grocery stores are short on food. Well, the easy stuff is gone from grocery stores. And shelters are being set up in schools and such."

"My mom mentioned this in a text, and Ms. Jacobson checked, but she didn't tell me it was this bad. We got so busy about then, and we really had no time to chat about it."

"I think we should go on to bed now. Tomorrow, we should check out routes and put together a plan, or several, in case we decide to leave. Katie, if Manhattan becomes like some of the other towns, we may not have a choice about leaving."

"Okay. You're probably right. Let's just go to bed, and we'll figure it out tomorrow."

I'm exhausted and almost skip washing my face and brushing my teeth but do both grudgingly. Leo's snoring before I finish. It takes me several minutes to find a comfortable position.

Then I start worrying about Mom. It's a long time before I finally fall asleep.

Chapter 5

Saturday, Day 3

"Katie. Katie. It's time to get up."

"Okay, Leo. What time is it?"

"Almost nine o'clock."

"I feel like I just fell asleep. Last night was exhausting. I can't believe how busy the restaurant became. All those poor people."

"Yeah. Well, the entire town is now busy. Remember last night we talked about the people who were here?"

"Of course."

"It looks like there may be about double the amount. They're setting them up at the college, in the empty dorms. I guess it's good school's out so they can use those."

"What? How can that be?"

"The hotels are all filled. It happened while you were working. I thought people would just park on the street and sleep in their cars, or maybe those with gear would go to one of the parks and camp, or go on to Tuttle Creek. Those things did happen, but it still wasn't enough. The City Park, Northeast, and Cico are all full. Tuttle Creek, while not full, has a considerable number of people there. Frank Anneberg Park isn't quite as bad, probably because of its location and people forget about it."

"People are camping in our parks?" I ask dumbly.

"Yep. The town council called an emergency meeting this morning at the police chief's urging. He started calling people at 4:00 a.m. when his people called and woke him. They met at 6:00 and got the university president involved. I hear he was a little reluctant to include the college in these efforts but was finally convinced. They've also contacted FEMA. Lots of people weren't prepared for camping. They thought they'd find a motel room. Some went on when they couldn't, but most of those who stayed are either out of gas or had small kids and needed a break after being on the road so long and so late."

41

What's Leo talking about? There are a few dozen hotels. How can they all be full? There must be thousands more people in town than there should be.

"You said they didn't keep going because they ran out of gas? Are they out of money too?"

"No. We're out of gas—the town is. At least we are until the trucks bring more, which, the way I hear it, might be a challenge since nothing's moving on I-70. People are coming from KC in the east and Denver in the west. While I don't think we have many Denver people here, the road's a complete parking lot to Goodland. All the little towns on 70 have been hit hard and are in the same shape we're in. It's a mess."

"I'm glad I'm off work today. I can't imagine how bad the restaurant will be."

"Yeah, uh . . . listen, Katie, I think we should leave."

"Why is that? All of these people will go home as soon as they realize the threat has passed."

"Many of them can't go home until the fuel arrives. I don't think the fuel will arrive until the roads clear. I suspect part of the reason the roads are so clogged is cars ran out of gas and were abandoned. The cleanup could take a while. And with so many more people here, I worry about our safety. You had nice families in the restaurant last night, but I guarantee not every person who has arrived in the last fifteen hours is nice."

My mind is screaming, *No, I'm not leaving*, but my mouth says, "What about our jobs?"

"I talked to my foreman this morning. He doubts we'll be working until this evens out. No fuel will be a problem. And I suspect fuel isn't going to be the only issue. Food is also going to be a problem. It's already happening in other places where small towns have been wiped out—the restaurants are out of food to cook, and the grocery stores are running low on easy-to-make stuff. If your restaurant runs out of food, how will they get more? Food delivery trucks will have the same trouble as fuel trucks. No food, no restaurant. I suppose the ad agency could stay open, but I think forfeiting your internship makes more sense than staying here."

"How would we go?" I ask. "If the roads are clogged, can we even leave?"

42

"I think we should take state and local roads. Casper's on the outer edge of what's being affected right now on I-25. People fleeing Denver used it to head north. Speaking of, you should probably check in with your sisters and make sure they know what's happening here so they can prepare for it there."

"Prepare?"

"Fill their gas tanks, buy food and water, and make sure they followed through on your folks' *Plan A*. Oh, which reminds me, there are now several thousand cases of E. coli and typhoid throughout the US and even in Canada. Cities all over the US are affected. It doesn't seem to be localized. They're using the term 'bioterrorism' since the only explanation can be a deliberate outbreak. How they're being spread is still unknown, but people are being cautioned to wash fresh produce, fully cook their meats, and drink only bottled water or water that's been filtered or boiled. So I suspect there will be a bottled water shortage also."

I sigh deeply. "It just keeps getting worse. Individually, these aren't really events that'd cause us any trouble here, but they sure are. I guess we should go."

Then I have a new idea. "Leo, could we maybe just go to a different town? All of these people came here, let's go somewhere else. We could camp for a few days or something, then come home."

"I don't think so, Katie. I think we should go somewhere we know we have a place. It's the safest and smartest thing to do. I'd hate to end up like these people in a town with no food, no fuel, and no water."

"But we could go somewhere not on the freeway and we wouldn't have this issue."

"Are you sure? Do you know for certain the terrorists are finished?" he asks.

"No . . . but if they aren't, we could still be driving right into trouble."

"True, but it's a risk we should take. Going somewhere I know you'll be safe is what we should do."

I let out a big sigh. "Okay, Leo, if you're sure it's what we should do."

He pulls me into a hug. "Yes, we should. After I saw all the people in town last night, I topped off my truck and the bed tank. I even bought a couple more fuel cans and filled them. Remember yesterday I said we should take both vehicles?"

"Yes, I'm okay with that."

"I've changed my mind."

"Why? I thought we agreed taking our stockpile of stuff to Mom and Jake's would be the best thing to do. I know we've sent things ahead, but . . . "

"I think we should drive straight through, and I'll need your help. I went out for a bit this morning and bought a utility trailer. It's nothing fancy but should do what we need it to do. I need to work on it a little to get it ready. Can you start getting things packed while I finish it? I'd like to leave here by noon."

I'm not very happy about leaving, but I know Leo's right. I'll try to look at it as a vacation—just until things settle down. "Yes. Let me call Calley and Angela, then I'll call the restaurant and leave a message at the ad agency service. I wonder where my mom is today. Hopefully she's not in a town struggling as much as Manhattan is."

"It sounded like she was in an okay place yesterday? And when she texted you, she knew about the traffic problems, so she probably knows to avoid certain areas. She'll probably make it to your home before we do."

"I hope so."

Leo kisses me and leaves the apartment. I look out the window. The utility trailer is hooked to his truck. It's nothing special. About eight feet long and made of some kind of wire. The back is tall, and the front is short. There's plywood stacked in it. Leo has a couple sawhorses and other tools next to it. He must have gotten those out of the storage closet on the balcony before he went down.

I'm a little bummed we're not taking my car. Yesterday, when he said we would, I was happy, even though I didn't want to drive alone all that way. Then, when he said we may have to dump it, I was really unhappy. Now, we'll just leave it here. I wonder what condition it'll be in when we return. I have a full tank of gas . . . will someone steal the gas? Will someone steal my car?

I get my phone and begin my calls—Angela first.

Angela lives in Casper, where Calley and I grew up. Well, we sort of grew up in Casper. We moved to Wyoming from Oregon when we were in junior high. Angela and Sarah, already adults and going to college, stayed in Oregon. A few months after we made our move, Malcolm was born.

I still laugh when I think about discovering Mom was going to have a baby. We were on a road trip to check out Wyoming and find a place to live. Mom was sick the entire trip, even threw up on one of the realtor's shoes. That was pretty funny. I half think we bought the property because Mom felt so bad.

When we got back home, Mom and Jake invited Sarah to visit for the weekend. Even though college was out for the summer, she had an apartment and a job in her college town. Angela was already living in an apartment in Alto and came over while Sarah was there. Jake barbecued and it was fun.

After we ate, Mom and Jake said they had an announcement to make. I thought it was just an official announcement about us moving, which seemed kind of weird since we all knew about it already. I was wrong.

The big announcement: they were having a baby.

Malcolm's ten now, and I miss him like crazy. The best thing about bugging out is I'll get to see him soon.

Chapter 6

"Hey, Katie."

"Hey, Angela. So . . . I guess I'm bugging out."

"Are you? Did something happen there? Oh, I bet it's the hordes of people, with you being on I-70 and so close to KC. Is that right?"

"Yeah. You already know about the people?"

"It's all over the news. They're here too. Not as bad as other places, but lots of Denver people are making their way here, and some are already here. Tim went out for more stuff last night as soon as we heard. He filled our cars and gas cans. We wanted to be sure to have enough to get to Mom and Jake's place, you know, in case we need to bug out too. He bought more dry goods and water also. Good thing he did after the food and water announcement this morning. Things are going nuts."

"It really is nuts. There are so many people here—they're camped in the city parks. The college is being opened for them. All the gas stations are out of fuel. And I think we're running low on bottled water and food too. Leo says we should leave."

"Leo's leaving with you? You finally told Mom and Jake about him?"

"Mostly."

"What's mostly mean? Never mind. I'm sure you have plenty to do to get ready. We're staying here for now, but Tim has things ready to go if we need to. I'm packing more stuff. Things I don't want to leave behind . . . just in case. We're not sure if he'll be working next week. They called all of the crews back home yesterday morning after the first attacks. Figured everyone's mind would be elsewhere and it's too dangerous."

"Yeah, same with Leo. No work yesterday. He called and told them he's taking some time off. I'm calling Calley, then calling my work and internship. You talk with Calley or Sarah?"

"Sarah's fine. Billings is starting to see people come in, I guess from the bridge going out in Seattle, even though it seems super far away. She says there aren't any problems at her place. I sent Calley a text but haven't heard back."

"I hope if anything really bad happens, she and Mike go to Mom's place," I say. "Even if they have to bring Mike's family. Mom wouldn't do well not knowing how Calley is doing."

"For sure. Hey, let me know when you're on the road. You coming here on your way? Or maybe just come here a few days. Things will probably blow over and we can have some sister time."

"Hmm. Good idea. I'll have to go to Mom and Jake's to visit but stopping and seeing you and my little Gavin boy would be great. Of course, you might have to bug out too."

"Yeah. I really hope not. We would, of course, but I don't really want to. And, now that I think about it, maybe it would be best for you to just go to Mom's place."

"Yeah, you're probably right. And no one wants to have to bug out, Angela."

"True. Talk later?"

"Yes, of course. Uh . . . Angela?"

"Yeah?"

"There's something I haven't told you."

"Okay?"

"About Leo."

"Yeah, so? What is it?"

"We . . . well, we're pretty serious."

"Duh, Katie. I figured that out on my own."

"Uh, right. I guess you probably did. But did you figure out he's living with me?"

She doesn't say anything. I think maybe we were disconnected. "Angela? You still there?"

"Yep. I'm still here. I'm just . . . surprised, I guess. Remember when I told you Tim and I were moving in together? You were very much against it. You told me it was God's plan for marriage not . . . what was the word you used? Cohabitation?"

"Yeah, sounds like what I said." I'm feeling a little ashamed.

"Oh, I know you were saying it with love and had my best interest in mind. At the time, I thought you were being rather prude, but now, I totally understand. Tim and I only lived together a short time before the wedding, and not even officially, but I wish we would've waited. I think the excitement of being newlyweds would've been increased if we would've . . . you know, *waited*."

I close my eyes and think about that word . . . *waited*. Leo and I had been dating for a couple months and had waited. I was beginning to think he was the one—the one I'd marry. I hadn't thought we'd stop waiting.

But one day, we were out for a bike ride and stopped at this community use cabin for a picnic. We started a fire, had our food, and the next thing I knew, we were no longer waiting.

And I was totally okay with it. Sure, I know what the Bible says about waiting until marriage. And also about cohabitating. Here I am, a person who thought she might be a missionary and share God's love with the world, actively engaging in sin. Sure, we all sin. But to deliberately sin . . . has this put me outside of God's will?

"Not to be mean, Katie, but I think you should really consider what you're doing. How long have you been living together? Can he move out—go back to wherever he was living before?"

"Since the beginning of February."

"Oh. You know, let's talk about this when we see each other. We'll try to visit while you're at Mom and Jake's place. And I think you should talk to Mom too. You know, if you're thinking choosing to live together—instead of subjecting Mom to another wedding—is the best choice, I think she'd disagree."

"You're probably right," I answer, then whisper, "She doesn't know we live together."

"Well, duh. I figured, if you hadn't told me, you certainly didn't tell Mom and Jake. You know, she's not going to be mad. She'll be surprised. We all kind of thought you were on fire for God, and now this . . . anyway, I'm glad to know you're human."

"Human? Of course I'm human. Why would you say that?"

"Katie, as much as I love you, sometimes I thought . . . well, I kind of felt like you were *too* good. Like I'd never be as good as you. I so often wanted what you had but couldn't see *how* I could get it. Does that make any sense?"

"Oh, Angela, you can get it. You just have to ask and be willing."

As I say this, I realize I can have it again too—I can have the feeling of fire in my belly, the incredible desire to serve, to share the love of Jesus. I'm no longer sure I'm called to the mission field—in the traditional sense—but I can get right with God and share His love with my family and friends, maybe even strangers.

"I don't know, Katie. Let's talk about this more too."

"We will, Angela. And I do know. God loves you. He's done great things in your life, and He wants to do more. He wants you to love Him back. I'm going to talk with Leo too. I think maybe things need to . . . I don't know, change."

"Maybe so, Katie. Keep me posted on your trip. We'll talk later."

"Talk later. Bye."

I want to think about what Angela said, but now's not the time to dwell on it. I try Calley next, but she doesn't answer. I leave her a message, letting her know things are bad here and I'm taking off for Mom and Jake's place.

Please, God, please keep all of us safe.

My first prayer in months. It's not much, but it's something.

The relationship Calley and I have is interesting. We're so very different from each other. When we were younger, we got along great—playing together and even having our own form of communication, to an extent. We looked very much alike, with similar body structures, crazy curly hair, and the same green eyes. She was very small as a child, and people often thought we were twins.

As time went on, we started to annoy each other. I guess it's pretty common among sisters, but it wasn't very comfortable. I suppose it was a little bit of sibling rivalry, plus me being the younger, annoying sister, along with different personalities.

Calley was very studious and exact in nature. She liked things to be a certain way, and she excelled in school—especially math. She had a small circle of very close friends. Mike, now her husband, was one of her best friends before they started dating.

She has a very unique style about her, choosing to wear clothing depicting her favorite anime characters. She's short, barely five foot tall, and curvy. She struggles to keep the weight off, like all of the females in my family do, since even a little extra weight can be a problem with her height.

While I take great pains to keep my crazy hair under control, her hair continues to have a mind of its own, which she allows. I'm now taller than Calley, at five foot four, and my wardrobe choices tend to be casual as opposed to quirky. Our childhood language is long forgotten.

Mom recognized we were having trouble getting along. I suppose it was pretty obvious since we fought often. Even though she would've preferred we have a close relationship with a special bond, she didn't harp on us about it. She let us each have our own space and learn to pursue our own interests.

While Calley did things like debate team and playing video games, I was a cheerleader and focused on my art and church youth group.

Even with our differences, we were expected to behave appropriately, and Mom wouldn't put up with us fighting. Instead, we tended to avoid each other and make snide remarks in hushed tones. Mom would often hear, and we'd get *the look*—or more.

I'm not really sure when things started to shift. Maybe at Calley's college graduation. I gave my perfunctory congratulations on her degree, and she hugged me tight. She said something like, "Katie, I'm so glad you're here. I know I haven't always been the best sister, but I love you."

After that we started talking more and would sometimes meet for lunch. Even with an associate degree in business, she still works at the same coffee shop she's worked since high school. She says she plans to find a "grown-up" job soon, but she loves the hours and flexibility of the coffee shop.

Plus, with tips, she averages fifteen dollars an hour, and that's hard to beat in a town like Casper. Since her wedding last year, she's been a little more serious about looking for something else. I think she's waiting for the perfect job, and I'm not sure how easy it will be to find. She may have to lower her standards a bit.

While our relationship is better, we don't talk very often. It's not just me she distances herself from. She does the same thing with Sarah and Angela. We try to reach out to her but are often rebuffed.

She does it with Mom, too, but Mom calls her on it. Sarah has started pointing it out to her also. Then Calley will pout a bit. The last time we were all together was before her wedding. Even though it was a happy occasion, she was still weird with us.

My next call is the restaurant. We're only open for dinner, but Mr. or Mrs. Lowery should be there. Will they terminate me, or just let me have some time off? I'm not scheduled for a shift until Wednesday, so they have a few days to find someone to cover me.

Mrs. Lowery answers. She says she completely understands, and I should go home to my family. The next few days may be challenging for the restaurant if food deliveries don't come in. They're probably fine tonight, but Monday night might be lean. I thank her for being so understanding and tell her I'll let her know when I'm returning.

I leave a phone message on the ad agency's machine, letting them know I'm leaving town and will call on Monday.

I need to shower and dress for the day. I wonder what the appropriate attire is when bugging out?

I choose khaki pants, a T-shirt, and a light button-up shirt to go over it. I suspect I'll lose the top shirt as soon as the day heats up. I put sandals on, then rethink and decide on tennis shoes.

Leo and I had talked about the possibility of this day when Mom and Jake sent the backpack. I know anything I can't live without should go in the pack. It's pretty well packed already. I get out my suitcases and start putting together the rest of my clothes. I'm thinking about the food we need to take and realize I'm hungry. I wonder if Leo's eaten? Even if he has, he can probably eat again.

We have a small cooler for fridge things, but the less the better. Then I think about the freezer and the stuff in there. Should I cook some of those?

We have a few pizzas, some frozen burritos, and little bagel pizza things. I could cook all of them, and we could eat them cold while on the road. I also have several packages of frozen meat, which I can leave frozen and pack in the cooler right before we go. Mom does this when we go camping; lets it thaw in the cooler, then cooks it.

Breakfast first. We have plenty of eggs, a full dozen plus four. I fry the four for breakfast and put the dozen on to hard-boil—more traveling food. There's a half-full tub of plain yogurt we'll finish and a jug of orange juice. Once I have everything ready, I go down to see Leo.

"It's looking good. Hungry? I made breakfast."

"Hey, great. Do you mind bringing my plate down here? I'd like to get this wrapped up and don't really want to stop."

The trailer already looks very different. The sides have plywood going up four feet, and the top is covered too. He made some kind of bracing out of 2 x 4s and attached the plywood. We now have an enclosed trailer.

"Leo, this looks great. If it rains, our stuff will stay dry."

"Our stuff will stay *dryer*. I doubt it's fully watertight, but it'll help. I'm almost done. It went pretty quick."

"Let me get our food. I'll eat here with you and tell you my plan."

While Leo and I eat, I tell him what I'm going to do with the food. He thinks it's a great idea, especially since we won't want to grab food along the way because of the foodborne illness issues. I ask Leo if he's heard any more news. He says, with the sawing and drilling, he hasn't turned on the radio. I tell him I'll check when I go upstairs and have it on while I'm packing.

"You know, Leo. I'm feeling a little bad about just leaving my car here. You think it'll be vandalized?"

"Yeah, I think there's a good chance it'll be."

"You said people are stranded here because there isn't any gas, right?"

"Yes, that's what I'm hearing. I believe it to be true."

"Do you think anyone would want to buy my car? It has a full tank, and we have the two five-gallon cans. Your truck uses diesel, so we can't really use the gas from the SUV or the cans."

"Maybe. I don't know how people are fixed for money. When you were thinking of selling it, did you research the price?"

"A little. It's a four-wheel drive, so that increased the value a bit. I think the Blue Book was twenty-six hundred. I was hoping to get twenty-two for it."

"Hmm. And you want to sell?"

"I'd rather sell it than have it destroyed and get nothing. You know, I only have liability. It's not worth having full coverage on something so old with such a low value."

"I don't know how we could sell it this quick. And you wouldn't be able to transfer the title over. It's a good idea, but I just don't see it as a real possibility. What we could do, maybe, is rent a storage unit and lock it in there. Might be a better choice than leaving it on the street."

"You think so? Could we do that?"

"Can you call the one on Eureka and see if they have a unit available? I imagine they do with school just ending. Lots of seniors are gone now, and some might have used a storage unit while living here. We have to make this quick, Katie. I still want to leave by noon."

"I'll make the call and get my packing done. Do you still need to pack?"

"Mostly done. I'll only need a few minutes. It'll take some time for us to load up, though. If we can get a storage unit, we can stop there on the way out."

The price for a garage unit is amazingly high at $110 per month. I figure, one month and I'll either be back or never coming back. I make the reservation over the phone and pay with my credit card. They tell me to bring my own lock. I'm pretty sure I have one in my dresser. And it's a combination, so I don't have to look for the key, only remember the code. Not always an easy task.

After taking care of the reservation, I turn the oven on to heat so I can make the food. While it's preheating, I pack the stuff in my dresser drawers. I finish as the preheat cycle is done.

I'm making a game of this. I put the burritos in and set the timer for twenty minutes. The cook time is thirty-five to forty, but I want to put the bagel pizzas in during the last fifteen or so minutes so they can cook too. I get the bagels ready on the cooking sheet. Now the game begins.

I want to have my closet emptied and packed before the bagels need to go in the oven. I'm making good progress until I get to the back of the closet. I don't even know why I have some of these clothes in here. I don't wear them. As the timer goes off, I make a decision. Leave them behind.

The bagels are in, and I shut the suitcase. I find a reusable grocery bag for my shoes. I tie a second pair of athletic shoes, my favorite running ones, on to the backpack. Like the clothes, a few shoes are still in the closet.

Next, makeup and toiletries. These are pretty easy since I use one of the toiletry-organizing roll things. The clear plastic bags Velcro to a large piece of material, then it all rolls together and Velcro's shut. I do have to pack my hair products separate and put those in a carry-on bag, along with some other miscellaneous stuff. I'm not finished, but the timer's beeping at me.

The bagel things look done. The burritos, bursting open, are also done. The two cheap pizzas go in next, directly on the rack to give them a nice crisp crust. Twelve minutes. That's how long I have to finish my packing and bring everything to the living room.

I finish emptying the bathroom. I have the nightstand by my bed left. I keep my jewelry and some keepsake items here. The jewelry, most of it costume, is stored in individual boxes or bags. I put all of these in a gallon-sized Ziploc and tuck it in the carry-on bag. I find a reusable grocery bag for the keepsakes.

I take a look around my apartment. I'm an artist, and I have my art on the walls. I have a few pieces lined up on the floor. I'm hopeful there will be room to bring it all. Maybe, with the trailer . . .

The timer goes off. I'm happy with my progress. I take the pizzas out. The counters are full of pizza, bagels, and burritos. Once they cool, I'll package them for travel. I peek out the window to see how Leo's doing on the trailer.

While the trailer looks great, there also seems to be trouble.

Chapter 7

Leo's talking to a couple of guys. Just normal, average-looking guys, but something's seriously off. One guy, almost as big as Leo, is wildly gesticulating. The other guy—smaller but rougher looking—is standing stock-still with his arms crossed. Leo's standing tall and strong with his arms by his sides. He shakes his head several times and gestures down the street. After a few minutes, the guys stalk off.

My phone rings. It's Leo.

"Who were those guys?"

"Guys who thought we have stuff they should have."

"What? What do you mean?"

"They saw me finishing the trailer and suggested we may have fuel to get out of here. I convinced them this was just a project I've been working on. At least, I think I convinced them. I'm glad the gas tank we got for the bed of the truck looks like a toolbox. How close to ready are you?"

"I have all my stuff packed. The food is cooling and needs to be packaged. Then we need to load. Oh, and I got a storage unit."

"Good. That's great. Listen, Katie, I don't think we should leave the truck alone. I think we need to keep an eye on it, so one of us should be here while the other one loads. Can you start bringing stuff down? Only light stuff, then we'll switch off."

"Uh, yeah. Sure."

I think Leo's being a little intense about this. Surely people wouldn't try to steal our truck in broad daylight. And, seriously, we've been out of gas less than twelve hours. Could people really be that desperate already?

I take my first load of stuff. As I'm descending the stairs, I remember I didn't check the balcony storage unit. Our bikes are in there. The tools Leo is using are kept in there, plus some of his other things are there too. About my paintings, I've decided I'm taking all of them.

"Here's the first load, Leo."

"Super, Katie."

"Oh, hey. What are you doing with the bike rack?"

"Trying to figure out how to mount it on the trailer so we can get our bikes loaded without taking up trailer or truck bed space."

"Good idea. I figured we'd just put them in the bed of your truck like we usually do."

"Yeah. I should've planned this a little better. I could've bought a few more things this morning. I think I have something I can use in the storage unit. Can you stay here while I look?"

"Of course."

"Katie, don't act friendly. We don't need people stopping to chat."

"Yes, boss."

Leo's back in few minutes carrying two totes.

"Find what you need?"

"Yes. I can make it work. I want to go ahead and load the trailer first. Everything we can get in there, we should. I brought these totes, but I'm thinking the totes would make a nice load in the truck. Then we can tarp it all. We can put things we need in the bed too. In the back seat of the truck, our backpacks and any gear we need on the road will be there for easy access. Let's load it last."

"All right. What do you want me to bring down?"

"How about you stay here. I'll make some very fast trips, and when I need a break, you go. Bring anything."

"Leo, I want to bring my paintings. They should go in the trailer. Can you bring them first?"

"Which painting?"

"All of them."

"All of them? Katie. No."

"Yes, Leo. I'm okay with leaving my furniture and anything we don't need, except my paintings. I want to bring them."

Leo lets out a big sigh. "Okay. I'll bring them first. They'll need to be in the trailer."

"Thank you, Leo. Also, I don't know what all is in the storage area. I meant to look but forgot. I know our bikes are there. Do we have anything else?"

"Not really, just some tools I'll bring with us. Be right back."

He gives me a quick kiss. True to his word, he's back in a flash. He has an armload of paintings—looks like most of the ones I had stacked by the wall in the bedroom. He puts them in the trailer.

Next trip, he's back with more paintings—the rest from the floor and a couple off the wall, plus a tarp. I help him put the tarp in the trailer at the front, then we put the paintings on the tarp. He goes for the rest. Once they're all in, we wrap the tarp around like a burrito.

"You know, Katie, I think it'd be better to layer a few totes on the bottom and then put the paintings near the ceiling. Better use of space. Let's grab the two I brought and see."

He's right. We can fit the two totes and two more easily going widthwise, add a third going long ways with one on top of this, then the paintings on top. He goes after more totes. Once we have the six totes arranged how we want, the paintings fit nicely on top, against the front of the trailer.

"I thought you wanted the totes in the truck?"

"Yeah. That was before I knew we were going to be a traveling art show." He winks at me and takes off for another load.

My turn now. I pack the food I made into zipper bags and tuck them in the fridge. Several more trips by each of us, and we have almost everything loaded.

We seal up the trailer and attach the bikes to the back. Leo's right, he made it work. It seems even more secure than the usual mount.

"What do you think, Leo? You want to go do a walk through, then I'll fill the cooler and we can go?"

"Yeah. I think it's a good idea. I took a listen to the radio, and it doesn't sound good. We should get going."

"What doesn't sound good?"

"They're saying FEMA's delayed in arriving. With so many cities being affected, they're spread too thin. Water's an issue. They're still recommending to boil or purify all water. The sporting goods stores are out of purification systems now, even iodine and swimming pool chlorine. They were recommending bleach, but that's all sold out too. We need to go before things get worse, before people start freaking out."

"Okay." I sigh. "Yes, let's get going. You go take a walk through and then I'll pack the cooler."

"I'll go ahead and fill the cooler while I'm in the apartment. Is there anything else you need?"

"My purse. Everything else is loaded. My backpack's in the back seat with yours. I took my emergency kit and a few other things out of my car. I'm ready except my purse."

"Okay. Go get it and then I'll do my thing."

I go up to the apartment and take a final look around. I find a bag I missed earlier, shoved in the closet. Everything else that should go is loaded. I really like this apartment and hope to be back soon. I want to take another minute to mourn over what I'm losing, but instead, I shake my head and get going. I move the cooler into the kitchen for Leo to have easy access, grab the things I need, and go on down.

Back at the truck, Leo hands me the fancy zapper stick.

"What's this for?" I ask.

"I heard what sounded like breaking glass. I think it came from the next block over. I think you should get in the truck and lock it. Keep this handy. I'll go and take a final look around, then bring the cooler down. I'll be quick. If anything seems amiss, call me immediately."

"Okay." I climb in the truck and lock the door, holding on to my zapper stick like it's a lifeline, as Leo heads to the apartment.

K-thunk. K-thunk. Several guys are up the street. There's more *k-thunks*, accompanied by laughing and cursing. What are they doing? Trying to break into cars?

There are at least six of them. I lose count as they move around the vehicles, mostly because they're dressed so similarly—black wife beater tanks, baggie black pants, sunglasses, and black beanies, even though it's way too hot to be wearing something like that. While we certainly have crime in Manhattan, and a few motorcycle clubs have been known to cause trouble, we're not really a big gang town. Even with my limited knowledge, these guys scream *gang* to me.

"Get away from my car or I'll shoot!"

My mind barely has time to register the new voice before several shots ring out. I hit the floor. My heart's pounding through my chest. There are several more shots—I lose count at eight. The laughing from the gang is gone, but the cursing, along with screams of anger and pain, continue. A couple more shots sound off until there's only the screams of pain.

My phone rings.

"Leo! They're shooting. I think it's done, but I'm pretty sure people are hurt."

"I know," he says, sounding a lot calmer than I think he should be. "I heard it. You're in the truck, right?"

"Yes. I'm on the floor."

"Okay, good. We're going to wait another minute, then I'll come and get you. I'd have you drive my truck, but with all of the cars on the street, the trailer might be a challenge for you."

"Uh-huh. Are we going to go see if we can help them? The hurt ones, I mean?"

"No, Katie. We're not."

"You don't think we should?"

"No. I think we should get out of here. This town is turning into a powder keg, and I don't want you in any more danger. We're going to drive from here directly to the storage unit. Then we're going to head somewhere safe. I don't see any movement. I'm coming for you now. Once we're a few blocks away, I'll call 911."

"Okay. I'm ready."

Leo's at the truck in seconds. I grab my purse and my zapper stick and step out. He tells me to crouch as he puts the cooler on the passenger's seat. He then hustles me to my SUV as we walk in a stoop, keeping close by the cars parked on the curb.

"Turn your car around and go the other direction. I'm going around the block and will catch up with you. It'll be too hard to navigate the truck and trailer on this street to follow you. Don't stop for anyone."

I agree and start my car. Leo moves behind the car in front of me and crouches slightly while he watches me get maneuvered around and headed in the right direction. I do a four-point turn and take off.

On the drive to the storage unit, I'm amazed at the number of people on the streets. Not many cars but many people walking and some on bikes. Passing by one of the local parks, it resembles a tent city.

I begin to breathe easier when I notice Leo behind me within a couple of blocks.

The SUV fits nicely into the rental unit. I lock it, write down the combination on two pieces of paper, give one to Leo, and put the other in my wallet. I climb in with Leo and we head out in a hurry—as much of a hurry as we can with the busyness of Manhattan.

I'm still shaking from the adrenaline pumping through my body. I shudder involuntarily.

"You did well, Katie. Getting on the floor was smart."

I nod but say nothing for a couple minutes. Then I start crying. I'm pretty sure Leo can't understand me through my tears, as I tell him,

"It was so strange. They were checking the cars and trying to open doors. They kept kicking the cars and hitting them with things. Then I heard a guy tell them to leave his car alone, and one of the gang guys just started shooting. I couldn't see what happened next since I was on the floor."

Leo pats my leg. "I heard the banging and hustled to get the cooler down the stairs. I had just opened the door when I heard the guy shout and the shooting start. I think there were at least four different weapons involved, but they all sounded like handguns."

As I'm pulling myself together, I look at the clock on the dashboard. 12:22. We're only a little later than Leo's target time of noon.

Getting out of town is slow going. With the traffic and the way I'm blubbering after the shooting, I'm very glad Leo's driving.

"How's the trailer pulling?" I ask a little while later, after my tears have stopped.

"It's fine. It's not very big, and even with the plywood I added and being full, the weight's still good."

"I can probably drive when we get to someplace less congested if you want."

"Yeah. Once we're in a better place, I'll let you take the wheel for a while. US-81 should be a good place for you to drive. Not curvy at all and, of course, flat as a pancake. You get ahold of your family earlier?"

"I talked to Angela. I left a message for Calley. I never even thought of calling Jake to let him know we're on the way. I should. And I should see if I can reach my mom and find out where she is. Did you make the 911 call after the shooting?"

"I did. They already knew about it. Said several people had called."

I nod. A shooting in broad daylight, I'd expect the emergency calls to be made. I decide to start my calls with Jake first.

"Hey, Katie."

"Hey, Jake. We're coming to your house. Manhattan got overrun with people leaving KC last night." I decide not to tell him about the shooting incident so close to my apartment.

"Oh, Katie. I'm sorry about this. I do think it's a good idea for you to leave, though. Drive straight through if you can. You heard about the water and food poisoning? You have enough stuff so you don't need to stop for food?"

"Yeah, I think we'll be fine." We talk for a few more minutes about Jake worrying over my trip, then about a wedding he's going to this afternoon, and then about the latest updates on the attacks—they don't think it was caused by suicide bombers; the bombs were remote detonated.

Jake finishes with, "I guess we'll know more as time goes on. Keep me posted on your progress. I look forward to meeting Leo, even though I wish it were a real vacation and visit you were on."

"Okay, Jake. I'll talk to you later."

It takes us almost two hours to get far enough away from Manhattan to be able to travel at something resembling a normal speed.

Listening to the radio and checking my Google Maps app, we decide to stick with the side roads as much as possible. We already knew we didn't want to go on I-80 near Cheyenne but had thought the interstate would be okay near where we were.

Only, we're now hearing reports of Lincoln, Nebraska, seeing refugees. That's east of where we planned to get on I-80, but not worth the risk. Instead, we'll catch Highway 36 west, then head north crossing over I-80.

We turn off the radio and plug in my iPod for music. Everything's going well when we reach a little town in Nebraska about twenty-five miles south of the interstate. Things are still quiet here.

"I think we should fill up, Katie. We're at about half a tank. The stop and go coming out of Manhattan didn't do our fuel mileage any favors."

"Sounds good. I need to use the restroom anyway."

Leo pulls to the pump while I head inside. When I come out of the bathroom, Leo's at the counter.

"Hey, babe. You ready to go? You want any snacks?"

"Maybe a soda. We have the stuff I packed from home."

"I think I'll grab one also."

At the refrigerator case, Leo grabs not one but three sodas. I arch an eyebrow at him.

"You may want to get more than one too. My card didn't work for gas. The guy here says the system's down. There's some sort of cyberattack. Guess we should've checked in on the news once in a while."

"A cyberattack? You mean someone's taking out the internet?"

"Pretty much. It's probably nothing. We'll listen to the radio when we get in the truck."

The radio catches us up on exactly what's happening.

"We're receiving reports of dozens of financial intuitions offline by what is believed to be the result of a malware cyberattack. The affected banks are unable to offer any online services, which has shut down credit and debit cards, online banking, and ATM machines. While it is a Saturday and most bank branches are closed, people are prevented from withdrawing money directly from branches since the computers cannot be accessed for these records. We're assured these attacks are being addressed and services should soon return to normal.

"In addition to financial institutions going down, social media giants Facebook and Twitter, along with YouTube, Google, and Yahoo, are unavailable due to what is believed to be a distributed denial-of-service taking these out.

"With so many people turning to social media and online searches to stay up to date on the latest news, this is causing extra panic. The affected sites hope to resolve these outages as soon as possible. 911 operators are being inundated with calls reporting downed status of websites. Please do not call 911 to report any websites being down. Please reserve 911 for true emergencies only. We'll have more on this developing story as information becomes available."

"Yikes, Leo. This doesn't sound good. I don't care about Facebook being down, but is the money we have in our banks safe?"

"How much money you have in the bank, Katie? A hundred bucks?"

"Nope. Around thirty. Less than usual, but I rarely have much in there."

"I don't think you should worry much about your money. We were smart to pull out more cash yesterday. I got most of mine. The bank didn't like me taking it out and tried to talk me out of it. If I haven't told you, I'm sure glad your folks sent the bug-out bag to you. We'd be in a world of hurt right now if they hadn't. It got us started and helped us make some wise decisions along the way—having cash on hand is one of those. The general population's likely freaking out right now."

We're both quiet as we continue listening to the news updates. There really isn't any new information about the attacks or the food poisonings, only a staggering announcement of the mass amount of life lost from the combined events.

We cross over I-80 without incident and are soon in the small town of Ansley, where we plan to head west. We listen to the radio off and on and discover the cyberattacks continue to evolve and increase. There are now many blackouts across the US due to the power stations being hit. The government has taken the internet completely offline, and even traffic lights have stopped working. It's a mess. No, it's worse than that. With everything else already going on, it's a mess on top of a mess.

We start looking for a gas station on 83 but don't find anything until we reach Valentine. The gas station, like the rest of the town, is dark.

"Looks closed, Leo."

"Yeah. I think the power's out here."

"We okay on gas?"

"We're okay. I'll put some in from the cans I bought last night. We'll use the big tank if we need to farther down the road. You think you could drive for a while? I'd love to shut my eyes."

He pours the fuel in the truck while I move around to the driver's side. I adjust the mirrors as needed. I'm a little nervous about driving with the trailer attached. I've driven Leo's truck before, and it handles fine. Jake has a very similar truck, just older, so I'm not new to driving pickup trucks.

From Valentine, we're heading west on US-20. We discussed taking 20 into Wyoming, which would put us in Lusk, but decided that was too close to Cheyenne, which is too close to Denver. We'll head north into South Dakota and go into Wyoming on US-18, then head to Newcastle. Leo makes sure I know which road to head north on before he dozes off.

Everything is going fine until shortly after midnight, when a deer darts out in front of me.

I briefly consider swerving but realize, with the trailer attached, I'm likely to wreck. I whack it hard, then skid to a stop.

"What's happening?!"

"I hit a deer. She came out of nowhere. Do you think she's okay?" I'm shaking so hard I can barely get the words out.

"Turn off the truck, then scoot over here. I'll get out and see."

Leo walks to the front of the truck, then over to the side of the road. He walks around the truck a bit, then climbs back in.

He starts the truck and carefully pulls forward. I feel a bump.

"What's going on Leo? Did I break something?"

"The deer was stuck underneath. You rolled her full-length, and she was caught under the trailer. I'm going to pull forward a bit and check for damage. One of the turn signal lenses is shattered, but I didn't see anything else."

"So . . . she's not okay?"

He reaches for my hand. "Sorry, Katie."

Feeling terrible, I simply nod.

Leo pulls forward to a wide spot and takes a flashlight with him when he gets out. I start to open my door.

"Can you wait here, Katie? The deer is a mess and I need to move it off the road. You don't need to help."

"I can help."

"I know." He shuts the door.

I watch in the side mirrors as he walks back to the deer and moves her off the road. It takes three trips to fully clear the road. I'm a little sick thinking of the damage I'd done to her. I'm fine with hunting. Even though I don't do it myself, I totally understand it. But this, I don't like. It's not the same at all.

After moving the deer, Leo walks very slowly around the trailer and truck, stopping often and looking underneath. He then pops the hood. After about ten minutes, he gets back in.

"We may have some good fortune. With the way you hit her, we only lost the lens cover, and the lower radiator hose came loose. I was able to tighten the hose. I have some tape to cover the lens with. I didn't find anything else, but we'll take it slow when we start out to make sure nothing's going on. I think the brush guard and the winch helped keep her out of the grill. You mind holding the flashlight for me while I tape the lens?"

He locates the tape in a small tool case he has under the backseat. It takes only a few minutes to get the tape on the lens. Leo takes over driving. True to his word, he drives very slowly for a couple miles, listening for anything not sounding right. He pulls over at a wide spot.

"Something wrong?"

"Don't think so. I'm going to do another walk around and check under the hood to make sure."

A few minutes later, he's back in the truck.

"I'll take her up to speed and then check again."

After a few miles at highway speed, he pulls over and repeats his walk around. Getting back in the truck, he says, "Looks like we dodged a bullet, Katie. I'm going to drive from now until daylight, then I'll do another walk around when we have full light. Hopefully all is well. Why don't you get some sleep?"

"Yeah. I think sleep is a good idea. I feel terrible about hitting the deer."

"I know you do, honey. It's one of those things. You did really well not crashing after you hit her. Pulling the trailer, it could've been easy for you to lose control."

Chapter 8

Sunday, Day 4

It's still dark when I wake, feeling the vehicle slow. I have drool stuck to the side of my cheek. *Ick.* Wiping my face with the back of my arm, I sit up. While it's mostly still dark, there's a hint of light in the east.

"Where are we?"

"Just past Newcastle."

"We're in Wyoming? That's great! What time is it?"

"Not yet five. It'll be full light soon. I still want to check the truck in the daylight, but we need some fuel. Nothing was open in Newcastle. All of the pumps had out of order signs on them."

"What road are we on?"

"Wyoming 450, heading east toward a town called Wright. I'm not sure which way to go from there to get to your folks' place and avoid traffic. Now that you're awake, I think I'll turn the radio on when we get going."

"I've been in this area before. Wright isn't too far from here. They might have an open gas station."

"Maybe. I'll add some just in case. If they're closed, we can put more in after we pass through the town."

"You need help?"

"Nope. I'm good at it now with the practice I've done over the last several months." He winks at me as he shuts the truck door.

Even though it's June, it's a little chilly this morning. I pull the light blanket we have in the truck around my shoulders. Then I realize my bladder's full, so I step out to take care of this business. Back in the truck, I snuggle into the blanket and close my eyes.

With the practice he's done, the transfer still takes several minutes. When he returns, I ask, "You think we'll have enough fuel to make it if we can't find a station open?"

"I think so. The auxiliary tank is sixty gallons. Let's look at the map, but I think it's less than four hundred miles from here. That should use less than half the tank."

There's a Wyoming map in my map collection, provided by Mom and Jake as part of the bug-out bag, and we stretch it out between us.

"Here we are." Leo points to a spot.

"Yep. One of my mom's friends lives around here. We visited a couple of times, not that I could ever find her house." I shrug. "We're in the grasslands . . . um . . . let me think, it has a special name. I'm surprised it isn't on this map. I'll think of it. Once the sun comes up, it'll be beautiful. It's pretty flat looking with rolling hills, but it's kind of deceiving. Off the road, like where Mom's friend lives, there's gulches and rock formations. It's pretty amazing, almost like a hidden land."

"Sounds like we'll be in for some scenery after daylight."

"Yeah, but watch out for the antelope. They like to dart out in front of you. Oh, I guess I should say pronghorn. One of my professors really gave me a talking to over calling them antelope, 'Don't you know the difference, young lady? Contrary to the song you may know, the antelope do not play in North America. Pronghorn. We have pronghorn. You want antelope? Go to Africa.' Man, he really let me have it. To be honest, I don't know anyone living in Wyoming that calls them pronghorn, even the hunting licenses say antelope."

"Some people are just sticklers, I guess," Leo says with a small laugh. "I'm looking forward to seeing the antelope."

"Yeah, well, don't hit one. We don't need a repeat of my performance last night."

"I'll be careful. So, we'll stay on this road into Wright, then we could go north to I-90. I can't imagine we'd have any troubles on 90 there. It should be far enough away from any of the towns with the bridge attacks. We can take 90 into Billings and then drop down. This route might give us the best chance for finding fuel too. Even though I'm sure we'll be fine, it'd be best to get a fill."

"You think going through Billings is a good idea? There's lots of people there, and if there isn't any power, how can we get fuel?"

"Last news we heard indicated scattered blackouts. Maybe Billings isn't affected? What are our other options?" Leo asks.

I point to the map. "We could take this road across here from Wright. It's a little state highway and would drop us onto I-25 north of Casper. But Angela said Casper had people from Denver, so that might not be smart."

"If Casper has people from Denver and they're already north on 25, they may have made it to I-90 too."

"Maybe. Or maybe people stopped in Casper. It's hard to know," I say with a shrug. "This road that drops on 25 is quite a ways north of Casper. I think it's a better risk than I-90. And then, at Buffalo or just past Sheridan, we can go over the Bighorns to their place."

"Looks good. Let me see if I can figure out the mileage." He spends a few minutes using the key to try to estimate it.

"I think it's a little over four hundred. With regular driving, we'll be fine. It's the stop and go that's hard on this truck's fuel consumption. Pulling the trailer isn't helping either. But we should make it. Of course, going over the Bighorns will also use fuel. Maybe, when we get to Buffalo, we can find out more about Billings. It may be worth going that way if it sounds okay."

"Sounds like a plan. You hungry?"

"Starved."

I get out and stretch. I'm still cold so grab a sweatshirt from the back seat.

"You want a burrito?"

"Might as well. It's better warm, but I can choke it down."

"Not me. I thought it was pretty terrible. There's three left—you can have them all. I'll take the bagel bites. Everything else in the cooler is uncooked. At least we have jerky and tuna packets. Tuna for breakfast. Yum. Oh! Thunder Basin National Grassland."

"What?"

"That's what this is called. I remembered. Closer to Wright, there's even a mine called Thunder Basin. That's how I remembered the name. I was thinking about the huge trucks there. Malcolm was totally mesmerized by those trucks when we drove by them. Wait until you see."

It's full-on daylight now, so Leo walks around the truck looking for any issues from me clobbering the deer. He finds nothing new. We listen to the radio and discover the power outages are very widespread, with more places affected than not. Cell service is also spotty, with some carriers completely down. The internet is still out. More people have died from E. coli and typhoid. It's all quite a mess.

When we drive past the mine, it's completely quiet. No large dump trucks driving around for me to point out to Leo. I'm not sure why, but this makes me cry. I know it's completely silly, but I can't help it.

We're in Wright shortly after 7:00 a.m. The gas station is open. There's a sign on the diesel pump telling us to go inside for service. Leo moves the truck over to the edge of the lot where we can see the front door.

"Wait here?"

I answer with a nod.

He steps out of the truck, then reaches under the seat and pulls out two soft-sided handgun cases. He unzips one. "Katie, this is the semi-auto .22 you've shot before. It's loaded and ready to go—just click it off safe." He motions to the small tab on the side. "I'm going to leave it on the seat. You know how to use it if you need to."

The gun faces toward the steering column. He gives me a small wave as he walks into the building.

A few minutes later, a guy comes out the door with Leo behind him. The guy heads over to the side of the building as Leo walks toward me, giving me a thumbs up.

"They have a generator. He's going to fire it up. It's ten dollars a gallon. I bought ten gallons. Told him I'd see if we could come up with any more money. The guy seemed fine, but I didn't want to flash my cash around too much. Besides, I only had a hundred on me. Give me a minute."

Leo steps out and hollers over to the guy. "The wife says to fill it. Okay by you?"

"Okay by me, if you got the cash. Need to see it before we go over the amount you already paid. You understand," he yells back.

I get into my purse and decide the guy is getting all ones. I produce a combination of tens, fives, and ones plus a single twenty, to total an extra $150. "Tell the guy the 'wife' didn't have any large bills."

Leo laughs. "Keep an eye out, Katie. Should be fine, but let's stay alert."

It is fine. It takes almost the full $250 to fill the truck and bed tank. The little left Leo puts in one of the gas cans. Leo shakes hands with the gas guy and we head out.

There's a small rest area in Wright we make use of. I take in my toiletry bag and a change of clothes. Leo does the same.

As we're getting out of the truck, Leo says, "Katie, take the zapper stick from your backpack."

"What?"

"I think we need to be cautious. This looks like a quiet place, but you never know. I'd feel better if you took the stick with you for your safety. I'm doing the same thing myself." He lifts the left edge of his shirt so I can see his holstered pistol.

"I had no idea you were carrying it. When did you put that on?"

"When we left home yesterday."

"Why didn't you tell me? And how'd I not see it?"

"Didn't think about it. Maybe since it's on the left side? I had it on last night while you were driving and I was in the passenger's seat."

"I guess."

"Is this a problem, Katie?"

"No. Not a problem. I know lots of people who carry all the time, or did when I lived in Wyoming. It's just not something I'm used to from you, and it makes me wonder how things changed so quickly."

"They did change quickly. And I think they're going to continue to change. We need to be ready. Will you take the zapper stick?"

I agree and take it with me into the bathroom, which I have all to myself. I'm happy I packed a washcloth in my bag and can take something resembling a sponge bath.

We both seem to be in good spirits when we get back in the truck. We decide we need another snack break and I'll try to reach my family.

I try to call Angela but get a no service message. Same thing when I try each other family member. Next, I text Angela, and it seems to go through. I let her know we're in Wright heading toward Midwest. Tim, Angela's husband, is from Midwest, and his dad still lives there. A few minutes later, Angela texts back. I let out a gasp. *Oh no!*

Chapter 9

"Leo! Angela says there was a fire in Manhattan. A bad one. Listen: *'I'm so glad you left Manhattan. There was a report on the news about it. A large fire broke out. They were getting it out when the power went out.'*"

"Oh no," Leo says. "I'm going to see if I can reach Bob and see what he knows."

"Okay. Let me text Angela. After the fire part she says, *'We're picking up Tim's dad and then going to Mom and Jake's. Let's meet in Midwest. You remember where he lives?'* Something must have happened since they're going to Mom's place too. You mind if we take a break here so we can meet them?"

"Not at all. I think it's a good idea. Might be smart to be together."

I send my text. *"Sounds good, Angela. We'll see you soon."*

Leo tries to call Bob and is surprised when the phone connects and starts to ring. He puts it on speaker so I can hear. He uses a different service than me, so maybe his company has things figured out to keep them working.

"Hello?"

"Bob? It's Leo."

"Yup. I know. Good thing you left town when you did. It's a disaster here."

"Heard there was a fire."

"Yup. There still *is* a fire. Aggieville is burning."

"All the guys are okay?"

"Far as I know. Haven't seen Stinky Pete. Think he may have took off, same as you. They're having a tough time putting the fire out. When the power went out, the water pumps went on backup generator or something, but the flow is down. Less flow means less water coming out of the hydrants. It's not good. Think I'll take off too. I'll likely be on foot. Someone stole the gas out of my rig overnight."

"What? They siphoned you?"

"Nope. They punched a hole in my gas tank. Mine and several others on the street. Should've found a place with a garage, I guess."

Leo and I catch each other's eye. I like Bob. He was one of the people Leo used to room with. He was always nice to me. I even set him up with my friend Bree, but they didn't really hit it off. I nod at Leo.

"Hey, Bob. Hold on a minute, okay?" Leo puts the phone on mute.

"Let's offer him my SUV, Leo. Where would he go?" I ask.

"His folks are in North Dakota. Guess he'd go there."

"That's right. I remember talking to him about it. Should be clear to there, as long as he watches out for deer." I smile weakly. "Then, when this is all over, he can bring my car back to me. You think there's enough gas for him to get there?"

"Probably close. You have a full tank plus twenty gallons. He can tie the cans on the bumper or the luggage rack."

"Do it."

He takes the phone off mute. "Hey, Bob?" Leo says.

"Yeah, buddy? Thought you and your lady forgot about me."

"Not a chance. My lady has something for you. Go ahead, Katie."

"Hi, Bob."

"Katie, you doing okay?"

"Yeah. You know if my apartment is in the line of the fire?"

"Not so far. But who knows what will happen. Should be okay. It's not likely the wind would shift toward your place."

"What about the storage units on Eureka? Any trouble there?"

"Not that I know of."

"Good. I rented a unit to store my SUV. Why don't you go and get it? You can head out to your folks' or someplace else."

"Yeah. I'd go to my folks. I appreciate the offer, but there's no fuel in town."

"It has a full tank, and there's also a couple of gas cans. Might not get you all the way home, but you might find fuel along the way. We just fueled up in a small town where the station was using a generator. It was crazy expensive, though."

"I have some cash. Thanks, Katie. I appreciate it. Think I'll see if Bree wants to go with me."

"Bree? I thought you and her didn't like each other much?"

"Yeah, well. We didn't. But we ran into each other a few more times, and I guess we do like each other. Saw her last night, and she's pretty scared. In fact, she's so scared she stayed at my place last night. On the couch, of course."

"Of course. I know Bree." Bree and I were very good friends until Leo moved in with me. She then pulled away from me a bit, saying she didn't think living together before marriage was okay. I completely respect her thoughts and am very much beginning to fully agree with her, but I do miss our friendship.

Bree comes from a very conservative Christian family. Her parents are even overseas somewhere in the mission field. They left the year she started college.

"Please do take her with you. With her folks out of the country, she doesn't have anywhere to go, that I know of."

I give Bob the unit number and the combination, then ask him to give my best to Bree and to call, if he can, when they get to his parents' place.

Soon, we arrive in Midwest. It's not a very big town, really nothing more than a wide spot in the road, but still, I manage to get us turned around trying to find Tim's dad's place. We finally find it when we see Angela and Tim's truck with a long, well-loaded flatbed trailer and Angela's Jeep both parked against the curb. We circle around the cul-de-sac and park across the street.

"Katie, I don't want to leave the truck. While I doubt what happened to Bob could happen to us, it's not worth the risk. I'll wait here."

"Yeah, good idea. I'll be right back."

Angela must have seen us because she comes running out. She's wearing flip-flops with jeans and stumbles a bit while navigating off the curb and on to the street.

"Katie! I'm so glad you're here!" she cries, pulling me into a tight hug, her long hair tickling my nose. She's about two inches taller than me and has lost weight since I saw her last summer. Not that she was heavy, but she still had a little to lose from being pregnant with Gavin. She pulls away, eyes filled with unshed tears. I blink, noticing my own tears.

She pulls me close again, saying, "And you're not going to believe this. Calley's going to Mom and Jake's too. Mike's folks, also."

"What? I don't believe it. I thought she was always adamant about staying put? What changed?"

"Something happened yesterday to Mike. He's okay, but someone attacked him at the gas station. Mike's parents were the ones who suggested they leave this morning. I've been texting with Calley, but they hadn't decided. Then, after you texted, we told her you were here, and she said they were packing to go. They're going to meet us at the Kaycee rest stop."

"That's so great! Not about Mike getting beat up, but about them coming. Mom will be happy. You hear from Sarah?"

"They went to Mom and Jake's last night after the power went out. Tate's family is there too. You heard they bought a camp trailer to stay in?"

"No, I don't think so."

"Yeah. I haven't been able to reach them since they got to Jake's. I tried Jake, too, but his phone goes straight to voicemail or just cuts off, and their landline gives me an 'all circuits are busy' notice. But, when they were still in Billings, the plan was to make a few trips back to their place today to get more stuff, if it seemed safe enough."

"Safe enough? Are there safety issues? Other than Mike getting hit?"

"Things are happening everywhere. Shootings, stabbings, all kinds of stuff. Haven't you been listening to the news?"

"Not much. Guess we should a little more. Are you almost ready?"

"Tim had to convince Art we need to leave. He was supposed to be ready when we got here. I've been packing things up. Not much really worth taking other than the memorabilia stuff."

"Have you heard from Tim's sister?" Tim's sister left home a few years ago after their mom died. No one really knows where she is. California, maybe.

"Nope. Thought maybe we would with everything happening. Tim's upset about it. So is Art. Is Leo planning on getting out of the truck? I'd love to meet him."

"Let's go over there. We heard about a problem a friend had back home, so Leo wants to stay with our stuff."

"Sounds smart. It's probably okay here, but better safe than sorry."

Leo steps out of the truck when he sees us coming over. I do the introductions, which are only slightly awkward. Then I tell Angela I should help her so we can get going.

"How are you all set for fuel?" Leo asks.

"I think we're good. Tim filled up as soon as we heard about people fleeing Denver. He filled our gas cans and bought a few more too. They're all in the back of his pickup. We're leaving Art's car here. It's a piece of junk, and he won't have any gas in it anyway. He can ride with Tim. I'll have Gavin with me. We're meeting Calley and Mike up the road."

Leo looks at me. I nod and give a big smile.

"That's great," he says. "I bet you're both very relieved."

We answer yes at the same time. I kiss Leo and tell him we'll try to hurry.

Inside, I give Gavin plenty of hugs and kisses. While I often talk with him on FaceTime, I haven't seen him in person since last summer. He's so big.

During the thirty minutes we spend getting everything ready that Art tells us he can't live without, I think about Calley and how amazing it is she's going to Bakerville. Out of all of us, she's always been the most vocal about Mom and Jake being "crazy preppers," to the point of being mean about it.

First, she didn't think anything could possibly happen. And if it did, she and her husband, Mike, would stay in Casper; she was adamant. They're buying the house Mom and Jake owned in Casper, on contract. Mike's parents live next door.

Calley married the boy next door, who also happened to be her high school sweetheart. They'd been dating since they were sixteen and were married last summer. Mike also has a sister who lives in Casper.

Calley said they'd all band together and be fine. I don't really know how they would be, since Calley barely keeps any food in the house. Maybe Mike's folks do?

I suspect the neighbors across the street from Calley and Mike are also preppers, at least on some scale. Sue and Adam always grow a huge garden and have several fruit trees, plus they home-can and dehydrate. Mom, Calley, and I were over there admiring Sue's garden one day, when Calley said, "I think, if the end of the world hits, I'll just hang out with you."

That got Mom all riled up. She said, "Calista Marie, if someone said that to me, I'd be sure to tell them what I really thought of their statement. It'd include something like, 'You've had the same opportunities to prepare for an unknown future as I've had. The fruit trees and tomatoes plants are available for you to purchase, just like they are for me to purchase. The store is full of food you can buy and store. Instead, you choose to put your head in the sand and have the gall to say you'll show up at my house if things get bad.' I'd likely have several other choice words to say and finish with something like, 'I'll meet you at the door with a shotgun.'"

Calley just stared at Mom. Sue looked amused. I wanted to be anywhere but there.

Mom continued, "You are my dear child, Calley, and you know how much I love you. You and Mike will always be welcome at our home. We've made plans to include you and, of course, your sisters and their families. Sue has always been a wonderful neighbor and good friend to us, but it's completely inappropriate to think she and Adam are planning to care for you and Mike."

Mom then turned to Sue and added, "Sue, you and Adam have built a wonderful place here. I know you've spent a lot of time and effort on this. And you know Jake and I have often been inspired by what you've done, and tried to replicate it. Casper may not be the safest place if there's ever a . . . *situation*. I'd hope, if it ever did become apparent it was time to leave Casper, you could help convince Calley, Mike, and his family of this, and you and Adam would come with them to our place. All of you would be welcome and a needed addition."

Mom looked back at Calley and added, "I fear it would take many of us working long, hard days to survive. Calley, we read the *Little House on the Prairie* books, and you were amazed at how hard Ma and Pa worked. If there was ever a grid-down situation, we'd all be working that hard and harder, day in and day out, just to eat. We'd also have to think about security. We'd need you. We'd need Mike. We'd need his mom, dad, and sister. We'd for sure need the skills and knowledge Sue and Adam have."

Sue hugged Mom. They pulled Calley and me in also. Sue, who had lived somewhere in the south before she moved to Casper—I can never remember where—said in her sweet, slow way, "Mollie, dahlin', that's one of the sweetest things I've heard. And Adam and me are gonna take you up on it if we ever have a need. We'll bring your gal kicken' and screamin' if we have to."

Chapter 10

I'm wiping down the bathroom when Angela says, "Guess that's about it. Tim and Art are hauling things out, and I'm just about finished with the kitchen. You have room in your cooler for some of Art's stuff?"

"Yes, sure. We've eaten most of our prepared food—just some sandwich fixings left, some frozen meat, and a few miscellaneous things. There should be room for some stuff."

"Okay, thanks. I have the fridge emptied out. Most of the things went into the garbage, and the rest I put in my cooler. The freezer has some things worth taking."

I put the freezer items in a grocery sack while Angela moves the garbage bag near the front door. We lock the windows and take a look around. No telling when Art will be able to come back.

Angela grabs a cat carrier, with a cat already inside making plenty of noise, expressing his unhappiness at being locked up. I'd forgotten he had a cat. He also has a dog.

"What about the dog?"

"Died over the winter. He was pretty old. I thought I told you?"

"Don't think so. Let's go, Gavin. Time to go see Grandpa Jake," I say to get Gavin moving.

"Grandpa Jake! I like Grandpa Jake. Papa going to see Grandpa Jake too?"

"Yep. Papa and Snowball are both going to see Grandpa Jake."

"And GrandMo? See her with Grandpa Jake?"

"I hope so. GrandMo is on her way home from her big trip. She couldn't take the airplane, so she's driving. She might be there when we get to their house. You'll get to see Malcolm too. And the goats and chickens."

"Yay! Let's go see goats and chickens. They like Gavin. They play with me."

I'm laughing, thinking, *Yeah, they're running away from Gavin,* but don't say anything. Instead, I pick him up and hug him. I almost forget the bag of fridge and freezer stuff, so I go back for it. Angela grabs the garbage bags, sits them on the porch, and locks the door behind us.

Leo walks over and introduces himself to Tim and Art, shakes hands, then starts helping secure the load onto the trailer. Tim has his two ATVs, assorted gear, totes, and more already on. There's plenty of room for his dad's stuff, with space leftover.

"Okay. Guess we're ready," Tim says after returning from putting the garbage in the dumpster. "Dad's not too happy, but he'll get over it. You hear anything from Calley?"

Angela checks her phone. "Nothing new, but you know reception is terrible here, even when the phones are working the way they're supposed to."

"Yeah. That's true. We'll stop before we get on I-25 so you can check for messages. What's in the bag, Katie?"

"Some stuff from your dad's freezer. I'll put it in my cooler. I have some frozen meat I put in when we left yesterday. It was still mostly frozen this morning. These frozen things should help it all last longer."

"You guys hungry?" Angela asks. "You need to eat?"

"We still have a few things in the truck. We're fine. You?"

"We ate before we left. I have snacks for Gavin. We'll be there in, what, about five hours? Maybe we can stop at one of the picnic areas in the Bighorns. You think, Tim?"

"Yeah. Let's make a plan when we find Calley and Mike. Stay close, Angela. Katie, you too."

Our little caravan is soon on its way. Kaycee is usually less than forty-five minutes, but with the increase in traffic once we hit I-25, we don't know how long it'll take today. I'm excited and surprised Calley's going to be there. I truly never thought she'd leave her house. The attack on Mike must have really shook her up. Poor Mike.

In an hour and a half, we're at the rest stop. There's a gas station at the rest stop turn off with a big NO GAS sign out front, which answers my question of whether we might be able to add to our fuel in Kaycee. I've been to this town many times when driving through and knew the station was here. I had hoped they'd have something figured out like the station in Wright.

The rest stop is full of people. Calley and Mike are already waiting for us. Calley sees me walking over and runs toward me. She grabs me in a huge hug, which completely surprises me. She's usually not one to show much affection.

"Katie, I'm so glad you left Manhattan. I saw on the news Aggieville's burning. Well, lots of places are burning, but Aggieville is one of them. Did you hear what happened to Mike? Someone tried to beat him up."

"Angela told me, but I don't know the details. He's okay?"

"Yeah, but he looks like crap." She gestures to him, and I have to agree. He has a black eye, cuts above his eyebrow and on his swollen nose.

"Jeez. Why?" I ask.

"Don't know. He was on his bike and pulled in for gas. He thinks the guy might have thought it was his turn instead of Mike's. Mike ran his card—this was around noon before the hackers ruined the banks—and the next thing he knew, he was on the ground. Mike didn't even get much of a return on the guy. Kicked back a few times, but nothing else. Several people pulled the guy off. He ran off before the cops got there. Mike wouldn't go to the hospital, but I had to go get him. He was seeing double and couldn't drive. Can't even drive now. I'm driving our Tahoe, and his dad's driving Mike's truck."

She gestures toward Mike's Chevy pickup parked along the edge of the rest stop, hauling a tarped utility trailer with wooden sides. From the shape of the tarp, I suspect the item in the center is the Harley Sportster he bought last fall. Mike's dad and mom are standing near the truck. They see me and give a wave, which I return.

"That's crazy. How'd you get his bike home?"

"Called Adam. Sue and him were both off yesterday, so we waited until they showed up. They're keeping an eye on our place and Mike's folks' place, but said if things get bad, they'll join us. Mom invited them before. I showed Sue how to find us on a map since they haven't been there."

"Good they're watching your place. What about your work?"

"What work? Mine called me Saturday morning and said it was too dangerous to work right now with the attacks and increase of people." She gives me a look, waiting for me to respond.

I answer with a nod and motion for her to continue.

"Anyway, this was before Mike was attacked. I guess he was one of many. Things were bad all over town, and I didn't know, but my bosses did. Then, when the cyberattacks happened, they sent out a new text message saying they'd let us know when we would reopen."

"It's good they were looking out for everyone. A coffee kiosk would be a dangerous place if someone wanted to harm you. You'd kind of be a sitting duck."

"Yeah, that's what Mike said. He called his shop and told them about the jerk beating him up. They said they were closing until things evened out. No one was bringing cars in to be worked on anyway. They'll call when he should come back to work. 'Course, they said that before the phones went out—now, who knows?"

"Mike's parents? Doesn't his dad work?"

"Yep. He's also off for now. His work requires computers and internet. He got a text saying they'd be shut down until the cyberattacks stopped. They took their systems completely offline. He thought he might have to go in and help, but they did it at headquarters in Oklahoma or wherever they are, instead of trying to deal with things here."

"Have you guys been getting phone calls and texts okay?" I ask.

"Hit or miss. The phones will ring but no one is there. That's what happened when my supervisor tried to call. The text came through a few minutes later. I've tried to call Mom and can't reach her. You think she's okay?"

"Probably. I suspect her service is messed up, like Jake's is. Let's try to call her." I pull out my phone. "Straight to voicemail. I'll send a text."

I send a text to Mom, letting her know we're all on our way to her place. I know she'll be excited about Calley and Mike. We walk over to the rest of the group. About that time, I get a text failure notice on my phone. Figures.

I say my hellos to Mike and his parents. Mike, his sister, and parents are all very tall. His dad and he are over six feet, and his mom and sister aren't much shorter. All have varying shades of red hair, with both men exhibiting a Dutch beard. The beard without mustache isn't a look many men can pull off, but it works with their pale complexions. In addition to all being tall, they're what I think of as sturdy. Not overweight but big boned.

Tim is introducing his dad to Mike and Roy, Mike's dad, and I'm struck at the size differences. The Curtis men are pale and red-haired, while the Carpenter guys are dark-haired and olive-skinned. Where Mike and Roy are tall and robust, Tim and Art are short and slight. Oh, Tim's appearance is deceiving. From working on the oil rigs, he's pure muscle. It's just not noticeable unless he's wearing a tank top.

I glance around and notice Mike's sister, Sheila. I wave to her; she returns the wave and starts to walk over. She and Calley are very close.

80

Sometimes it's a little hard for me since I think they're closer than Calley and I are.

"Hi, Sheila."

"Katie. You look good. I like your setup over there. Great way to carry your bikes. The trailer looks like something Mike would put together," she says with a laugh, causing her strawberry blond curls to bounce.

Where Calley, Angela, and I have naturally curly hair, I know Sheila goes to a lot of trouble to style hers so it has just the right amount of spring.

I'm impressed it looks as good as it does today—you know, with bugging out and all. I noticed her mom looks pretty good too. I'm suddenly feeling self-conscience but shoo the sensation away.

Sheila and her mom, Deanne, both have a lighter shade of red as opposed to the more brilliant shade of red the men of the family were blessed with. Calley once told me Deanne and Roy met because of their shared hair color. They were two of the few red heads in their community college.

"It kind of does look like something Mike would construct." I laugh. "Leo did it. I think he's in the bathroom, but I'll introduce you soon. You driving your mom's car?"

"Yes. Dad's driving Mike's truck, and Mom's driving Dad's truck. It's musical vehicles. At least Calley's driving the right one—my old Tahoe. I guess you heard my husband left me. Took off with a girl he met at a convention in Denver. He was living there, last I knew. That's where the divorce papers came back from anyway. Hope he's okay."

"I'm sorry, Sheila." I don't know what else to say. I thought he was a jerk the first time I met him. I think he's more than a jerk for leaving Sheila for another girl. I don't wish him to be unwell, but still . . . he's a jerk.

Once Leo's out of the bathroom, I introduce him to everyone he has yet to meet.

"Well, we going to stay here all day?" Art huffs.

"Everyone ready to go?" Tim asks, giving his dad a look. There are nods and yeses all around.

Ever practical, Leo asks, "How is everyone on fuel? I think it's just under three hundred miles."

Calley speaks first. "We're all good. When Mom sent those crazy packs a few months ago, surprisingly, we did things she suggested and then some. Mike has a—what do you call it, sweetie? A saddlebag?"

"A transfer tank," Mike says. "Thirty-six gallons plus a couple of filled Jerry cans. My dad has a few five-gallon cans too. Our four vehicles all run on gas, so we can share. When Mollie and Jake sent out the *Plan A* text, I told my parents and, though they thought we were all nuts, they filled up too."

Mike's dad mutters about how it did seem ridiculous, but now they're glad they did it.

Mike gives a quick bob of his head. "We did wait until morning, though, since it was so late and we were in bed. Worked out okay since the mass amount of people didn't get to us until Friday night. Wish I would've thought to fill my bike on Friday, then maybe I wouldn't look quite so pretty right now."

We all offer courtesy laughs, and Deanne gives him a hug.

"All right, so this is everyone?" Leo asks, looking around.

I do a quick mental count. Eleven of us going to Mom and Jake's. They said they were planning for us. And I know it's true with the lodging they'd put in and increasing their food and supply stores. Plus several features they added while building their place.

I have to admit, I'm not even sure Calley knows about all of the aspects of the homestead. We've never spoken of it, so if she does, she's great at keeping the secret.

Angela, Tim, and I had what Mom and Jake call the "grand tour." I think Sarah knows from something Angela said before. I haven't told Leo about it. That'll be up to Jake and Mom to do.

I hope they don't decide to give him the grand tour. In my mind, this means they'll think the worst is yet to come. Could these terrorists do something worse than they've already done?

"Katie? You okay?" Leo asks, and I notice everyone's staring at me.

"Oh . . . uh, yes. Tired. Thinking of what a crazy few days it's been. And I just remembered, I hit a deer last night. I know it seems silly considering everything else that's happening, but . . ."

"You poor dear," Deanne says, wrapping me in a hug. "Hitting a deer is never good. At least you're okay and didn't wreck. Let's get you home. Have you heard from your mom?"

"I hope she'll be there when we get there. I haven't heard from her since yesterday. I let her know we were leaving, and she texted back she was happy about it. I sent her a text a few minutes ago to let her know where we are. Tried to call, too, but just got her voicemail."

"Let's get there and see," Tim says. "I'll take the point, if no one minds? Leo, you want to pull up the rear?"

"Sure. Sounds good. You know a place to stop and eat? Everyone brought food for lunch?" Leo asks.

"Yeah, we'll stop on the way over the Bighorns. Oh, and you agree we should go past Sheridan and cut over, instead of Buffalo? Is it shorter? Roy, do you know?"

Roy says he doesn't know and hasn't been that way. We decide to take the Sheridan route. Going over the Bighorns will take about the same amount of time either way, but where we'll end up should be closer to Bakerville. We'll stop somewhere in the mountains for lunch.

Our convoy is on the road. Eleven people in seven vehicles, towing three assorted trailers. I'm sure we're quite the sight! I hope Jake's ready for all of us. I know he and Mom have always said they would be, but Mom isn't there. *Please, Lord, let my mom get home soon.*

Chapter 11

I-25 continues to move along, although there's considerably more traffic than any other time I've traveled this route. When we merge with I-90 and continue to Sheridan, traffic increases. A few miles before we reach Sheridan, it's backed up and is slow going.

This is very un-Wyoming. A Wyoming traffic jam tends to be more of the "deer crossing the highway and we have to stop for them" brand, as opposed to traffic congestion.

"What do you think the problem is?" I ask Leo.

"Looks like they're stopping people when they're exiting the interstate, which is blocking the right lane. And the left lane is all gawking to see what's happening. Then, a line of people getting back on the interstate is causing further slowing."

"Why would they be stopping people?"

"Maybe they're trying to prevent what happened in Manhattan from happening here? Maybe they're out of gas and lodging, so they're keeping people moving along."

"How do you think people have even made it this far?"

"I don't know. Maybe they got out early and were able to get fuel along the way. It must be about—what? Four hundred miles between here and Denver? Not terribly far on a normal day, but with the fuel shortages . . . Could they be coming from somewhere else? What states are the car tags?"

I watch for a few seconds. "Mostly Wyoming. Some Colorado and South Dakota. And I saw a couple others I didn't recognize and couldn't make out."

"Hopefully the road we need to take won't have anyone blocking it. Do you know how big the towns are we need to go through?"

"No. I don't think I've ever been this way. I went over the Bighorns at Buffalo before, but never this way. I can't imagine the towns are much. Wyoming doesn't have a lot of large towns. Sheridan's pretty good sized compared to most. It's one of the larger towns in Wyoming. Must be somewhere around eighteen thousand, I guess."

"A regular metropolis."

"Ha. Yeah. I know. The others we'll go through are smaller. And since they aren't on an interstate . . ." I raise a hand. "Of course, with the power out and all of the attacks, who knows what we'll run in to?"

We drive in silence for the remaining miles to our exit, several miles beyond Sheridan. We both breathe a sigh of relief when we discover only our little convoy is taking the exit we want, and there doesn't appear to be anyone stopping traffic.

We continue through two little towns without any issue, then reach the Bighorn National Forest. The road we're taking is a seasonal road closed during the winter months when the weather turns bad. It's been reopened since mid-May. Even though there's no snow near the road, we can still see plenty on the higher peaks.

I've done some hiking in the Bighorns before, a little farther south, with Jake and Mom. It's a beautiful area, and there's hardly any traffic. No one's in front of or behind us, and we've met only two cars so far since passing the last town.

Even as beautiful as it is, I soon find myself dozing off. I'm not sure how long I've been asleep when I feel the truck slowing to a stop.

"Everything okay?"

"There's a picnic spot here."

"Oh, good. I'm hungry, and I could definitely use the bathroom."

"Me too, on both accounts."

We all pull in and take turns using the single vault toilet. Calley and Deanne take coolers over to a picnic table. I go to our truck and find the lunchmeat in the cooler, along with condiments, a loaf of bread, cheese, and a bag of chips to add to the lunch collection. With everyone contributing, it turns out to be quite an array of choices. The conversation is, of course, centered on the terrorist attacks.

Angela says she heard on the radio that the illnesses had been tracked to restaurant buffets and salad bars. Someone had been purposely poisoning them. The cyberattacks are worse, and the stock market and all banks will be closed for the week because of the damage done by malware inserted during the cyberattacks. The internet's completely out, with no idea when it'll be working again. The only bright spot is there hasn't been a new attack of any sort today. Hopefully it stays this way.

It's very quiet here. We're still seeing very little traffic. In the time we've been here, we've only had one car go by in each direction. After we eat, we decide to rest for a bit. Blankets and pillows are put out in a small grassy area, and others sit in their cars with the seats back.

The relative quiet of the forest is interrupted by the sound of a motor. I look up to see a van traveling on the road in the direction we're headed. Less than a minute later, a loud screech and the squeal of tires fills the air, followed by the sound of metal slamming into metal and glass breaking.

"Angela! Can I take your Jeep and see if anyone's hurt?" Leo yells, while running to his truck.

"Yes, of course," Angela responds, while Tim and Mike both say they'll help.

Leo grabs the large first aid kit from his truck, and the three are quickly in the Jeep. Tim takes Gavin's car seat out of the back and Leo hops in. While he pulls out, Leo yells to us, "Stay alert, everyone."

All of us are standing together, not really sure what to do. Many expressions of, "I hope everyone's okay," are uttered. Roy and Art are sitting at the picnic table nearby. Angela's holding Gavin, and he's kicked up the bottom edge of her shirt.

"Angela, are you carrying a gun?" I say, with more dismay in my voice than I intended. Calley, Sheila, and Deanne all look at us.

"Uh . . . yes," Angela answers hesitantly.

"When did you start carrying a gun?" Calley asks.

"Friday morning. Well, I bought it Friday morning. After Mom and Jake sent out their *Plan A* and we did those things, we started talking about it."

Angela meets my eyes, then continues in a rush. "I've shot Tim's pistol several times, and both of Mom's pistols. Plus, remember the mini-class we took with Mom last year? I've been thinking about it since then. I've tried several rental guns at the gun range when we've gone shooting. I just couldn't decide what I wanted. I finally made my decision and bought it."

"And you feel okay carrying it around?" Sheila asks.

"Mostly," Angela answers with a slight shrug. "It's a little strange, though. We went to the range after I bought it, and I practiced drawing and shooting. I need to work with it more, for sure. I plan to spend some time on it once we get to Mom and Jake's place. Maybe I can take another class from the neighbor now that I have my own gun. I want to get my concealed carry permit."

"What kind is it?" I ask—not that I know one gun from another, but it seems like the right question.

"It's a Sig Sauer 9-millimeter P320 Compact."

"Wow. Sounds . . . fancy."

"It's very nice. And it's convertible. I can change it from a compact to a subcompact, or even to a full-size. I don't know if I'll use that option, but it's nice to have options."

"I don't really know what you just said," Sheila says. "Your gun can get bigger or smaller?"

"Yeah. Pretty much. This—" she motions to the holster "—is the medium-size version. The smaller, compact version is for putting in a small purse or maybe on a thigh holster. You can wear it on your hip, too, of course, but it conceals real nicely. This one does, too, but the subcompact is smaller. The full-size is bigger. But my gun can't get bigger or smaller unless I order the things needed to convert it. I'm not sure I'll do that since this is the size I want."

"Oh, okay," Sheila says, sounding and looking completely uninterested.

Living in Wyoming, we're all pretty used to guns. Mike and Tim are both carrying today, Leo too. It's kind of a surprise Angela has a gun, but not overly so. I wonder if Calley does? I'll ask her later.

We stand around trying to make small talk but are really wondering if everything's okay. A few minutes later, Angela's Jeep pulls into the picnic area. Tim, alone, steps out.

"It's, uh . . . not good," he says.

Angela goes over to him.

He wraps her in a hug. Once they release, he looks at the rest of us. "Two cars, pretty much head on. One car had a driver only. She was gone when we got there."

I gasp and shake my head. Others make similar noises and gestures.

Tim gives a somber nod. "The minivan was carrying what seems to be a family. Dad's gone, and Mom isn't looking too good. Two young teens in the back. They're alive but in bad shape. We can't get our phones to work to call for help. Do any of you have service?"

We all check. Angela and Sheila show bars but can't dial out. Head shakes all around.

"Okay. We talked about how to transport the kids. Deanne and Roy, Mike said he thought using the back of your Yukon might be good. We can load your things in the other vehicles."

"Yes, of course," Deanne says, while she and Roy go to their SUV. I go to Leo's truck to rearrange the back seat so some of their things can fit in. In just a short time, we have the back seat and cargo area empty with everything lying around; we'll work on putting it in the other vehicles while they get the kids situated for transporting. I bring over a tarp and several blankets to lay down in the back of the SUV.

When I step away, Tim says, "Leo asked if you could come back. He said you two took some first aid classes and he could use your help, if you're up to it."

"Um, yes, we did." I bite my lip. "I can help."

"Good. We'll need Leo's truck to move the wreckage out of the road. You want to drive it, or the Yukon?"

"Yukon. I don't know about driving the truck on the hill with the trailer. I can do it on flat ground without curves, but this . . . I don't know."

"I'll drive it. You follow me."

Tim turns to everyone else. "Can you all be ready in a few minutes? Get all the things stowed away. I'll honk three times when we're ready to go. Deanne, Katie needs to help. She'll drive the Yukon for now, okay?"

The accident is less than a mile down the road, around a curve. With the positions of the cars, I think the uphill car was on the wrong side of the road. I stop about a hundred yards back near where the road flares have been set up. Tim stops near the minivan; Leo waves me forward.

"Where should I go?" I ask out the window.

"Let's get the children loaded, then we'll move the cars out of the way. I'd like you to sit with one while we load the other."

I put the Yukon in park and turn it off, then walk over to Leo and the children. Both are covered with space blankets and look to be unconscious. Each is wearing a cervical collar from Leo's kit. I take a look around and ask, "Where's Mike?"

"Over there. There hasn't been any traffic and we put out several flares, but he thought he heard a vehicle, so he went to stop them before they drove up on us."

"Is there another car?"

"I don't know. Could've just been you and Tim coming down. Sound travels weird in places like this."

We soon see Mike walking back toward us. His face is white, and he's moving very slowly.

"Leo," I say softly, while gesturing toward Mike.

"Mike," Leo shouts over to him, "you'd better sit down. You don't look too good."

Mike gives a slight nod and walks to the edge of the road to lean against a tree.

Tim has the minivan attached to the winch.

"Leo, I think this is ready once we have the kids loaded and out of the way. Is the mom . . . ?" Tim asks.

Leo's face clouds as he shakes his head. "Couldn't help her."

Mike, Tim, and Leo all three carefully carry the boy using the roll-up stretcher we have as part of our emergency kit. He looks to be about thirteen and skinny. Not bad skinny, just not filled out yet skinny. He reminds me of a long-distance runner I knew in high school. He moans a little when they move him but doesn't wake up. I wish we had a second stretcher so he could be moved less, but we'll need it to move the little girl.

Leo and Mike walk back, as Leo says, "Katie, go on over to the Yukon while we move the girl."

I do as he asks and look over the boy. I can see Leo has put a makeshift splint on his leg out of a couple of sticks and an Ace wrap. There's blood on the wrap, and I wonder if he has a compound fracture.

They're soon back with the girl, who's awake and whimpering. She's younger than the boy by a year or two. I start talking to her softly, telling her she'll be fine. I hope it's the truth. The blankets and pillows from our truck and several more, likely out of Angela's Jeep, are positioned around the children to keep them from moving.

"Katie, hop in the passenger's side. I'll move this somewhere safe while we clear the road. You watch over the children. You know what to do for them." It wasn't a question he was asking; it was a statement.

He had advanced medical training in the service and specialty classes afterward. At one point, he considered becoming a paramedic. He's taken EMT training but has yet to follow through with certification. Recently, we've taken a couple of first aid classes together. It was pretty redundant for him and didn't come close to what he already knew, but he went along with me.

It takes about five minutes to clear the road, then they use branches to sweep as much glass off as possible.

Leo comes over to the Yukon. I start to ask, "What about . . . " The girl's sleeping or unconscious again, but I don't want to finish my question. I don't want to ask, *Are you just going to leave the dead parents on the side of the road?*

"Not much we could do. Left them in the vehicles and covered them. We'll send someone back here as soon as we get to town. I'd like you to ride in the Yukon. I don't know what it's going to be like for the children. The boy has a compound fracture at minimum, plus whiplash affecting both of them.

"If there was any way to get help to them, we wouldn't have taken them out of the van without a backboard. But with no phone service, plus the distance and the gas issues . . ." Leo lifts a shoulder. "This seems the best choice. At least I hope it is. I don't know. Let's just try to get them to a hospital safely and quickly."

He gives me a smile before raising his voice. "Tim, we're ready to go. You want to honk to let the others know?"

The horn on Leo's truck blares three times.

"I'll drive my truck right behind you," Leo says. "If you need to stop, stick your arm out the window and signal me."

The rest of our group slowly drives up. Mike, still looking a little pale, returns to the passenger's seat of his truck, with his dad driving. I wonder if it's from seeing the victims or overdoing it after the beating he took. Calley's right behind Mike's dad. Mike's mom is next with Sheila. Sheila steps out and comes over to the Yukon.

"Am I still driving this?" she asks Leo.

"Please. Katie will ride with you and monitor the children."

Roy is driving slowly down the road, followed by Calley, Deanne, and Angela. We join the caravan behind Angela, with Leo following us. Tim and Art take the final position. Roy sets a slow pace to keep from jostling the kids around. They have both woken up several times but never really became aware. One time the boy was moving more than I would've liked, and I thought I'd need to have Sheila stop, but he settled in again.

It's over an hour before we reach the town of Pryor. We have no trouble finding the small, well-signed hospital emergency room.

"Pull in the emergency bay." I motion with my arm.

The rest continue to the parking area. Leo stops, not in the bay but not in a spot either. He's running this way.

"How are they?" he asks from a distance.

"No changes," I say, as he goes into the hospital. He hesitates for a moment at the door, the door that would automatically open if the power were still on. It's cracked slightly, so he pries the doors apart and slips in.

I carefully open the back of the Yukon. Sheila and I stand nearby but out of the way. It's only a minute before the gurney's here.

Leo's with them. "Katie, can you come in with me? Sheila, here's my keys. Please have someone park my truck, then come in. They may have questions for you since you were in the car with the children. I think it'd be best if someone stayed with our vehicles at all times. We'll be out as soon as we can. Can you send in Mike and Tim?"

Leo and I do our best to answer questions. We're in the lobby when Mike, Sheila, and Tim join us. The hospital staff ask us to stick around; they've called the police by radio.

An officer arrives within ten minutes. Leo tells what we know, and the officer asks if he's sure the other three are deceased. He replies he is. Leo hands the officer three driver's licenses, from the mom, dad, and lady driver. He takes our information, including where we're headed, along with the names of everyone in our party.

Leo asks the officer, "I know we're really not supposed to know anything about the children we brought in because of privacy laws and such, but is there any way you could find out if they'll make it? I don't need specifics, just an idea if they'll be okay . . . physically, I mean. I assume the driver and passenger were their parents. That never really goes away."

The officer gives him a long look. "Give me a few minutes. I'll see what I can do."

He returns in about five minutes.

"The boy has a compound fracture. He'll need surgery. We don't handle surgeries here, so he'll be transported to Prospect or Billings. The doc said whoever stabilized it did a fine job. That you, Leo?"

"Yes, sir."

"The neck braces were also a good call. Both have moderate cervical injuries and concussions. I can't give you much more info than this. I need to talk to the others in your party and get a quick statement

91

from them. The county sheriff and highway patrol are going to handle the recovery effort."

"Thank you, Officer. I appreciate what you could tell me."

Our group is gathered back around the vehicles after quick restroom breaks. Once everyone finishes giving their statement and the officer leaves, Calley says, "I can't believe the refineries were hit."

Leo and I look at each other.

"What are you talking about?" Sheila asks.

"The oil refineries. On the radio. You didn't hear?"

"We didn't have the radio on," Sheila answers.

"I didn't know either," Angela adds. "Calley told me, and we found a radio station giving an update. The station's on auxiliary power, so they're only broadcasting every so often and only giving important news. The president's talking tonight, and it seems the refineries in the Gulf, plus several other big ones throughout the country, exploded around noon our time. The Casper one wasn't mentioned—too small I suppose. Neither was that one on I-80, but lots of others. More than half of them, I think."

Leo shakes his head. "This will really complicate things. I had hoped they'd get the cyberattacks and malware issues solved. Then trucks could start running again to bring food, fuel, and other essentials. If the refineries were hit— " he shrugs and shakes his head " —we may have a serious shortage."

"I thought we got most of our gas from other countries. I know we drill some, but not all of it," I say.

"We import crude oil from other countries and drill it here. Then the crude oil is turned into gas at the refineries. Nearly all of the gas and diesel sold in the US is produced in the US," Tim tells me.

"How close are we to your parents' place?" Leo asks.

"Around an hour. I've been to the recreation area we saw coming into town with them before. It didn't take much more than an hour to get to it."

"Is this the only town between here and there?" Leo asks. He's been amazed at the distances between towns in Wyoming.

"No. We still go through Wesley, the town Jake works in. Won't be far to their place once we get to Wesley," Angela offers.

"Is there a grocery store there?"

"Yes, a couple," I say.

"I think we should buy all of the shelf-stable food we can. It might be even longer before trucks are running to restock the shelves. Hopefully they'll be open. And if gas stations are open and pumping, we need a fill. You'll have to use your cash with the banks down."

"What are we talking about here?" Mike asks. "Are you saying we should spend all of our cash buying food and fuel?"

Leo very carefully and calmly says, "No, Mike, I'm not trying to tell you how to spend your money. Not at all." He gives Mike a slight smile before looking around the group. "I do want to spend some of the cash I have on hand for food and fuel, if possible. And tomorrow, I might do the same thing if given the opportunity."

He reaches for my hand. "I'm very grateful Katie's parents are welcoming me to their home. They don't know me. They know I love Katie, and that was enough for them. With the bridge explosions putting us out of our home in Manhattan, the cyberattacks taking out the banking and electrical grids, and now the new explosions taking out our ability to make fuel, this is a huge deal."

"It really is," Tim agrees. "This could very well set us back to a time in history before we had the conveniences we have now. In the past, people didn't run to the grocery store when they needed food. They produced it themselves. What they couldn't produce, they traded the neighbors for or they did without. We may very well find ourselves in the same situation. Having food on hand will be a big help. It won't last forever, but it might last long enough to figure out how to produce all we need."

Mike nods. "You're right, man. You too, Leo. Calley and I have always kind of laughed at Mollie and Jake. When they lived in our house, when it was still their house, I thought it was super funny the buckets of food they had. They've always told us to go to their place if there was a problem and to bring my family, but we wouldn't have left Casper if I wouldn't have been blindsided at the gas station yesterday."

His hand travels absently to the side of his head. "If things could get worse . . ." His voice trails off as he looks at his wife. "I know Calley will be safer. My mom and sister also. Me too, I guess."

"I have money," Calley says. "I brought all my tips."

I find this kind of funny. Calley's a cheapskate—big time. She's always saved more money than she spends. When we were young and living at home, she saved her tips in her room until she had enough to put in the bank. The "enough" varied. Malcolm used to say going in her room was like going in the bank. I have no doubt, while she has some bills, she also has lots of change. This is verified when she pulls a coffee can out of her car.

"Most of it's in rolls, but some is loose," she says. "I guess the store won't mind, but it'll be a pain to pay."

"Let's get into Wesley and see what's open," Calley's father-in-law suggests.

Chapter 12

When we roll into town, we see the first market is open and is doing a brisk business. The gas station we passed was open but had a sign out front saying *No Gas.*

"There's another market up the road," I tell Leo. "They have a gas station too. Maybe it'll be open."

"How much cash do you have, Katie?"

I count it out. I've only used the $150 for the crazy expensive gas this morning. "Looks like $737 and some change. Several dollars in change. Not Calley's crazy amount, but probably ten dollars or so."

"I think you and whoever isn't driving should start shopping here. I guess that's just Mike, Tim's dad, and you. The rest of us should try to find a gas station. I'm going to pay for anyone who doesn't have the cash needed. It could be high, like this morning's place. If the other store is open, I'll get them all started there or see who wants to come back here. I'll pick you up soon."

"Okay. Will we run out of space?"

"Sheila's car is still empty. You know what to buy?"

"Same stuff we've been buying. Rice, beans, cans of things."

"Instruct Mike if he seems he needs it."

"Mike's kind of a picky eater. There are only certain things he likes. Might not be easy."

"Do your best."

Leo tells everyone what he's thinking. Tim's dad, Art, offers to drive Angela's Jeep to the gas station so she can shop. He says Gavin, asleep in the backseat, can stay with him. Apologizing for not having more, he gives Angela all of his cash—thirty-eight dollars.

Mike says he thinks he can drive if Calley wants to shop. It's only a short distance, and shopping might be more of a challenge for him—his head is pounding.

Calley fishes in her purse and pulls out a small bottle of ibuprofen. She gives him two and a bottle of water. She kisses him and asks, "You have enough money for gas? For both my car and your truck? Katie said they paid ten dollars a gallon this morning."

"Yeah. I have enough. But whatever's left won't be much. You kept the money you took out of our account, right?"

"I have it."

"I'll try to make a run through the grocery store with everyone else. You think I should spend all I have?"

Calley thinks a moment before answering, "After gas, you probably won't have much." She reaches into her purse and hands him several bills. "Use this. I'm going to keep back some money. I want to give Mom and Jake some when we get there."

I can see Leo wants to say something but doesn't. Instead, he says, "I'll walk the women to the door, make sure all seems well. You each have a flashlight? It's probably dark inside."

I take mine out of my purse. Angela turns on the flashlight app on her phone, and Calley gets a small flashlight out of her car. Though the store is busy, everything seems fine.

"If I'm not here when you all finish, wait outside, close to the store. Angela, you look like you can handle things if they turn sour." He motions to her waist.

"Yes." Angela doesn't look as sure as she sounds.

Inside, it's surprisingly quiet and calm, considering how busy it is. An employee greets us at the door.

"Glad you brought flashlights. We have lanterns around, but it's still dark. Use this black sharpie to mark the price on the packages. If you find something without a price on the shelf, holler for one of us. We're around helping. Cash or local checks only at checkout. Same goes for the liquor store inside. If there are things you want from there, you may want to pop over there first. It's clearing out fast. Well, the entire store is clearing out fast, so . . . " She shrugs.

We thank her and start in.

"I think one of us should go to the liquor store. Bottles of booze might be good to have."

"Angela, this isn't a time for drinking." While none of us are big drinkers, Calley has never been a fan.

"Not that, Calley. It's good for cleaning wounds and also for trade. I've read about it. I'll go in there. I think I know what to get. Can you guys grab things for me if it's something you think I'll want and it's running low? I'll be back shortly." She takes her cart and heads for the liquor store.

Calley shakes her head. "Where should we start?"

I scan the aisle markers. "Let's go over there." I head toward what I think is where the dry beans and rice should be located.

"What does Mike like?" I ask.

"Pasta, hamburgers, stuff like that."

"Not going to be able to get hamburgers."

"I know. It'll be fine. Mom has so much food it seems kind of crazy to buy more. And she'll have hamburger. Of course, it's probably deer or antelope. He won't like that much. Elk isn't bad if they have that."

The shelves have been hit hard. We move through, grabbing what we can.

"I need another cart," Calley says.

"I'll go get us each a second cart."

Angela comes out of the liquor store. She has three paper grocery bags in her cart. She sees me and gives a small wave.

"We need second carts. You probably will also," I instruct.

I push and pull two empty carts. Angela pushes an empty and pulls the one with the already-purchased alcohol.

Calley has a fully loaded cart when we reach her.

"Jeez," Angela says, "you guys got a lot already."

"Lots of it's big stuff, so it's really not as much as you'd think. Angela, don't worry about taking out things from mine. Let's just keep going." She nods and we keep going.

In the soup aisle, Calley says, "Mike doesn't like soup. He doesn't want to drink his meals."

"He might need to learn to like it," Angela says.

When we think we're done, we decide to go down the aisles again. Angela says she'll wait up front.

"Why is that?" Calley asks.

"I'm going to be out of money. I gave Tim half of the cash we had. I wonder if I even have enough for what I have in my cart."

"Don't worry," Calley says. "I have money, and Gavin needs food."

"I have money too," I add. "This is a group effort. I just wish we could call Sarah and see what she needs."

They both nod in agreement. Our second trip down the aisles finds several more things we either missed or decided against the first time. They seem more appealing now that we know just how bare the shelves are.

97

At the checkout stand, Calley goes first. Her bill is impressive. Mine's just as impressive. Angela's no slouch either, and Calley and I each help her pay. She bought the booze with her money, so it's not like she didn't already spend plenty. As we're finishing, Leo walks up beside me.

"Hey, Katie. Everything go okay?"

"Yeah, sure. We're done. The shelves were kind of bare."

"Same at the other store. I bought quite a bit. It's stowed in Sheila's car. There's a ranch store open I'd like to go to next. The cashier gave me directions. The gas station was open. It was fifty bucks for five gallons, which was all we were allowed. We each got our five gallons."

When we get out in the lot, Sheila's pulling in. A fair amount of the space in her SUV has already been taken, but with some creative arranging, we're able to add our purchases and still have space left.

Leo tells everyone about wanting to go to the ranch store. He says he's not sure what they'll have but thinks it'd be worth a stop, saying he and I can go alone if everyone else wants to head on.

"I think we should stay together," Deanne says. "In the store, I heard people talking. They're starting to get scared. I think scared people can do unpredictable things. I'd hate for something to happen to anyone, like what happened to Mike."

Everyone agrees. Leo shares the directions he was given so we can meet if separated. Art asks to stay in the car and entertain Gavin, saying he'll keep an eye on everything. Roy says he'll join Art. He whispers something to Mike, and Mike nods. Then Roy gives Mike some money.

As we walk to the building, Leo asks Tim, "You think Mr. and Mrs. Caldwell could use more animal feed?"

"They keep a pretty good amount on hand but could probably use more," Tim says.

"What all do they have?" Leo asks.

"Nasty chickens and ducks." Angela makes a face. She hates birds.

"Cute goats," Tim adds. He loves the baby goats. "Plus, they raise pigs and sheep during the summer. I don't think anything else. They talked about rabbits, but there are so many wild ones around they could just eat those."

"Would you be willing to get whatever you think they may need for their farm? Feed and maybe even seeds and starts if they have them?" Leo asks, while handing Tim money.

"Yeah. Sure. I'll buy some things too. I think they like heirloom seeds. I'll have Angela help me. I can do a little rearranging of my trailer to fit the bigger stuff."

Near the door of the store, there's a cage with propane tanks. "Do you think we should buy a few of those?" I ask Leo. "Might be good for the grill."

"Yes. Great idea, Katie. We'll get a few when we check out. Don't let me forget. But there's something else I want to make sure we buy first." He gives me a slightly cryptic wink.

Inside, everyone splits up. I stay with Leo. I can't imagine anything I need to buy in here.

Leo sees the gun counter and heads over there. Oh, so this is why we're here. The gentleman behind the counter says, "No gun sales. I can't run the background check."

"I have a concealed carry permit issued in Kansas. Will you be able to use it in lieu of the background check?"

"Yep, no problem. Wyoming recognizes Kansas permits."

"Thank you, sir. And I can take it with me today?"

"You betcha. No waiting time in Wyoming. I'll be over in the next aisle if you and your lady see something you'd like to look at."

I'm pretty sure the guy winked at Leo. I have no idea what that was about.

"Katie, I know we talked about this Friday morning, but things have changed since then. I'd like you to find a handgun and a rifle you're comfortable with. I'll teach you everything you need to know to use them. I saw your sister with her gun on her hip. She's smart to have it. You need one too."

"I don't really think so. I have the zapper stick, you know."

"Sure, and it's fine for its purpose. But a stun gun is nothing more than a minor deterrent. While it may slow someone down, it's not likely to completely stop them. A guy my size, it might not do much. Plus, how close do you have to be to someone to zap them?"

"Pretty close," I agree.

"Mm-hmm. And I really don't like the idea of you having to be that close to someone meaning to harm you."

"How about mace?"

"Same deal. You'd have to be pretty close. And the wind would have to be right."

I nod in agreement. I'm not very happy about it but concede, to a point. I don't know if I could shoot anyone. Then I think about Malcolm and Gavin. Okay, yeah. If I needed to shoot someone to protect one of them, I could do it.

Calley steps next to me. "You buying a gun, Leo?"

"Yes. For Katie."

"Good idea. I wish I could get one, but Mike says, with the computers down, I won't be able to. He brought his revolver, his plinking rifle, and his shotgun. I used to shoot Jake's .243. I'm sure he'll let me use it again if I need to."

"I have a concealed carry permit. I can buy without a background check. It's frowned upon to buy for others, but I think the guy here will let me if you want to get something. Katie's getting a pistol and a rifle."

By the time we're finished looking, I've picked out a .40 caliber handgun and a carbine—that's what Leo called it. Apparently, it's a rifle but shorter. Calley has the identical pistol and a new rifle, which she says is really for Mike. She'd prefer *his* .223 since she's already comfortable with it. Calley chooses a new .223, and I have a .22. Leo would've liked to see us both get .223s, but there's only the one.

He says a .22 rifle has a decent amount of stopping power with a well-placed shot and it'd be good for coyotes and things. He also says, quietly, the rifle choices aren't very good, but these are better than nothing.

We get extra magazines for each, holsters for the handguns, scopes for the rifles, and lots of ammo, plus a few other things.

When we're done, we find Angela and Tim back at the stovepipe pieces. Man, this store has a little bit of everything.

"Hey, Angela. What are you guys doing?" I ask.

"We're trying to decide if we should buy stovepipe."

"What for?"

"Oh, I know," says Calley. "Mom and Jake's new cabin they put in last year. Mom said she bought a stove from a friend but still needed pipe. I don't know if she ever got any."

"Right." Angela bobs her head. "I don't know either. We're talking about heading to the house and asking Jake. They're open until 4:30 today, so we could come back. It's not far."

Leo looks at his watch. "It's after three now. You don't have time if it's forty-five minutes to their place. Let's just buy it. The sizes are pretty much universal, especially if we get a couple of adapters, so it should fit. We can always return it if it's not needed."

Leo picks out what he thinks he needs, asking Angela and Calley questions they really can't answer. He says he's probably getting too much, but too much is better than not enough. He picks up things from a few other sections while I wait out front.

He exits the store with his goods. "What all did you buy, Leo?" I ask.

"A little of this and a little of that. I wanted to be able to contribute things. Your parents are very generous to let me join you."

Angela and Tim have already purchased and loaded the animal feed and seeds. We use bungee cords to attach the piping to the trailer. Tim's truck and trailer are looking very hillbillyish. Everyone indicates they're finished and they just want to get to Mom and Jake's place.

It's almost 4:00 by the time we get everything loaded. Art had taken Gavin for a walk, and they return with Art carrying a small grocery bag.

"Hey, Tim," Art says, "when Gavin and I were walking, we stumbled on some kind of outlet store. They have all kinds of stuff. I had a little change so grabbed a couple of things. Got packages of fancy rice for ten cents each. Some cans of tomato sauce for a nickel. You all might want to take a quick look. They were doing a brisk business."

"Where's it at?" Tim asks.

"At the end of the block. There's another place across the street. Some kind of antique store, I think. It looked a little hoity-toity, so Gavin and I skipped that place."

"What do you all think?" Tim looks around.

Tim's trailer has almost zero space available with the bags of animal feed and lengths of stovepipe, along with the assortment of other items. The SUV Sheila's driving is full of food, and things are stuffed in every nook and cranny available in each rig. I dread the unloading process.

I don't know why, but suddenly I think about the girl and boy from the wreck and hope they're doing okay, or as okay as can be expected. And I hope they were able to get their parents and the lady from the other car so they can be buried.

"We're pretty well loaded," Leo says. "Does everyone feel like they have what they need?"

"I'm not sure," Angela answers. "You know, when Mom started getting serious about preparedness, she'd talk to me about the books she was reading. I've read some of them at her recommendation. They really made me think about what things could be like after . . . what's the phrase they use? The balloon goes up?"

Leo and Tim both nod while Angela continues, "Lots of times they'll even go scavenging after whatever event, which often seems to work out for the book characters. They'll go to the malls or find grocery store trucks abandoned on the side of the road. But here, I don't really see it as much of an option. I don't even think there's a mall anywhere around here except in Billings, which isn't someplace we'd want to be. And this isn't a heavily traveled route for truck traffic. They'd have to be on their way to one of the towns around here."

"What are you getting at?" Calley asks.

"I guess, I'm wondering if we ought to take a minute and see if there's anything else we should buy. Tim kept back a little of the money he had for shopping—not much, but some. I don't want to pass up an opportunity today that could hurt my child in the future. In addition to the store Art found, there's a couple of discount-style stores on the way out of town located right next to each other. They may be open, and if they are, we should stop. Plus, I feel better about the idea of making my purchases now rather than scavenging for things later."

"I think it's a good idea, Angela. We're pretty full, so everyone keep in mind the space available," Mike's mom, Deanne, says.

I'm not really interested in more shopping. I'm tired after having been on the road since yesterday. Angela is right, but . . . *ugh*.

Tim goes back to the salvage store with his dad. The rest of us go to the other discount stores. Calley and I each give Tim some money to add to his dwindling amount.

Angela leads the way to the other stores she mentioned. I'm surprised to see both stores are open.

Mike offers to stay with the vehicles and Gavin. The rest of us split up between the two stores. Leo pulls Angela aside and hands her some money. At first, she tries to refuse it but eventually nods her head and accepts what he offers. Leo and I go to separate stores. He asks if there's anything I'd like.

"I don't know. I'm so tired I can't even think. Should we be concentrating on food? Both of these places carry food, I think. The one over there has clothes. Maybe they both do."

He hugs me for a moment while the others head toward the stores. Angela makes a motion to ask if I'm going to join them. I nod.

"Food's always good," Leo says. "Plus anything you think you might need. Underwear, socks, another pair of shoes—things wear out. Angela made a good point about salvaging, but in a remote area like this, it could be a challenge."

"Okay."

"You need some money?"

"I have probably three hundred. I'll probably fall asleep before I can spend it all." I smile and start walking toward the store. I turn around and ask, "Any special requests?"

"Gummy bears. I'd like some gummy bears."

The store is well picked over, but I find enough things, including gummy bears, to almost fill my cart. Angela comes by with her cart heaping. She has lots of clothes for Gavin, but larger sizes, too, for him to grow into, I guess. There's also baby clothes in the cart.

She sees me looking and says, "No. Not yet. But who knows? Plus, Sarah and Calley. And maybe you could need baby clothes if you and Leo get married. I'm going to look for diapers too."

I finish and go to the truck. While I did buy quite a bit, I still have over $150 left. Sheila and Deanne are already out there, along with Roy. I'm surprised Calley isn't here—I didn't see her in the store when I left. Sheila's playing with Gavin, and Mike's nowhere to be seen.

Roy's working on some kind of contraption with a tarp and plans to attach it to the top of the Yukon. He's waiting for everyone else to come out so we can load it and then get it in place. I let him add my purchases to the mound on the tarp.

Within five minutes, Calley and Mike walk hand in hand from the other discount store. Everyone else is back and trying to get things loaded. I'm impressed with some of the purchases. Besides for food, clothes, and shoes, there's bedding, camping supplies, boxes of dishes, pots and pans, and many other things. The items suitable for the tarp contraption are added and spots are found for everything else. It's not easy!

While we're finishing loading, Tim and Art drive in. Tim gets out and says, "Wow. That place was something. It was pretty busy, but they had a ton of stuff. Most of it's out of date but dirt cheap. I filled several boxes. We had so much stuff that we ran out of room. My dad has a box of things under his feet and another in his lap."

"Let's see if we can find a spot for it all so Art can be a little more comfortable on the ride to Jake and Mollie's," Roy says.

A little more fiddling and everything is loaded. The final leg of our journey is quiet.

At 5:00 we're getting very close to home. We listen to the top of the hour radio update. They briefly go over the refineries being targeted today, give a recap of the cyberwar (I notice it's no longer called a cyberattack), the food poisonings, the bridge explosions, and the airplane/airport explosions.

Then the announcer says they won't be on the air again until the president speaks at 9:00 p.m. eastern, seven o'clock our time. They want to conserve fuel since they don't know how long he'll talk.

We turn the radio off after the announcer signs off. Tim has the lead, and soon our little convoy is bouncing along the two-mile-long private gravel road to Mom and Jake's. And bouncing is almost an understatement. The road is worse every time I travel it.

I mentioned it to Mom once, and she said, "It keeps the riffraff out." I guess it would. We're only going about ten miles per hour, and it still seems too fast.

As we crest the top of the hill, I get my first glimpse of their homestead. They've put a lot of effort into developing what they call a "food forest" by planting trees, vines, and berries. The vine and berry plantings along the road look green and healthy. The dwarf fruit trees along the backyard wall are peeking over the top, with their green leaves waving gently in the slight breeze.

Beyond the house, the larger fruit, nut and—someday—firewood trees look strong and healthy. The chickens and goats are roaming the pastures, and there are a few new structures dotting the landscape. Even though I've never officially lived here, I feel like I'm home. And it's good to be home.

Chapter 13

Malcolm is by the garage, jumping up and down. I'm very surprised when Jake's parents come out of the garage apartment. I wasn't expecting to see them. I hope nothing happened in Prospect like what happened with Mike.

Sarah, Tate, and his parents are joining the group. There's quite a collection of people here.

But not my mom. I don't see her anywhere.

Jake's hugging Calley and visiting with Mike. Then Angela's hugging Jake. I catch his eye, and he motions to me. I hurry over for my hug. Angela pulls me into the group crush.

"Jake, I thought we'd never get here," I tell the man who's been a father to me for more than half my life. Jake gives me a big smile, showing off the dimple in his left cheek.

"You made it. You're here." Jake drops a kiss on my forehead. "It's all good now. Heard about the trouble your town is having. I'm so glad you left before it started."

Are those tears in Jake's eyes? I hug him tighter and say, "Yes. Leo was the one who said we should. Come over and meet him."

"Not sure I can." Jake gives a small laugh.

I signal to Leo as we try to move from the crowd. "Leo, this is Jake," I say.

Leo offers his hand. "Leo Burnett, sir. I'm pleased to meet you."

Jake dips his head. "Jake Caldwell. Thanks for helping Katie get home."

"Yes, sir. Thank you for allowing me to join Katie and all of you here. I appreciate it."

"You're welcome," is Jake's slightly awkward response.

"Mom's not here yet?"

"Not yet. Hopefully soon," Jake replies, in a voice which barely hides his distress.

I don't know what to say, so I simply nod. I feel as distressed as Jake looks, so I change the subject. "We brought lots of stuff, Jake. Leo and I brought things from home, and we all stopped and shopped in

Wesley when we heard about the latest attacks on the refineries. I can't believe how bad this is."

"I know. The refinery attacks will really be a challenge to overcome. It sounds like they hit all of the big ones. Maybe we'll know a little bit more when the president speaks tonight. Oh, by the way, we're having a community meeting tonight. We set it up last night for the same time the president's now scheduled to speak. We'll put it on the radio there. Not sure what the turnout will be, but you can join us."

"Okay. We should probably try to unload some things tonight. Maybe we should start before we go. You think, Leo?"

"Actually," Jake says, "why don't we hold off? The Snyders are going to be down here in a few minutes. I invited them for the grand tour."

"The *full* grand tour?" I'm surprised by this and don't even try to hide it.

"Yes. Thought it might be a good idea. Good idea for all of you," Jake says slowly.

I think about what this means. Jake and Mom have spent a lot of time and an insane amount of money. At times, they questioned what they were doing since it was, in some ways, a struggle. When other people bought new cars, they stuck with their paid-for vehicles and put the money toward preparations instead. The features they added when building this place seemed a little . . . well, nuts, at times. And if Jake wants to show everything off, then he must really be concerned.

"You think so?" I ask.

"I don't know. Maybe. With everything that has happened, I'm not sure what to think."

"And Mom's not here. What are we going to do? We need to get her home." I'm barely able to keep my voice from cracking.

"I'm not sure how we could, Katie. I don't know where she is. I haven't heard from her since yesterday, and there's too many routes she could've taken. We just have to wait."

I can't keep it together any longer and I start to cry. Jake pulls me into a hug.

"Things seem grim right now. But I know your mom. As much as we want her here, she wants to be here and is doing everything she can to get home. She'll make it home. I *know* she will. I'm upset about this, too, honey. I wish she'd drive in now or I knew where to even start looking for her. There are so many routes she could take to get home. I don't even know where to start. It'd be like looking for a needle in a haystack."

Sarah asks Leo what's wrong. He whispers a response, and the next thing I know, she's hugging Jake and me too. Soon, Calley's there also. Then Malcolm. Angela is nearby with Gavin. Once again, we're in a crush of bodies.

Loud enough for everyone to hear, Jake says, "We all wish Mollie was home. It's hard not knowing where she is. With where she was last time I heard from her yesterday, I would've expected her home by now. I'm not going to tell you I'm not worried—I am.

"I'll also tell you, Mollie was being smart about this trip back. Did you all know she had a get-home bag stored at her boss's house? She took it as a checked bag when she went last winter. What we packed for her was the prototype for the bags we did for all of you.

"Thursday night, she did her own version of *Plan A* by visiting the convenience store near where she works and buying some supplies. Lots of convenience store food and drinks. Then, Friday morning, she bought more food and supplies, including a bicycle from SuperMart.

"When I talked to her yesterday morning, she was in Vale, Oregon. I had a text from her yesterday midday, and she was somewhere in Idaho. She was making a point of staying off the interstates and choosing state and county roads to get home.

"If, for some reason, she had to abandon the car, she's got the bike. She's not as adept on a bike as Katie." Jake gives me a slight smile when he says this. "But she'll do fine. And if she has to abandon the bike, she'll walk. You all know we've been doing quite a bit of hiking and backpacking over the past few years. She knows what to do."

I look around as Jake finishes. I'm not the only one crying.

"Until we know something more, all we can do is wait. Mollie and I have an agreement not to go looking for the other one unless we know where to look. It'd be a fool's errand. Waiting is all we can do." The sigh that escapes Jake tells me it's not what he wants to do.

"We'll have the community meeting at seven, when the president's scheduled to speak. Before we leave, I'd like to go over a few things with everyone. I invited Evan and Doris, so we'll wait until they arrive. Shouldn't be but— " Jake pulls a strapless watch out of his pocket and checks the time " —twenty minutes or so. In the meantime, let's discuss sleeping arrangements."

Everyone's suddenly talking at once. Some are discussing the president's upcoming address, some talk about Jake's announcement of going over a few things, some ask questions about where my mom might be, and others discuss where they might be sleeping.

"Wait." Jake moves his hand. "Maybe, first, we should do introductions. I just realized, with the extended families here, not everyone knows everyone else. And there's so many of us . . . it could get a bit confusing. I'll start. These are my parents, Alvin and Dodie Caldwell." Jake gestures toward my adopted grandparents.

Grandpa Alvin lifts a hand, while Grandma Dodie dips her head.

"Tate, can you introduce your family?"

"Uh, yes. Of course. I'm Tate, married to Mollie's daughter Sarah. This is my dad, Keith; my mom, Lois; and my older sister, Karen."

The *older* statement earned him a pop on the arm from Karen.

"Hey!" Tate rubs his arm. "They were visiting Sarah and me from Tulsa when everything started."

Jake prompts Tim to go next.

"I'm Tim. This is my wife, Angela, and our son, Gavin. My dad, Art Carpenter, is over there." He gestures with his left arm, and Art gives a little wave.

Mike quickly says, "I'm Mike, and this is Calley." He puts his arm around Calley, then points to his parents. "These are my parents, Roy and Deanne Curtis. And my sister, Sheila Stapleton."

Tate adds, "Garrett. Our last name is Garrett."

"I think I've met everyone here at least once," I say. "But just in case, I'm Katie. This is Leo." I nod to him.

"Leo Burnett," he announces.

"I think all of you know Malcolm?" Jake asks, as Malcolm gives everyone a shy wave. "And you all know me, or else you wouldn't be here."

"That was a little weird, Jake," Angela says. And we all, including Jake, laugh. It was a good icebreaker.

"Okay, so let's get lodging figured out. My parents are in the apartment off the garage. Tate and Sarah brought a camp trailer they'll be staying in. Tate's parents are in the bunkhouse." He gestures toward the bunkhouse, which we can't see since it's on the other side of the garage and back another hundred yards, at least.

"Angela, I stumbled into this little cabin yesterday. It's a little . . . rustic . . . but nice. I thought it'd be good for your family. Art, too, at least for tonight, if you don't mind."

We all look at where he's pointing. It's small but adorable, and I kind of wish it was for me.

"It's fine," Tim says. "We don't mind my dad staying with us."

Jake dips his chin. "Well, I think it may be a little cozy for more than a day or two, but we'll sort it out," Jake says.

"It's a Tiny House," Angela says. "It looks cute. Isn't it cute, Gavin?"

Gavin has no idea what his mom is talking about but agrees. "*Cuuuute*, like Gavin."

This draws plenty of laughter.

"You sure are cute, Gavin," Jake says. "Roy, Mike, the cabin should be good for your family. You should all fit fine. I haven't aired it out yet. Malcolm, can you get the key to the cabin and open all of the doors and windows?"

"Sure, Dad. I'd better hurry. The Snyders are pulling out of their driveway." Malcolm gestures to the top of the hill. "Oh, and Dad, don't forget you have pizza in the oven." Malcolm is off at full speed.

"Oops, I did forget about the pizza."

"I'll take care of it, Jake."

"Thanks, Sarah. There are four more ready to go in the oven after you pull those out. We'll have to scrounge up something else to feed everyone tonight. Katie and Leo, you two will be in the house. Leo, I have the guest room ready for you. Katie, you'll have the basement room. We'll get everything situated soon. Let's wait for Doris and Evan to come down and then we'll finish."

"Sure, Jake," I say. "I know you said we should wait to unload, but I brought a cooler of frozen things. You think I can put those in the freezer?"

Angela, Calley, and Deanne all say, "Me too."

"We have room in our freezer. It's in the garage," Grandma Dodie says.

"I'll get it, Katie," Leo says as he, Tim, Art, Mike, and Roy all make their way to the vehicles. I take a good look around . . . I sure wish Mom was here.

Chapter 14

Mom and Jake bought this place as bare land. At one time, it was part of a cattle ranch. The acreage was sold to a real estate investor and divided into fourteen residential parcels. The investor had bought when the market was terrible, and it took him a long time to sell the parcels. When Mom and Jake found this place, only one parcel had sold, so they had their choice. Now, everything is sold.

I had really hoped they'd buy one of the lots on the creek. While they did like those lots, they felt this parcel suited them better, especially since the creek lots were three times as much, didn't have water rights, and weren't on high ground. Jake likes the high ground. I do have to say, the views from their place are incredible.

While this is high ground, it wasn't the highest spot available. Mom and Jake's friends, the Snyders, live farther up the road, and the old original ranch is another half mile beyond their place. The ranch is unoccupied but still used for farming. Jutting off from the ranch is a two-track heading up into the wilderness. It's not used much, except by four-wheeling enthusiasts.

Jake and Mom have thirty acres, which, when they purchased, seemed like enough. They both wished they would've bought two lots and tried to buy the one adjoining theirs, but it sold before they could figure out how to make it work.

Mom says the people who bought the lot are very nice, so she's okay with it. The neighbors don't live here yet, but they've built a shop, house a fifth wheel in it, and visit as often as they can. Mom says they're supposed to start construction on their house this fall. Now . . . who knows?

Mom and Jake's house is a series of connected rectangles. They designed it using very basic design principles to keep the costs down.

Their gravel driveway is on a private gravel road. When pulling in, the oversized detached garage and shop combination is slightly right of the driveway. It's the first rectangle, with the long sides going east–west. It's taller than a regular garage, with a lofted area for storage.

Mom says the garage is way too big, dwarfs the house, and is an eyesore, but Jake says it looks and works just fine. I know he'd like to have a second shop, about the same size, so he can buy a boat and camp trailer. Mom and Jake both say, "Maybe someday." But now, I wonder if someday will ever arrive. Our world has changed so much.

My daydreaming is interrupted by the arrival of Doris and Evan. Doris gives Angela, Calley, and me hugs, then oohs and ahhs over Gavin. I introduce her and Evan to Leo, and they're then introduced to any of the others they don't yet know.

Jake and Grandpa Alvin return from the barnyard area, having quickly done the chores.

"I saw everyone come in," Doris tells Jake, "and it looks like you've got some goods to unload. I thought you all may be a little crunched for time, so we brought some snacks down. It's an assortment of things."

As she's talking, she's opening the tailgate on the truck and emptying a cooler. Evan sets out paper plates and napkins and opens two bags of potato chips and a cooler full of drinks.

"Thanks so much, Doris. You didn't need to bring food, but I'm glad you did. I put a few pizzas in the oven, but it won't be enough for all of us," Jake says.

"I started putting things together after you and Sarah were helping us unload earlier. I needed to empty the freezers out. I would've made more pizzas and chicken but didn't realize everyone else would be here. When I looked out the window and saw the vehicles all pulling in, I added the sandwiches, meats, cheese, and other things," she says with a shrug.

Lois and Karen help Sarah bring out Jake's finished pizzas. Once everything is spread out, it takes only a few minutes for our large group to fill our plates and start eating. While there is enough food, I can see there won't be much leftover after this crew finishes. Good thing Jake had Sarah put in more pizzas.

Jake takes a few minutes to eat a slice of pizza and a hard-boiled egg. He washes it down with a big drink of water, then clears his throat.

"Before we go to the community center, I want to take a few minutes to show everyone around here. This will be a quick tour since we're on a time limit. We can spend more time on it later if needed.

"When Mollie and I first started looking for new property, we knew we wanted some place private and out of the way. We also knew we wanted to have certain things set up so, if there was ever a reason, you all—our friends and family—could use our place as a retreat, or as some people may call it, a bug-out location.

"We built the house to have a dedicated guest room and the loft for overflow guests, plus a bedroom in the basement. We added the studio apartment off the shop. Then we added the bunkhouse, which has bed space for at least eight—twelve if we add in the futons. Last year we bought the cabin over there, which, though slightly smaller than the bunkhouse, also sleeps eight—ten with the loveseat sleeper sofa things. Doris, you know about those since you helped Mollie make the slipcovers for them."

"Sure, I've even been in the cabin, the bunkhouse, and the studio. Cute places."

"Yeah, thanks." Jake gives a distracted nod. "Yesterday, I was offered, as Angela named it, the Tiny House. Sarah and Tate brought their camper down, plus I have a few other ideas if needed, so we're in okay shape for lodging."

There are murmurs of thanks all around.

"We also wanted to have a small farm so we could provide as much for ourselves and any people joining us as possible. Over the years we've built up a decent amount of food in storage. Our goal, which started shortly after Malcolm was born, was to have a year's supply of food for each of us.

"At the time, we had a family of seven. Then, when we moved here, we included my parents in those numbers. As the girls have married, we've added on to our supplies to accommodate for spouses. We've also added for family members we thought might be joining us. Right now, I can't for sure say we have a year for each of us, but we have a decent amount."

More murmurs and some disbelief on many faces. Doris mouths to Evan what looks like, "*A year for each of them?*"

"One thing I really want to stress is things don't look very good right now. Things didn't look good last night when the lights went off. Lights going off for a short time wouldn't be too big of a deal, but from what I heard about the way the cyberattacks were done, major systems were broken and need to be repaired before power can be restored."

Pretty much everyone agrees this is what they understand also.

Jake continues, "Now, today, with the refineries being targeted . . . it could be quite a while before things return to normal.

The people who are stranded in other towns will be stuck there until fuel can be brought in. I suspect we'll get fuel from other countries, but it could take some time. So, you all could be here awhile."

"Jake, I'm sure there's lots to be done here, so be sure to tell us how we can help. I know with Mom gone it's probably not easy."

"Thanks, Sarah. And it's true. There's lots to be done, and many plans we may need to make. We'll all need to work together, especially if this does become a long-term thing. One of my concerns is the terrorists, or whoever they may be, aren't finished with us yet. I was worried about an electromagnetic pulse being set off, which would destroy the power grid. But they seemed to have found another way to do this—with the cyberattacks. It doesn't mean they won't use an EMP, but I hope it's less likely."

I look around and a few people look confused, others are nodding.

"One thing Mollie and I added here was a safe room. I'd like to show you all this so you know about it and can go to it if needed. Those of you here now—you're family. Most of you by marriage, but still family. Evan and Doris, you know Mollie and I consider you family also. I'd still like to ask all of you to keep this confidential. Can everyone do that?"

Safe room. That's what he's calling it. Interesting. I suspect it's because it sounds better than *nuclear fallout shelter.*

Jake makes sure he's seen a nod or heard a yes from everyone.

"So, let's go around the house. Sarah, do you think the rest of the pizzas are done? Can you go ahead and pull them out of the oven? We'll just leave them out for people to grab a slice. Then please join us," Jake says, while walking toward the house. Malcolm is practically skipping next to him. Sarah heads into the house via the front door. The rest of us follow Jake like little ducklings.

Jake opens the small mudroom at the back of the house. This is the direct entrance into his and Mom's room and the basement.

"Malcolm, will you hold the door for everyone to get in?"

"Sure, Dad."

With Malcolm as the doorman, Jake leads us down the stairs. The staircase ends directly in the large rec room, housed under Mom and Jake's bedroom and Mom's office.

The rec room features a foosball table, a large table for games or cards, a small chess table, plus a small corner bar. For seating, there are chairs around the tables, a rocket heater bench, two comfy chairs, and two futons.

The floor is painted concrete, in a medium gray with a high gloss topcoat, and several area rugs. The walls are white and covered in artwork done by all of us kids, with most being my work but several from Malcolm, who also loves to draw and paint. The ten-foot ceilings in the basement add to the spaciousness. There's a decent-sized window—big enough to crawl through in case the house was on fire or something.

I know Alvin and Dodie plus all of us kids have been down here, but the extended families haven't, and I quickly find out Doris and Evan haven't when Doris says, "Wow! I had no idea you had a game room down here."

"Yeah," Jake says. "We don't use it much. Mainly when the older kids are here and we want to spread out a bit."

"It's very nice," Doris adds, while everyone else says something similar.

"Thanks." Jake motions to the door on the left wall. "This door here is to a guest room. Katie will be using this room."

Then he points to a door straight ahead at the bottom of the stairs. "This goes to the bathroom." He opens the bathroom door but doesn't go in. "It's sort of like a Jack and Jill bath. So this part has a half bath, open the door there and you'll go into the room with a tub and shower combo. Then another door leads to another half bath."

"It's not really what realtors call a Jack and Jill bath, but it makes sense," Angela says.

I don't know what it's called. I've never seen a bathroom like Mom and Jake have, but I do understand why they have it. And so will everyone else shortly.

"Okay," Jake says while closing the bathroom door. "We'll go out the rec room through here." He motions to yet another door.

Once we've all followed him into the main basement area, there are murmurs and gasps as everyone gawks at all the shelves and storage cabinets. Some of the space has even been divided into smaller, locked rooms.

On one wall is another escape window, but it's not like the windows in the game room and bedroom, which pull in lots of light. This one is altered slightly so only a small amount of sunshine will come in. There's nothing wrong with the window itself, but the window well is closed off, preventing light from filtering in.

"We designed this section of the basement to act as a storage area," Jake says. "Pretty much, these things won't be accessed unless needed. We keep the day-to-day food upstairs in the kitchen and mudroom pantry. I'm not sure if you noticed the ceiling in here is a little lower than in the game room."

Quick glances up and nods of acknowledgment follow.

"And this door here goes to the bathroom we saw from the rec room—it has a dual door and also has a lower ceiling. We wanted to make this part of our safe room by providing extra mass above head. When we poured the basement, we had a cement ceiling put in. These are pretty common in Europe but not used much here. The cement ceiling gives a little more strength and security to our structure.

"We had the basement done to have ten-foot ceilings throughout. In this section and the bathroom, we manually lowered the ceiling after construction was completed by adding a sturdy loft-type feature, dropping it down to seven feet at the bottom of the beams. It's great for storing things like toilet paper, paper towels, and other similar items. In some sections, we put sandbags on the loft instead of using it for storage. This extra mass gives us, essentially, a fallout shelter."

Everyone's pretty quiet. I notice a few eye rolls and looks exchanged.

Jake continues to walk to the back of the basement, stopping when he reaches a bookshelf against the back wall. He pushes the side of the bookshelf and it slides a bit. He pushes a little more, and it folds into the cabinet next to it like an accordion. There's a collective gasp.

"What do you have here, Jake?" Grandpa Alvin asks.

Jake opens a door and steps into the room the moving bookshelf exposed, turning on a light.

"Take a look, Dad. You can all come in, but it'll be a little tight. It's not very big, only 16 x 12. This is the space under the mudroom at the front of the house."

Jake gestures at the right side and back walls and continues, "These are bunk beds folded into the wall, pretty much Murphy beds. It takes just a minute to fold them out, and when they aren't needed, they're out of the way."

The back wall has two sets of these folding bunk beds, and there's one set on the right-side wall, for a total of six bunks.

115

"We also have folding chairs and a couple of card tables over here. It's kind of sparse but not terrible. The curtained area has a toilet with an attached sink. The faucet's a hand-pump style, which pulls from the water tank here." He motions to a large water container with a sticker prominently advertising thirty-five gallons on the side.

"With the dropped ceiling and sandbags, combined with the cement ceiling and a plan to add additional sandbags in the room above, this room provides a little extra security in case of heavy fallout. It could also double as a safe room if we needed a place to hide out."

"Pretty nice, Jake. Might be a little cozy for all of us, but good thinking," Grandpa Alvin says and starts to walk away.

"Hold on, Dad. There's more."

Chapter 15

"This really would be too cozy for everyone, but six people can easily sleep in here." Jake makes a sweeping motion, encompassing the safe room.

"Plus, four more cots could be put out, making tight sleeping quarters for ten—more if needed. It'd be fine for a few days. And see the door between the bunks on the back wall? It opens to a tunnel, which connects to the garage. The plan would be to move the livestock to the garage, and I can care for them in there without having to go outside. Since there are several more than ten of us, let me show you an extra option."

Jake leads us out of the safe room and over near the storage area egress. He opens the window and says, "This egress does double duty. The wooden grate above can easily be lifted, and the ladder on the side takes you out of the basement in case of a fire or other emergency. But there's also a special feature."

Jake reaches the back wall of it and pops something off, swinging a section of the planks open. I catch Leo's eye and he nods. I can tell he's enjoying this and can't wait to see what's next.

"This opening in the window well goes into a tunnel, which connects to the root cellar." Jake pops on a light and the tunnel is suddenly illuminated. Again, gasps and awes from the group.

"The entrance is short, only about four feet high, so you'll need to watch your head. Then it'll open to six feet. Leo, Dad, Mike . . . you'll have to stoop a bit. Roy, you too, I think." He gives Roy a nod. "Everyone watch your step. There's another door in about ten feet. We'll let Malcolm lead and he can open the second door."

"Yay, Dad! I can do it."

This garners several small chuckles over Malcolm's enthusiasm.

Jake and Mom told me before this is a marine door with a fairly tight fit. I'm somewhat reminded of a submarine tour we took years ago when living in Oregon.

After going through the marine door, we continue on another twenty feet where Malcolm opens up another door, then takes a minute to slide a shelf out of the way. We all file into the root cellar.

Those tall guys among us are visibly happy to, once again, be able to stand upright. There are lots of wide eyes but very little conversation other than a few murmurs of surprise.

"So, here we are." Jake looks to the gathered group. Leo has a big smile. Many others look confused.

It's not much to look at, nothing more than a basic, slightly rustic root cellar. Well-stocked shelves sport a fine layer of dust, and the dirt floors give an earthy aroma. I'll admit, I wouldn't want to have to be locked up in here for any length of time. But given a choice between this bleak and musty room or radiation poisoning . . . yeah, it's a pretty easy decision.

Roy's the first to ask what many are likely thinking. "So it's a root cellar? Or another safe room? Or is it a bomb shelter?"

"Well, its first function is root cellar. Then it's a fallout shelter or a safe room. While a direct explosion here would be unlikely, I don't know how well this would hold up. We built it to have a safe place to go and to provide protection from fallout from a nuclear weapon."

Now there are more than murmurs with people all talking at once.

"Wait, wait," Jake says. "I want to answer but don't even know where to start. I did hear one of you say you didn't know we were survivalists. We're not, at least not in the way the media portrays. We do live a lifestyle of preparedness. When we were still topside, I shared how we've been working to have food on hand for all of those we care about. This is no different. We want to provide for you by offering a safe shelter. It's likely we'll never need to use this place and Mollie and I threw some money away. That's just fine.

"We needed a root cellar anyway, and adding the tunnel to connect made sense to us. We look at this like an insurance policy. It's here if we need it. Same with the food storage, though we do eat much of the food we store. I'd like to show you the rest if you want to see, but we're on a time schedule. We can look now and answer questions later, or I can answer questions now. What do you want to do?"

I think everyone agreed to complete the tour. Angela, Tim, and I had this tour together before. I was a little weirded out by the fact they built a fallout shelter, so I completely understand the others' reaction. I look at Sarah and Tate and think they've had the tour also. I can't see Calley and Mike, and I don't know if they've seen this. Probably, but the way Calley has been—maybe not.

"Like the basement room under the mudroom, this has extra protection in case of heavy fallout, with several feet of dirt on top of the space. The extra protection is also helpful for the root cellar aspect. We store our garden produce down here, especially the root vegetables and home-canned items. There's also water and a few other things. This part we're standing in is what we call the midsection. Through here is the front section where the door from the yard enters."

Jake opens the door dividing the two rooms. It's a simple wooden door, not a marine version. There's a tight-sealing steel door at the base of the stairs entering the root cellar for extra security. The doors entering from ground level are basic wood, similar to root cellars everywhere. A stack of already filled sandbags are at the ready, stacked on either side of the door, to add protection.

Ideally, Jake told me when I had this tour, a proper shelter would have a corner or a turn, but it didn't make sense with their root cellar construction. Especially since they wanted the root cellar to appear to be only a root cellar and not scream fallout shelter.

"At the back of the midsection, we have more shelves, which slide aside and open to what we call, you guessed it, the back section."

Moving to one of the shelving units, he pushes it to the right, revealing a wooden door. He opens the door to show another tunnel. This one is small, only four feet in diameter, and has a wooden floor added to give a level surface. There are several shelves along both sides, making a narrow passage. Jake does the same thing to a shelving unit on the left, pushing it and opening an identical tunnel.

"These are nothing fancy. We put in a couple of 48-inch x 10-foot culverts to act as sleeping pods. The shelves on either side take up a little space, but the extra storage is worth the squeeze to get by. Then we have a six-inch foam mattress at the back with a short headboard shelf. The mattress is larger than a twin but smaller than a full. It'll be great for one person and cozy for two but doable for a short time.

"The shelving here at the front contains shelter-specific items and provides a place to put your stuff if you have to stay in here. On these shelves, and in other places, we have provisions to make things comfortable. We have enough supplies in the root cellar area for twenty people to stay for two weeks plus an additional two weeks' supply is stored just inside the reinforced basement for easy access.

"To give a little extra space, the tunnel we came through from the basement can be opened for sleeping. We even have presanded plywood in one of our outbuildings, which can be brought down here if needed. The plywood will give a flat surface, like in these culvert bedrooms. It's all a little rustic. We would've loved to be able to make this one of those million-dollar shelters you may have seen on TV."

This gets Jake some chuckles.

"But we did what we could. I mentioned the lowered ceiling in the basement. The bathroom, like the basement safe room, has a layer of sandbags above the ceiling. This gives a little extra mass in a room which might be . . . um . . . visited fairly often. The cement ceiling, combined with the storage items in the loft, provide enough protection to use the basement as a pass-through, going from the safe room to the cellar, or accessing the bathroom from either, in all but the heaviest fallout.

"In case of heavy fallout, we have a couple of compost toilets on standby. Not aesthetically pleasing, but better than nothing. Again, we hope to never need this." Jake looks around the room, trying to make eye contact with everyone present. "But we have it if we do."

"So, with the root cellar, we can all fit down here if we needed a . . . uh, shelter?" Tate's mom, Lois, asks warily.

Jake nods. "Combining this section plus the safe room gives us space to house thirty people fairly comfortably if there was nuclear fallout. It's very likely, where we are, a nuke strike wouldn't happen nearby, and our fallout would be minimal. So minimal the basement storage area would provide enough protection—at least this is what we think from our research.

"That said, there's always the chance of a wild strike and we could get more fallout than what we expect, which is the reason for the extra protection of the safe room and root cellar. So, I know this isn't the cheeriest thought, and we have no reason to think there will be a nuclear attack, but I wanted to make sure all of you knew what we have, just in case.

"And I'll be honest, even though we feel twenty in this section and ten in the other is about as cozy as we'd want to be, if there really was a nuke strike, we'd likely want to squeeze more people in. It definitely wouldn't be fun, but saving as many lives as possible would be worth a little inconvenience."

At his last statement, Jake looks around and sees people nodding.

"I'm pretty impressed, Jake," Roy says. "Even if it isn't a million-dollar shelter, it seems like it'd do the job. How'd you determine twenty people would fit in here and ten in the other space?"

"Good question. We found some info on fallout shelters recommending a minimum of ten square feet per person or to temporarily crowd in at five square feet per person. The two root cellar rooms are about 250 square feet, not including the culvert bedrooms. This gives over twenty-five square feet per person based on the twenty people count. The safe room space is 192 square feet, giving just under twenty square feet per person. The beds provided are for twenty and ten, but we could increase these numbers substantially if we hot racked it."

"Hot racked? What's that?" Tate's sister, Karen, asks.

"Bed sharing or sleeping in shifts. It's common on some Navy ships, especially among the enlisted. It's called hot racking because the bed might still be warm from the last person sleeping in it," Roy offers.

"Right," Jake says. "It doesn't sound overly pleasant but is for sure an option. In the Navy, usually people are on different shifts, so it's not a big deal. In a small space, it'd be harder since there isn't really any place to go. Those not sleeping could be playing cards at the table or reading, but it would be awkward.

"With the front and middle rooms of the root cellar, plus the sleeping tubes, we have about 330 square feet. Plus, we could really stretch the numbers by including the access tube to the marine door, which would be another eighty square feet. Using those numbers, we're over four hundred square feet, or forty people, giving ten square feet each. The safe room could bump to twenty people easy, and even more if we utilized the tunnel to the garage for space."

"So you'd allow sixty people between the two rooms with ten square feet each? Double if you really wanted to cram people in?" Roy asks.

Jake says yes, and many people are nodding as they've followed along with the math.

"I can't imagine it'd be very pleasant but can see it would be survivable. What about air supply? There's enough air down here for all of us?"

"Good question, Roy. A normal root cellar needs circulation, so intake and outtake air vents are added. You can see these in each of the rooms. Ours are a little different than some. Right now, they're basic vents. But for each of the intake or outtake air vents, we have a small battery-operated fan which fits into the bottom of the vent pipe after an extension is added.

"The intake is positioned to bring air in while the outtake is turned to push air out. The vents themselves are pretty basic—PVC pipe going straight out, then curving so it's down-facing, preventing particles from falling directly into the pipe. Also helpful to keep our free-ranging chickens from leaving anything down the vent we don't want."

This garners a few laughs.

"We've also added a few filters as an extra precaution. The filter at the ninety-degree curve is made out of felted wool, and a foot from the opening into the room is a filter made from cut-to-fit carbon pads.

"The little fans help move the air around, but to be sure to keep the air fresh, we have a few homemade Kearny Air Pumps. These are manual pumps which remove stale air and usher in fresh air. Mollie found an article online for ventilation and cooling of shelters, which introduced us to the simple, yet effective, Kearny Air Pump.

"And it also had many suggestions on manually ventilating a shelter using large homemade fans and bed sheets. We have the supplies for these stored in case we need them. Ventilation is definitely important, and the fans will also help cool the air since it can get hot with just the heat from so many bodies. The safe room has a similar ventilation setup."

"That's good, Jake. Sounds like you guys did a lot of research. I know I speak for Deanne and Sheila when I tell you how grateful we are you invited us. And as nice as this is, I hope we never have to stay in here." Roy gives a big, corny looking smile.

"I completely agree. And we'd probably better get going." Jake ushers everyone out through the front section of the root cellar instead of the tunnel back to the basement.

"For those who wish to go to the community center, we should probably get a move on it," Jake says.

Evan and Doris have been mostly silent during this grand tour. Evan now says, "Jake, thank you for showing us your safe room." I'm amused he called it a safe room. "It's pretty great. And thank you for offering it to us, in case we do need it. I'm sure I speak for everyone here—your secret is safe with me."

Everyone nods and agrees. There are many more thanks like the one Evan gave.

"I hope you'll all come to the community center," Evan says. "We had a meeting there last night, and I think it's important for the entire community, which now includes all of you, to find out what may come next for us, depending on what the president says and how the community may handle this."

We make our way up the root cellar stairs. Once we're outside, I ask Leo, "You want to go? I think I should, and I hope you think you should, but it's up to you."

"Yeah. I think I do. Sounds like it could be important."

I'm very tired but agree it's important. I know, as soon as we get back, I'm not going to want to do anything but go to bed.

As we make our way to our vehicles, Malcolm and Gavin go into the apartment with Grandma and Grandpa. It looks like most everyone else is loading up for the meeting. Jake has a five-gallon water container in each hand, as does Evan. They look deep in conversation and not very happy.

Calley touches me on the arm. "Katie, did you know about the shelter space?"

I can't tell if she's asking because she didn't know and is feeling left out, or if she thinks I feel left out. I decide to proceed with caution. Calley has a way of easily getting her feelings hurt and then pouting.

"I knew."

"Good. I was afraid you may not have seen it yet, and I didn't want you to be too surprised. Mom and Jake swore Mike and me to secrecy when we visited after announcing our engagement. I have to admit, I was a little surprised they hadn't showed me before then."

I think back . . . Angela, Tim, and I had our tour after Calley's engagement was announced, so we saw it around the same time. Oh, we knew about the basement—the rec room, guest room, funky bathroom, and the storage sections. And we knew about the root cellar. They just hadn't opened it all up before.

"I saw it after you," I tell her. "Remember, though, they always said we should come here because they had many plans put in place. I think they probably hinted about the shelter. I never put it together, though."

"I agree. Thinking back, they definitely hinted. I'm glad they did all of this, even though it seemed silly for so many years. Now, I think they were probably pretty smart. After they showed Mike and me, we'd make jokes about it. Some not very nice ones. Then we were joking about it one day, and it didn't seem as funny. Especially when we started paying attention to the things going on in the world. I don't know how I never realized what a mess things were before then."

I nod and mumble my agreement, as she says, "Mike thought we should start buying a few extra essentials. In the beginning that was really just Dr Pepper and pasta. But then, when they sent the backpacks, we started buying more things to keep on hand, like they suggested. I even created a week-long menu, bought everything for it, and then put it in storage. I did this four times. Now, we'll eat from this food and replace it—well, mostly. Sometimes I still struggle with making it to the grocery store.

"We added a few other things, too, mostly just bags of beans and rice. It was kind of hard finding things that sounded good. You know, Mike likes what he likes and not much else. I do hope we never have to spend much time in the shelter. Not my idea of fun. Well, we'd better go. It looks like everyone's getting ready to pull out."

Jake, Evan, and Doris had been talking near the truck. The three of them still look very unhappy. I wonder what that's all about?

Chapter 16

"Your folks have created quite the place," Leo declares as we pull out of the driveway.

"Yes. They've really spent a lot of time and money on it. There've been so many times I thought they were a little crazy for putting so much effort into it. I even thought we were missing out on things over the years because they focused their money on preparedness."

"What'd you miss out on?"

I pause while I think of how to answer. What did I miss out on?

"Oh, nothing much, really. The house we had in Casper was a used double-wide. We could've afforded a new, nicer place, but they chose to buy one for cash. Mom said not having a house payment gave them a lot of freedom. I guess it did since the money they saved was used to put in the fallout shelter. Still, growing up I would've liked a nicer house, something like the one we had when we lived in Portland. And new cars. They've had the same cars since they were first married."

Leo doesn't say anything, and I wonder if he thinks I'm being childish. Now, it seems the choices made by my parents over the years were genius. I have a place to live, out of harm's way of the people escaping the cities, plus we have food and comfortable beds. If things get worse, we even have Jake's "safe room" ready for us.

When we arrive at the community center, it's still several minutes until the president is supposed to speak. A few dozen people are already milling around, as more arrive. Doris sets up a radio and speakers, then finds a station she thinks is broadcasting. A few minutes later, an announcer declares the speech will begin shortly.

The gathered crowd, now numbering well over a hundred, begins to move in closer to the picnic table holding the radio and speakers. As people check their watches and cell phones for the time, there's an increase in tension. The announcer makes a quick statement, saying they expect the president to come on at any moment.

Within seconds, without any music or fanfare, the president begins his address.

"Good evening. I'm speaking to you tonight to give you a report on the situation our country is facing. The loss of life over the past

several days has been staggering. My prayers and condolences go out to all who have lost loved ones. I regret to say, the assaults upon our nation continue, with the latest attacks of our oil refineries today at 10:22 a.m. eastern time.

"Today's incidents further complicate our already vulnerable position. Friday's attacks on our cities' bridges caused a mass exodus from the affected cities as our citizens tried to find a place they could feel safe. The small towns and communities of which our people fled to have had a very difficult time accommodating the abundance of new inhabitants. Resources were rapidly depleted. We enacted a program to send aid to the areas in most dire need.

"The cyberwar, which began yesterday, complicated this aid when the bulk of our nation's power grids were taken offline. One of our main goals was supplying fuel to these areas so people could return to their homes. The lack of electricity impeded this process. The destruction of more than half of our US refineries, and several refineries in other countries, means we now face a certain worldwide shortage of fuel."

There are many gasps and cries in the crowd. I hadn't heard about other countries' refineries being attacked and had simply assumed the world would come to our aid.

"We will bring our unaffected refineries to their full capabilities, and we will rebuild our destroyed refineries. Our financial institutions have been impaired by the cyberwar. Because of continued attacks on our systems, we were left no choice but to take the internet offline. This prevents the use of credit cards through the online network. ATMs are also unavailable. As a result of all financial records relying on internet access, I've declared a banking holiday, beginning tomorrow and continuing through this week.

"The American Stock Exchange, the Nasdaq Stock Market, and the New York Stock Exchange, after consultation with the US Securities and Exchange Commission, and in light of the outrageous attacks on America and continued cyberattacks, will also be closed for the week. Our hope is we can stop the cyberwar and remedy any damage caused within this time.

"The cyberwar has taken almost every power station offline, either fully or partially. For most people, this power outage is simply

an inconvenience, not a tragedy. We are providing as much help as we can to healthcare facilities that require power to operate. Backup systems are in place and believed to be functioning.

"Do remember that, with summer temperatures and the lack of air conditioning, you want to do what you can to keep yourself cool. My experts tell me a wet T-shirt can help lower your core temperature. You can also use small, manual, handheld fans to provide additional relief. The very young and the elderly are most susceptible to heat exhaustion. These people who are most likely to be affected will need extra care and monitoring.

"While it seems we're in dire straits, I assure you, the functions of our government continue without interruption. We're working to get help to those who have been injured and taking precautions to protect our citizens from further attacks. The search is underway to find those who have carried out these malicious attacks. Once located, they will be dealt with and brought to justice.

"Within our borders, we're experiencing many instances of violence in our cities, including riots, looting, arson, and other criminal activities. In the areas which have been hardest hit, the National Guard is being brought in based on requests from individual governors.

"I ask the help of every person—whether in the cities, small towns, or rural areas—to band together during this distressing time. It will take all of us working with one goal in mind to come through this time intact. The goal of preserving our great nation and citizens. The goal of preventing riots and destruction. The goal of not just getting through this travesty but of enduring and becoming a much stronger nation because of it.

"We will never forget. We will move forward and come together as one nation, indivisible. Thank you. Good night. God bless the United States of America."

There are several seconds of silence before the radio announcer returns.

"We'll replay tonight's presidential address in its entirety at 8:00 p.m. tonight and tomorrow at 7:00 a.m. and 1:00 p.m. Now, for local news, we have reports of scattered burglaries and looting in various businesses throughout our county and surrounding area. We *have been asked to pass on the request from local police to remain at your homes from dusk to dawn. While a curfew is not officially being established, anyone on the streets during nondaylight hours will be deemed to have nefarious intentions and will be stopped, with arrest likely. This request remains in effect for the duration of this crisis.*

"Please remember to continue to boil or otherwise purify all water from public sources or use only bottled water. We don't believe the water supply in our area was affected by the terrorists but know this could change. If you're unable to purify water at home due to the power outage, you can obtain purified water at City Park in Wesley and Pryor, Prospect Chamber of Commerce, and the Rendezvous Museum parking lot in Rendezvous.

"We're still operating on backup power. To conserve this power, we will drop our broadcasts to 7:00 a.m., 1:00 p.m., and 7:00 p.m. beginning tomorrow. We'll also broadcast any time there's an urgent alert via the Emergency Alert System. Our sister station, KWDI at 870 AM, will broadcast at 5:00 a.m. and 5:00 p.m., in addition to any EAS broadcasts. We welcome donations of diesel fuel to use in our generators at either of our station locations. Thank you and good night."

No one says anything for about five seconds, then everyone begins speaking at once. It's near pandemonium.

Doris starts disconnecting the radio and speakers when a man with a very scraggly beard, cropped hair, and many tattoos, who's carrying not only a sidearm but a rifle strapped across his back, steps onto the bench attached to the picnic table holding the radio.

It shifts and would've tipped over had Evan and Doris not quickly applied pressure on the opposite side. Evan continues to hold the table while Doris tries to quickly remove her equipment from harm's way. The guy standing on the bench simply scowls at them, then practically screeches.

"People, people. We've all heard the president. It doesn't sound like the power's coming back any time soon, and with these latest attacks, we're going to have a gas shortage. And you heard him say, *exactly what I said last night*, we need to band together. Those who have things the rest of us need are required to share."

If I thought it was chaos before, it was nothing compared to what erupts now. Leo gently grabs my elbow and moves me slightly away as the group starts pushing inward.

"Now wait a minute, Morse," a man is yelling. The guy on the picnic bench must be Morse since he's looking around to find the source of the clamor. Suddenly, someone else is by the picnic table, and he looks enraged.

"What is it you want, Bosco?" Morse asks. His right hand goes to the butt of his gun. He briefly massages the handle before removing his hand so he can point at Bosco.

In a very loud yet controlled voice, Bosco answers, "Your version of the president's speech is incorrect. He said we should band together, true. But he was speaking in the context of not rioting and stealing. Which, unless I miss my guess, is what you are implying you'd like to do—stealing from others who have things you think *you* need."

"I'm not suggesting stealing," Morse blares. "I'm saying people who have more are obligated to give to people who have less. I have no doubt people like you, Snyder, and Caldwell have things the rest of us need. You're required to share. The president said so."

I look at Jake. He looks mad enough to spit nails but is trying hard to keep control. A glance at Evan verifies he, too, is furious.

It's the one Morse calls Bosco who responds first. "You, Dan Morse, aren't only twisting what the president said, you're completely delusional. After you took off in a huff last night, Evan Snyder and Jake Caldwell collected fuel cans and went into town, bringing back fuel to everyone who needed it. I happen to know a few people were short on cash but needed to fill their can, and Evan and Jake covered it.

"I haven't seen you offering to help people out. All you've done is whine about *your* needs. You haven't offered one constructive suggestion—only convoluted opinions of what our president asked of us, which, again, wasn't for this to turn into a Communist nation of share and share alike."

"You see? Exactly, what I'm saying." Dan Morse is nearly hysterical now. "Snyder and Caldwell have so many resources they can run into town on a whim! The rest of us can't do that. It's their responsibility to make it so we can. You think Caldwell's being helpful? He's not. He's selfish and not at all interested in helping his neighbors. He even has a whole new group of people with him—people who'll be a drain on our already depleted resources."

Now Jake's not the only one trying hard to keep control. I can barely hold my tongue. This guy is some piece of work.

"You're not only an idiot, you're a sorry excuse of a human being, Dan Morse," Bosco says, then he turns to the rest of those gathered. "I think we all know the type of person Dan is. He's not one of us. No matter how long he lives in Bakerville, he'll never be one of us. Those of us who've lived here for generations aren't opposed to new people moving in when they benefit our community, like the Snyders, Caldwells, and many other new residents we've welcomed recently.

"But people like Dan Morse are not what we're about. People like Morse are little more than a parasite, attaching themselves to others and doing their best to suck them dry. Morse doesn't even have a job. He brags about the fact he doesn't have a job. And here he is telling the rest of us, who bust our butts each day to provide for our families, what we have should also belong to him. They have a name for that, folks. It's called Communism."

And then, things really fall apart.

Chapter 17

Dan Morse launches himself at Bosco. Bosco was mostly facing Morse and saw him coming, but he wasn't able to get out of the way. They connect, hard, and both land on the ground with a groan. It's a combination wrestling and punching bout, with people either moving away or trying to break them up—and a few cheering for their favorite.

Evan moves Doris well away from the fray as Jake gathers us up like little chicks.

Soon a voice, louder than the rest, bellows, "Enough. That's enough." I can't see who it is, but he seems to have some authority as the group breaks up and manages to separate Bosco and Morse from each other. Once the crowd has parted, I recognize Jake's friend Phil Hudson.

Phil is a huge man—extremely polite each time I've met him, but one not to be trifled with. Mom says he reminds her of a slightly smaller version of Shaquille O'Neal. While not the seven-plus-foot tall, over three-hundred-pound Shaq, he's still over six foot and, I'd guess, around 250 pounds—all muscle, as near as I can tell. His shiny, shaved head and closely trimmed full beard are even reminiscent of Shaq. Retired Coast Guard, having served twenty plus years, mostly on a Cutter, he's shared some interesting stories.

"Dan. Terry. Bloodshed isn't going to help anything. Acting like hooligans completely goes against working together as a community. Which, I suspect, is what both of you would like to see happen. Dan may not have expressed himself very well, but I'm sure he's concerned for his fellow neighbor more than himself. Isn't that right, Dan?"

Looking like a deer in the headlights—well, a bloody deer, considering his nose is spurting and he has a cut above his eye—Dan responds without much conviction. "Yeah. Sure. Exactly what I meant. We can't have— "

Phil cuts him off. "Thank you, Dan. And, Terry, I know you. I know you go out of your way to help people. People appreciate what you give to our community. In fact, as I look around, I see a caring community. We're a group with much in common. The biggest thing we have in common is we live here on purpose. Some of you, like Terry, grew up here. Your parents lived here, your grandparents, maybe even your great-grandparents. As an adult, you may have left for a while, but you returned."

Several people are nodding along.

"The rest of us found this place and knew it was home. Many, like my wife and I, were enchanted during our first visit. We can't imagine living anywhere else. Part of what makes this place so special is the people. Not just in our community, but Wyoming as a whole. Wyomingites are a breed apart. Whether native or transplanted, we have a uniqueness all our own. I'd say, those who don't are the ones who don't last in Wyoming."

This gets chuckles and cheers.

"Maybe, what we need to do is figure out who needs help. I wasn't at your gathering here last night, news of it didn't reach us until today, but I hear Jake and Evan were able to get fuel for people to run their generators and such. I went into town today—just returned shortly before this meeting—and I can tell you, it's fortunate they went last night. There's no fuel to be had. Food's another issue. SuperMart and Albertson's are picked dry."

This causes many reactions among the crowd. I can't say I'm surprised, not after being in Wesley yesterday. But I still feel tears stinging my eyes. Out of fuel. Out of food. What'll happen?

"Friends, friends." Phil pumps his hands to quiet the group. "I'm not going to lie, this is concerning. I know most of us keep our pantries fairly well stocked. And with the restaurant and the snack shack at the ski resort the only places to dine out, we're cooking at home most nights.

"When we do get into town, we expect to go into the SuperMart and have the truck late and many of the shelves empty. Seems we're often at the end of the line here for getting restocked on things. We only had this happen one time before we realized the need to keep extras on hand. Well, I should say, my lovely wife, Kelley, realized it'd be smart to keep extras on hand."

He blows a kiss to his wife, which draws a few weak smiles. I'm pretty sure he's making light of their pantry. Mom's very good friends with his wife, and while they don't talk openly about it, Kelley and Phil are also preppers. I'm not sure they're at the black belt degree of prepperhood my folks are, but they're preppers, nonetheless.

"I will say right here, right now," Phil continues, "while I know there are people in this community who'll go out of their way to help their neighbor, there will be no discussion or suggestion of taking things away from any person. What you own is yours and yours alone."

"But that's not fair!" Dan sputters.

Phil says nothing to Dan, simply gives him a look. Dan immediately quiets and looks at his shoes.

"So, again, maybe we need to figure out where we stand today. Who needs help today?"

"Excuse me," a lady from the middle of the crowd shouts out.

"Yes, Sally-Ann?"

"Yes, Phil. I saw on the news, before the power went out, FEMA and the National Guard, and a few other groups I can't remember, are trying to get to communities. When do you think they'll reach us?"

Leo softly whispers, "Never."

We haven't talked about this, but I know he's right. With the transportation issues and cyberattack, I doubt FEMA or the National Guard is even able to get to where they need to go. If FEMA is helping anyone, it's the people in the cities. With everything that's happened, a little community in Wyoming is going to be on its own.

Phil looks very somber as he shakes his head. "I don't know, Sally-Ann. Personally, I don't think we should count on any outside help. With what I was seeing on the news before the power went out, I'd say we're on our own. For now, at least."

There are cries of disbelief throughout the group.

"I thought that might be the case. Hoped I was wrong," Sally-Ann says.

"We're going to work together," Phil says confidently. "Right now, tonight, if you need help with food or water, or help at your house, whatever it may be, let's figure out how we can assist you. Maybe we should divide into groups.

"Those who need any type of help, move over near the playground. Those who can offer help, of any type, but don't need help today, let's move over by the building. If you could use some help but also have something to offer, how about going over to the memorial monument. The rest of you, I suppose, can go on home or mingle around. But before we break up— " Phil is raising his voice to be heard as people start to separate into groups.

"Before we break up, let's decide if we should meet again tomorrow night. I fear driving here will start being a problem with our limited fuel. Should we meet tomorrow night and then decide if we should continue? Evan? What do you think?"

"Uh. Yeah." Evan was obviously caught off guard by this question. "I think that sounds like a good plan. We can carpool, and for those with bicycles or ATVs, riding those might be a good idea."

"Or horses!" someone yells out.

"Yes, or horses. Good idea. Okay, friends. Let's get in the smaller groups. We'll figure this out," Phil says.

I notice Dan Morse is starting to slink away when Phil stops him. I can't hear what is said, but from the look on Dan's face, he doesn't like it. Phil points toward the needs-help group, but Dan shakes his head. Phil points to the third group, which needs some help but has things to offer. Dan looks at Phil and offers a rather rude hand sign, then stomps off.

As I'm watching him leave, I realize Jake's talking to me—to all of us.

"I'd like to see if we can help out. There's many people needing labor done. Would any of you be willing to help? I don't think we need anything from the others right now, so I'll go over to the building. If you'd like to stay and join me over there, that'd be great. We all know Dan Morse was completely out of line, but I do think it'd make a big impression on how you all consider yourself a part of this community. Would you guys mind joining me over by the building?"

There's lots of enthusiasm as everyone agrees. Tate's parents, who aren't much younger than Jake's folks, seem to be the most excited about the prospect of helping out. From the first time she met them, Mom said they're "salt of the earth," and judging by their willingness at the moment, I'd say she's completely correct.

When we get to the building, Phil and his wife, Kelley, are talking to Doris and Evan. Doris has a notebook and pen. When Phil sees Jake, he waves him over. The rest of our group and the others at the building—which includes Terry Bosco, looking a little worse for wear, and maybe a dozen others—wait patiently. I recognize a few of the faces but can't put names to anyone else.

After a minute or so, Phil says, "Thank you all. I'm not really sure how we should best go about this. I've asked Doris and Kelley to be kind of the secretaries of this endeavor. Kelley and I are going over to the people needing the most help. Evan and Doris will take the other group. I wanted to ask Jake and his wife, Mollie, to find out from each of you what you can offer to others. However, I just found out Mollie isn't home. She was away on a business trip and has yet to return.

"Jake assures me he's still more than willing to help as needed, along with his family who have arrived from affected cities. Now, I've seen Jake's writing before, so hopefully one of his lovely daughters will assist him in taking notes on how each of you can help our community."

This gathers a few courtesy laughs. Sarah moves over by Jake to help him. Kelley offers her a small notebook and pen, then Phil, Kelley, Evan, and Doris walk off to their assignments.

"Well," Jake says, "I'm not too good at this stuff. Phil said we should get a rough idea of how you'd like to help out. Sarah will write it down. We'll need to discuss how to go about things. Without communication, and possibly limited transportation, we're going to be challenged to fill people's needs. I'll start. As Phil said, my family's here. Sarah and her husband, Tate, came down from Billings where things are getting dicey."

Apparently, no one, including me, knew of trouble in Billings.

"Tate's parents were on vacation, visiting, when all of this started."

Now people are saying how terrible it is to be caught away from home during a time like this.

"My daughter Angela, her husband, Tim, and their little boy, plus my daughter Calley, her husband, Mike, and his parents and sister are from Casper. Things are turning dangerous there. Mike had a run-in yesterday at the gas station."

This is a friendly group, and now they're commenting on Mike's bruises.

"And my daughter Katie and her . . . friend . . . Leo, are here from Manhattan, Kansas, where Katie is going to school. As you all may have heard, a fire started at the college there. It was burning out of control on the last report. Thankfully, Katie and Leo left a few hours before."

Someone taps my arm and says how fortunate we were to leave before the fire started.

"My seventy-five-year-old parents are at my house. They only live in Prospect, but with the way things are, I couldn't bear not having them with me."

Again, many people are saying things like "of course," and "definitely best to have them with you."

Jake nods. "I wanted to introduce you to everyone. It's possible we may all be working closely together during this time. And I have to admit, after what Dan said, I felt the need to clear the air. And to make it clear, while I'm completely committed to helping this community, I am first committed to my family. And I can guarantee, we will not be a drain on this community."

"None of us believe that dirtbag Morse, Jake. He makes things up as he goes," Terry Bosco says. His voice has a decidedly nasal quality, which wasn't present before he was punched in the nose.

"Okay, thanks, Terry. So let's get started. I can help with water. We have a working pump. And I have some food items I could donate to a community coffer. I also have quite a group here who can help with labor."

"I can help with water and adding some food also," Terry says. "I might need a few days to recover before I do much physical labor. My wife—she didn't come to this soiree tonight, but she's a surgical nurse practitioner with a practice in Prospect. She'll help any way she can."

"Terry Bosco? B-O-S-C-O? And your wife's name?" Sarah asks.

"Yep, correct. Her name is Belinda."

Sarah smiles in thanks.

"Alex and Natalie MacIntyre." He spells it out for Sarah. "We know things."

This gets a laugh from the group. And now, I realize who these familiar faces are. Jake and Malcolm attended their daughter's wedding yesterday. I met them all last year when I visited.

Alex releases an embarrassed laugh before going into detail about the things they know. The MacIntyres teach immersion classes on homesteading and living without power. They know about growing crops, livestock, preserving food, even building sheds and cabins with primitive tools. As he's wrapping up his spiel, he turns to Jake. "You know a lot of these things too. You should add them to your list."

"You're right, Alex. But some of the stuff is more Mollie's specialty, and until she gets home, I'd prefer to focus on the stuff I'm comfortable with."

"Oh, sure. Of course, makes sense."

I can tell Alex feels bad about mentioning something that'd bring up my mom.

"Well, we're happy to help people learn what they need to know," Alex says. "And, like Jake, I have a whole bunch of people at my place. We had guests in for our daughter's wedding on Saturday, plus people here for classes last week and a family who came in for this week's classes. Boy, the stories they have about their journey here . . ." He shakes his head.

"After they shared their experiences, everyone figured they'd better just hunker down for the duration. Only Natalie and I are here tonight, just to get a feel for things, I guess. We'll bring the adults along tomorrow night. How many of us are there, Natalie?"

"Fifty-nine total, with fourteen under the age of sixteen—five of those are our children. Two from the family who had trouble on the road. The others are our nieces and nephews here for the wedding."

Alex nods and says, "We have varying degrees of skill levels, but we'll be able to help with labor and offer assistance where we can. We won't be a drain on the community's resources either. And to copy Jake, we're committed to helping our community, and we're committed to our family and those at our place."

The remaining people gathered offer similar items. When there's only one family left, Jake turns to them and says, "I'm sorry. We haven't met. Jake Caldwell."

"Yes. Hello. Sam Mitchell . . . ini. Sam Mitchellini, and this is my wife, June, and our children. We're, uh, new to the community."

"Welcome." Terry Bosco shakes Sam's hand. "Glad you're here. Don't know where you're from, but I suspect being here, during a time like this, is better than most anywhere else. Where's your house?"

"We don't have a house yet. We're living in a camp trailer. The land we're on connects with Phil Hudson's place."

"Oh! I know where you are," Natalie MacIntyre says. "I wondered whose trailer was there. I thought that land was owned by some guy down in Alabama or somewhere."

"It is," June says. "He's letting us buy it on contract from him. We're so fortunate to have found it. It was a friend of a friend situation."

"Good to meet you all, Sam, June, and children." Jake shakes hands with the adults. "You all are set up well enough to be offering help to others? There's nothing you need?"

"I have to admit," Sam says, "we wondered about going with the group that can help but also needs things, but right now, we're in good

137

shape. Things could change, of course. But we'd like to help where we can, while we can."

As he's speaking, I notice Leo watching him. Leo has a look he gets sometimes, a look that tells me he's trying to sort something out or remember something important. I'll have to ask him about this when we get a minute.

"We can also add to the community workforce and help with water," Sam continues. "We're fortunate the property owner had a well put in, and we have a generator to run the pump. It's not the best tasting water, but it's okay."

"Let me guess, it's a little on the salty side?" Jake asks.

"Yes! It sure is."

Each of the Bakerville people lets out a small laugh. Apparently, they all have salty tasting water.

Phil, Kelley, Evan, and Doris are walking toward our group. I'm kind of surprised they're done as quickly as they are. Their groups were much larger than ours.

"Well, folks, it's not bad at all," Phil says. "Mostly, today, people need water. Jake and Evan brought water along with them. We've asked people to check their cars for containers so they can take water home with them from here. Sally-Ann, who lives across the street, was going home to get containers to pass out. She says she has several empty soda jugs. A few people are helping her. Sounds like everyone's fine on food today, and for several days. Can I see your list?" Phil asks Sarah.

He spends very little time looking it over. "Good. This is good. Alex, I think we're going to need your expertise. Yours too, Jake. You two have excellent water catchment systems. I think we're going to need to replicate the systems throughout the community. Maybe not today, but if the power doesn't come back on, then soon."

"Whatcha mean?" one of the women asks.

"We'll want to collect as much water as we can," Phil says. "Collected water can be used for watering the garden, washing, flushing the toilet—even for drinking. Right now, I'd say the people getting water out of their well are, for the most part, using a generator. It's possible the stored gas available will run out before the power comes back on. If that happens, no generators."

"Okay." Jake glances at Evan. "Let's see if we can get people enough water to tide them over until tomorrow night. Looks like they're coming back from Sally-Ann's now."

"Phil?"

"Yes, Sam?"

"We brought water to share also."

"Great!" Phil enthusiastically clamps Sam on the shoulder. "Let's get this done."

Combined with containers people had in their vehicles and what Sally-Ann provides, those who really need water are able to get enough until tomorrow night. It's good Sam brought water also, since Jake's and Evan's isn't enough for everyone.

Almost as soon as Leo and I start the short drive home, he says, "I know Sam from somewhere."

"Really? I wondered why you were looking at him so intently. Where do you know him from?"

"That's the thing, I can't figure it out. I'm sure it'll come to me. I wanted to talk with him but couldn't find an opportune time to start the conversation. Plus, I'd be embarrassed asking him how I know him."

I laugh a little. "My mom does that all the time. She never forgets a face, and she'll often say, 'I'm trying to figure out how I know you' to people. It used to embarrass me quite a bit. Then, one day, I found myself doing the same thing to the lady behind me in line at the grocery checkout. What do you think about the fight between Dan and Terry?"

Leo takes a moment before answering, "I think Dan Morse may be a problem. He seems a little shady. It sounds like something happened last night. I heard another snippet of a conversation. Seems Dan was the one who called last night's meeting. At the meeting, he called Jake out for having solar power. Terry Bosco put an end to it last night also. Then Mr. and Mrs. Snyder told everyone it was necessary to work together, really work together, not the way Dan Morse was suggesting, which the way I heard it was taking from people."

"Pretty much what he was saying tonight before the fight broke out?"

"Yep. Dan's definitely one to watch out for. I noticed he left instead of sticking around to get or offer help."

I don't really want to think about a neighbor being a problem and decide to change the subject. "What'd you think about the talk from the president?"

"It was fine. Hard to hear what we'd already suspected—there will be a fuel shortage. I did hope he'd know more about when he thought the cyberattacks could be stopped and the power brought back on, not that I really expected this info."

I nod but say nothing as we pull into the driveway of our current home.

At the house, there's a brief discussion on playing a card game we love, affectionately known as Whoopee, but it's decided an early bedtime's in order. I'm beat, so I'm completely behind this decision.

Chapter 18

Monday, Day 5

I'm slow to arouse from my heavy slumber. I'm pretty sure a noise awoke me, but I hear nothing now. I give a small stretch and roll over to sleep a little longer. Then I hear the noise again—a knock on my door. Now I'm fully awake and remember I'm at Mom and Jake's house sleeping in their basement bedroom.

A small voice accompanies the knock. "Katie? Katie? Are you awake?"

Malcolm.

"Yeah. I am now." I try to keep the grumpy out of my voice.

"Can I come in?"

"Sure. Come in."

Malcolm opens the door and pokes his head in. "Jeez, Katie. I thought you were going to sleep all day."

"Mmm. I could. I'm still pretty tired. What time is it?"

"Almost nine. You should get up. Sarah made breakfast. She saved you some, but it's probably pretty cold by now. Leo got your truck and trailer unloaded. Wow, you brought a lot of paintings. They're really good."

"Thanks, Little Buddy. I don't think Leo was too happy with me for packing them, but with the fires back home, I'm glad I did. I'd hate to lose them. The things I left behind I'm okay with losing, but those paintings . . . they're special to me."

"Yeah. Well, I like them. They're in the living room. Dad said you might want to hang a few up and bring the rest down here. You guys really brought a lot of stuff. Most of it's in the garage. They're working on Tim and Angela's stuff now. Mike's got most of their stuff done. I think Dad's gonna go out for supplies again today after everything's unloaded."

"Supplies? Like groceries?"

141

"Maybe. I think he's looking for other things too. Mr. Evan and Dad have been getting things the last few days. Not just for us, but to help the whole neighborhood—all of Bakerville, really."

"Okay. Let me get dressed. I'll be up in a few minutes."

"Sure, Katie. Oh, and do you mind not calling me *Little Buddy* anymore? I'm pretty old now and not so little. I'm going to be as tall as Calley soon and then I'll probably be as tall as you. And pretty soon, I could be as tall as Dad. Maybe even taller than Dad—maybe as tall as Mr. Hudson."

I can't help but laugh at this. "Yeah, sure. Sorry. I'll try to remember. But if I forget, you can remind me."

My full bladder encourages me to head to the bathroom before dressing. I briefly consider showering. I give myself a sniff. Yep, I stink. Makes sense—I haven't had a shower since Saturday morning. With Mom and Jake's off-grid system, I can happily enjoy a hot shower. But first, breakfast.

I find the still slightly warm plate Sarah left for me in the kitchen; it's something resembling a breakfast burrito. She put the tortilla on the plate, with scrambled eggs, sautéed peppers, black beans, and sausage. I add sour cream and salsa.

There's a lot of activity outside, so I quickly put the breakfast items away and rinse my plate. I'll save it to wash the next time dishes are done. Mom and Jake have a portable dishwasher kept in the utility room, or at least they did last time I visited. Mom rarely uses it. She'll pull it out when we're all visiting, but for day-to-day dishes, they're washed by hand.

Outside, Leo and Jake are over by the Tiny House. Leo gives me a wave when he sees me.

Jake turns, smiles, and hollers, "Hey, Katie! Good to see you. Figured you were pretty tired after your trip. You get some breakfast?"

"I did, Jake," I holler back while making my way toward them. "Malcolm woke me, said he thought you might be going to town?"

Once I'm close enough for normal conversation, Jake says, "Yeah, I think I will. I was thinking last night about going to Pryor to get some more sheep."

"Uh . . . I forgot you had those weird sheep. I thought they were more goats."

"They only look like goats. They're American Blackbelly sheep, a hair sheep. No wool."

"Seems weird not to have wool. They're pretty cute."

"It does, but they're so much easier to care for. We're raising them to eat."

"Eww, Jake. You didn't have to tell me that after I just told you how cute they are!"

Jake gives me a smile. I know this is the way things are when someone has a producing farm. And I suspect when the chops are on my plate, I'll fully enjoy them.

"I bought these feeder sheep from a guy outside of Pryor. The meat is exceptional, very mild compared to a lot of lamb. Our plan was to give these a go for a couple of years, and if it all worked out, we'd start a small flock. I think it might be smart to go ahead with our flock now. I'm going to head to his place and see if he'll sell me a few starters."

I say nothing for a minute, remembering Mom had said they were trying to keep their farm chores under control while they decided if they even wanted to continue with a farm.

"Jake, I thought you guys were thinking of phasing out of farming?"

"True. We were feeling pretty burned out. Especially me. We decided not to take on anything new this year and try to get caught up on some of the maintenance around here. I made a good dent in it earlier this week. And if it weren't for everything going on, we definitely wouldn't be adding things to the place. But food may be scarce for a while until trucks are running again. Makes sense to raise our own if we can."

Leo nods and I say, "I understand."

"I'll need to go by the feed store and possibly the hardware store to get some fencing. You guys picked up some great stuff yesterday."

"We got a lot of things for sure. I think Leo bought a roll of fencing and some posts."

"Mr. Caldwell needs something a little different for the flock than what I found. What I got is good for putting around a garden."

"Please, call me Jake. You can call my dad Mr. Caldwell until he asks you to call him something different. The fencing you brought will be perfect for extending the runways I've made near their main pen. The breed has a reputation for being a little skittish. We're still seeing that with the ones we have, so instead of letting them out to run around, we've made an alley for them out of cheaper fencing."

I look out at the sheep pen and see they're hanging out by their house. "When do you let them out in the runway?"

"Usually late afternoon. Don't want to give them too much time to get into mischief. I need to let the goats out. My folks, at least, will be here, so they can roam around for the better part of the day."

"You don't keep them penned up?" Leo asks.

"Some. The pens are a barrier to keep them safe from predators. We make sure to keep them secured at night. During the day, if someone's here, we let them out. If we have to go somewhere, we put them back in the pen. The boys stay in their pen while the girls are out. We don't need any 'cohabitating' going on unless we arrange it. We often let the males out for a while in the evening. Even fifteen minutes helps.

"We still feed hay but don't need nearly as much as if we didn't let them out. Which is something else I should find—more hay. I bought some of last year's from a friend and picked up the rest of what he had available on Friday. I know another guy, who I heard had some left from last year. It might be a hard year for hay if machinery doesn't have fuel. In fact, maybe I should make a run to his place right now."

"Sounds good, Jake. I'd love to go with you to look at the sheep. Can I take a shower while you're gone to check on the hay? I'll be ready when you get back."

"Of course, Katie. That's fine. You want to ride along, Leo?"

"Yes, sir. I'd like to go, but I wonder if I ought to take my own truck and trailer? That way we have space in case something else comes up we should buy."

"Good idea. Let's do it. I'm going to find Malcolm. I think he has Gavin over at the bunkhouse, trying to keep him out of Angela's hair while she gets the place set up. I'm thinking about lodging for Art. Maybe I should see about moving him into the bunkhouse. He seems to get along well with Keith and Lois."

The bunkhouse, where Tate's mom, dad, and sister are staying, is on the north side beyond the garage and near the big draw running through the property. It's a nice place. It's not a bunkhouse in the traditional sense of a big room with a bunch of bunk beds; it's more like a small, two-bedroom, one-and-a half bath apartment with two sleeping lofts.

I suspect Art would get along great with Tate's dad, so staying there will probably be fine. Both are talkers and would likely easily lose track of time.

While Jake goes to find Malcolm, I tell Leo I want to check out the Tiny House and say hello to Angela. It needs a few steps and has cinder blocks in place as a temporary measure. There's a front window looking out on the porch, and the open door has a window.

"Knock, knock. Angela?"

"Come on in."

She's in the kitchen working on putting things away. They only brought the essentials and things she'd really hate to lose. Since she and Tim own a decent-sized house; it would've taken a full-size U-Haul, at least, to get everything they own here. I know when she left, she was sure this would be a temporary stay until the power came back on and the people who'd arrived from Denver could go back home. Now, with the refineries exploding, it could be long term for all of us.

The angry howl of a cat reverberates throughout the little place.

"Where's Snowball?"

"I have him locked in the bathroom. He's not very happy about it."

"I can tell. Can I have the nickel tour?"

"Katie, it's a Tiny House. You can get the whole tour standing at the front door," she says with a laugh. "It's really cute."

I have to agree; it's really nice.

"Do you have electricity?"

"Not yet. Jake gave us lanterns and flashlights for last night. Jake says he might have a plan."

I nod, anxious to see the place. I decide to explore the loft first. It's interesting but should work for them.

Back downstairs, Angela steps out of the kitchen so I can check it out. "It's definitely a one-butt kitchen," Angela says. "Tim loves it, thinking it'll get him out of cooking. I plan on lots of grilling, though, since we don't have appliances in here. He'll be in charge of grilling. Jake put that there this morning." Angela motions to a wooden section in the otherwise granite countertop.

"I guess the previous owners took the stovetop out, but Jake gave us a little stove to cook on. It's an alcohol stove, like the kind used on boats."

"Hmmm. Why'd he have a stove for a boat?"

"I asked that too! I guess Mom bought it online to use in the cabin Calley's staying in, but they decided to go with a two-burner propane cooktop instead."

"Ah, so they just had it stashed in their stuff?"

"Yeah, it and probably a hundred other things they found a good deal on that they can use 'someday,' not that they're hoarders or anything." Angela and I laugh.

"Right. Of course, now . . . "

We're both suddenly serious, as Angela says, "Mm-hmm. Now all of the stuff might come in handy."

I decide to change the subject. "Did you eat breakfast this morning? Sarah left me a breakfast burrito. I assumed she cooked in the house."

"Yes, she did. She made enough for everyone. Sarah asked Calley and me what we thought about pooling resources. Instead of everyone making individual meals, we rotate cooking for the group. We like the idea. They're going to talk with their extended families about it."

"I like the idea too. You know, if Mom was here, she'd already have everyone agreeing to it and a schedule made." We both laugh at this, but then, once again, are suddenly silent.

"She'll get here, Katie. I know she will, even if she has to walk. Jake said she was in Idaho last time he talked to her on Saturday. I'm sure she's made it even closer. She probably ran out of gas and is biking now. Not her forte, but she'll be fine."

"You're right. I guess I now know how she felt thinking about something like this happening and wanting us here. I didn't need the bug-out bag she sent me since we were able to load up and drive. But getting that bag really made a difference for me—for us. Leo and I started looking at the world and how things are. We sort of became preppers too. In the few months we've had it, we really put aside a lot of things and learned some valuable skills."

"I was impressed you knew how to help Leo with the kids in the car accident."

I shake my head. "I don't know much. I took a CPR and first aid class in March. Last month, I took the advanced version. Leo let me look over his EMT books and stuff. I planned to take another course, maybe even take a real EMT course, but with this, I'm not sure."

"Wow, Katie. I had no idea you were still interested in medical stuff. I know you talked about being a doctor when you were younger, but with your art, I thought that was your focus."

146

"Oh, it is. I wouldn't want to be a doctor or nurse, but it seems smart to know things like this. Not as a profession, just to be able to help people, like the kids in the wreck. And some small towns have volunteer departments, so maybe that'd be a possibility. I don't know, though. I'm glad I didn't see the parents or the other lady who died. Leo hasn't said anything about it, but I suspect it still bothers him. Did Tim say anything?"

"Yes. We talked about it last night. Art was very supportive and told him how wonderful it was he went to help. Tim said it was bad but didn't give details, which I'm thankful for. I guess, with no gas, there will be less car accidents."

"True. I think I'd rather have gas, though."

She nods in agreement. The rumble of a diesel engine causes us to look out the front window. Jake's white truck rambles by. I'd best get a move on it so I'm ready when he returns.

"How's the bathroom?" I ask.

"Not nearly as nice as the rest of the place. Take a look."

I take a quick peek at the unfinished bathroom, trying to not let the cat out. I bet Angela's loving the compost toilet and camping shower.

"Hey, Angela. Want me to fill your shower bag for you so it can get warm?"

"Ha-ha. Very funny." She pauses for a moment. "Not a bad idea, though. Tim would probably love a hot shower later. I think I'll use the house today, but I know he'd prefer the privacy of our place. Of course, with Art sleeping on the futon, there's really not a whole lot of privacy."

"Yeah. Jake's coming up with a plan for Art."

Angela nods. "As terrible as this all is, it may be good for Art. He seems to have more energy today than he's had since Tim's mom died. It's good to see him doing things. Usually he's not even out of bed until midday. Gavin made sure he was up bright and early this morning. So early, Art went and helped Jake with the chores. Well, I'm not sure how much help he was, but he went over there."

"Did you help feed the chickens?"

"No! I don't like those things. The ducks either. Well, the ducks are kind of cute and they don't peck, so they're a little better. But I don't really like either."

"You like to eat them."

"Somewhat. And not duck, just chicken. Oh, hey, guess what we found upstairs?"

I shrug.

"There's built in play areas. A sliding table for LEGO blocks, kind of like the one Malcolm has only smaller, plus lots of little cubbies. It'll be fine for Gavin, and we can close off the stairs. I'm going to have Tim build a railing around Gavin's bed to keep him from falling out. Even though the bed platform is only six inches off the ground, he rolled out last night and it woke him up. Oh, and look over here."

We take two steps toward the kitchen where she shows me a little space under the stairs. Gavin's highchair is sitting here along with a TV tray holder.

"Jake says he thinks it's a desk cubby. It's great for Gavin's highchair, but it'd be cute to have a little work desk there. Jake's going to take me shopping in the basement later. He says they have quite a few things that should work in here. It's great we got the stove pipe yesterday. He has a woodstove he thinks is small enough to use in this place but didn't have enough piping for it. Of course, I can't imagine still needing to be here when it's cold enough to need a fire." There's a quiver in her voice, which matches the quiver of her lip.

I gently wrap my arm around her shoulders. I wonder how long it'll take for gas to start producing. Which reminds me . . .

"I never asked. What about work for you and Tim?"

"Oh. It seems so long ago since all this started, I almost forgot we even have jobs. Or we did."

Tim works in the oilfield. His company contracts out to plug abandoned oil wells. He often works out of town Monday through Friday, and sometimes for several weeks at a time. Before they had Gavin, this wasn't too bad since Angela would go visit him on the weekends. Now, she really doesn't like it when he's gone for weeks on end.

Angela has her realtor's license. While she does sell houses, she's also a leasing agent and makes most of her money from this. After Gavin came along, she dropped her hours to thirty per week. There are some days she needs to be in the office, like the first of the month for collecting rent, but otherwise, her schedule is fairly flexible. She has a neighbor watch Gavin while she works. Tim and Angela even bought a small rental house last year. It needed a little work and took longer than they expected, but they're now recouping their investment. I guess all that may change now.

"So what about work?" I prod.

"Good question. Their rig was supposed to go back in service today, and they were scheduled to leave at 4:00 a.m. for Northern Colorado. We already had a lot of refugees or whatever they're called by Saturday morning, and with the reports of the highways, they pulled the plug on working the rig until things calm down. The guys already out on rigs were called home. Then, when the cyberattacks happened Saturday, Tim reached one of the other guys on the FRS and the guy said they were shut down until the power comes back on. To lay low and be safe."

"What's an FRS?" I ask.

"A walkie-talkie thing. They use them when communicating at work. He'd tried calling and texting first, but nothing was working. He turned the radio on and tried a guy who lives pretty close to us. The foreman had sent out a group text telling everyone about the shut down and asking everyone to turn their radios on and try to reach crew living near them, so it worked out well. He'd tried to raise Tim on the FRS about fifteen minutes before, so had his on to try again. Funny thing was, the text came through a little bit later.

"After Tim found out he was done with work for now, we decided to check in with my boss by driving over to his house. He said the same thing. No power means no phones, which means no business. He'd also heard about some of the violence already happening with the extra people in town, and told us we should either hole up at home or get out of town. We stopped and checked on our renters—they were doing okay.

"The whole phone thing was so weird. I guess it's done now, though. I haven't been able to send texts since we were at the rest stop in Kaycee. Haven't received any either."

"We were mostly able to stay in contact with Calley. She had called Saturday and told us about Mike being attacked. We let her know we were packing to leave. She didn't decide until Sunday morning. We contacted you, made arrangements with Calley to meet, and you know the rest."

"Speaking of Calley, I think I'm going to go and check in with her. Then I need to get ready. I'm going with Jake and Leo to look for more supplies."

"I heard they wanted to make a trip. Not sure there will be many groceries. You know how bare it was yesterday. And after the president's speech, I'd say everyone likely went looking for all they could."

"He's looking for some specific things. Hey, did you know that back pen with goats in it is actually sheep?"

"Oh, yeah. I forgot they had some of those hair sheep things." We both look out the living room window where we can see the goats. The *real* goats; the hair sheep aren't visible from here.

"Jake wants to get enough to start a herd so there's plenty for eating."

"Ewww. No. I'm not eating them."

I laugh when the response I expect is delivered. Angela isn't much of a meat fan. She'll eat chicken and a little hamburger, and she loves bacon and pepperoni, but that's about it. She prefers vegetables, beans, and pasta.

"And I think sheep are a flock not a herd," she tells me smugly.

I ignore her and ask, "You want to go see Calley, or are you staying here?"

"Staying. I still have those few boxes to empty and a whole lot more stuff in the garage. Not sure what to do with it all. If you see my husband, can you send him over?"

Chapter 19

It's not far to Calley's cabin. The Tiny House is set perpendicular to it and only about twenty feet from the front door. I wonder why Jake put them so close to each other?

The cabin was added last year. It's a prefab building, somewhat like the Tiny House, but larger. The front door is open, but the screen's shut. Angela doesn't have a screen door. That might be something good to try and find for her today.

I knock softly and wait. I can hear talking but don't see anyone in my line of sight. I knock again, a little louder.

"I think someone's at the door," Sheila says. Her face appears moments later.

"Hey, Sheila."

"Oh, hey, Katie. How are you? You get enough rest?"

"Yeah. I'm good. Been up a bit. I was visiting with Angela and getting the tour. Cute place."

"It is. So is this one. You want to come inside? We're just organizing things."

Inside, Calley's stepping out of the front bedroom, and Sheila excuses herself to go to the back.

"Hi, Katie. Feeling better?"

"Much. Thanks. How are you? How's Mike today?"

"Mike's doing okay. His head's still hurting quite a bit. I think he should've gone to the doctor, but you know how he is."

I nod. I do know how he is, but he's not my husband to make comments about, so nodding seems like the safest response.

I glance around. Sheila's right. This place is cute. Last time I was in here, it was still unfinished.

"You been in here before?" Calley asks.

"Not after it was finished. Turned out nice."

"It really did. I like how it has a cottagey feel compared to the bunkhouse. Mom told me she tried to make it shabby chic."

We're in the main room, an open space with a seating area, small dining room, and a kitchenette along one wall. "Mom loves those," Calley says, gesturing to two pale green slip-covered loveseats. "She found them each on sale, and Doris helped her make the covers for them so they match. They're pull-outs."

"Mm-hmm. Doris said something about those last night. What do you mean pull-outs?"

"You know, beds," she says, while making a motion showing how they flip out.

"Oh, yeah, sleeper sofas? Or sleeper loveseats, I guess."

"Exactly. Twin sized. Mom pulled them out once and made me try them."

"And how were they?"

"Pretty much like every sleeper sofa. Maybe a little better. They both kind of fold out onto the floor, more like a camping mattress. There's no bar underneath at least. The one without arms is kind of strange for sitting in. Not bad but weird not having an arm rest."

"This place is really cute. What's Mike think of it?"

"He's okay with it. Wishes we had the bunkhouse instead. Since it's more of a western theme, he likes the ruggedness of it."

I continue looking around the cabin, checking out part of the loft and the rest of the main floor. I avoid the loft Sheila's using, plus the second bedroom on the main floor that Roy and Deanne are staying in.

When we get to the bathroom, Calley notices me looking at the water pitcher sitting next to the sink. "We don't have running water here. It's too far from the house to connect and too rocky to dig an underground cistern like the bunkhouse has. There's water on the front porch in the barrel. There are two buckets in the shower with water to flush the toilet. We have a solar shower heating up outside. Did you see the Berkey system on the counter in the kitchen?"

I nod as she continues, "We'll fill it up for drinking water. The pain is going to be keeping the barrel full. And if we have to be in here in the winter . . . I don't know. I guess we'll bring the barrel in the house. It'd freeze outside."

Once Calley finishes giving me the tour, I ask, "Where's Mike and Roy?"

"Not sure. Maybe over at the garage still unloading. He's supposed to bring things here he thinks we need."

"Thanks for the tour of your cabin. Seems like it shouldn't be too bad, other than the water situation. Even that shouldn't be terrible. You could always shower in the main house."

152

"Yeah, true. Oh, did you hear we're talking about rotating cooking and stuff? And I know Jake could use some help with everything he has going on. It's a lot for one person. Jake said we should all take today and get settled. He said maybe we could all talk after the community meeting tonight."

"Sounds like a good idea. I'd best get going. I'm riding along while Jake and Leo go sheep shopping."

"You think they'll be looking for more supplies?"

"I suspect so. Don't know what's out there, though."

"Hold on just a minute," Calley says. She's back shortly, handing me what looks like a small makeup bag.

"I have some money left from yesterday. Please take it and buy anything you think we can use. Spend it all if needed. I thought a lot about what Angela said yesterday, about needing to scrounge for things we need. I'm happy with the stuff we bought yesterday but realize, with all of us here, things could run short."

I nod. "I'll do what I can. Anything specific you want me to look for?"

She leans in close. "Condoms and baby things."

"Okay . . . those are complete opposites."

"Yeah. We haven't really been trying but haven't been using protection, so I could be pregnant now. In which case, I need baby things. If I'm not pregnant, I don't want to be right now, so I need condoms," she explains in a quiet voice.

"Makes sense." I give her a hug and start to leave. Sheila and Deanne come out of the back room. It's obvious both have been crying.

"Katie, can we give you money too? Please buy anything we can use," Deanne says, handing me a wad of bills.

"Sure. Yes. Any requests?" I ask, silently pleading she doesn't order condoms.

"No. Whatever Jake thinks is needed. We're so grateful to be able to join everyone here. Jake and Mollie have made so many preparations. We want to be able to contribute something more than the few things we purchased yesterday. In fact, Sheila, why don't you go see if your dad has any cash on him? If he does, have him give it to Katie. Calley, you think Mike has money?"

"He doesn't. We combined what we had left last night."

Sheila and I step out the door together while I throw a "see you later" over my shoulder to Calley.

A few steps away from the cabin, Sheila shoves several bills toward me and whispers, "Can you pick me up some cigarettes? This should be enough for a couple of cartons. Marlboro Reds would be great, but whatever will be fine."

"Uh . . . right. Sure. I guess I can do that. Is it a secret or something?"

She doesn't say anything for a couple of beats. "Yeah, I guess it is. I told my parents I quit. So if you could keep it quiet, I'd appreciate it."

Oh, great. I hate having to keep secrets like this. "I won't say anything, but I can't imagine you'll be able to keep it quiet for very long. Living in the same place, they'll smell it on you. And, well, I guess you know you shouldn't smoke in the cabin."

"Of course I know that. Look, if you don't want to get them for me then don't. Your judgment, I can do without."

"Sheila, I'm not judging you. I have no opinion at all on whether you smoke or not. Lots of people smoke—not a big deal. What I would have a problem with would be if you expected me to lie for you. I won't announce the cigarettes, but . . . "

"Oh, I know all about you, Katie. Believe me, I'd never think someone like you would *ever* tell a lie."

I feel my eyes stinging with tears, the scorn and mocking . . . where is this coming from? I look down and quietly say, "I'll do what I can."

Chapter 20

Sheila and I finished our short walk in silence. We find all of the guys at the garage, except Jake, who's not yet back from gathering hay. With all the stuff we brought, the garage resembles a warehouse instead of a place to park cars.

Leo sees me and strolls over. He gives me a questioning look, but I shake my head and attempt a small smile. He moves in to kiss me on the cheek.

Sheila goes to her dad and pulls him aside. She purposely avoids looking in my direction. I hate conflict. At the same time, I'm glad I somewhat stood up to her and let her know I won't lie for her.

"We didn't get to talk much before. You feeling good? Well rested?" Leo asks.

"Yeah, mostly. I'm not really tired but feel like I could sleep, you know?"

"Yep. I suspect some of it's the stress of the situation. It's easy to want to shut down. I don't think you're the only one experiencing it."

I nod. "I'm going to take a shower. I want to be ready when Jake gets home."

As I start toward the house, Sheila runs over to me. "Here's a little more money. I'd love some chocolate if you can find any. I know my mom would appreciate it also."

I tell her I'll do my best.

I try to hustle in the shower, but it's still over half an hour before I'm ready to go. I'm so thankful for the solar system providing hot, running water. I towel dry my hair, put it in a bun, and do my makeup. I grab my purse so I don't have to go back downstairs and can leave when Jake and Leo are ready.

In the front yard is an unfamiliar vehicle towing an enclosed trailer. There's a sign on the trailer, but the angle doesn't allow me to read the writing. I don't see Jake's truck, but do see he and Leo are talking to a gentleman. I walk over to see what time we're leaving. Once I know, I'll go visit with Sarah. When I'm closer, I can see the trailer signage indicates a solar system company.

155

"Hey, Katie," Jake says when I approach. "This is my friend Dwayne. He set the solar system up. I emailed him before the cyberattacks about buying a backup. He saw my email and responded, but with everything down, he drove over here."

"Hello, Dwayne," I say.

"Nice to meet you, Katie. Jake was telling me you and Leo were in one of the towns severely affected by the displaced people."

"Yes. We were in Manhattan, Kansas, but we were able to leave before things got too bad for us. A fire started Saturday afternoon. We talked with one of our friends, and it's pretty bad. He was trying to leave also. Someone had punched a hole in his gas tank and stole all his gas."

"I didn't hear about this," Jake says. "I'm glad you and Leo were smart and got out of there early."

Jake gives me a look I interpret as, *I'm so thankful you're safe,* then turns to Dwayne, "So the system you brought, it's a used system just like the one I have?"

I don't pay much attention as they discuss the current solar systems and the changes Jake's thinking of.

It sounds like they've made a deal when Leo says, "Excuse me, sir?"

"Yes?" Jake and Dwayne both answer.

After establishing Leo wants Dwayne, he says, "Mr. and Mrs. Caldwell have done a great job of setting things up. The two larger cabins have small twelve-volt solar systems. Each has a small fridge, a few outlets, and a few LED lights. I don't think you could run much more."

Dwayne nods in response.

"And Mr. Caldwell was able to get another place yesterday, the little place over there, which is without a system. I was wondering if you had a small system that'd work to power both places and possibly another system for what they call the bunkhouse?"

"Hmm. What are you wanting the system to provide power for?"

"I'm not sure. Nothing much, I'd say. It just seems with more use, a bigger system might be better."

Jake hasn't said anything but looks like he wants to, when Dwayne says, "What kind of system do you have on the building, Jake?"

"It's one of those basic RV systems. We keep the system off when it's not in use, except one sunny day each month I fire it up, make sure the batteries get a full charge, and turn things on. It's been fine for temporary lodging, but Leo's probably right. It may be a little light for permanent housing.

"That said, I think we'll have to make do. I have a backup system for the cabin and the bunkhouse, so if something happens to the primary, we can pull it, but I can't afford new, larger systems. You've just about tapped me already, Dwayne." Jake lifts his hands in surrender while giving a wide smile.

"Sir, I'd like to get the new system. That is, if Dwayne has something that'll work. It's the least I can do for you letting me join Katie here."

I can see Jake wants to say no. But I can also see Jake's thinking it over and trying to decide what would be best.

"Leo, Katie, can I talk to you two for a moment? Dwayne, we'll be just a minute and I'll be back with cash. Oh! I just remembered, we spoke once about adding a wind turbine, just a small one that could sit on top of the house. You have one of those with you?"

"I do, Jake. You can put it on top of the house and tie it right into your system. It has a manual braking system, so you can shut it down when you get one of those super blows. It's six hundred bucks with everything you need to hook it up."

"Okay. Let me think about it."

As we walk to the house, Jake says, "Leo, I appreciate you wanting to contribute. I have a few concerns about putting in a larger system. Mollie and I had talked about a twenty-four volt for the bunkhouse. Let me tell you why we decided to stick with the twelve-volt."

"Of course, sir. I certainly didn't want to overstep. I was simply thinking, since he was here and Angela and Tim's place is without power, it'd be a good time to add it."

"I agree. And it might be. Let's discuss for a moment."

We're in the living room and Jake motions us to the seating area as he continues his thought. "One of the reasons we went with the smaller systems, besides for the fact they're inexpensive, is operational security. If you're the only house on the hill with lights, you can make yourself a target. With the smaller system, we have a decent amount of power during the daytime and can do things needing electricity, plus run the fridge. At nighttime we're limited in the amount of power we have, which means if the fridge is running, we can have one or two low-voltage LED lights and that's it.

"One light looks more like a bright flashlight than a house with power. We have lanterns and small solar lights for additional lighting. It's still a risk, which is why all of the houses, except Angela's since it's new, have black-out curtains in place, which do a good job holding the light in. So I'm not really opposed to a twenty-four-volt system setup the way you suggested, powering both places, but if we have this, we should discuss if it's worth making ourselves more of a target."

"Good point, sir. I have to admit, I didn't think of that. And with the location of the cabin and the . . . " He hesitates, looking for the proper term.

I help him out by adding, "Tiny House, Leo."

"Yeah, sure. Tiny House. With these both being on the south side and more visible from a distance, I can see how we'd definitely want to be careful with the lighting. Do you think it's as simple as a training issue? The people living in the two houses working on their awareness?"

"I'd like to think so, Leo. But I know it's hard to not want to turn all the lights on in the house. Of course, we may be looking at a whole new world with lots of changes. Keeping the lights off is just one more change."

"I think it'd be okay, Jake," I say. "Plus, having the extra power during the daytime will make many things easier and allow the houses to be more independent, without everyone needing to be in here."

"That's true, Katie. And now, since we're discussing it, I wonder if it wouldn't be a good idea to put the system I'm buying on one of the houses instead of keeping it in storage. I wanted a second system because I was concerned the attacks might escalate to an EMP. It still might, of course, but with the cyberattacks, it seems they've found a great way to cripple our power system. An EMP doesn't seem as likely to me now.

"Leo, if you're sure about contributing toward a system, I'm okay with it. I feel a little bad about you spending your money, but it may not be worth much for long anyway. And if things get back to normal, Mollie and I will reimburse you for your part."

"That won't be necessary, sir, but I do appreciate the offer. Back to normal is likely to be some time off. With you allowing me to stay here, I suspect it could be looked at as rent payment. Like you say, money may not be worth much. I emptied out everything I could to use as we need. I'd like to use it while we can."

"Well, we'll discuss this when things return to normal. What do you think about putting the used system on the cabin and connecting both the cabin and the Tiny House to it?"

"Great. Let's do it," Leo enthusiastically agrees.

I decide I don't really need to be involved any further in this discussion so excuse myself after asking if they're still planning to go look at the sheep.

"Yes, for sure," Jake answers. "We'll wrap up with Dwayne and head out. What are you planning to do?"

"I thought I'd go see Sarah. I haven't spent much time with her yet."

"She's out in the main garden working on the weeds. I've spent less time on the garden lately than I should've. She has Lois and Karen helping. She said they'll do the kitchen garden next and see what all they can harvest for dinner tonight. Should be quite a bit of greens and things ready."

"Okay, thanks, Jake. I'll go see her. Let me know when you're ready to go." I give Leo a wave and head toward the bunkhouse. The main garden isn't far from there.

Mom and Jake set the area up so the water catchment on the bunkhouse and the bunkhouse's outdoor kitchen are the main water sources for the garden. They do have to use the water well sometimes if there's a long time between rainfalls and the rain barrels empty out, but for the most part, the catchment works well.

Because of the fencing around the garden, I can't see Sarah, but I hear the three of them talking. At the gate, I call out, "Hey, Sarah! You having fun in the garden?"

"Katie! Well . . . yes. Kind of. We're making good headway for sure. I enjoy working in the garden. I think Lois is enjoying it also, but I'm not sure about Karen." She gives a light, airy laugh.

Sarah, always a picture of elegance, even while weeding a garden, is wearing a large floppy hat, stylish sunglasses, a long summer dress, and adorable sandals. While in college, she took to wearing dresses and adopting a vintage 1950s style. She's the tallest of the females in our family, at five foot seven, and has the same curvy figure we all share. And like each of us, she has to work to keep those curves from getting out of control.

Her sleek brown hair is often in a shoulder-length Pageboy, fussed over with soft curlers and a scarf to keep it smooth at night, and often a fifties-era fashion hat during the day. Perfect eyebrows and bright red lips complete her classic look.

The rest of us girls have crazy, curly hair, but Sarah's is almost stick straight and somewhat fine. Angela, Calley, and I deal with our curly hair by keeping it long; Mom combats hers by cutting it super short into a pixie. I sometimes wonder how Sarah got fortunate enough to not have our kooky hair. While today's look isn't in line with her normal, classic look, it's still very becoming on her. More 1970s Flower Child than 1950s Pin-Up Girl; she's even without her usual vibrant lip color.

Lois and Karen both talk at the same time.

"I love it," Lois says.

"Not my favorite thing," Karen says.

I laugh at all of them. "Looks like you have a nice pile of weeds already. You going to give those to the livestock?"

"Yeah. Jake said to put half in the compost pile the chickens work. The other half we'll divide between the goats, sheep, and pigs. I'm going to start helping with the milking tomorrow." Sarah smiles. "He has another goat they'll be adding to the milking herd on Wednesday."

"Really? One that kidded recently?"

"Yes." My sister nods. "Two weeks ago on Wednesday. There's also a goat ready to kid anytime. He's asked we keep an eye on her. Once she kids, we'll move her and her baby, or babies, over to the other pen. Malcolm knows what to do, and I'll help if it happens while Jake's gone. She's kidded before, so we'll just keep an eye out and then move her over when she's finished."

"Wow. That'd be fun. I've never been around when one of the goats kidded. I'm going with Jake and Leo to look at the sheep. Maybe she'll wait until I get home."

"Maybe. It might not even happen today. Jake says she's marked on the calendar for tomorrow."

"Oh, good. Maybe I'll be around. I have a few minutes before we go. Can I help?"

"Sure you can," Karen says. "In fact, you can take over for me if you'd like."

"Karen!" Lois fakes a look of surprise.

"Just kidding, Mother."

We chitchat while we work on the weeds. It's a conscious effort for all of us to keep the conversation light. When it starts to drift toward the situation we find ourselves in, we make a point of returning to the easy chatter. I wonder if it might not be better to just let out our true feelings, but since I'm leaving shortly, I don't want to get into anything too deep. There will be plenty of time for that later.

After about thirty minutes, there's the beep of a horn. I'm not sure if this is Leo or Jake calling me, but I decide to go see if they're ready. Dwayne's truck is gone, and Jake, Leo, and every other guy staying here walk out of the garage.

"We got the solar systems," Leo tells me. "Dwayne gave us manuals and lots of information for setting everything up. I think it'll be fairly straightforward."

"Did you buy two?"

"Three. Plus batteries for storage. They'll last forever as long as they remain dry. Worked out a good deal. Would've bought more, but he had other stops."

"That's great, Leo."

Chapter 21

Everyone's discussing their plans for the day, which start with unloading the hay Jake brought home and continuing to organize the items everyone brought from their homes or bought along the way. It seems Sarah's husband, Tate, and his dad, Keith, went to Billings yesterday to get as much stuff from their rental as they could. They stopped at some stores, but the town was a mess.

While they were in Billings, Karen, Tate's sister, went into Prospect with Jake. At Jake's urging, she bought clothes and shoes for all of them, including winter gear. She was, understandably, upset about the thought of still being here when winter arrives. It's only June now, and we all hope things will be back to normal and we can go home before then.

The thought of not being able to go home almost brings me to tears. While I'm not sure Manhattan's where I want to live out my life, I did want to finish my degree. It seems such a waste to put so much time, money, and effort into my degree and not get it done. Of course, with the world in such a pickle, I wonder how much call there will be for graphic design.

"Okay, Katie?" Leo asks, and from the tone, I know I'm supposed to answer.

"Huh? What'd you say?"

"I'm going to go and help unload the hay. We should only be a few minutes, then we'll go. Okay?"

"Yes. Of course. I'm ready. I'll pop in and say hello to Grandma Dodie. I think Gavin and Malcolm are in with her, so I can see the boys also."

I only visit for about fifteen minutes before there's a knock on the door. It's Jake letting me know it's time to go. He's given Grandpa Alvin a NOAA alert radio and put him in charge of monitoring it while we're gone.

"You all be careful. Remember what happened yesterday. You had a close call," Grandpa Alvin says to Jake.

I look to Jake as he nods and says, "We'll be careful. You too. Lock the gate behind us when we leave. That should discourage visitors."

"What was that about?" I ask as we walk to where Leo, Tim, and Tate are milling around by the vehicles.

"I'll tell everyone in a minute. I'm kind of surprised you haven't heard yet."

When we get to the trucks, Leo tells me, "Tim and Tate are also going. While we were unloading the hay, we talked about looking for a few other things and thought we might need the extra space."

"Sounds smart."

"Leo, Tim, did you hear about what happened yesterday while Karen, Evan, and I were in town?" Jake asks.

"Tate told me about it earlier this morning," Tim says. "Sounds scary. Glad all that was hurt was your car."

I look over to Jake and Mom's car and notice a groove across the hood showing silver instead its metallic teal color.

"What happened?" I ask.

"Some guy was taking pot shots. He scraped the hood," Jake says nonchalantly.

"Jake! That sounds so scary."

"It was, Katie, but we weren't hurt. Karen and I were both shook up. We learned a good lesson on paying attention and being careful. Yesterday, we didn't have a need to defend ourselves—we just got out of there. But I'm prepared if needed."

"Same here, Jake," Tim says, while Leo nods.

"I didn't think about taking a gun along," Tate says. "I guess I should. Give me a few minutes and . . . I'll be back." Tate says "*I'll be back*" in his best Terminator voice, garnering a chuckle from the rest of the guys.

I'm in no mood to chuckle. "Do you think it's safe to go?"

Jake looks at Leo, then Tim, and finally me. "Probably. We drove into a strange situation. I'm not entirely sure what was wrong, but one of the neighbor guys said the guy simply lost it and started shooting."

"And you don't think other people might lose it?"

"Katie," Leo says softly. "Sure, it could happen. But it's more likely to happen as time goes on. Now is the time we should be going out and gathering things we need. You could stay here."

I take a deep breath and focus on what Leo said. Even when the world isn't falling apart, bad things happen. And Leo is probably right, now is the time to go. The longer the lights are out, the more unstable things will become.

I give a slow nod. "You're probably right. I suppose the same thing could've happened before this mess started. I don't want to stay here. I want to go along and help."

"You really don't have to, Katie," Jake says. "If you'd rather stay here, it's totally fine."

I shake my head, now determined to go along.

"I think I'll grab my shotgun too," Leo says.

"Sounds good. I put mine in the truck this morning when I went after hay."

"I don't have one," Tim says. "But I brought my hunting rifle with us. Should I grab it?"

"There's probably no need," Jake tells him, as Tate walks up and says, "Ready to go."

"Hey, Jake, why's Alvin shutting the gate?" I ask, suddenly remembering their conversation.

"Oh, that. Yesterday had a little too much excitement. Shortly before you all arrived, one of the guys from the community came over. He wasn't . . . he was looking for assistance I wasn't able . . . I wasn't *willing* . . . to provide."

"It was that Dan Morse guy," Tate says with disgust. "It's smart to close the gate, Jake. I think we should probably do it all the time."

"You're probably right," Jake says with a sigh.

"What'd he want?" I ask.

"He wanted to use the freezer," Tate spits out.

"What?" I laugh. "Who cares about that? You didn't let him?"

Tate furiously shakes his head, while Jake solemnly says, "No, Katie, I didn't."

"Why not?"

"Give a mouse a cookie . . . " Tate says, but Jake just shakes his head.

"What?"

"You know, the kid's book?" Tate asks.

I shrug. "Maybe? But what does that— "

"It makes sense," Leo says. "If you let him use your freezer, what else will he want? It sounds like a simple thing, and I suspect he didn't exactly ask nicely to use it, but rather expected to use it. And the entitlement factor didn't set well."

"It didn't." Jake tips back his ballcap. "But I do still feel kind of bad I turned him away. Maybe, if I would've handled it better . . . "

"Nope, Jake," Tate says firmly. "That guy's crazy. He shouldn't be anywhere around here. I definitely don't want him around my wife. And if he comes back . . . " Tate doesn't finish his thought, just asks, "Are we ready to go?"

Our drive is fine and mostly uneventful. Jake's leading the way in his pickup, towing his large utility trailer. He has several dog kennels in the back of the truck to secure the sheep in. He and Mom have talked about buying a stock trailer, but with the size of their livestock—small—it hasn't been needed.

Tim's truck is next, pulling his long flatbed trailer, with Tate riding shotgun. Leo and I are in the rear, towing Leo's trailer.

When we reach Wesley, we try to see if things are much different than yesterday. At first, there isn't anything noticeable. The combination hardware store and lumber yard on the edge of town appears to be open. The two discount stores are both open and doing a booming business. None of the gas stations are open.

The grocery store Leo and the others went in yesterday has a line outside it. We can't see the one Angela, Calley, and I shopped in from the road. There's a taco wagon type place open, which surprises me. With the power out since Saturday, I wonder how they've kept their perishables from spoiling?

We have a few tense moments when we arrive at Jake's friend's house to buy the sheep. His friend greets us with a shotgun.

Once he realizes it's Jake, everything's fine, but I was pretty scared at first. I guess it makes sense for him to be cautious. Things have changed in the last few days.

Jake's able to make a deal for a young ram—younger than he was hoping for, but his friend assures him he'll be ready for the task within a few months—plus a mature ewe, a yearling ewe, and two just weaned ewes.

The guy selling the sheep is quite the talker and spends some time sharing how hair sheep can breed year around, so Jake can really build the flock fast. He says it's likely we'll even get twins from the older ewe, maybe the yearling, too, since this will be her second lambing. The young ones will likely only have singles.

Before we leave, Leo makes a deal with the guy selling the sheep for a tow behind camp trailer. The sheep guy directs us to his dad, who lives next door, to buy a small motorhome. While there, Leo negotiates for beams from the dad's backyard sawmill business and even manages to finagle us some fuel.

The fuel is a real surprise. The guy gets farm delivery and is feeling fuel rich and cash poor. We make a deal for fifty gallons of diesel and thirty gallons of gas.

Afterward, we go into Pryor for more supplies. I'd love to stop by the hospital and check on the children from yesterday, but I know they won't be able to tell us anything.

Pryor's having something like a sidewalk sale, but nothing is on sale—it's all full price or more. Tim stays with the sheep while the rest of us buy what we can, which is some household goods, food, garden plants, and a little fresh produce. I'm even able to get the items requested by Calley, Sheila, and Deanne.

Then Jake gives us directions and we head to the lumber yard.

Before we go in, Leo asks Jake, "Sir, did you have a plan beyond your fencing needs?"

"Not much, Leo. What are you thinking?"

"I'm thinking this may be our last chance to get the materials we need. Maybe we should overbuy? I know you said you have the materials for a greenhouse on hand. Are there other things we should have on hand?"

"Maybe so. I don't even really know what we might need. Part of me feels like we have plenty, but I know that's wrong. We could never plan for everything."

Leo nods, then says, "I was thinking about winter. The motorhome and trailer, plus Tate and Sarah's trailer, aren't going to be very comfortable come winter. Katie's told me about the wind and says it's even worse here than Manhattan."

He looks to me for confirmation, so I add, "Yes, it's true. And the wind is biting cold."

Tim, a Wyoming native, nods in agreement.

"No doubt," Jake says. "The wind and the cold combination can be pretty bad. Each winter we've lived here, we've dropped down to negative twenty or lower. Add in the wind and . . . well, it's pretty cold. Tate and I were talking about this. I had him buy some plywood and insulation so they can skirt his place. It'll help, but it still won't be perfect."

"I bought those things. They're part of our massive amount of stuff we have at your place." Tate makes a sweeping motion with his arms.

"Good idea," Leo says. "When Katie and I were going to your place last night, she pointed out the neighbor that has a big shop but no house yet. She said he and his wife visit but don't live here? They have a camper in their shop?"

Jake gives a single nod. "Yes, yes they do. It's a fifth wheel. You thinking we could move the trailers in the garage when winter hits?"

"Well, we could. But I was thinking we could build little sheds around each of the trailers and the motorhome. Then the garage would still be available. I think we might need it for other things."

Jake nods several times. "Excellent idea. We could leave Tate and Sarah's trailer on the side of the garage and build a lean-to off it. We'd already have the one wall done. That what you picked the beams up for?"

Leo nods, while Tate raves, "Sounds good. I suspect Sarah would be much warmer in something like that. You know how hard it is to keep her warm."

"Yes. And we could make it a little larger—not a whole lot—so there could be space put in a woodstove, provided we can find one," Leo suggests.

Jake leans against the pickup. "We could do rocket mass heaters."

Leo looks a little puzzled, so I say, "Did you see the woodstove in the bunkhouse or in the basement room?"

"Yes . . . Oh! I guess I didn't really put together how it works. The heat from the stove warms the rock, and the rock slowly lets off the heat?"

"Exactly," Jake gushes. "The woodstove in the living room at our place is the same concept, but the pipe is encased in the brick and it's more of a masonry heater. We have a rocket heater in our room too. I wasn't so sure when Mollie first told me about them, but they work amazingly.

"The best part is, they're easy to build. We'd need stovepipe and bricks or heavy-duty cinder blocks. I have one metal barrel, but we'd need a few more. For Tim and Angela's place, I have a small woodstove. We could do brick around it like we did inside the house—just make it a smaller version. In fact, maybe we should rework the cabin Calley's family is staying in to do the same thing. The more heat we can trap, the less wood we'll need. And wood may become scarce with everyone using it this winter."

Jake pulls a small notebook and pen from his pocket. "Leo, what will we need for building the sheds?"

Leo thinks a minute. "Tate, you like the idea of staying where you are and having the lean-to?"

"I do. I think it'd be a good solution."

Leo nods and spends a few minutes writing in the notepad. The rest of us say nothing. Tim and I make faces at each other the way siblings do, then Tate gets in on the act, causing me to giggle.

Leo looks up from his paper and asks Jake, "Where do you think the motorhome and trailer we got today should go?"

"You bought one for you and one for Art?"

"Maybe. That was my first thought. But I did hear you and your dad talking about your brother. If he and his family come here, they should have one. Then Art and I could bunk together."

Jake is visibly moved. Not only because he misses his brother and is worried about him, but also because Leo would think of this. Jake says nothing for a moment while he composes himself. Even so, he needs to stop and start again.

"Thank you, Leo. That's a good plan. Do you think using the backside of the garage to build another lean-to would be good?"

"How long is the garage?" They go over measurements and details, where to put the lean-tos and the greenhouse Jake wants to build.

I can see Leo's wheels turning while he works out what he's thinking. Finally, he says, "Have you thought about attaching the greenhouse to the house? You all enter through the door by the garage, but the other door is supposed to be the main entrance? You could put a greenhouse and sunroom combination there and even pipe some warm air into the house and vice versa."

The look of shock and awe on Jake's face is priceless. He mutters, "I don't know why I didn't think of that." Then, loud enough for us all to hear, he says, "Excellent idea. Are your building skills good enough to do these things? The greenhouse I planned to add on to the processing room wouldn't have been anything wonderful to look at. But if we're adding it to the house, it shouldn't look like a cobbled together mess."

"Yes. I can do it. I'll need some help, but it's within my skillset. I wish we would've looked at what you bought for the greenhouse before we left. We'll have to do our best."

"I have the list I used." Jake digs in his wallet and brings out a piece of paper that's been folded many times. There's more figuring and planning as they attempt to work out the details of the new attached greenhouse.

"You have a patio across the back?" Leo asks.

Jakes tells Leo it's poured concrete and there's going to need to be some serious rearranging so my mom doesn't lose her outdoor kitchen and entertaining space.

Leo nods and starts writing on his notepad again. In just a few minutes, he says, "Okay. I think I have it. We'll do the twelve-foot-wide greenhouse off the main house. Tate's trailer off the garage, a second lean-to off the back of the garage for the small camp trailer, and the motorhome off the processing shed. We'll tie it in to the wall, building it out to fit. Sound good?"

Everyone nods and agrees. I can't help but think what Mom's going to think when she gets home and sees the new addition to the house.

"What do we need to get for the rocket heaters?" Leo asks.

Chapter 22

The shopping takes just about forever. Leo works on the building materials while Jake gets fencing supplies and buys more livestock items, plus things for growing various crops. Tim and Tate also find items they think they could use. As they pay for and load the purchases, I realize why we brought all the trailers—we need them.

I'm kind of surprised by one of Jake's purchases. He bought meat rabbits. Mom and Jake have lots of wild rabbits around.

"Jake, I thought you eat wild rabbits?"

Jake looks a little surprised. "Well, yes. We have. The first couple of winters we hunted rabbit, but they don't have much meat and were kind of gamey and stringy. Your mom and Malcolm didn't like them much at all. I didn't mind them, but they weren't my favorite either. Plus, the numbers aren't reliable. We had quite a few last year but not many this year. And with the predator problem . . ." He lifts his hands.

"Not to mention, many people will likely be hunting them for food. Your mom had a friend in Casper who raised domestics and gave us a couple she butchered. Those, we liked fine. You've had them before, haven't you?"

"Oh, yeah. I don't think I was home when Mom made those. But I've had rabbit in a restaurant before. It's fine."

Jake nods. "I think these will be fine."

He bought three young females and one young male, plus a dozen cages that can be stacked in towers of three, some of the feed the rabbits are currently eating, several large bags of another kind, and a few smaller bags. He also bought an unassembled metal shelving unit, a dozen Rubbermaid dish tubs, and a large storage tote.

"Jake, what are the dish tubs for?" I ask.

"I want to be able to set up another fodder system. We have one system we use during the winter, plus supplies to put together two more and quite a bit of stored grains. The shelving unit, dish tubs, and large tote will work for another system. The bags are assorted cereal crop seeds, winter field beans, and clover."

Mom once sent me a picture of trays of wheatgrass on shelves. "Huh. So the fodder is the grass Mom grows?"

"Exactly. We set it up by the basement window during the winter. The ambient light helps it grow. We don't cultivate much, just enough to give the goats and chickens some fresh stuff when the snow's on the ground and they can't get out as much. With the addition of the sheep and rabbits, plus the likelihood we won't be able to get hay and commercial feed for a while, we'll increase the fodder production. We also plant a small amount of root vegetables just for the livestock. We'll need to increase it next year if things don't get back to normal."

I hate that Jake is mentioning next year. I give a fake smile. "Ah. Makes sense. I do have to admit, it's hard to think about eating the rabbits. They're so cute."

"I know. The rabbits, the sheep, the goats . . . they're all cute. These rabbits need a couple of months to grow before breeding. He told me of another place to stop in Wesley with New Zealand rabbits. I hope to get another buck and two more does there so we have a variety of blood lines."

"The different breeds are okay to cross?"

"Should be fine. Californians were produced by crossing different breeds. I can't remember which ones right now."

"Okay, sounds good. I'm going to see how Leo's doing."

It's not long until we've finished loading.

"Whew. What a shopping excursion. I have about five dollars left from the cash Sarah and I had, combined with the cash my parents gave us. And I'm pretty sure they gave me all they had," Tate says.

"I still have some money," I offer.

"I have a little, too, but not much," Jake says. "I've spent most of what I brought along."

"I have money," Leo says. "Is there someplace else we should go?"

"I want to see about a few more rabbits in Wesley, plus we might see someplace else we want to stop," Jake says. "The grocery stores didn't look too good driving through, at least the ones on the road. There are a few resale shops that might be worth looking at. One for clothes, one for housewares, and one full of all kinds of junk."

We end up finding clothes, assorted footwear, bedding, and belts. Leo suggests the belts when talking about how I planned to carry my new pistol; he reminds me I only own a couple of fashion belts.

The used housewares store has lots of useful things: cheap doors and windows for the building projects, tile, brick, and even a screen door and a small table for Angela's house. The junk store is just that—

junk. But they do have a huge selection of heavy-duty work clothes, which we buy in assorted sizes.

While we find almost everything on our list, there are some building supplies Leo wanted but couldn't get, plus they didn't have everything needed to make three rocket stoves. Jake says they'll keep looking.

Three hours later, all of us except for Jake pull into the yard back at the farm. Jake wanted to make a quick stop along the way to check in with his martial arts instructor. We offered to stay with him, but he waved us on, telling us he'd be along shortly.

Grandpa Alvin unlocks the gate and lets us in, and I immediately look around to see if Mom's home. She isn't.

However, the terrorists have struck again.

"They hit the railroads today," Grandpa Alvin says. "Took out the tracks in many places, collapsed tunnels, and blew up bridges and rail yards. There was even an explosion in Montana, east of Billings, at a place called Jones Junction, that resulted in a chemical spill from one of the tanker cars."

"I didn't even know trains were still running," I say. "I figured they would've stopped when the power went out."

"Not sure if they were running. I think they just blew them up where they sat. It sure seems they, whoever *they* may be, are determined to stop supplies and people from getting from place to place," Grandpa Alvin says.

"We have dinner just about ready," Sarah says. "You all want to get the sheep and rabbits settled while we finish? We'll eat over at the picnic area by the swimming pond."

I take the produce we got in the house. I'm not quite sure what to do with it all, so I leave it on the table for now. At least it's out of the heat.

Leo and I start setting up the rabbit cages while everyone else, except Sarah and Lois, who are working on dinner, get the sheep housed. I suddenly realize I've been thrust into the life of farmer and homesteader. While we have it better than most, the entire nation is essentially back to living like Laura Ingalls.

Without any warning at all, my face is wet with tears. I bend my head and let them flow. Once the tears start, I know there's nothing I can do to stop them. The sadness, the fear, and the reality of living in a new world are sliding out of my eyes.

Leo's arms are immediately around me. He doesn't even ask why I'm crying or what's wrong. He doesn't tell me not to cry or say everything will be fine. He simply holds me and lets me grieve. As the voices of the others come closer, he gently leads me away from our workstation.

"Hey, Tim, we have two of the cages assembled. They're ready for the bucks to go in one and the does in the other," Leo shares as we step away.

At his truck, Leo puts down the tailgate and hoists me up. There's a nice breeze, which earlier Jake said will likely lead to a thunderstorm. He was happy about the rain, saying they haven't had any for a couple of days. I suppose that's another thing I'll learn to be happy about. We'll need the rain to help the crops, which will be an essential part of our survival.

Even though Mom and Jake have what seems to be a large amount of stored food, it won't last forever.

With this thought, I'm struck again with the realization of just how fortunate we are. The choices and sacrifices Mom and Jake made over the years will make a difference in our lives in this new world. I know it wasn't always easy. Angela told me Mom wondered more than once if they weren't being silly.

She loved the idea of traveling, but with the farm, this was limited. They do go on camping and hiking vacations, which they love, but Mom has always had a dream of traveling the country, or even the world, by backpack.

I suddenly realize she may be traveling by backpack right now. I'm pretty sure this isn't fulfilling her travel dreams.

Jake's truck is coming up the road as I try to pull myself together. He's stepping out of the truck when Sarah calls everyone over to the picnic area. Mom and Jake put in a big triangle, just like old farms and ranches used, to ring for dinner. It's effective.

"Thank you, Leo. I'm sorry I lost it. My emotions are all over the place."

"Ah, Katie. It's completely understandable. There were several people with damp eyes this morning, and not just the women."

I dip my head in agreement. "Well, I'm starving. Let's go eat."

Sarah and Lois have prepared quite a feast. There's a large salad made out of fresh greens, radishes, tiny carrots, and microgreens from the garden. The microgreens and carrots, Sarah explains, are plants that needed thinning.

The main dish is grilled bone-in chicken with a variety of cooked veggies to clear out the almost-past-its-prime produce in the fridge. Angela made dinner rolls. Malcolm was ecstatic about this. He loves Angela's rolls.

"Jake, are you planning on going to the community center tonight for the meeting?" Sarah asks.

"Yes, I think it's best for me to go," he answers.

"Lois and I would like to join you," Keith quickly adds. "We met some real nice folks last night and would love to participate in your community as much as we can. 'Course, I'll be watching for flying fists and ducking as needed."

This garners a few chuckles, and a sour look from his daughter Karen.

"I'd like to go along also, Jake," Grandpa Alvin says. "Your mother wants to stay here and watch Malcolm and Gavin, if everyone else wants to go."

Malcolm looks slightly disappointed he won't be going.

"Sure, Dad. We should take as few vehicles as possible. Even though we're good on fuel, it's smart to conserve."

"I think I'll stay behind and keep Grandma company," Tate says.

Leo claps Tate on the shoulder and nods his head. Jake gives them both a strange look, then a new look crosses his face—a look of understanding, I guess.

"Sure, Tate. That's fine. I've been thinking about the water problem some people are having. I have a generator I no longer use because the recoil rope and spring broke on it. I was supposed to fix it but have kept putting it off. I have a new spring and rope, so I thought maybe we could fix it and then rig it to work the well at the community center. Does anyone have the skills needed to get the well pump operational?"

"Shouldn't be too difficult," Roy says. "If we have access to the breaker box, we could add a plug on the wall coming from the breaker. Then you can plug the pump into the building's power or plug it into the generator. Of course, that's provided you have the wires and everything needed."

"I might. We have wiring stuff leftover from various projects. Let's see if we can find what we need and get the generator working to take with us," Jake says.

"You think we can have our own meeting when we get back? There are several items we should discuss and plans we should put in place. We'll have cookies to encourage everyone to join us." Sarah looks around the group with a smile.

"Sure, Sarah. Good idea. I'd like to go over some emergency preparedness things also. It'd be good for everyone to know what to do in case something big happens here."

Tim and Tate go with Jake and Grandpa Alvin to grab the generator. Jake asks Mike to take his dad into the tool shed to look for the parts he needs.

The rest of us, even Gavin, start clearing the food and dishes. The picnic area near the swimming pond, one of several developed picnic spots scattered around the property, is lovely.

There are trees and blueberries planted around the pond and several tables and benches. A propane grill and makeshift countertop provide a usable space. But I really have to wonder why we're so far from the kitchen as we clear and haul things inside. At least Sarah moved the dishwasher into the kitchen. None of us want to hand-wash if we don't have to.

"What's the building over there?" Leo asks, pointing to a small rock structure near the swimming pond.

"The sauna."

"Really? Nice. Is it made out of . . . rocks?"

"Sure is. They have a ton of rock here, so as they cleared the area, they used what they could. See the small mound over there, at the top of the small draw?"

"Uh . . . yeah, I guess so."

"It's an icehouse. It's double walled, both walls made out of rock with insulation between. And then downhill from the icehouse, deeper in the draw, is a cold house—at least, that's what Mom calls it."

"Cold house?"

"Yeah, it's kind of strange. The icehouse—you know, where they store ice so they can have it year-round—has a drainage pipe, so when the ice melts, it can exit the building. The drainage pipe runs down the hill into the cold house. It then drains into a trough. Stuff you want to keep cold is placed in the trough. The water keeps it chilled, kind of like a fridge . . . but not really."

"Huh. Interesting concept. Does it work?"

"I guess. They made ice and put some in the icehouse the first winter to test the setup. Mom said it worked but is very labor-intensive, so they never tested it again. I suspect we'll be using it this winter, unless the power comes back on before then."

"Your folks could be pretty popular next summer if they have a shed full of ice."

I have to laugh a little at this. Who would've thought ice could promote popularity?

Chapter 23

Roy thinks he has everything needed to set the water system up. Leo and Art filled four five-gallon jugs with water to take to the community center in case they can't get the well going. Angela and Karen raided Mom and Jake's stash of recycled gallon and liter containers to take for people who don't bring something to carry water. They decide to preemptively fill them here.

We're all sitting over on the covered porch visiting when a portable radio comes on with a loud squawk. *"Ladies and gentlemen, your attention please. We've just received word the president will give an emergency address at 9:30 p.m. eastern daylight time. Again, the president will give an emergency address in approximately one hour. We will broadcast the address in its entirety. This message will repeat every ten minutes until the address. Thank you."*

"Well, that's interesting," Grandpa Alvin says. "Must be about the railroad attacks today, don't you think?"

"Maybe so, Dad," Jake says. "I'm kind of surprised he's talking a half hour later than the previous addresses. Seems he'd stick with the same time, figuring people might be expecting it."

"You think Doris and Evan heard about it, Dad?" Malcolm asks. "Will they bring their radio and speakers again so everyone can listen?"

"Not sure. Maybe I ought to see. We need to be taking off in a few minutes to get to the community center anyway. I'll swing up there, then stop and pick up everyone riding with me. I can squeeze in five. Dad, you with me?"

"Yep. Still going and planned to ride with you. I'll grab four others and meet you out at the road so you don't have to pull in."

"I don't think you need to go to the Snyders' house," Angela says. "Looks like they're starting down the hill now. Might want to stop them, just in case."

I volunteer to go to the road while everyone else scrambles to get ready.

Doris and Evan slow when they see me waving at them.

"Hey, what are you doing?" Doris asks.

"Oh, you know, just flagging you down. We wanted to make sure you heard about the president speaking tonight at 7:30."

"Sure did. We were going to stop in and tell you all. Are you going to the community showdown? I mean, *meeting*?"

I laugh. "Yeah. I hope it's a little less exciting tonight."

"You and me both!" Evan chimes in. "I'm too old to be breaking up fights."

Jake's and Leo's trucks start—those diesels are not quiet. Someone's much quieter gas truck also starts.

"Here comes your family," Doris says. "You riding with one of them or you want to ride with us?"

"I think they saved me a seat. We're trying to take as few vehicles as possible to save on fuel."

"If we have a meeting tomorrow night, three of you can get in with us, but we can figure out rides better tomorrow. See you there."

The Snyders pull away as Jake pulls up and says, "Leo had to take his truck so you can ride with him. Tomorrow, maybe we'll see about carpooling with the Snyders. See you there."

I wave and think how funny it is he says the same thing Doris did. Leo's alone in his truck. It would've been smart for us to hop in with Doris and Evan.

Buckling my seat belt, I say, "Doris already had the speakers, so we're all set. Hey, why didn't Tate want to go?"

Staring straight ahead, Leo gives a slight shrug.

"Leo? What aren't you telling me?"

"It's nothing, really. Tate thought it might be best to stay behind."

As we bounce down the gravel road, I think about this. "He's staying to protect them, isn't he?"

Leo confirms this—Tate stayed at the homestead because the idea of Grandma and the children there alone concerned him. Thinking about it, I'm suddenly worried.

I know Mom and Jake never considered their chosen retreat could be infiltrated by evil. But now, with the confrontation Jake had with Dan Morse, things have changed. Of course, I expect Morse will be at the meeting and not lurking around our homestead.

As we pull into the community center, I look for the ATV Dan sped off on last night. There are several Quadrunners, side-by-sides, and assorted motorcycles. These multipurpose vehicles, usually restricted to off-road use only in most states, can be legal for all but interstate use in Wyoming. I remember when we first moved to Wyoming and I was incredibly amused to see a Quadrunner in downtown Casper. There's an ATV similar to Morse's, but where is he?

"I don't see him either," Leo says, reading my mind. "It's fine, Katie. I suspect he'll be here."

Jake's immediately bombarded with requests for water. Angela starts handing out bottles, telling people to transfer it into another container if they can and bring the empty back. If not, bring the empty back tomorrow. A few people begin drinking from their bottle right away.

I almost start crying when a little girl, no more than four years old, says, "I'm so thirsty, Mama. Can I have a drink now?" I decide to make sure the little girl's family takes home plenty of water tonight. I grab another bottle and walk over to them. Their first bottle, a two-liter once holding root beer, is more than half gone. A boy around Malcolm's age is now drinking from it.

"Hi, I'm Katie."

"Hi, Katie. I think we've met before. Your mom is Mollie?"

"Mm-hmm. She is. I'm sorry, I don't remember."

"We sat near you all at last year's rodeo. Malcolm and Tony are friends and chattered the whole time. We live just over the hill from your parents. I'm Olivia. This is Tony and Lily."

I do remember now, but I have to admit, she doesn't look anything like the lady I met last year. She's a tiny wisp of a woman, several inches shorter than my five foot four. I suspect she barely weighs a hundred pounds. Her makeup-free face boasts eyebrows and lashes so light they appear nonexistent. Her white-blond hair is slicked back in a tight bun and looks more like a crew cut than the full head of flowing blond curls I remember.

She's only a few years older than me, having had Tony right out of high school. Her tired face seems to have aged at least a dozen years. I suspect most of the aging has happened in just the last few days. She looks as tired and scared as everyone else.

"Of course. It's nice to see you again, Olivia. Lily and Tony have both grown a lot since last year. Malcolm too. I couldn't believe how big he was when I first saw him. I guess that's the way it goes." I realize I'm rambling a bit but continue on. "Is your husband here also? I can't remember his name."

A cloud comes over Olivia's face. "Jason works on an oil rig. He was in North Dakota when the planes came down. His wasn't due home for another week. After the bridges went out, they talked about shutting down early but didn't. He would've left anyway, but they were in company trucks and he's not a company driver. Last time we spoke, they were given a choice of staying and finishing out their week or heading home. He was planning to come home.

"Then the phones went out and the refineries were hit, so I'm not really sure what's happening now. I'm hopeful he'll be home soon. I know the country will be needing oil, but it's hard to be here alone without power and things. I can't even get the well working. We had some bottled water, but it ran out last night. I only found out about the meeting today when someone stopped by my house earlier." She gives a visible shudder. I wonder what that's about?

"I'm so sorry. I hope your husband's on his way."

"Thank you. Is Malcolm here? I'm sure Tony would love to play with him."

"He's not. He stayed with our grandma to help take care of our nephew. My sisters and their families are all here. My sister Angela is the one handing out water at Jake's truck. Have you met her before?"

"No, I don't think so. Is she the one who was married last year?"

"That was Calley. She's over there." I point to where Calley and Mike are standing, talking with a group of people. From the gestures at Mike's eye, I believe his beating is the topic of conversation.

"We have another sister, Sarah, but I'm not sure where she is. Around here somewhere. There's a whole lot of us, and sometimes our mom can't even keep us straight." I try to make something resembling a joke. I fail.

"Where's Mollie?" Olivia asks, looking around.

Now it's my turn to look sad. "My mom was in Oregon for work when this all started. Jake last heard from her on Saturday. She was somewhere in Idaho. We think she may have run out of gas. She'll be biking or walking home, I have no doubt."

Olivia reaches out and hugs me. I do my best to hold back my tears; at least one escapes.

"Well, Olivia. I'm glad to see you made it." I feel Olivia shudder at the unknown voice. She lets go of me.

Dan Morse is standing next to us. Leo was right about him showing up.

"Yes. Thank you," Olivia responds.

"Where's Jason? He send you on your own?" Morse asks.

"Yes. He wasn't able to join us."

"Hmm. Interesting. I would've thought for sure he'd be here . . . considering he wasn't available to chat when I stopped by today and all." Morse smirks as he crosses his arms.

Tony steps closer to his mom. His little fists are balled up, and he looks ready to spring into action. Lily is oblivious, sitting on the ground playing with a doll. Olivia says nothing.

"Well, I guess I'd better get this meeting started," he says. "They need me to keep things equitable here. Otherwise, we'd have a few people hoarding everything and letting everyone else go without. Then there's the problem of bringing outsiders into our community to take all of our resources." He looks directly at me when he says this.

While my first instinct is to practice some of the Krav Maga I've learned on him, I decide to follow Olivia's lead and say nothing.

As soon as he's far enough away to not hear, Tony whispers, "I don't like that man, Mama. He's not a good person."

Olivia, obviously shaken, hugs Tony close and says, "Thank you for standing next to me. You helped me feel strong."

"You are strong, Mama. But I'll always protect you. Especially when Dad isn't here. We can't let that man know Dad isn't home."

Olivia nods and hugs Tony even tighter.

Dan Morse is standing on top of a picnic table calling for everyone's attention. I look around for Leo. He sees me and gives me a wave as he walks over. People are ignoring Morse and continue to talk and mingle around. His voice gets louder.

Phil Hudson taps Evan and Jake on the shoulders, then motions for them to join him. Evan looks okay with it, but Jake—not so much. His shoulders sag as he follows a few paces behind Evan, who's on Phil's heels.

Phil stops next to the picnic table Dan is standing and yelling on. He raises his hand in a call for quiet. As people notice, they stop talking and moving around, and in less than a minute, he has everyone's attention. Even Dan Morse is silent as he glares at Phil.

Phil moves his arm in a motion to indicate Dan has the floor and can begin. But before he can speak, a dirt bike comes tearing in the driveway. Instead of stopping at the parking lot, the bike continues to the gathered crowd. With a final roar of the engine, the bike is shut off and a lady I don't know steps off.

"Terry! Terry Bosco! Are you here?"

Chapter 24

Many people murmur, and one person yells out, "What's going on, Belinda?"

"Has anyone seen Terry?"

There are many "no" and "not today" responses.

"Terry's gone. I can't find him anywhere. I thought he'd show up here." Belinda's close to hysterics. A woman nearby goes to her, wrapping her in a hug.

"The coward probably took off on you, Belinda," Dan yells. "You know he's all talk, and when things get tough, he can't handle it."

"You shut your mouth, you . . . you . . ." Belinda sputters. "You don't know anything. You don't like Terry because he called you out for being a Bolshevik and a vagrant."

Dan says nothing but has an increasingly smug look about him.

"More trouble, and somehow I suspect Dan Morse is part of it," Leo whispers.

"Belinda, when did you last see Terry?" Phil asks.

"After lunch. He was going fishing, then to my parents' place. He never made it to their house. My dad's out looking for him. My mom's at my place with TJ."

"Okay," Phil says, "we need to put together a search party. There are a few things that need to happen here also. Jake Caldwell brought a generator, and one of his family thinks they may be able to hook it up to the well. Can someone with a key help Jake get the access he needs?"

"You bet. I'll help Jake," someone yells out.

"Thanks. There's been some water handed out tonight. If they can get this going, there can be more. Get what you need for drinking, cleaning, and flushing. We're all fortunate to live out here on the edge of nowhere with our septic systems. I suppose you all know, just add water to the tank and flush. Gravity should still do its job, and you won't have any problems. I've advised Jake to take the generator home with him. We'll plan on continuing to meet at seven each evening to catch up on events and get people water."

"Well isn't that just great," Dan says. "There isn't any reason Caldwell can't leave the generator here and we can get water at our convenience."

"Actually, Dan, there's several reasons." Phil speaks slowly to him, like he's explaining something to a child. "The first reason is, it's Jake's generator and he's offering us the use of it. There's a very good chance, if it were left here, it'd magically grow legs and walk off. I'm not going to take the time to explain the additional reasons to you. If you need water, see Jake.

"For those of you who weren't here last night, if you have a need other than water, see my lovely wife, Kelley. If you were here last night and something new has come up, Kelley's your girl. I can't promise she can solve your needs tonight, but she'll do her best to help.

"Those who can help search for Terry, head over to my truck. We'll likely be searching on foot, so we should pile as many people in as few vehicles as possible to conserve fuel. Belinda, you okay to drive your bike?"

"Of course. I drove it here, didn't I?" She shakes her head. "I'm sorry, Phil. I know you were asking about my mental health right now. It's not great, but I can keep it together." With that, Belinda starts her bike and takes off.

Leo gives me a kiss and tells me he's going to help with the search. Tim, Mike, and Art join him. Sarah, Karen, and Lois are hovering near Kelley. Calley and Angela signal to me they're going with the search party.

I shake my head. I need to stay here, to stay near Olivia.

Doris has the speakers set up and announces to everyone still gathered around that she'll stay until after the president finishes speaking, for anyone who wishes to listen. Dan Morse takes this as his cue to slip away.

I watch as he heads for his ATV. I wonder if he's going to get a water jug or just leave. I have my answer shortly as he turns his ATV on and hightails it out of the parking lot. I swear I can feel Olivia relax next to me.

I check my phone. It's 7:25, almost time for the president. I turn to Olivia. "Did you bring containers to put water in?"

"I did. When Morse stopped by today, he mentioned he'd made arrangements for people to be supplied water."

I raise my eyebrows.

"I'm now well aware he didn't arrange for anything. I suspected he was full of hot air, now I have confirmation."

I nod. "Let's get your containers as soon as the president's finished. Hopefully they'll be able to get the well working, but if not, we'll send you home with enough to last until tomorrow evening."

The radio lets out the squawk, which now accompanies it coming back on the air. I wonder if it's intentional by the station. I think a bell or even a horn would be much better.

There is no announcement from the radio station. Instead, the president immediately begins his address.

"Ladies and gentlemen, I come to you tonight to share additional heartbreak. The attacks on our country continue. At approximately 6:30 p.m. eastern, a series of explosions affected our nation's railway system. Railroad bridges were destroyed, tracks were mangled, and tunnels were collapsed. There were many derailments. Commuter, passenger, and freight lines were all afflicted. At this time, due to continued communication issues, we do not have a complete accounting of the destruction. My prayers continue to be with all affected by these acts of terrorism."

There's a long pause, and I half wonder if he's finished. I'm not the only one, as I notice people glancing around and several shrugs in response. We soon discover he has more to share.

"Around the time we received the first reports of the railroad catastrophe, I was privately notified of the loss of several members of Congress in separate events."

There's a collective gasp in the gathered crowd.

"My fellow Americans, your elected officials were targeted. They were murdered in cold blood. At this moment, we can confirm the loss of twenty-eight senators and one hundred forty-two representatives. We're working hard to make contact with every member of Congress so we can help protect the remaining members.

"My wife and I are deeply pained by the losses, which began on Thursday evening and continue through today. We believe we share this pain with all in our great country and even around the world. These losses are something we will carry with us through all of our days. The tens of thousands of Americans who have lost their lives

will never be forgotten. Our senators and representatives will never be forgotten.

"We continue to search for those responsible for these atrocities committed on our soil and to our citizens. We will leave no stone unturned in our search for justice. And as you hear my words today, you can be assured we will find justice.

"During this difficult time, we must remember to be united as Americans. We shouldn't be fighting and trying to destroy each other. Save your anger for the enemy, not your neighbor, not your fellow American. The looting and vandalism must come to an end. We're working tirelessly to provide needed assistance to the areas hardest hit by the travesties of the last several days.

"None of us will forget these trying times. We will go forward into a new world. A world where we can once again live in security and freedom. Thank you. Good night and God bless America."

There's nothing additional. No one comes on to tell us which members of Congress were killed. The local announcer doesn't add anything. There's only silence.

The gathered crowd is also mainly silent. We're a small group, with so many having joined the search for Terry, and many are hugging each other. As I look around, most are quietly crying. I realize my own eyes and cheeks are wet. I don't even know when my tears started.

After a bit, I touch Olivia on the arm. "Whenever you're ready to grab your jugs, I'll be over by Jake's truck." I motion to his truck in case she doesn't know which one is his.

She nods, her lip quivering as she fights to hold back tears.

As I'm walking over to the truck, Doris stops me and envelops me in a big hug. "Killing our senators and representatives makes it feel very personal. It also makes me wonder who they'll target next."

My eyes go wide.

"Oh, not us. But I worry for my daughter. They could decide to target law enforcement. She was still working her job in San Jose when the phones went out."

I forgot Doris has a daughter who's a police officer. "I'm sorry, Doris. You must be so scared."

"Yes. Not knowing is the hardest part. I know she'll stay on the job as long as she feels she can make a difference. After that, she'll head here. Like you and your family, we've discussed the possibility of things falling apart. I do have to admit, I thought it'd be a quick attack, not these little attacks, which seem to really be tearing us apart and inciting extra fear."

"It's good you had a plan. Maybe she's already on her way."

Doris smiles weakly and nods. "Maybe."

I give her another hug, then continue to the truck. I look around for Jake but don't see him. He's probably trying to get the well pump working.

Olivia and her children walk over. "Here you go, Katie." She hands me the empty water jugs we'd passed out full earlier. "I emptied them into containers I brought along. You know anything about the well working yet?"

"Not yet. Jake was still out here until after the speech, so they haven't been working on it long. Roy thought it'd be fairly simple. I can give you more water from the jugs here if you need to leave."

"We can wait a bit and see if the pump starts working. I don't want to take too much, just in case it doesn't."

Olivia and I mill around, sticking together but moving from person to person and chatting. We're all in various stages of upset and are a very somber group.

While Olivia and I are visiting, I find out she lives just over the ridge behind Mom and Jake's house. As the crow flies, it's less than half a mile.

After about half an hour, Jake announces the water is working. There's a rush of people gathering their containers and heading toward Jake.

"We can use the kitchen and the outside faucet," Jake says. "Those of you with really large containers, go to the outside faucet. Smaller containers, come with me to the kitchen."

It's coming on twilight by the time the last person's container is filled. Olivia is near the end, and I help her carry the jugs to their car.

As we reach her little red economy car, several vehicles pull into the driveway. The search crew is back. We stay where we are while they park.

Leo walks over and wraps me in a big hug. "We found him. It seems he fell in a gully and hit his head on a rock . . . or maybe multiple rocks. Happened several hours ago. He probably died pretty quickly."

I gasp and Olivia utters, "Oh no. Poor Belinda. Does she know?"

187

"Yes. Her dad told her. She got there right when we were leaving."

"Did *you* find him?" I ask.

"Phil found him. I was nearby when Phil hollered out asking for help. It was . . . not good. I kind of wish Belinda's dad could've kept her away. I heard she's a nurse, but still, it's her husband."

Angela and Calley walk over, both holding their husbands' hands. None of them look too good.

"I'm glad I wasn't close enough to see anything," Angela says. "Leo and Tim say it was bad. And we heard about what the president said about all of the congressmen being murdered. Sounds like they're not only trying to destroy the country, but also make it difficult to rebuild."

Jake walks over, shaking his head. "I heard about Terry. I'm sure Belinda appreciates you all helping in the search. Definitely not the outcome I would've expected, but good Belinda knows. Not knowing would be very hard."

Tears immediately come to my eyes since I'm sure he means we don't know about Mom. I look at Angela and Calley and see the same tearful looks.

"You guys ready to head on home?" Jake asks. "I know it's late, but I'd like to have a family meeting before we shut down for the night."

I look toward the community center and see the rest of our family walking our way. Keith and Roy are carrying the heavy generator between them. Tim and Leo run to help.

"Olivia, you think you'll be good on water until tomorrow night?" I ask.

"Oh, yes, Katie. We'll be fine. Thanks so much for your help."

I catch Jake's eye. He gives a slight nod.

I move closer to Olivia. "Come over tomorrow. Jake and Mom have a shower you can use."

She smiles and nods. "What time?"

I look to Jake, who says, "I think we're going to go on another supply run tomorrow. You want to go along, Katie, or stick at home?"

Although I'd like to go, I know I'd better stay home and help out. "I'll stay home." I turn to Olivia. "Stop by late morning?"

Chapter 25

We're in Mom and Jake's great room for our family meeting. We pulled the kitchen chairs in, and Jake brought in a few camp chairs, but we're still short on seats. People are sitting on the staircase, on the woodstove hearth, and on the floor. Our group of twenty can really fill a room.

Grandpa Alvin starts with talking about the president's latest announcement. He and Grandma Dodie seem pretty distraught over it. They watch a lot of political stuff on TV and know the names and faces of many people in Congress.

Jake talks briefly about the death of Terry. Too much death in one day. Of course, death seems to be the norm for the last several days. Too much death every day since Thursday. I don't even know how many people have died since the attacks started.

Jake leans forward in his chair. "Okay, so one of the things I want to discuss is a follow up to the root cellar tour last night. Mollie and I have a binder with a list of things to do if we discover there's been an attack and we need to move to the shelter.

"With the communication issues we're facing right now, I'm not sure if we'd even have much notice, but I'm hopeful an alert would come over the NOAA radio. I have my mom and dad monitoring the radio as best they can, and we keep one in the kitchen over there. The binder goes on the shelf under the radio, included with the cookbooks." He holds up a binder.

"The spine says *ERG* for Emergency Response Guide. I know it's late, but I want to at least get started on our plans of who will do what in case of an emergency. We have a few copies of the shelter information in here. I'll pass those around. There aren't nearly enough for everyone, so you'll have to share, and others will just have to listen and you can read later." Jake hands out six stapled copies of two or three pages.

"The shelter preparation is only one part of our guide. I'd like to go over this tonight, and then maybe tomorrow night we can look at another section. Of course, our *Plan A* is another part, but we're way past that."

Sarah quickly says, "*Plan A is* what Mom and Jake had in place if it seemed something strange might be happening. They had shared this with us kids. It's the last-minute trip to the grocery store, the bank, and the gas station."

This received lots of nods. Apparently, almost everyone else was in the loop for *Plan A,* even if they didn't know what it was called.

"Yes, exactly," Jake says. "So for the shelter, I also have this list Mollie put in a plastic sleeve. We can write on it with a dry erase marker so we can decide who does what. It's the back page of the handout I've given. I think we should just look at it. The front pages give the details of what to do, which we can look at if needed tonight. Mostly, I'd like to just get the assignments made, and you can follow up on the how-to later. Sound good?"

There are nods and yeses all around. For the next fifteen minutes, we talk about who will do what if there's ever an alert of a nuclear strike. I lose track of who has what job, other than Grandma Dodie is in charge of making sure Malcolm, Gavin, and the dogs are in the shelter right away, and Angela and I are to cover the garden with plastic.

Jake says there's some controversy on whether this will help much since we could be in shelter for some time and lose the plants due to neglect, but they've decided it's worth a try. Others are to do things like get the food out of the fridge, move sandbags around, and move the livestock.

I'm glad there's a guide to follow and Jake made a list of who does what. Jake says he suspects the Snyders will be down to help, and he's going to talk to a few other neighbors tomorrow, offering them shelter in case of an extreme emergency. He says he's not going to give the "full tour" but will tell them about the basement and to head here if there's an attack.

"Sir, Katie and Calley both purchased handguns yesterday, and I think they should start carrying them," Leo says. "I believe Angela also purchased hers recently. Can we use your range?"

"You definitely can," Jake says. "While we were out and about today, I was thinking it might be smart for everyone to carry. Did you know the Snyders are firearms instructors? I think we can ask if they'd give everyone a proper class or two, then we can use our range for practice. Mollie and I target practice quite a bit, but I'd like even more instruction from Evan. Until the last few days, I've only carried when hunting or hiking, and I'm not super comfortable with drawing.

"It's too late tonight, but I'll talk to him in the morning and see if I can set up a group training for anyone interested. I do want to make another trip tomorrow to see if we can find additional things, both for here and for the community in general. We'll sort out how to get everything done."

"Sounds good, sir," Leo says. "There's a definite urgency to continue to gather things. Many items are already scarce. Are there specific things you're looking for, other than the building supplies we still have on our list?"

Jake leans back in his chair, lacing his fingers behind his head. He gives two slow nods.

"Those things, plus more food, is always a good thing, both for humans and animals. And some of the livestock feed, like corn, can be used for both. Additional building supplies to have on hand, clothing, everything we think we might need.

"I'm getting to the end of my cash, but like we've discussed, I think it'd be best to have goods instead of money. There's a couple of little towns north of us that might be worth going to—a few feed stores, lumber yards, and small mom-and-pop grocery stores. Not sure what we'll find, but it's worth a look."

"Think you could go early, and we could have the afternoon for shooting?" Angela asks.

"Yeah, let's try it. If you don't want to go but think of things you'd like to have, make a list. No promises, but we'll try. Mike, you feel up to going along tomorrow?"

"You know, Jake. I'd like to, but at this moment, I'm feeling pretty terrible," Mike answers.

"I'll go," Roy and Keith both say at the same time, while Art says, "Count me in."

"Me too," Lois says.

Tate asks Sarah if she'd like to go and she, rather reluctantly, I think, agrees.

"Okay, great. Let's hit the road by 8:00 a.m. Before we go, I'll check with Evan about having lessons in the afternoon."

"Katie gave me change back today from the money we sent with her," Calley says. "I want you to take it, Jake. Use it all."

Calley isn't the only one; almost everyone digs money out to give to Jake. Malcolm grabs a small bag for the money to go in.

As the money is going in the bag, Jake says, "I think it's important we all remember we're now living in a finite world. The supplies we're going after—well, some of them are going to be very scarce for a long time. We need to make the most of everything we have. From this point on, nothing's disposable. While we're not on food rations at the moment, let's do our best to not waste any. Malcolm, take only what you can eat."

"Dad, you know I can eat a lot," Malcolm says with mild disgust.

"True, but I also know sometimes you think you can eat more than you can. The old phrase 'your eyes are bigger than your stomach' comes to mind."

"I have no idea what that means." Malcolm shakes his head.

Grandpa Alvin jumps in and says, "Sure you do. Like when cake looks really good so you ask for a huge piece and then you can only eat half of it."

"Oh . . . yeah. I guess I might have done that once or twice. So did someone make a cake? I'll only take a small piece."

"No, there isn't any cake right now. It was just an example," Jake says with a small smile.

"Okay, I'll only take what I can eat. But if it's not enough, can I get more?"

Everyone laughs a little at this, as Jake says, "Probably, as long as everyone else has enough."

Lois waves her hand. Jake acknowledges her with a smile.

"So besides food, should we be conserving other things? Like if we open a can of corn or something, do we save the can?" Lois asks.

"I think so, yes. Sarah, you've always been good at recycling. Can you organize something so we can keep things we may need? Right now, save everything. Then we can reevaluate as time goes on. This isn't just kitchen-related things—worn out or outgrown clothes, shoes, tools, anything you use. So if it breaks, tears, whatever, still keep it just in case. We never know what use we may find for things."

Sarah speaks up, "Jake, before we finish, can we talk about dividing chores and duties? I know we won't be able to 100 percent figure things out right away, but starting a plan would help."

"I think figuring a way to share the chores would be good," Art says. "Some of you probably know, I have a pretty bad back."

I catch Angela's eye, and she gives me a slight shrug. Not to sound terribly mean, but Angela and Tim think Art's bad back and numerous other issues are either based in hypochondria or boredom, or a combination of the two. The doctors haven't found anything really wrong with him that getting a little fresh air and doing some stretches wouldn't help. I tune back into what Art is saying.

"Even though I'm sometimes feeling poorly, I'd like to help out. Watching you and little Malcolm milk the goats and feed the chickens this morning made me think, maybe I can do something like that. I'd like to try at least. You do those things only in the morning, or at night also?"

Tim and Angela both have a look resembling shock.

Jake also seems a little surprised as he says, "That'd be great, Art. Sometimes we have to milk in the evening but not until the kids are weaned. Right now, it's mornings only. They do all still need food and water in the evenings. I took care of that before we went to the meeting. I'll need to go out and lock the chickens up when we're finished, but that's it for tonight. You interested in helping in the morning?"

"You bet. I'll set my alarm. What time?"

"We'll start chores around 5:30."

"Okay. Angela and Tim, you mind the alarm going off so early? It's just my phone, so it'll play softly. I'm glad the phones are at least still working as clocks and alarms."

Jake bobs his head in agreement. "I have a few battery-operated, travel alarm clocks, and we have several larger windup alarms . . . might want to hold off on those unless you want to wake the whole house, though."

"I think the phone will be fine. Then, tomorrow, I'll make sure to get the place Leo bought for me cleaned up and move on over so my early morning chores don't bother you, Tim. Okay?"

"Yeah, sure, Dad. Not a problem at all for you to set your alarm to help with the chores," Tim says with a bit of a stutter.

"I appreciate my beautiful wife and my mom making all of the meals today," Tate says. "If we're making a kitchen rotation, I'd like to be in on it. Sarah and I usually share the cooking and cleaning at home, and this should continue here."

Sarah gives Tate a look I can only describe as adoring. Many others chime in on the cooking and cleaning, and it's soon decided these chores, along with caring for the gardens, will be put on a schedule.

Deanne is put in charge of the schedule and will try to have it set up tomorrow. It's decided breakfast, for now, will be self-serve based on what people brought along.

Jake rubs a hand across the back of his neck. "Okay, so, tomorrow will be a busy day. We'll get the chores done, make a run to town, do some shooting practice, plus get Art and Leo set up in their new places."

As the group breaks up, Leo pulls me aside. "Katie, I'd like you to come with us tomorrow."

"Sorry, Leo. I've already decided to stay and help out here. Plus, Olivia's coming over with her children to use the shower."

Leo purses his lips. "I'll see if Jake can do without me. I'll stick around in case you need me."

"Why?"

"Terry's death . . . it wasn't an accident."

"What do you mean?"

"He didn't just fall and hit his head. His head was bashed in. I think it was meant to look like an accident, but it wasn't. Phil saw it too. He had one of the other neighbors, a retired police detective, take a look. Evan, who's a retired police officer, and the one they call Deputy Fred were there also. Everyone thought the same thing—it was staged. We don't even think he was killed where we found him. The blood wasn't right."

I don't know what to say about them suspecting murder. Instead, I say something really dumb, "It's good Mom and Jake have lots of retired police officers and military in the neighborhood. Lots of government workers too. Mom said more than half of the retired people are state, federal, or military retired. Good to have a cop when you need one, even if they're retired."

Leo gives me a strange look. Then I start to cry. I have no idea why I'm crying . . . again. But I am. Leo holds me tight and says nothing. It only takes me a couple minutes to get myself together this time.

"I'm sorry about this, Leo. I don't know why I keep crying."

"I understand. Things are an absolute mess right now, and having this murder happen so close to here . . . well, I'm concerned."

"You think it's Dan Morse?"

"Seems likely with the trouble they had last night at the meeting . . . and the meeting the night before. If it is, he didn't seem too fond of Jake either, which is worrisome. And he seemed way too fond of the lady you were talking with tonight. He was watching her. But just because it seems likely, doesn't mean it was him. Someone could've had a beef with Terry and took advantage of his fight with Morse, choosing to take out Terry and cast suspicion on Morse."

I nod, agreeing it makes sense. "Olivia. Her name's Olivia. You think he'd hurt her or Jake?"

"I don't know. Probably not if we were still living in normal times. But right now, he likely realizes we're on our own. There's no sheriff to call. We have Deputy Fred, but I don't think he's an actual deputy. I think he's a jailer. Of course, like you said, there are many retired police officers around here.

"I think I've met a dozen just since last night, even three couples that were both police officers—husband and wife. And I've met *more* than a dozen retired or former military. There are even a few lawyers and at least one judge. They could set up quite the judicial system here, if needed. I wonder what brought all of these people here? They aren't even from the same places. It's pretty interesting."

I shrug, not really understanding what Leo's getting at.

Chapter 26

Tuesday, Day 6

I made sure to set my alarm so I'd be up before Jake and everyone leaves. It goes off at 6:00 a.m., but I hit the snooze several times and finally crawl out of bed closer to 6:30. I notice I'm pretty achy and figure it's my lack of exercise the past few days. A run is in order this morning.

Art, true to his word, is helping with the chores; he's walking one of the goats back to the pen. When Mom's home, she does most of the milking. Jake helps, but he always says his hands are too big since the goats are dwarfs instead of full-size. Malcolm was taught how to milk and has been milking just about every day with Mom gone.

Malcolm's practically giddy at breakfast because the goat Sarah was keeping an eye on kidded overnight. She had triplets, and Malcolm helped move them to what he calls the "nursery pen" so the other goats won't bother the new mom and babies.

Jake arranged shooting lessons with Evan. Evan is going on the supply run this morning, so lessons will be later. He and Doris are out of cash, but Jake made an arrangement to help him get things he finds and needs in exchange for the lessons.

"Jake, I'd like you to take the cash I have left. Please spend it on whatever you think we can use." Leo hands Jake a bundle of bills.

"Sure, Leo. I'll do what I can. I want to make sure we're prepared for today. I was thinking others might start to realize we're in this for the long haul. They might think cash is no longer king. Can you and Katie give me a hand?"

"Me too, Dad?" Malcolm asks.

"Yep, you too, Buddy. How about you grab some of those plastic grocery bags, maybe a dozen or so, then meet us in the storage section of the basement."

"Sure, Dad. Be right there."

In the basement, Jake opens a closet. It's full of small toiletry items like you'd find in the travel aisle of the grocery store, plus matches, four-packs of batteries, candles, disposable diapers packaged in plastic zipper bags, small packages of feminine hygiene products, airplane-sized bottles of booze, and a few other things.

"Wow, Jake. Quite the stash."

"Yeah. We put this stuff together specifically to use for barter. I don't want to take too much of it today, but put one or two of each item in the bags Malcolm brings down. Don't fill them too full. I don't want it to be evident how much we have of anything."

"All right. Sounds like a good plan."

"Leo, can you grab one of those boxes over there and put a couple of small propane canisters in it? Throw in some rings and flats from the canning shelves too. And let's grab a case of quart jars and a case of pints. Open the packaging but leave them in the box for ease of transport. I'm going to grab a couple cans of diesel and gas also."

"Uh, sir . . . Jake, do you think this is a good idea?" Leo asks.

Jake gives him a questioning look.

"I mean, do you think it's safe to flash these things around?"

"Oh, well, that's something to think about. I'll definitely be discreet. But I have to admit, I'm glad Evan's coming. He'll be security."

"I'm glad he is also, sir," Leo says. "I think you should be prepared for anything today. Everyone who feels comfortable going armed, should."

Jake scratches his arm as he shakes his head. "Truthfully, I don't think any of us, except Evan, are used to carrying on a daily basis. Tim and Tate have done quite a bit of shooting. I carry when hunting and hiking because of the bears and mountain lions here.

"So just the three of us and Evan. None of the others have shot enough to feel okay with it. Or, in Keith's case, it's been so long he isn't sure of himself. He did say he's happy to bring a shotgun, but he doesn't want to carry a handgun. Sarah and Lois both say they'll wait until after they have training. Same with Roy."

Leo nods in understanding. "Better to have people unarmed than not knowing what they're doing. That could be a recipe for disaster. It'll be good to get everyone some training. Hopefully no one will ever need to draw a weapon, but if they do . . . "

It's not long until Evan shows up and everyone loads to go. It's quite the caravan again. Jake's in his truck, towing his large utility trailer, and riding with him is Roy. Evan's also towing a trailer, the enclosed kind. Sarah, Keith, and Lois are with Tate in his Dodge Ram, towing his small utility trailer. Tim and Art are bringing up the rear, towing the flatbed.

As I watch them drive away, I wonder where Mom is. Will she get home today?

"You want to go for a run with me?" I ask Leo.

"Sure, a short one. Let's get ready and I'll tell Alvin so he can . . . so he knows."

I shake my head, wondering if we're going to have to be on alert for danger every waking minute from now on.

We go about three miles round trip. While we're running, I think a lot about our new life and especially Terry's death. It all seems so senseless—the plane crashes, the bridges, the food poisonings, the cyberattacks, our elected officials being assassinated, and Terry being killed so close to our new home.

After our run, I head inside to get ready for the day. I'm just out of the basement shower and going to the garden to help Angela and Calley when Olivia's car pulls into the driveway.

I holler over to my sisters, saying I'm going to get Olivia situated and then I'll be out to help. Angela gives me a wave; Calley laughs and says something I don't fully catch but sounds like, "Sure you will."

"Hi, Olivia!" I shout in greeting while she's helping the children out.

"Hey there, Katie. Thanks so much for setting this up for us. We're a little early. I hope that's okay?"

"No problem. I think Leo may still be in the shower. We just returned from a run. Should be just a minute or two."

"That's fine. I wonder if I could take some extra water so I can wash a few things? We're starting to run low on clean clothes."

"Sure. Did you bring jugs? Or better yet, did you bring your clothes? We can stick them in the wash. Can't dry them, but we can wash them."

"Your washer's working?"

"Solar panels. As long as the sun's shining, there's enough power for the washing machine. Do you want to run home and bring a load back?"

"You think that'd be okay?"

"Why not? No one's doing laundry right now, as far as I know. We can put the load in after you all shower."

Leo walks out of the house. After greetings and brief small talk, he says, "Shower's free for whoever's next."

"You want to run and get laundry?" I ask Olivia. "Tony can start his shower, and I'll play with Lily."

Olivia agrees. I take Tony and Lily in the house, show Tony the main-floor guest bathroom, and sit with Lily in the living room while we read a book. Olivia returns within twenty minutes, knocking at the front door. One look at her face and I can tell something's wrong.

Before I get a chance to ask, she says, "Dan Morse was at my place when I got back there. He made it quite clear he knew I'd come over here. He left after a couple minutes, but I think he may be watching my house. I didn't want him to know we're doing laundry, so I put the clothes in this box."

"Good thinking."

What is up with that crazy guy? I can only assume he has a thing for Olivia. I briefly consider telling Olivia about Leo's concern but decide against it. She's freaked out enough. Instead, I say, "There's something strange about that guy."

"You're telling me. He seemed very nice at first. A little off, but harmless. Now, he seems even more off and not so harmless. I half wonder if he didn't have something to do with Terry dying. Do you know if it was an accident?"

I decide to play dumb. "I don't know much. Maybe we'll learn more at tonight's meeting."

When Tony comes out of the bathroom, Olivia and Lily take their turns in the shower, then we put their laundry in to wash. While it's washing, I check with Angela and Calley in the garden but see they're about done. Sarah, Lois, and Karen really did a good job getting the garden under control yesterday.

I help Leo clean the motorhome—his new house. Art will take the small trailer. Malcolm shows Tony his newest LEGO set while Olivia and Lily wander around visiting the livestock, garden, and who knows what else. When the washing machine completes its cycle, they take the wet laundry home to hang on their line.

As Olivia's getting ready to leave, I caution her to be careful and to let me know if she needs anything.

Leo and I have the motorhome ready for occupancy and have started organizing the building materials. A few minutes before one o'clock, a vehicle begins to pull the hill. Ah, these wide-open spaces and the way sounds travels. Makes it hard for cars to sneak up on us.

"Right on time. Sounds like our group may be home," Leo says.

I nod in agreement as the hood of Jake's pickup crests the hill. We continue to watch, then both look at each other in amazement when we notice the third vehicle back is a frozen food company home delivery truck with Tate hanging half out the window, waving like a madman. He then gives the horn a little toot.

"This ought to be good," Leo says, as we move toward the driveway.

Chapter 27

Tate barely has the frozen food truck stopped before he's bouncing out. The excitement of the group arriving home and Tate's horn honking has everyone gathered around, all talking at once.

Those who just returned have huge smiles on their faces—but none as big as Tate's. When Sarah walks up, Tate wraps her in a hug, lifting her from the ground before twirling her in a circle. She throws back her head and laughs. He sets her on the ground with a kiss.

"She's full up. Well, mostly."

Several questions ring out. Tate raises his hand. "Wait, wait. I'll tell everyone about it. Just give me a minute." He lets out a noisy breath and hugs Sarah close.

"We were in a little town in Montana. Everyone but Sarah and I went into the feed store. Since this was our third or fourth stop, we stayed with the vehicles, just to keep an eye on things. It was only a few minutes later when I saw this home delivery truck pull up.

"The guy got out and hung a big sign off the truck, saying he had items for sale. You all have probably seen the same thing parked alongside the road. We used to see one guy in Oregon at a park all the time. Anyway, I told Sarah I was going to go see what he had. An ice cream sandwich sounded kind of good.

"He had another guy with him in an older Toyota truck, and both of them were in their delivery-man uniforms. They were selling for double regular cost in cash or trading for things. I bought Sarah and I each a sundae cone, with plans to buy one for everyone when they came out of the feed store. While Sarah and I ate our cones, we noticed lots of people going over but not many people buying things.

"I figured most people were caught without cash, so they couldn't purchase treats. I noticed the guys had a sign out listing things they'd trade for. A few people went away and soon returned with trade items. I started wondering why they came in two different vehicles. Gas is in short supply and was one of the things they wanted to trade, so why two vehicles?

"When everyone came out of the feed store, I let them know I'd buy them an ice cream but also mentioned my thinking on why the two vehicles. Evan suggested maybe they planned to sell all they could and then leave the delivery truck. So I wondered if it might be worth trying to make some big purchases. At that point, I wasn't sure what all they had in it since I'd only asked for the cones."

"Yeah," Evan adds. "Once Tate mentioned the extra car, it seemed they might have just brought a few things to get rid of and then planned to ditch it. But it did seem worth finding out more."

Tate bobs his head like it's on a string. "Exactly. I asked Evan if he wanted to go over with me while I got cones for everyone and see what we could find out. Turns out, one guy is the warehouse manager at the company's DC—the distribution center. The other guy's a route driver and does the route in the town we were in, plus many other little towns.

"They have everything on generator, keeping the frozen stuff frozen, but are running low on fuel. While they were taking cash for things, they really wanted diesel, gas, and propane. It seems they've kind of taken over the DC, may have even moved their families into the offices. They didn't come right out and say this, but we pieced things together and that's what we think.

"Jake and Evan had both brought fuel, and Jake had a five-pound propane he brought to trade, along with several one pounds. While there are lots of ice cream treats—or there were, at least—the truck is full of lots of other things. Seems the DC had just received a restock on Friday before everything fell apart."

Evan interrupts, "They hadn't even loaded all the trucks yet. And they did plan to sell what they could, load the Toyota with anything left, and ditch the truck. They have several more trucks at the DC."

Tate nods. "So we got the fully loaded truck for Jake and Evan's fuel, propane, and a few other trade things like—"

Sarah jumps in, "Diapers, feminine products, booze, you know, the stuff Jake brought along."

"I found it surprising they'd want to sell food," Lois says. "If I had a warehouse full of food, I'd want to hold on to it."

"I asked them about that," Evan says. "They said they don't have the fuel to power all the freezers much longer, so they're trying to home-can some of the meats. Jake offered a dozen canning jars and I had a box of lids. This truck's really loaded, but from the looks of it, most everything is breaded or processed. No steaks or things that can be prepared for long-term storage. Smart on their part. Still, they either have a whole lot of food at the DC or they really misjudged how much to get rid of. I've never been to a warehouse like that, so I don't really know what it might be like."

"What about the truck?" I ask.

"We told them when this is all over, we'll take the truck back where we met them so they could pick it up," Tate says. "They gave us a look like they didn't think things would be over any time soon."

"So how's the freezer work?" I ask. "Does it keep things frozen as long as the truck's running?"

"Yes, exactly." Tate bobs his head. "Or we can plug it in to keep it freezing. There's all kinds of stuff—assorted styles of chicken, beef, bacon, fish, potpies, pizzas, and stir fries, plus lots of ice cream. Once we finished our deal, the guys took off and we offered to sell food to anyone still wanting to buy. There weren't many people who had cash, but we did trade for a few things. And we handed out ice cream treats to everyone gathered around, so we do have a bit less of the treats than we started with."

Everyone comments on how nice it was to pass out ice cream to people.

"I have to admit," Jake says, "I feel a little bad about how we did this deal since it wasn't really their stuff to trade away. But I guess we'll see a lot of this if things don't change rapidly."

Several of us nod in agreement as Jake continues speaking, "Evan's going to choose some things for Doris and him since some of his stuff was used for trading, and he's also taking it as partial payment for the shooting lessons, along with some meat he and I made a deal with on Saturday at a little mom-and-pop store. The bulk of the foods are precooked, heat-and-eat things.

"I think we'd be smart to use the truck stuff first. We can plug it into the solar-powered outlet in the garage and share power with my parents' freezer, but the sooner we empty it, the better. Most of the meals are pretty highly processed, so while it will fill our stomachs, it's not the best nutrition. I also bought a few TV dinners at the mom-and-pop store, so we'll definitely have our fill of processed foods."

Sarah waves a hand. "You know, I'm not a fan of processed foods. But as busy as we are, it'll be helpful to have these quick meals now. That'll free everyone up to do other things. I think, once all of the truck food is gone, we should work on emptying out the freezer in the basement."

"Agreed," Jake says with a nod. "We'll talk more about the plans for that. Looks like Doris is on her way down here." Jake turns to Deanne. "Do we have enough lunch made so Doris and Evan can join us?"

"Yes, I think so. Especially if we can add ice cream for dessert," she answers with a smile.

When Doris arrives, she hears the tale of how they brought home the truck filled with frozen foods. Tate and Evan tell it with even more flair the second time around. After lunch, we all enjoy an ice cream treat, then ooh and ahh over what the truck contains.

While the contents of the truck aren't split evenly between our tribe and the Snyders, it does seem fair. Jake put quite a bit more in for trade goods and ended up with about two-thirds to Evan's one-third. Jake also brings out some of the meat from a previous shopping excursion.

When the power went out Saturday, Jake and Evan went into town for fuel and whatever else they could find. The town's chain stores were closed, but a small mom-and-pop market was open. The owner offered Jake all the meats and cheeses in the refrigerator area, plus everything in the freezer case.

I think Evan had planned, at the time, to pay for a portion of it, but trading for our gun training seems smart. Jake puts this all in the delivery truck with the rest of their stuff and asks Evan how it looks.

It's decided Evan and Doris will leave their portion in the truck in a designated area. They're using their generator to keep their freezers going right now, while Doris tries to preserve as much meat as possible via canning and jerky. She borrowed one of Mom's pressure canners and had just finished two canner loads before coming down.

We should probably be doing the same thing. One of my finds in Pryor yesterday was a large amount of spring greens, which need to be dehydrated or something. I'll have to talk with Sarah and Angela to see what they think we should do. Or maybe they should just be the focus of meals for a couple of days. Could we freeze them?

Jake and Mom have two freezers. One is in their mudroom pantry, always plugged into the solar system. The second, in the basement, is usually on the grid electric but is currently connected to the solar system.

Because the solar system isn't huge, they can't keep both freezers connected at the same time, so Jake's been swapping the power by using some kind of timer device to keep things frozen and using the generator as backup.

Grandpa and Grandma's freezer in the garage is on the garage solar system. Even though everything is okay now, it makes sense to have only one freezer connected to the house for simplicity's sake, if nothing else. Plus, I wonder how smart it is to use the generator so much with the fuel issues. No, freezing isn't a good idea.

I've never canned. I know the basics from helping Mom years ago. I didn't find it to be an enjoyable job at all. I do remember some things need to be pressure canned and others can be water bath canned. I wonder if Sarah or Angela know? I don't think Calley does. Mom used a book when canning. Maybe, if we can find it, we can do the canning on our own.

As I'm thinking of canning, I realize Evan's asking who all is going for weapons training. It seems all of us except Grandma Dodie and baby Gavin want to go. Malcolm's told he can go along too. Jake bought him a new .22 the other day, and it needs to be sighted in.

He has a single-shot youth model .22 he's shot a lot. In fact, he's taken one of Evan's lessons before. Nothing in-depth, just basic safety and training. Rumor has it, Evan nicknamed him "Dead-Eye" after his marksmanship skills. I wonder if I'll get a nickname? I doubt it'd be as cool as Dead-Eye.

Chapter 28

We divide into groups based on experience so Evan doesn't have all of us at one time. There are more beginners—the class I'm in—than intermediate, so he divides the beginners into two groups. He takes my group first. Even though I have my newly purchased handgun, I'm told to leave it at home. Today, I'll use one of the school guns.

We spend over an hour in the classroom learning about gun safety before we go out to the range. Most of this I've heard before, *"All guns are always loaded. Never let the muzzle cover anything you aren't willing to destroy. Keep your finger off the trigger until your sights are on the target. Be sure of your target."* But somehow, it seems a lot more serious knowing we'll soon be putting these rules into practice.

When we finish in the classroom, Doris gets the second group of beginners to start their classroom training while my class heads to the shooting range. Jake joins to assist at the range.

To say I'm nervous would be an understatement. Sure, I've shot before with Leo and a .22 rifle with Jake, but to think I'll learn to use my personal handgun and become comfortable enough with it to carry on my body is almost overwhelming.

The shooting range is outdoors. They've set it up with two areas, with a third larger range in a different location. The two ranges are backed by a wall of dirt, similar to the setup Mom and Jake have.

Lois, Karen, and Sarah are in my group. They look as nervous as I feel. When we get to the range, Evan gives us the range rules. These include the rules we learned in the classroom plus, *"Keep the gun unloaded until you're at the firing line and the range is declared 'hot.' Immediately stop firing if you hear 'cease fire.' When the range is cold, there can be no handling; weapons are emptied, left open, and laid on the firing bench. Only Evan can declare the range 'hot,' and only then can we commence firing."*

I'm so nervous my mouth goes dry. I'm pretty sure Evan realizes how I'm feeling. As he's setting us up in individual positions on the firing bench, he ushers me over. "Katie, I have the perfect gun for you to start with."

My stomach falls and my eyes bulge. On the shooting bench is an extremely large handgun. From what we learned in the classroom, along with the little I already know of guns, it's some kind of revolver. Maybe the kind that Dirty Harry guy carried in the movie Jake likes? I'm not sure, but I know I'm not going to enjoy it. Guns kick, and with the size of that gun, I'm sure to land on my bottom if I try to shoot it.

"Uh . . . Evan, I think that gun's way too big for me."

Evan smiles, showing off his crooked front tooth. "Your mom said the same thing when she took her first handgun class, and I set her up with this. Trust me. You'll be fine."

"Okay. I guess. What is it?"

"It's a Colt Python .357 Magnum. We'll load it with .38 Special rounds. I know you're thinking, 'This is a big scary gun, and it's going to knock me down when I shoot it.' It won't. It really absorbs the recoil. And loaded with the .38s, it should be just fine for you."

Uh-huh. I'd like to believe him, but I seriously have my doubts. He then goes on to help Lois, Sarah, and Karen. They're also all shooting .357 revolvers—but none look as scary as mine. They're much smaller.

The one Sarah's given is my mom's revolver, which Jake loaned Evan for the class. Evan tells Sarah it's a Ruger SP101 without a hammer. I remember Mom mentioning this gun before, how she thought she'd love it for concealed carry because the lack of a hammer is supposed to make it snag free—which I guess means easy to draw. But she found it hard to shoot. Something about a heavy trigger pull. She still keeps it but doesn't conceal carry it. She calls it her "house gun."

Sarah must remember this too. "Didn't my mom decide she doesn't like this gun?"

"I don't think she loves it," Evan answers. "She still practices with it on a regular basis and can shoot it just fine, more than fine. But she keeps it at home instead of taking it out since she prefers her Springfield for carrying."

Evan makes sure Karen and Lois are all set. Then Evan helps each of us determine if we're right or left eye dominate, and we do several dry fires, making sure we're observing the safety rules. He asks us all if we're ready to live fire. The other three nod eagerly. Me, not so much. I'm still wondering why he gave me this giant gun.

Evan declares the range "hot." We're each told to put on our ear and eye protection, then are each instructed to put in only one round under his watchful eye, with Jake standing by to assist as needed.

Evan's between Sarah and me at the range bench. We're in seated positions, using beanbag-like things to secure our guns. Evan says it'll help us get the feel for it, shooting from this position instead of starting out standing. We'll soon see how much fun this can be. I'm very doubtful and am really feeling a knot in my stomach. *What was I thinking?*

When I went to the gun range with Leo and shot his little .22, it was fun. Sure, he went over all of the safety stuff and made sure I knew the range rules. But I never felt this ache in my stomach. I can't explain why I feel it now. Somehow, I manage to get set up. I'm trying to calm myself with deep breathing.

"Take a deep breath and let it out. Take another deep breath and let it out. Then pull up on the slack in the trigger. On your third breath, take it in and let it out partway, then gently squeeze the trigger."

It takes me two cycles of the deep breathing before I feel comfortable enough to squeeze the trigger. I'm shocked when it goes off. It not only scares me a little, but it doesn't have much kick at all. And I even hit the target. Not right on the bullseye, but not too shabby. Most shocking of all is, it wasn't terrible. Not terrible at all.

We continue practicing for quite a while. I shoot somewhere around twenty-five rounds, with my comfort level and aim improving each time. We each have an opportunity to try all the guns available. Evan was right, the big scary gun I shot first was the most comfortable to use. I really liked it the best.

Toward the end of our shooting, we all switch to standing position. I'm so glad we didn't start with this. I can't believe how tiring it gets.

We finish as Doris is bringing down the next group. I notice it's not only the other beginners but the intermediate people also. Doris will work with them on the alternate range, while Evan works with the beginners.

After the beginners and intermediates are finished, people with more experience—like Jake, Tim, and Tate—will practice drawing to help increase their comfort level. Like Malcolm, Jake has a new rifle or two that need sighting in, so that's also on the agenda.

Leo's going to sight my new rifle in for me, then I'll shoot it tomorrow or the next day, and Mike's going to sight the one Calley picked out. Right now, Leo's on transportation detail, hauling people back and forth for the classes.

I feel good. Even a little proud. My arms and back hurt slightly, but in a way that reminds me I did something I wasn't sure I could do. The four of us "beginners" chatter to Leo on the way back to the house about how great it was and how we can't wait to do it again.

"It's good you want to shoot again," Leo says. "I think the plan is daily range practice so you can get comfortable. You'll take your own weapons tomorrow for another class with Evan or Doris, then we'll start using the range your folks have."

Karen looks a little crestfallen. "I don't have a gun."

"Me neither," Lois and Sarah both add.

"I think there's a plan in place for that," Leo answers.

Leo drops us off and returns to the shooting range to help as needed. We start talking about dinner. Even though Calley and Deanne are in charge tonight, they're in the current beginners' class. We decide we'll handle it and unanimously vote to serve a variety of single-serve main dish meals out of the freezer truck, along with a big salad from the garden. Since we're cooking for such a large group, we'll use the oven in the house and the oven in the bunkhouse.

Grandma Dodie joins us in the kitchen with Gavin, while Karen and Lois take dinners over to cook in the much smaller bunkhouse oven. We quickly assemble a salad and are soon regretting our decision to use the oven as the house rapidly heats up. We move to the covered deck on the north side to enjoy the shade and the slight breeze. We can hear the shooters on the range quite well from here.

"The sky's clouding up. I wonder if it'll rain." Sarah points to the mountains.

Grandma Dodie says she thinks it might; the breeze has a crispness to it. Hopefully the shooters will finish before the rain hits.

Lois and Grandma Dodie seem to get along very well. They're soon conversing about everything under the sun.

When the conversation turns to the situation we're in, it halts a bit until Grandma Dodie says, "None of us really want to be here. Alvin and I'd much rather be at home, but we're glad Jake came and picked us up. We're stubborn enough we would've stayed there as everything collapsed around us. Even if the town started burning, like Katie's town did, we would've been hard-pressed to leave. We sure hate asking for help. Jake knows this about us and didn't push. Instead, he made it seem like our idea to come out here. I'm glad."

"We were so scared at Sarah and Tate's place in Billings," Lois says. "Things started going bad fast. Even though nothing happened right by their house, we kept hearing sirens and knew there was trouble. After the bridges were hit, more people came into the city. We never did figure out where they were coming from. As far as we know, there weren't any bridges hit close by. Seattle, sure . . . but that seems way too far away for Billings to be affected. I don't know."

No one says anything for a bit, then Lois starts again, "When Sarah and Tate suggested coming here, we didn't want to. We'd only met Jake and Mollie the one time at Sarah and Tate's wedding. We knew they had a little farm but had no idea it was like this. We were sure we'd be imposing. And I still think we are, but at the same time, I can see how having a few extra hands to help will be beneficial. And, truthfully, I'm very thankful we're not in Tulsa right now. I can only imagine how bad it is there."

At this, Karen begins to cry. Sarah pats her arm but says nothing. Lois and Sarah are also misty eyed. Not Grandma Dodie. She remains steadfast, staring into the distance. I silently step away to check on the food in the oven and allow them a little time.

After checking on the oven in the main house and finding a few things ready, I poke my head out and ask if it's all right for me to go check on the bunkhouse food.

"Of course," Lois says, "but let me go along in case things are ready."

I grab two large cookie sheets to carry the dinners back. As we walk to the bunkhouse, Lois comments on how the shooting has stopped. We both look toward the Snyders' house and see a truck pulling away from the place followed by a second.

"Looks like Jake and Leo," I say. "I guess they're on their way back. Good, the food's about ready."

The few dishes in the small oven are finished. We add additional meals to the oven, which can cook while our group starts on what's ready.

Sarah and Karen have set things out on the back patio. With the dishes from the bunkhouse, we have quite a spread. Along with two large bowls of salad, there's an array of frozen convenience meals:

chicken alfredo, spaghetti, macaroni and cheese, lasagna, sweet and sour chicken with rice, and roasted turkey with vegetables.

"We put more in the oven in the bunkhouse," Lois says.

"Perfect." Sarah taps her mother-in-law on the hand. "There are still potpies to come out of the oven. They took the longest to cook. Should be ten minutes or so, so we can start with this."

The trucks pull in the yard, and everyone unloads. They're a jubilant group. Especially Malcolm, who asks over and over, "Did you see me shoot? That's why they call me Dead-Eye. I like shooting the handgun and my new rifle, Dad. *It's* amazing."

Jake tells Malcolm he did really well and to go wash for supper.

Deanne and Calley thank us for putting the meal together as others chime in.

"If you all need to wash up, go ahead," Lois says. "It's ready now."

Everyone scatters to wash the gun powder and assorted gunk from their hands. Once everyone has gathered back, Grandpa Alvin says, "I know there may be others here who don't believe the same as I do, and I respect that, but I think we should express our thanks to God for this meal. Jake, would you do the honors?"

Jake, never really comfortable speaking in public, and especially shy about praying out loud, takes a deep breath before saying, "Of course. Our Heavenly Father, we thank You for this meal and the hands which have prepared it. Thank you for bringing us all together. I ask You watch over Mollie and bring her home to us safely. Amen."

Several amens follow.

Jake's prayer, while short and slightly awkward, really touches me. Is God calling me back? Mom and Jake have a neighborhood Bible study they go to. Maybe I could start going with them?

I realize I'm woolgathering when Leo touches my arm and asks if I'm ready to grab some food. I tell him to go ahead, I need to see if the other dinners are ready. Sarah catches my eye, and we go together.

Once we have the remaining dinners brought out, I fix my plate. I share a potpie with Sarah, which turns out to be sirloin, and take a little lasagna, chicken alfredo, and sweet and sour chicken along with salad.

"Did we make much of a dent in the freezer meals?" Tate asks, still looking proud over his deal.

"Nope. Not really," Lois responds. "We didn't even touch the skillet meals, pizzas, and appetizers."

"Everyone has done well at clearing out and organizing the garage, so I'm going to pull the freezer truck inside," Jake says. "The less people who know we have it, the better. And as soon as we can get it emptied out a bit, we'll move everything to the small freezer I keep in the processing room. It'll use less juice than the truck, and we can get rid of the truck all together."

Everyone agrees this is a good idea.

"I'm on cleanup," Tate says. "Who's helping me? Sarah, Mom— not you. If you cooked dinner, you're not cleaning up." Tim and Leo both volunteer, and Art says he'll help Jake with the chores.

"We'd best hurry," Jake says. "There's another meeting at seven tonight. Mom, did you monitor the radio today?"

"I did," Grandma Dodie says. "Except for the time we were fixing supper. I left it in the apartment while we were on the deck. I didn't even think about taking it with me."

"That's fine, Mom. Was there anything new?"

"Why, no, there wasn't. The last update I heard was right after the girls came back from shooting. There was talk on the cyberattack and the assassinations, but nothing new was announced."

"Does that mean things are getting back to normal, Dad?" Malcolm asks.

"I'm not sure. It's good there were no new attacks today. That'll definitely help."

Chapter 29

To conserve fuel, almost everyone packs into one vehicle. Thanks to needing to take the generator, five of us don't fit, so we wait for the Synders to come by and pile in with them. Leo and I ride in the bed.

I had suggested Sheila and Karen ride with us since Jake's truck was packed full, but Angela said, "Nope. We're all riding together." Then she raised her eyebrows at me and gave me a goofy look. Grandma Dodie stays home with Malcolm and Gavin. Tonight, Tim stays behind.

Leo and I sit close to each other, leaning our backs against the cab. We talk about everything and nothing on the way to the meeting. We hold hands and pretend like all is normal. I'm very glad we have the truck bed to ourselves.

We're getting close to the community center when Leo says, "I want to talk with you about something."

"Sure, what's up?"

"Well, you know how we've been together as a couple for a while now?"

I'm suddenly concerned. The way his voice sounds isn't the normal Leo. I cautiously answer, "Yes?"

"And you know I love you. I mean, you definitely know, right?"

"Sure. What's going on?"

He sighs. "It's just that . . . well, I want to be sure we respect the rules of your parents' home. Even though I'm living out in the motorhome now and not staying in the house, I want to . . . well, I guess I want to do things right. I think we ought to not . . . I don't think you ought to come for any, uh, visits to the motorhome."

I search his face, trying to understand exactly what he's saying. He's a bit flushed, and I realize it's a blush. He's embarrassed. *Oh!* No visits to the motorhome . . . I get it. Maybe we're on the same wavelength and both are feeling conviction about not living together until marriage. Even so, I can't resist having a little fun with him.

"Okay, I understand what you're saying. And how long do you want to not have these . . . visits?"

Leo gives me a small smile. "I think we should wait until we get married." My heart skips a little beat as he continues, "And believe me, I want to marry you. I'm not asking you right now, in the back of a pickup truck on the way to a meeting that's sure to be interesting, but I will. I promise you, I will."

I let out a big sigh. "I know you're right. I've been thinking the same thing. If I'm being honest, I've never felt completely right about us living together. You know, as much as I enjoy being with you, that's a big part of why I didn't tell my mom and Jake about us living together. I felt a little guilty."

"We'll start fresh, Katie. We'll do this right. I know living together and everything that goes with it is commonly accepted. Like you, I felt a little guilty, too, but since everyone else was doing it . . . I don't think I want to be like everyone else. I have to wonder if a good reason we're living in such a mess right now isn't because of the moral decay of society."

"Wow, Leo, such big words." I smile and give him a playful jab to the arm.

He laughs. "Yeah, I've been thinking about it some. I heard Jake and Malcolm talking about a Bible passage they'd read, about how husbands are to love their wives as Christ loves the church, and it got me to thinking. Even though I was going to church almost every week, I haven't exactly lived a life based on the Bible. I want to change. I want to be . . . more. More for you, and I definitely want to be more for the children we'll someday have."

I can't help but smile. "Thank you, Leo."

We pull into the driveway of the community center. There are more people here tonight than last night. Everyone's talking about Terry's death, the assassinations, the power outage, and the lack of news. Many thought it strange nothing new happened today.

A few suggest it's part of the plan, the terrorists have done enough damage and can now just sit back and watch Americans fight Americans. After all, look what happened to poor Terry. A terrorist didn't kill him. I saw the word *accident* referred to in quotations several times when Terry's death was mentioned.

Dan Morse is here but standing back from the group. He appears to be listening but not participating. Many of the people we met last night and the night before are also here.

Even though the president isn't supposed to speak, Doris hooks up her speakers and turns the radio on a minute or so before seven so we can listen to the evening update.

Without preamble, the announcer says, "*It is 7:00 p.m. mountain time. Our reserves are running low, so we'll be dropping our broadcasts to one time per day at 7:00 p.m. We will also broadcast any time there's an urgent alert via the Emergency Alert System. Our sister station, KWDI at 870 AM, will broadcast one time per day at 7:00 a.m., in addition to any EAS broadcasts.*

"*Folks, today, I feel like no news is good news, at least on a national level. We haven't heard of any new attacks. Of course, our country is devastated by what has happened over the previous several days, but we're hopeful.*

"*Unfortunately, the news near home is not as good. An incident at the Prospect hospital resulted in many deaths. A gunfight of some sort broke out followed by a fire, which consumed the building. With the lack of water, the hospital was a total loss. Among the dead were several doctors, nurses, staff, and patients. We don't really have the exact details on what happened, we just know the end result.*

"*With the loss of the hospital and medical personnel, those in need of medical attention should go to the urgent care on First Street. For advanced medical needs, the hospital in Billings is functioning at limited capacity. There is not an ambulance service, so you're encouraged to find your own transportation to Billings if you feel the need to go there. You could also try Cody, but we're unsure of their status. Our attempts to reach out to our contacts in Cody have failed.*

"*Because of local incidents such as this, you're asked to stay in your home from sunset to sunrise. Remember who the enemy is. Your neighbor didn't crash airplanes, destroy bridges, or assassinate senators. Remember, you live in Wyoming. We're a different breed than most. We're tough. We have to be. Cowboy up and get through this.*"

Silence. No sign off, nothing.

A lady standing near us says, "Oh no, not the hospital."

Several others say, "What will we do?" or, "I don't have enough fuel to go to Billings or Cody," and similar things.

I think about the boy and girl we helped in the car accident. Were they transferred to Prospect? The police officer said the boy would need to either go there or Billings for surgery. I pray it was Billings and he's still safe.

Phil Hudson walks over to the picnic table, which has become the speaking area.

"Good evening, friends," he says loudly. "While we ponder this latest tragedy, which is hitting way too close to home, let's talk about today's needs for us right now. Jake and his crew have the generator running, so you can fill your containers.

"Kelley, Doris, and Sarah will be around if any of you need to add your name to the *available to help* or *need assistance* lists. If you need assistance, see either Kelley or Doris. Ladies, wave your hands so people can see where you are. Good. Sarah's the one to see if you can help out others. Sarah, let us see where you are. Okay."

Phil pauses for a second, dropping his shoulders and letting out a sigh. "Belinda asked me to share with you, there will be a service for Terry tomorrow. They took him into Prospect today, but because of the amount of work the mortuaries have, they've made arrangements to bury him at home.

"The service will be tomorrow afternoon at three o'clock. In the interest of supporting Belinda and conserving fuel, I'd like to suggest we meet tomorrow after the services instead of waiting until seven. Kelley and I also thought we could have a potluck of sorts when we meet."

"I think it's a wonderful idea," Doris says loudly. "I'll bring pulled elk in a barbecue sauce."

"I'll bring baked beans," adds another lady.

Someone says she has lettuce in her garden and will bring a salad.

Tate whispers to Jake, and Jake nods. "We'll bring assorted appetizers," Tate announces.

Many others add what they'll be bringing. Several people remain quiet.

"It sounds like we'll have plenty of food," Evan says. "Phil, do you think we need to limit people eating the food to only those bringing something?"

"Not at all," Phil answers. "I think everyone who attends the funeral to support Belinda and TJ should know they're welcome to the meal following the service. If you don't want to join the service

216

or the meal, come between 5:30 and 6:00 for water. Does that sound good to everyone?" He looks around for agreement.

I look at Dan Morse, who's shaking his head and making grandiose gestures. I guess he doesn't like the sounds of it. I also suspect he isn't going to be paying his respects at the funeral tomorrow. I do think he'd like to show up for the meal, though, and the way Phil phrased it, he won't be welcome.

I wonder for a minute if he could be hungry. Maybe they're out of food at their house and this is part of his reasoning for wanting to get things from others. I have no problem with feeding hungry people, but this guy is so strange.

Olivia and her children are near the playground. I tell Leo I'm going to go visit. He tells me he's going to see if he can help with the water.

"Hi, Olivia. How was your day?"

"Okay. I really appreciate the . . . uh . . . things you did today. It was a huge help."

I appreciate how discreet she is and give her arm a light squeeze. "Of course. Will you go to the funeral tomorrow?"

She sighs. "I'm not sure. Belinda and I are kind of friendly—at least, enough to wave and say hello when we see each other. But I don't really want to take the kids."

I nod in understanding. "Maybe we could ask Jake if they could stay at the house. My grandma would probably love watching them. Of course, Malcolm and Tony would have a great time, and she wouldn't have to watch them much. She'll probably have Gavin, and Lily wouldn't be much of a bother."

"I appreciate the offer, but I think I've imposed on your family enough."

"How's that?"

"Today . . . you know."

"Oh, that wasn't a big deal at all."

"It was to me. I really appreciate it. I think I'll pass on the services. Besides, while I don't want the children to go to the funeral, I wouldn't feel right about coming to the dinner without them."

"Oh . . . I'm sure Phil didn't mean it like that. Surely he'd realize parents might not want to take the kids to the funeral but would bring them to the meal." I say it, but then I wonder. Would he? "Give me a minute. I'll be right back."

I search out Jake to see if he can mention this oversight to Phil. When I find Jake and explain, he agrees Phil wouldn't have meant children had to go to the service, and maybe clarification was in order.

He thanks me and then heads off after Phil.

I visit with people I recognize but don't really know, then start back to Olivia.

Sarah stops me along the way. "Katie, want to help me tomorrow?"

"Maybe . . . " I say hesitantly.

"Good. We're going to watch the children while the parents go to the service. Since we didn't know Terry, it only makes sense."

"Okay." I shrug.

"Folks, folks. Can I talk to you for a minute?" Phil says loudly.

People begin to settle down as he continues, "I didn't realize earlier, there may be some parents who wish to pay their respects tomorrow but would prefer their children not attend. Totally understandable. There will be childcare here during the service and then families can attend the meal together. Many of you've met Sarah Garrett, Jake Caldwell's oldest daughter. She's going to take care of the childcare, along with the help of her sisters and other relatives. I know your children will be in good hands."

Since Phil had gestured our way, all eyes are on Sarah and, by default, me. Sarah, never shy, waves to everyone and says loudly, "Thank you, Phil. We'll be here by 2:30, so you can begin to arrive then."

"Perfect," Phil says. "Looks like the water line is diminishing, so if you need water, hustle on over. And remember, Kelley, Doris, and Sarah are around if you need help or can offer help."

As Phil walks off, Olivia walks over to me. "Thank you for that, Katie. I appreciate it."

"Well, I didn't really do anything. I just asked Jake about it. Everything took off from there. I'm helping Sarah with the children tomorrow, so I'll get to play with Lily again," I say with a smile.

"Sounds good. We have our water, so we're going to head on home. I'll see you tomorrow."

Back at the house, Sarah's a ball of energy, planning for the childcare the next day. She can't wait to have her own children and is disappointed each month when nothing happens. I know she's starting to stress about it.

For the childcare gig, she's enlisted help from Angela, Calley, Sheila, and Karen. The six of us are in Mom's kitchen, discussing Sarah's plans while she jots down notes on an old envelope. Sheila doesn't seem at all excited about it, making several faces and comments about having to babysit.

"If you don't want to help, it's fine. No big deal at all," Sarah says.

"No. I'll do it. I wouldn't want anyone to accuse me of not contributing to the greater good or some such thing." Sheila turns on her heel and stomps out the door, making sure the screen slams behind her.

The rest of us look at each other with wide eyes.

"Well, that was . . . interesting," Angela says.

Calley immediately jumps to Sheila's defense. "She's just upset about things. She wasn't doing too well with her divorce, and now being here and not knowing how her ex is . . . it's a little much for her. She didn't mean anything by it."

"I'm sure she didn't," Sarah says kindly. "We're all upset and on edge. And you know we're worried about Mom and how she is. I feel like snapping sometimes too."

"Yeah, but you don't," Angela argues. "You act like an adult instead of a spoiled brat. Sheila—this isn't the first time she's done this. She thinks she's the only one who hates what's happening. Well, she's not. Someone needs to talk with her and tell her to knock it off because I've about had it up to here— " Angela motions to her well-shaped eyebrows " —with her stomping around and acting like a brat. Seriously, Calley. You should talk to her, because if I need to be the one to talk with her, it won't be pretty."

"Fine," Calley snaps. "I'll talk to her. You know, it's not like you're perfect either, Angela."

"I'm not saying I'm perfect. Did you hear me say I hate this too?" Angela practically screams. "I do. I hate it. I hate that I left my home. My job. My life. This sucks. You think I want to live in a house without running water and have to cover my poop with sawdust? You think any of this is fun for me?

"What about Katie? She doesn't even know if her apartment's still standing or if any of her friends are dead. Same with Sarah. Have you heard her crying, wondering if the people she went to school with and worked with in Oregon are dead from the bridges collapsing? None of us like this, but we aren't flying off the handle all the time and acting like big babies."

Calley, face full of anger and eyes full of tears, starts to say something, then stops. She suddenly drops her head and begins to wail. Sarah, Angela, Karen, and I look at each other. Sarah shrugs her shoulders and reaches out to Calley, who quickly pulls away. Sarah isn't dissuaded and gently gathers her into her arms.

"It's okay, Calley," she quietly croons. "We're all upset."

Calley dissolves into Sarah's arms as she continues to sob. "I'm sorry," she gulps. After a few minutes, Sarah releases her. Calley wipes her eyes and turns to Angela.

"You're right. We're all in a bad situation and none of us are happy with it. But Sheila . . . she's really playing the victim card, acting like it's all about her. I'll talk with her. It sounds like we're going to be here awhile. I don't want us all feeling like we have to walk on eggshells around her."

Angela gives Calley a weary smile. "Okay, that's good. And I'm sorry I yelled at you."

Calley nods and asks, "Sarah, did you say Grandma's going also?"

"Yes, Grandpa Alvin convinced her it'd be good to help us. I'm surprised she agreed . . . you know how she doesn't care for crowds. Lois and Deanne are going too."

Lois is a recently retired schoolteacher, so I know she loves children. She's in her midsixties, about ten years younger than my grandparents and around fifteen years older than my parents.

Mike and Sheila's mom, Deanne, is a year or two younger than my mom. She doesn't work outside the home, but she's an amazing homemaker with a Pinterest-worthy house. Maybe Calley should enlist Deanne's help in talking with Sheila. The mom and daughter duo seem extremely close.

"I'm going to ask Malcolm to gather some outdoor play equipment plus a few games," Sarah continues. "I know they have a playground, but I think we'll need lots of activities."

"Uh . . . Sarah," Angela says quietly, "you know the service won't last that long, right?"

Sarah just shrugs and makes herself another note. Sarah's still making and changing plans when people start to wander off to bed. Jake steps into the kitchen and asks how it's going. I can see Jake's getting tired, so I quietly tell Sarah it's time to wrap it up.

Art and Leo are both sleeping in their new places tonight. Both are parked in the driveway until the shelters can be built for them. Leo's thinking he'll wait on those as long as possible, with the greenhouse—which he's decided to enlarge slightly—and several other things having priority. It's possible we won't even still be here when winter arrives.

No new attacks today. I think this is a step in the right direction.

Chapter 30

Wednesday, Day 7

The continual ringing of the doorbell brings me out of a sound sleep. Someone is serious about waking up the entire house.

I'm dressed in shorts and a T-shirt. I grab a hoodie and slip into flip-flops, then start up the stairs. On the second step, I stop and consider going back for my handgun. I had the class yesterday, and I did well. But I've never shot *my* handgun, only the ones Evan had for us to use. I decide to leave it.

At the top of the stairs, I can now hear a very loud, frantic sounding voice. Jake's much calmer voice is also present. I can't make out what they're saying, so I walk through Mom and Jake's bedroom, into the office, and peer out from the woodstove surround, making sure to keep behind it.

In the living room, Malcolm and Jake are by the open door. Jake's comforting someone, but he's out of my view, blocked by Jake's body. Jake moves slightly, turning in my direction.

Tony, Olivia's little boy, is the one at the door. His face is streaked with tears.

"What happened?" I ask.

About this time, Leo carefully opens the front door and steps in. He has his sidearm—not pointed but held at his side.

"I'm not quite sure," Jake says calmly. "Tony's upset, but it's hard to sort out what's going on."

Tony visibly shudders, then takes a deep breath. When he speaks, he sounds calm, almost serene. "Someone came in our house . . . broke in our house. My mom and Lily are still there. She told me to run for help."

Tony's forced calm demeanor suddenly breaks down, and he's once again in tears. "You have to help. I don't know who else can help."

"We'll help your mom and sister, Tony." Jake rest a hand on Tony's shoulder, then turns to me. "Drive to the Snyders' house. Take the car. The keys are hanging in the cabinet in the mudroom. Honk the horn and wait in the car until one of them comes out for you or asks you to come in. Do not bang on the door, do not try to go in.

"When they recognize the car, they'll come out. Tell them what's happening and tell them Leo, Tate, Tim, and I have gone over there. Tell them I have the walkie on the channel we use for hunting. Malcolm, you get Tony some water and help him calm down. Leo, go wake Tate and Tim. Ask Sarah to come in here and stay with the boys."

As soon as he finishes speaking, I run out the door, quickly find the keys, and head to the car. Sarah comes stumbling out from her trailer. She's pulling a robe around her, and her feet are also clad in flip-flops.

Grandpa Alvin steps out from his apartment and says, "What's going on out here?"

"I don't have time, Grandpa. You'll have to talk to Jake."

I drive much faster than I should. The car slides on the gravel several times, and driving over the small creek bridge, I may have caught a little air.

I think about what Jake said and make sure I'm fully visible driving into the Snyders' place. My lights are on, and I give the horn a toot as I cross from the road into the driveway. I honk a few more times as I pull up near the big picture windows. I roll down the window so I can hear if Evan or Doris call out.

In the cool night air, there's a tinge of smoke. A woodstove burning in June? In the distance, the sky lights with a flash. Earlier, Jake said it looked like rain as he prepared the rain barrels attached to every roofline to accept more water. While the rain is always welcome, the accompanying lightning can spark a fire. I hope that's not what I'm smelling.

The time on the car clock tells me it's after 3:00 a.m., the infamous witching hour, and the Snyder house is fully dark. I honk a few more times. I wish I knew Morse code—I'd honk out SOS.

It feels like forever before the porch light, followed by a light in the house, turns on. The door opens slightly, and Evan yells, "Jake, what's wrong?"

I open my door but stay inside the car while I holler back. "It's Katie. Jake sent me. There's a problem with Olivia and her children."

"Katie, c'mon in here."

I slowly get out of the car. I don't think Evan's going to shoot me, but just to be sure, I walk out like I've seen in the movies with my hands fully visible.

Evan then fully opens the door. I don't see a gun in his hand and continue toward the door. He loudly says, "Doris, it's Katie from Jake's place. You can come on out."

I envision Doris barricaded in the bedroom, using the bed as cover with her weapon at the ready.

Evan ushers me inside. While he doesn't have a gun in his hand, one is on the side table near the door. It's unholstered. A second gun is in its holster nearby. It's not at all uncommon to see guns at the Snyder house, but to think one of them may have recently been aimed in my direction is a little unnerving.

Doris walks out of the bedroom, fully dressed, and I immediately tell them what I know. Doris goes to get the walkie-talkies while Evan returns to his room to dress. I'm left alone in the living room with their black lab, Danny.

Danny was Evan's K-9 when he was a police officer. When Evan retired, so did Danny. Danny's one of the sweetest dogs I've ever met and is amazingly well-behaved. I'm not exactly sure what Evan or Danny did when they were active on the force. I should ask some time.

Doris comes back with a hard-sided case. She opens it on the dining room table to reveal four walkie-talkies. She turns on each and checks to make sure they're working and on the correct channel. Evan arrives from the room shortly after.

"Okay, Katie. Did Jake say where they'd be? I'm not exactly sure where Olivia lives. Do you know?"

"Not really. She told me it's over the hill behind their house, maybe half a mile as the crow flies, but farther by road. I'm guessing it's the road going off to the right when we drive in, before the pond, but I don't really know. I'm sorry."

"Wait," Doris says. "You mean Jason's wife? The tiny little blond? They have a boy about Malcolm's age and a young girl?"

"Yes, exactly," I answer with a vigorous nod.

"They rent from the Styles. You've met Jason, he's an oil well worker," Doris tells Evan, then turns to me and asks, "Is he home?"

"No," I say, shaking my head.

"And the Styles are gone too," Doris says. "There isn't anyone else nearby. I don't think the walkies would reach that far if Jake's already left."

"Well, I'll try him when I get close," Evan answers.

"I'm going with you," Doris says, sliding her holster into her waistband.

Evan looks like he wants to argue but simply nods. "Might be a good idea. I'm stopping in my room, then we'll go. Katie, it looks like the porchlight's on down at your place—it must be on the solar system. You head on down the hill. If Jake's still there, tell him to wait for me. If he's not there, turn out the porch light."

I agree and start to walk out, then stop and ask, "What's in your room?"

"My gun safe."

Back at Mom and Jake's house, I quickly park. As I run inside, I notice the smoke smell is stronger. "Where's Jake?" I ask breathlessly to the room full of people.

"Gone already, along with Tim, Tate, Leo, and Grandpa Alvin," Angela says, looking nervous. I quickly go back and turn off the porch light.

"Why'd you do that?" Sarah asks.

"Evan said to turn it off if Jake was already gone so he'd know not to stop here."

"Makes sense," Sarah says.

"I think I'll go out and see if I can get a ride with Evan," Mike says.

"You can't, Mike," Calley says quickly. "You still get dizzy."

"I can help. You know I can."

Mike's dad shakes his head. "Normally, yes, you definitely could. But until you're better, it's not a good idea, son," Roy says gently. "I hate not being able to help also, but for me, it's a matter of lack of skill. I wouldn't even know what to do. Today's shooting lesson was the first I've handled a gun in years. It's best to know our limitations."

I think about this. Grandpa Alvin went along. I'm kind of surprised Jake let him go. Of course, with Grandpa Alvin, he isn't one to dissuade if it's something he believes in. Grandma said it well earlier about them being stubborn. About the time I complete my thought, we see Doris and Evan speed by. Mike leans back in his chair looking defeated.

"How about some coffee?" Sarah asks the group in an effort to change the subject.

Sarah puts water on to boil to use in the French press. The solar system isn't powerful enough to use things like coffee pots, hair dryers, and curling irons, but the French press option works just fine for coffee. I do miss being able fix my hair properly; ponytails and buns are going to get old quick.

Shortly after 4:00 a.m., I'm very antsy and decide to step outside.

"Mind if I join you?" Sheila asks, as I grab a flashlight from the kitchen.

"Sure, that's fine." Things are still not great with Sheila, so I'm less than excited. "You want to grab another light?"

"No, I'll just stick with to you," she answers.

I nod and we go out the front door.

This east-facing door gives us an immediate view of the impending daylight. There's a very light band of color showing across the top of the distant mountains. The illumination is so faint it's barely noticeable.

"Ewww. There must be a fire somewhere," she says, as we walk out the door and the smell of smoke hits our noses.

"Yeah," I say, wondering if the smoke's related to the trouble at Olivia's house.

Sheila lights a cigarette as we walk along the sidewalk toward the garage, taking the driveway in the direction of the gravel road.

"Um, Katie," Sheila whispers.

"Yeah?"

"You, uh . . . you think everything's okay with your friend?"

"I hope so."

"It's so scary. I would've thought Bakerville would be . . . safe. I guess that's the word. It's such a small town. It doesn't seem stuff like this should happen in a small town. Oh, I guess it's not even a town, but you know what I mean."

"I know what you mean. And I agree. It's one of the reasons Mom and Jake chose Bakerville. It's quiet and out of the way. But sin, it's everywhere. Adam and Eve passed on the desire to sin to each of us. We're born with it."

"Save it, Katie. I don't need a sermon about sin and your mythical God." Her words reach me like a smack across the face.

"Of course not. I wasn't . . . that wasn't what I meant. I was trying to say anything can happen. We live in a fallen world . . . uh, I mean. Jeez, Sheila. I know you aren't a believer, and I've tried to respect that. I'm not trying to preach at you, but I'm also not going to watch how I talk for fear of offending you. I say nothing when you use language I'm not comfortable with, and I'd appreciate the same consideration from you. You can't expect me to never mention my faith."

"Yes, I can. When you talk about those things, it makes me uncomfortable."

"That's certainly not my intention. But I can't be someone else when I'm around you, Sheila. I'm just me. The last few months, I've turned my back on God. I'm not going to do that any longer. Salvation is a choice. I made my choice as a young girl. Then, a few months ago, I . . . uh, I faltered. Now, I realize whatever happens here, in this messed up world, I need Jesus. And I'm not ashamed of that."

"You? Perfect little Katie faltered? What'd you do? Forget to pray before dinner?"

"Wow, Sheila. That was cruel."

"So what? You think just because you're a little goody two-shoes I have to talk to you a special way? I say what I think, that's just the way I am. You don't like it? Too bad. Calley told me all about you wanting to be a missionary. What a joke. You think people want your God? Believe me, they don't. You going and peddling your 'good news' or whatever isn't for anyone else anyway. It's just a way to make you feel good about yourself.

"You think you'll look good for Jesus that way? Because you won't. You know why? Because He's a fable, a fairy tale. He doesn't exist. Do you understand me, Katie Andrews? GOD. IS. NOT. REAL." Sheila is shrieking, almost crazed, with bits of spit flying out of her mouth and hitting me in the face.

I take a step back, not only to avoid the flying spittle but to give myself some room, just in case this escalates. I have no idea how a simple conversation has turned into . . . what is this?

I take a deep, quiet breath. "I'm sorry, Sheila. I never intended to upset you. I'll . . . I'll head back in now. You can keep the flashlight for when you're ready to go inside."

"Great. That's just fine. Here's an even better idea. Keep your preaching to yourself. Stay away from me. It's bad enough my mom and dad believe the same garbage you believe. At least they respect me

227

enough to keep quiet about it. You and your crazy parents need to do the same."

Whoa. My crazy parents? I don't think so . . . "Listen, Sheila. You can say whatever you want about me, but you won't say a thing about my mom or Jake. My mom, who isn't even here, and Jake have opened their home to you. Not just their home, but they're willing to share everything they have. They even planned for you to be here. Did you know that? Did you know they purposely purchased items to take care of you if something like this happened?"

"They didn't do it for me," she yells. "We all know they only did it so Calley and Mike would come here. Their precious little Calley, who also thinks they're complete religious whacka-doos. You know that, right? You know she wants nothing to do with your stupid religion? She thinks you're all a bunch of brainwashed idiots. Oh, but they still made sure to guilt her into thinking she had to escape Casper and drive us all here. So Mike had a little bump on the head. Who cares? We were stupid to come here. We should've just stayed there and let you holy rollers pray to your worthless God on your own."

"Enough, Sheila." Sheila spins around as I shine the light in the direction of the voice. Her mom, dad, and brother are all there. Tears are streaming down Deanne's face. Mike looks angry. I move the light slightly and see Calley standing quietly, several feet behind Mike. Roy speaks again, "You've more than made your point."

"No. I've not yet begun to make my point! You think I'm stupid enough to believe Katie or her family give a whit about me? You and Mom say things like 'oh, that's such a Christian thing for them to do,' but I know the truth. I know they're only doing this so they'll look good for others. Probably to look good for their silly God too. Just like you and Mom do.

"You go to church and pretend you're so much better than everyone else, but what about the rest of the week? You think I don't know what a couple of hypocrites you are? You used to drag Mike and me along to church with you, remember? All those people there were just the same. They'd be all sanctimonious inside the building, then, outside, they'd be smoking and cussing and discussing what they did the night before. Liars and fakes. That's all they are . . . all of you so called believers are just liars."

"Sheila, you can doubt the existence of God and you can believe whatever you want. But the fact remains, we're here by invitation.

Jake and Mollie have opened their home to us. You think it would've been better to stay in Casper? Even after what happened to Mike? You think we'd have any hope of surviving there for any length of time? Your mom and I had enough food in the house for two, maybe three weeks. You saw what we packed. How much food did you have? Because you didn't bring any out with you when you came to our house with your suitcase."

"We would've been fine," Sheila snaps.

"Would we? By eating what? Snakes and sagebrush? We don't even have a garden. I don't even have guns for hunting."

"Mike does. There's more than enough antelope and deer."

"I've never hunted," Mike says quietly. "I don't think it's the same as shooting at nonmoving targets. Not to mention, sneaking up on a wild animal isn't like walking up to a dog or something."

"Oh, fine. So you're with them, Mike? You didn't want to come here either. The only reason you did was because you were in so much pain. Calley used your injuries against you so she could come home to her mommy and daddy."

"My dad is dead. My mom is missing and may also be dead," Calley says, while rushing toward Sheila. "Jake has been nothing but nice to you . . . to all of us. Without my mom home, he has no reason to even welcome us here. You think it wouldn't be smarter for him to turn us all away and just take care of Malcolm? His own flesh and blood?"

"Give me a break, Calley. You don't even like your mom and Jake. I haven't said anything here you haven't said before. You told me yourself about how nuts your mom is. How she said she was a Christian, but then your dad died and she stopped going to church. Oh, sure, she'd drop you and your sisters off, but she didn't go. She and Jake can't even keep their marriage together. Weren't they planning on a divorce? So, what, their perfect God can't even keep their marriage together? What a fine example of wonderful Christians they are."

"My mom and Jake are examples of normal humans," I say. "They have struggled together and separately. The only reason they're still together is because of God."

"Katie's right," Calley interjects before Sheila can say anything. "Things haven't always been great with my mom and Jake. And my mom has had plenty of troubles over the years. Lately, though, things have changed. I can see a difference in her as she . . . gosh, I can't even believe I'm saying this, but I can see her growing in Christ.

"So much of the bitterness she had is gone. I turned away from God out of anger. Anger that he took my dad. Anger my mom was so upset all the time. Anger my life was different. When Mike and I became friends and I got to know you, I thought I'd found a kindred spirit. Someone who was also angry at God and we could be angry together."

Sheila starts to say something but Calley powers on, not even taking a breath. "But, Sheila, I'm not sure I want to be angry anymore. I'm tired of being angry at my mom. And I'm not even really sure why I decided I didn't like Jake. He's been nothing but good to me. To Katie, Angela, and Sarah also.

"Seems to me he's been pretty good to you, too, Sheila. I've heard a few of the remarks you've made, under your breath but loud enough for Jake and anyone nearby to hear. Jake doesn't call you out on it. You know what he does? He prays for you. He prays for everyone here by name. Did you know that? I didn't, not until Malcolm told me. They pray together for all of us."

"I don't want or need his prayers to his imaginary God. Don't you get that? Have I not made myself clear?"

"Oh, you've made yourself quite clear," Deanne says. The tears are gone, and her face is a mask of anger. "You've made yourself so clear, if you weren't an adult, I'd take you over my knee and then send you to your room."

"Ha. I'd like to see you try."

I suddenly wonder if this argument is going to come to blows. I also feel sorry for Sheila. I know I should just be angry at her, but we're ganging up on her. She's feeling trapped and is lashing out.

Roy must realize this too. He reaches out and touches Deanne's arm, then calmly and quietly says, "We love you, Sheila. I think everyone just needs to call this a . . . call this done for tonight. We're all nervous about what might be happening at Olivia's place. And also with our own lives—with our futures. Let's just go back in the house."

"You can go back in the house. I'm going to the little hovel everyone thinks is a cute cabin to crawl up to my tiny little cell and try to get some sleep. I'm done with all of you. I may be stuck here for now, but believe me when I tell you, this is only temporary. I have no intention of staying here any longer than necessary."

With that, she turns and starts to run away. She stumbles and corrects herself before she falls. I start to offer her the flashlight, but Mike says, "Don't, Katie. She'll be fine. It will just make things worse. When she gets like this, it's best just to let her be."

Chapter 31

In the house, the conversation lulls between subjects—except the subject of Sheila. We talk about what might be happening at Olivia's and what has happened over the past several days—none of us can believe it hasn't even been a week since our world changed.

Today is Wednesday; the airplanes were shot down last Thursday . . . the beginning of everything going wrong.

Angela and Sarah look very solemn. I suspect I do also. With Grandpa, Jake, and our men possibly in harm's way, we're a bit on edge. I glance at Grandma Dodie; she looks very tense. Her husband and son are both out there.

We're on the third round of coffee when the sun begins to peek over the horizon. The sound of the anticipated rain, pitter-pattering on the metal roof, provides background noise to our off and on conversations. Our exchanges now range from celebrity gossip, to TV shows, to movies, to the weather.

We now pointedly avoid anything that might be happening at Olivia's or why we're together in this room. No one talks about the attacks or the questionable world we now live in.

I'm still upset about the trouble with Sheila. The more I think about it, the more I believe it really has nothing to do with God, but something more. This strikes me as funny. Of course it's something more. It's the end of the world, just like the song. Only we don't feel fine.

We don't feel fine at all.

Malcolm and Tony are in the guest room trying to sleep. Gavin's curled up in a blanket on the floor. Penny and Scooter, Mom and Jake's little dogs, are curled up next to him.

Eventually, the rain lets up and Calley says, "I think I'm going to go back to our cabin. I'd like to try to go back to sleep. Mike, you want to join me?"

Mike sighs loudly. "I suppose I should. Maybe one of these days I'll be fully functioning again. Until then . . . " He gives a shake of his head. From the look crossing his face, I suspect he realized the shake wasn't a good idea.

"You'll be fine soon," Grandma Dodie says. "Head injuries can take a while to heal. I remember one time our younger son, Robert, crashed on his bike. Hit his head and knocked himself out. When he came around, he couldn't even remember riding his bike. It was a few weeks before his head stopped hurting. To this day, I don't think he remembers the crash. Other than that, he was fine. You'll be fine, Mike. Just give it time."

Calley and Mike say their goodnights. They aren't out the door thirty seconds before we hear an engine beginning to pull the hill. We all bounce out of our seats and gather around the windows. A wash of headlights, and soon, a vehicle crests the hill followed by a second.

In the dim morning light, we can just make out Jake's truck in the lead followed by Evan. We're tripping over each other as we make our way to the yard.

The smoke smell, still hanging in the air, is now old and acrid. Not the fresh scent of a wood burning fire, but a combination of wood, plastic, rubber, and who knows what else. The rain should've cleaned the air a bit, but instead, it just smells smoky and wet.

The truck lights turn off and people began to empty out as we rush over. The porch light on the house flips on, and Tony yells, "Mommy! Mommy!"

Tony runs toward Olivia as she quickly closes the gap. I walk to Leo and Jake, standing next to each other. Leo touches my arm and gives a slight smile. I give him a nod and ask, "Everyone's okay?"

"We're all fine. Olivia's house burned down," Jake says quietly. "Thankfully, the rain came at just the right time. Just in case, Tate stayed behind to make sure it doesn't spread."

A hush falls over the group. Olivia's holding Tony tight and speaking quietly to him. Lily's asleep in Doris's arms.

"We couldn't see any flames when we got there but could smell the smoke," Jake says. "At the time, we thought maybe someone had a fire going, even though it's June, or a lightning strike sparked something. You never know. We drove with our lights off, and then, at Leo's suggestion, walked the last bit, keeping the Styles' house between us and Olivia's place. We heard loud voices and a scream, then lots of crying. While it had been our plan to wait for Evan to arrive, it was too hard to do with what we were hearing."

Grandpa Alvin takes over, "We decided we needed to help right away. Jake gave me the radio, and I stayed behind to wait for Evan.

233

Leo's the only one of us with any combat training, so he put a basic plan together. Just as they were getting ready to go . . . "

"It was bedlam," Tim says.

Grandpa Alvin nods. "Yep. Suddenly, there were flames and the screams increased. At that point, Leo said, 'Let's go,' and they went. As much as I wanted to help, I stayed where I was supposed to. A shot rang out. I thought it was one of our guys but found out later it was from the . . . assailant. The radio cackled, and Evan asked where we were."

"I had found their truck and parked next to it. Doris and I were hotfooting it the rest of the way. I figured they'd be using the house as cover. We'd heard the shot and didn't know what to think. When Alvin answered and said he was at the house but the others had gone in, I wasn't too happy—thought it was a mistake. As soon as we got closer, I could see why they had to go. The house was almost fully engulfed."

"With the flames," Doris says, "we could somewhat see what was happening. I saw the bedroom window open and Olivia there holding Lily. She was trying to lower her out the window. Tim hustled over to the window and grabbed Lily from her. Jake and Tate were there shortly after and helped Olivia out. Right then, we heard a second shot. Evan and I weren't quite sure where the shooting was coming from. We knew where Jake, Tate, and Tim were, but Alvin had told us Leo was out there somewhere also."

"I was trying to cover them while they helped Olivia and her daughter out of the house," Leo says. "I had no idea you and Evan had arrived. Ideally, we should've each grabbed a radio. On the drive over, Jake mentioned he had enough for each of us but didn't think to grab more than the one to talk with you two."

Each of the men nods, as Jake says, "Definitely a learning experience. Communication is important."

Tim takes over the story. "Once we had Olivia and Lily out of the house, we hightailed it to safety where Alvin was waiting. I was kind of surprised to see Evan and Doris there. Leo must have seen us make it back to the house since he silently slipped in."

Leo shakes his head. "Not that silently. Pretty sure Evan had a bead on me."

Evan claps Leo on the shoulder. "Sorry, friend."

Leo gives a nod.

"Anyway, as soon as Olivia and Lily were safe, we stayed behind the Styles' house," Tim continues. "We had no idea, and still don't, who was shooting at us. Olivia said the person who broke in was wearing a ski mask. Can you believe that? Definitely a male by the size and the arm hair, but who he is . . . she's not sure.

"She has her suspicions but nothing conclusive. There wasn't anything we could do for the house. With no water, we could only let it burn. We would've been back sooner, but we wanted to make sure it didn't spread beyond their place . . . not that we could stop it with only the couple of rakes and a shovel we found in the outbuilding."

Evan runs a hand across the nape of his neck. "We got lucky tonight."

"Blessed," Grandpa Alvin corrects. "We were blessed. It could've been much worse."

With the sun starting to peek over the mountains, I take Olivia and Lily to the loft room and pull out the sleeper sofa and a sleeping chair. The chair is cot-sized and perfect for Lily. The twin-sized loveseat works well for Olivia.

Tony returns to the guest room with Malcolm joining him. They're chattering away; the elation in Tony's voice over his mom and sister being okay is evident. There's also sadness over losing his house and all of his clothes and toys. The poor family. A house fire at any time would be terrible, but now, when things are so bleak . . . I just feel so bad for them.

Jake and Evan put an empty fifty-five-gallon water barrel in the back of the truck. Then, five gallons at a time, fill it from the large collection barrel attached to the house. They'll rake and shovel the debris, plus add water to help ensure the fire doesn't restart. We're all hoping for a wind-free day.

Art volunteers to do the chores. He says he can handle all but the milking on his own. Malcolm, in charge of the milking with Mom gone, is given a reprieve this morning after the excitement of last night. Jake instructs Art to simply let the babies out, and they'll take care of milking the moms today. We can make do without today's milk.

"Jake, I'd like to help with the chores," I say. "No way can I go back to sleep anyway, not after all of this."

"Yeah, sure, Katie. I understand. You know what to do?"

"Not in the least," I answer with a shrug.

"I'll help," Leo says. "Under Art's expert guidance, we can take care of it."

Jake gives a weary nod. "Thank you. We'll be back as soon as we know the fire's out." Jake, Evan, and Roy pile into Jake's truck to return to Olivia's. Doris, obviously exhausted, takes their truck back home.

We've completed everything but letting out the baby goats when Malcolm stumbles out.

"I'm here. I'm ready to milk," he says.

"Jake said we can skip milking this morning and just put the babies with their moms," I say.

"Nope. I'll milk. With Tony and his sister here, we'll need it. You know, kids need lots of milk so our bones get strong."

"Is that right, squirt?"

"You know it is, Katie. I think that's why Calley's so short, she doesn't drink enough milk."

"Mm-hmm. I don't know, but milking this morning is fine. I can help, just tell me what to do."

"Art can help me. He's pretty good at it."

And with that, it seems I'm dismissed. Now, I feel like I could go back to sleep. Just as I'm toying with the idea, Jake, Evan, and Tate return. Roy stayed behind to make sure the fire was out. He'll walk home when he thinks it's no longer a threat.

"You know, as much as I'd like to go home and hop in bed," Evan says, "I think we need to go ahead and go out today. Take another team . . . an acquisition team, if you will, and see what else we can find. Jake, you still in favor of this?"

"I am. We could still use building supplies, and if there's any food around, it's always a good idea."

"Okay, I want to get the smell of smoke off me, then I'll be ready. Not sure if Doris will want to go after being out half the night, but let's assume she does. And how about we just take my truck? I think we should start thinking about our finite fuel supply. I'll hook the cargo trailer on."

"Sounds like a plan," Jake answers. "So how many can we fit in your truck? Five?"

"Six if we put the middle section of the front seat down. Let's do that. Doris can have the middle spot. She won't mind."

"We'll start getting ready. What do you think, half an hour?"

"About that. See you soon."

I'm not going. I'd rather stay at the house and help Olivia and her children, knowing today might be rough for them after losing their home and everything except the clothes they were wearing.

Angela asks if I'd mind watching Gavin so she and Tim can go. I don't mind at all and tell her so. Once again, Mike wanted to go out but was encouraged to stay home and rest. Each day, he gets a little stronger and has fewer dizzy spells, but I know it's wearing on him. Tate's the sixth person on the team.

It's slightly over half an hour before Evan and Doris return.

"Okay, team, we ready to roll? Who all's going?"

Jake points to those going. "We're ready, the four of us. You think we can be back around one again, even though we're starting slightly later than yesterday?"

"Don't see why not. The places we talked about going, I anticipate being easy in and out events. You agree?"

Jake tilts his head to the side. "I think so, yeah. I want to make sure we're back in time for Terry's funeral."

"Agreed. Doris has the meat ready. So we'll just need time to give it a quick reheat and put on appropriate funeral clothes to be ready to go."

"We can take care of heating the meat for you. Would that help?" Lois asks.

"Sure, that'd be fine. You can go in the sliding door. It's open. I have some bread and buns I pulled out of the freezer sitting on the counter. I don't think it'll be enough, but . . . " Doris finishes with a shrug.

"All right then, one o'clock it is. Whoever has lunch duty today, feel free to make it a light one since we have the potluck a little earlier than we'd usually eat supper. Sarah, will that give time for you to do any setting up?" Jake asks.

"Should be fine. If we can be there by 2:15, I'll be happy."

"Good. Evan, I suspect we'll be done with the funeral, the meal, and getting water for everyone by 6:30 or so. Would that give us enough daylight to have shooting lessons? I thought maybe Leo could train some of the more advanced people on my range, and the beginners could be with you and Doris on your two ranges."

"Should work fine. Leo and I spent a few minutes yesterday on the range. I'm confident he'd be an excellent instructor. Leo, you good with that?"

"Yes, sir. I'd be happy to help."

"Great. Sounds like everything's planned out. We should get this show on the road. Acquisition team, let's roll," Tate says, with a fist pump in the air. Angela, Sarah, and I giggle while Doris rolls her eyes. Most of the guys just shake their head.

I'm very pleased Leo stayed with us again today. As soon as everyone leaves, he says, "Hey, Mike said there was a problem with Sheila last night. You okay?"

"Oh, um . . . yeah. I'm okay. I feel kind of bad about it. I'm not really sure why she was so upset with me. Then, when her family came out, I think she felt attacked and it got even worse. I want to go and talk with her but think maybe I should give it some time."

"Mike says she's still in a snit. So I agree, give it time. Maybe later today. How about now you shoot your rifle a few times?"

"Sure. Can we use Jake's range?"

"Yep, they've dug out a hundred-yard alley. Your parents take the distance a little farther by stretching out from the alley, but we'll be fine sticking in the alley. We'll start at fifty and move back as needed."

"If you think I'm ready."

"I do. I think you'll be fine."

"Well, let's get it done. We plan to put away the mass purchases from our crazy shopping day in Wesley. It's still piled in various places. We've decided everything is being merged together and moved to the basement. I don't think DIY breakfasts will happen much longer. Pretty much, what people brought is diminishing. Grandma Dodie suggested we start having all our meals together to make things easier."

"It's a good idea, unless you're the one doing the cooking. Then . . . not too much fun."

"For sure. I heard you asked to be added not only to the cleanup rotation but also the cooking crew."

With a shrug, he says, "Figured, as long as they put me with someone who knows their way around the kitchen, I'll be fine. I can chop veggies and stuff. And I'm awesome on the grill."

"You are?"

"Of course. Don't you know us men have this special grilling DNA?"

I can't help but laugh as I realize he's pulling my leg.

"Living with the guys in Manhattan, I decided to teach myself how to grill. It's not really hard to press some burger together and throw it on a hot rack. I make a mean hot dog too."

"Well, okay then. I guess we'll have hot dogs on your cooking days."

The rifle practice goes well, but after we start, I suddenly realize Olivia and her children are still sleeping. I hope we aren't disturbing them. As we work through supplies today, I want to make sure Olivia and her children have whatever they may need. I can't even imagine how they're feeling after losing everything.

Back at the house, Olivia is up and moving around. She seems to be in surprisingly good spirits, considering. While she has her suspicions—Dan Morse—she can't confirm who broke into her house and set it on fire. She does believe he was there for reasons other than destruction of the home, but somehow, he didn't follow through.

"I had trouble falling asleep last night," Olivia says. "Both Tony and Lily were a challenge to get down. Once they were asleep, I started thinking and worrying about Jason. Soon, I was a blubbering mess. When I finally calmed down a bit, I decided to read. I had a candle burning in a mason jar, which wasn't great light, but sitting near it, I could see okay. I was just starting to feel like I could doze off when I thought I heard something outside."

She stops for a minute and stares off into the distance. "You know, I've been so on edge after realizing the trouble Jason would have getting home. And then Dan Morse coming around so much, and putting on a charade Jason is home . . . when I first heard the noise, I half wondered if it was my imagination playing tricks on me. When the sound came a second time, I thought maybe an animal was on the porch. With coyotes and such around, you never know."

I say nothing while she ponders her next words.

"I saw a shadow go by the window and knew it definitely wasn't a coyote. The shadow was man-sized. He must have known I saw him because the next thing I know, he was trying to get in. The door was locked, but I wasn't sure how long it'd keep him out. I ran to Tony's room first and told him to go out the back and run for help. I saw him slip the shoes on he'd left on the back porch, then Tony took off running.

"The front door splintered, and I ran into my bedroom. Lily had been sleeping in my bed. The noise woke her, and she was screaming. I locked the bedroom door, but there was soon banging on it. There was no way the door would hold for long if he wanted to get in. I quickly put shoes on and opened the bedroom window, busting out the screen."

Tears form in Olivia's eyes. She lets out a big sigh. "And I'm not really sure what happened. Something put him into a rage. I started hearing things breaking. In his rage, he must have knocked my candle over. Either that or he set the fire deliberately. It really doesn't seem like a little candle should've burned my house down." At that, the tears spill over, and she begins to softly cry.

I put my arm around her. I'm not really sure what to say, plus I don't think she needs to hear anything from me.

"I really don't understand. Why would he do this? Was he there to kill us? And why go into a rage like he did? He didn't even try to break down the bedroom door. Instead, just started these guttural screams and throwing things. I don't think he meant to start the fire. At one point, I heard him yell, 'Oh no.' And that's when the smoke began to smell very strong. I should've opened the bedroom door then, and Lily and I could've made a dash for the backdoor. I was just so scared, and Lily was screaming and crying . . . it was terrible.

"I'm not sure what happened next, but he must have left. I did hear a shot, and Lily and I both hit the ground, not sure where the shooting was coming from. Then I realized the fire was out of control and we had to get out. I lowered Lily out the window, then your brother appeared. Then Jake and your other brother helped me out. When the shooting started again, I immediately threw myself on the ground. I have some cactus in my stomach, but otherwise . . . I'm so thankful no one was injured."

I agree and give her a big hug.

"I sure appreciate being able to stay here. I'm not sure what we're going to do after losing the house. We're only renting but have been there since Lily was born. The Styles are good landlords. You know they were on vacation when all of this happened? Went to Florida to visit family. They called and checked in the day the cyberattacks started and said they didn't have any way to get home. I hope they're doing okay."

Fresh tears begin after this. Through her sobs, she says, "I just don't know what to do. We'll have to find someplace and make sure Jason knows where we are for when he gets home."

I stay with Olivia for several more minutes until she tells me she'd like to rest for a bit.

Chapter 32

We're able to get the food and other purchases stashed away from the shopping trips. I did keep out the gummy bears I bought for Leo and a few other things.

By the time the last of the stock is put in the basement storage spaces, all are overflowing. We've also utilized the upstairs and under-the-bed storage, along with putting things in closets and spaces in the bunkhouse and cabin. We tried to keep things organized in the manner started by Mom and Jake, but it wasn't easy. I'm not sure what we'll do with the new stuff coming in today. Maybe Jake has a plan.

About 12:45, I start watching for the team to return. Today's lunch—a giant salad, pieces of roast, and cheese—is ready and waiting. We're taking assorted appetizers from the freezer truck to the funeral meal today. We start cooking as many as we can in advance after Lois suggests keeping them warm in coolers by filling quart mason jars with hot water. We choose things that won't get too soggy in a cooler: pot stickers, assorted wings, and meatballs. We're also bringing some prepackaged food, like mini-donuts and pretzels.

Calley and Mike went to the Snyders' and grabbed the food they prepared. We gave it a reheat and used Lois's cooler method for it also. We pulled a couple loaves of bread out of Jake's freezer to add to Doris's bread collection.

Around 1:30, we're starting to wonder where the acquisition crew is. We go ahead with our lunch, putting theirs aside. At two, it's getting close to time to leave for the community center.

Leo pulls me aside. "I'm not sure what to think. Both Evan and Jake said they'd be back by one. We agreed it's important to return when planned so the rest of the family doesn't worry. Without communication, it's hard."

Grandpa Alvin and Keith walk over. "Whatcha planning, Leo? Think we need to go find them?" Grandpa asks.

Leo gives a slow nod. "Jake showed me on a map where they planned to go and the route they'd take. I'm just not sure we wouldn't be jumping the gun by going now. Sunset's about, when? Sometime after nine o'clock?"

"Sounds about right." Grandpa Alvin nods.

"I'd like to think they're just running behind. Maybe found something they couldn't pass up and it's taking a bit longer. And in that case, they might have strayed slightly from the route they planned. What do you think about going to the funeral and the reception, then, if they aren't back by the time we're done, we go looking for them?"

"Yeah. I guess that's smart. Not like Jake to be late for anything, but it could be what you're saying. With fuel the way it is, it makes sense to get what you can while out. I know Dodie's really starting to worry, but we'll wait and see."

Alvin talks to everyone else, and all agree it's probably something like Leo suggested and it's a good idea to give them some more time. I'm sure Leo is right, they found something they can't pass up, but there's a knot of worry in my stomach. Dodie definitely looks concerned, with her mouth pulled in a tight line.

We load our food and ourselves in Leo's truck and Sarah's car to go to the community center. I wasn't sure if Sheila would go with us. I hadn't seen her since the blowup in the early morning hours. She didn't help with getting things ready, and no one mentioned her. When it was time to leave, there she was. She seemed to purposely avoid my gaze as she climbed into the bed of Leo's truck.

Alvin's going to stay with us at the community center to help with the children, but most of the guys, along with Olivia, plan to go to the funeral. Art stays at the homestead. He says he wants to catch up on his sleep, but Leo tells me he's really staying behind to act as security.

Security for the homestead—have things changed so much in such a short time?

Leo asks if I'm okay with babysitting or if I feel it was divided by stereotypes—women babysitting while the men do other things. I assure him I don't need to go to the funeral and understand the guys wanting to, since most were on the search party and they'll also help with the burial.

As we're driving, I think a little about Leo's question on stereotypes. While the women have been doing most of the cooking, the guys have done a lot of the cleanup. We're all learning how to shoot, and guys and gals go out on the acquisition team.

Everyone helps with whatever chores need to be done. But there are some things done by certain people just because of their skills. Leo will likely always be better at construction than I am. But I'd probably be more likely to paint the finished structure since he's told me he hates painting and I enjoy it. Well . . . I love painting with oils on canvas, but painting walls is fine too. I still feel slightly artistic.

It makes sense to me we should do the things we're best at. Sarah wanting to take care of the children and figuring out who needs help during this time also makes perfect sense—those are skills she has.

We arrive shortly after 2:15 for the babysitting gig. It's not five minutes until the first people start to arrive. Cars and trucks are loaded to capacity, with many more people in them than there should be. One small car has so many people get out, I'm reminded of a clown car. Others show up on quads, side-by-sides, motorcycles, bicycles, and horses. I suspect bicycles and horses will soon be the main mode of transportation. I'm glad Leo and I brought our bikes.

There aren't a lot of children in this community, as it's primarily a retirement area. By the time three o'clock rolls around for the funeral service, I'm pretty sure we have every child in the community here. There are twenty-eight under the age of twelve, including Tony, Malcolm, Lily, and Gavin. We even have teens stay with us, preferring not to go to the funeral but, I suspect, not wanting to miss out on the meal either. I can't say I blame them.

Someone opened the community center hall so people could leave their food. The lack of windows really makes the building unsuitable to use without power, but at least things are protected from flies and other bugs. There's quite an assortment of dishes. Many are small containers with only a few servings.

The lady who said she had a garden brought a cooler with several gallon zipper bags of lettuce, and I help her take it inside. She apologizes for only having a half-used bottle of Thousand Island dressing and a small, unopened bottle of Ranch. I should've thought to grab a bottle of dressing from the house—which was one thing I purchased several of on Sunday's shopping adventure.

The older children start a softball game, with Grandpa Alvin acting as the coach for both teams and the umpire. Karen offers to assist with the ball game and encourages Sheila to also help. Sheila does go with Karen to the field but makes no effort to join in the game.

Dodie and Lois tend to the youngest children. Besides for Gavin, there's a few other very young ones. One, about a year old, is the cutest little red-haired boy dressed in full-on cowboy garb, including adorable little boots. There's a little girl just slightly older than Gavin and a baby who's not yet walking, but her mom told us she's starting to scoot and to keep an eye on her so she doesn't scoot away.

Sarah, Deanne, Calley, and I tend to those older than the baby/toddler group but not old enough, or not wanting to, play ball. Deanne and Calley are at a picnic table doing an art project with several kids. Sarah and I are on the playground with our group.

"I'm really starting to worry," Sarah says. "They should've been back by now."

I don't need to ask who "they" are since I'm also wondering where Jake and everyone is. They're now over two hours late.

"Maybe they did find something they didn't want to pass up and it's just taking a little extra time," I say, trying to be encouraging. The knot in my stomach is still there, but I do my best to pretend I'm not too worried. With Angela and Jake being gone, it's hard, but at least my significant other isn't with them. Leo is safe at the funeral. Safe . . . at least I hope he's safe. With Terry's death and Olivia's house burning down, maybe none of us are very safe.

It's close to 4:00 p.m. when the first people begin to return from the funeral. Leo, Mike, Roy, and Olivia arrive a few minutes later.

Walking over to Sarah and me at the playground, Roy asks, "Our people aren't back yet?"

"Not yet. I'm pretty worried," Sarah responds.

"Yep. On the way from the funeral service, we decided to give them until five and then we'll go looking. I'm going to find Phil and see if I can help set things up for the food part."

Olivia is looking rather nervous. "They're not back yet." A statement not a question.

I shake my head.

"You see Dan Morse here?" she asks.

"I haven't seen him. I don't figure he went to the funeral?"

"He wouldn't be welcome there. And Phil did make it pretty clear only funeral people could come to the dinner. I'm almost certain it was him last night. I wish he wouldn't have been wearing the mask, then maybe we could do something about it. I guess Evan went over and spoke to Phil this morning before they went on their . . . excursion."

"Really? I hadn't heard . . . makes sense, though. Did they stop and see him on their way out? Maybe that's why they're late."

"They did, but Phil said they only stayed about five minutes. I think pretty much everyone knows about my suspicion it was Morse, but since I have no proof . . . " Her voice fades off with a shrug of her shoulders. "There's Belinda and her family pulling in now." Olivia lifts her chin in the direction of the car.

Belinda speaks to people as she walks over to the picnic table that doubles as a podium at meetings. Along with her mom, dad, and son, she stands stoically as the crowd quiets.

"Thank you all so much for taking time to honor Terry today. TJ and I really appreciate the support we've received from all of you. Thank you, Ralph, for performing the service. Those of you who were part of the search party to help locate Terry, I'm forever indebted. I'm so thankful you found him, helping to give TJ and me closure. And thanks to all who brought food for us to share as we continue to fellowship and remember Terry. Mom, Dad, do either of you wish to say anything?"

Her dad shakes his head.

"Yes, everything Belinda said. Thank you all so much," her mom says.

I hadn't notice Phil step up, but he's there and shakes Belinda's dad and TJ's hand and then hugs Belinda and her mom. He turns to the crowd. "Thank you for gathering with us. We have the food out, and there are a few tables set up, but we likely don't have enough seating for everyone to sit at the same time. I see many of you brought your own chairs, so we'll just do the best we can. I'd like to ask Ralph to bless the food and then we can eat. Let's let Belinda and her family go through first."

Ralph steps forward. "Let us pray. Heavenly Father, as we're gathered on this day of Your will, we offer thanks unto You. Please bless the food we're about to receive in Your name. Please, Lord, be with the ones who have suffered loss, and remind them, Father, that all who mourn shall be comforted. Even today, Father, we give thanks, for all is in Your hand. Amen."

Even though I'm hungry, I'm not sure I can eat. My stomach is a mess from worry.

Leo walks over, puts his arm around me, and pulls me close. "Let's get something to eat. We're going to take off at five o'clock if they haven't shown. We'll go back to the house first, then drive the route backward from the plan they had. I'm taking Alvin and Keith. Phil

Hudson, David Hammer, and David's older boy are going with us. Mike wanted to go, but his dad talked him out of it, suggesting another day of recovery."

I nod and agree with the plan and a little food. I catch myself right before I tell him to call me if they're going to be late. The lack of phones is not easy to get used to.

The food line is fairly long, and I half wonder if we'll even get through it before Leo wants to leave. Sarah, Lois, and Karen are in line. The faces of each reflect the same concern I feel.

Leo and I do make it through the line. I take a modest amount of baked beans, barbecued elk, salad, and a few other things. I'm glad Doris sent such a large amount of meat and we brought plenty of appetizers; there really isn't a lot of food left.

A few minutes before five, Leo tells me they're going to go. He's sorry he can't help us get the food containers cleaned up, but he'll see us at home soon.

"We'll be back within an hour of full dark—around 10:30. Sooner if we find them before then, of course."

"Be careful." I hold him tight. "I'd really like it if you could bring the rest of my family home."

Grandpa Alvin waves at me as he and the others load into the truck.

I return to the gathering, which is winding down somewhat. There are still a few things on the dessert table, and I get myself a cookie, then join Olivia near the playground.

"How are you doing?" she asks.

"Worried."

"Leo say what their plan is?"

"Take the route Jake showed him, going backward. They'll be back by 10:30 with or without them."

"Hmm." Her eyebrows draw into a tight line.

We watch the children play. Lily's playing in the pea gravel with two cups, pouring gravel from one cup to the other. Tony and Malcolm are playing with a couple of other boys around the same age. Something like a game of tag, as near as I can tell.

People are starting to leave, and I look around for the rest of my family. Sarah and Lois are talking with Kelley Hudson. Deanne and Calley are starting to clean up the food. Grandma Dodie is with Gavin, walking him around while they look at things. I sure hope his mom—my sister—comes home soon. With both Angela and Tim in our missing group . . . I shut my mind down to prevent it from going there.

Sarah walks over and says, "It looks like people are leaving. We should go ahead and get our things. We'll need to make more than one trip. There's too many of us for my car. I guess we should've thought ahead."

I shake my head. "I didn't even realize."

She rests her hand on my arm. "I know. Me neither. Grandma Dodie's the one who said something about it. We've gotten used to piling into pickup beds over the last couple of days." She smiles, but it doesn't reach her eyes.

"Would you like to take a few people home?" I motion to the car. "I'll stay and work on cleaning up."

"Sure. I'll take Grandma and Gavin for sure. They're ready. Olivia—you and your children want to go this time? My car fits five, but it's such a short trip I think six will be fine.

"Maybe bring Jake's truck back?" I say. "There's a set of keys in the mudroom cabinet."

"Good idea. That way just one trip to get everyone else home."

Sarah pulls out of the driveway while I go over to help clean up the food. Belinda's still there visiting. She looks exhausted. TJ, her son, is about the same age as Malcolm.

"Do you play Minecraft?" Malcolm asks.

"Yes. Some. I don't play too much, but I like watching that guy on YouTube who plays," TJ responds.

I smile over the conversation. Malcolm loves to build things, whether with LEGO blocks, wood, or on a computer. He also loves to draw and paint; *I'm* pretty sure he gets that from me.

With most of the people now gone, there are very few vehicles still in the parking lot. Belinda appears to be saying her final goodbyes, with her mom by her side.

"Looks like we're leaving now," TJ says to Malcolm. "With my dad dead, I have to help my mom. I'll need to be the man of the house." His little shoulders sag. "I guess I'll see you later."

Malcolm bobs his head once. "Yeah, TJ. I'm really sorry about your dad. Maybe you can come over sometime. You think your mom will let you?"

"Maybe. I'll let you know."

As he walks toward his mom, Leo's truck pulls in—much faster than I think is safe.

Evan's driving while Leo and Tim in are in the bed. Phil Hudson and David Hammer both bolt from the cab when Evan is barely stopped.

"Belinda! Belinda! We need you. You and your mom," David yells, while Phil hollers for his wife to come quickly.

The first night I met Terry, he said Belinda is a nurse. I run toward the truck, wondering where Jake and Angela are. Who else is missing? Tate and Doris!

Then, Evan says words that almost stop my heart. "Doris and Angela have been shot."

Chapter 33

I quickly look around for Malcolm. He's running toward the truck. He's close enough I can throw my arms around him to stop him.

"Stay here, Buddy. Let them take care of Angela and Doris."

"No! That's my sister and my . . . my Doris. I can help. I know how to apply pressure."

"I know you do, Malcolm. But right now, Leo's there. Plus, Belinda's a nurse. She'll know what to do. Is her mom a nurse too?"

"I think so . . . or something."

"That's good then. The three of them have lots of training."

"Where's my dad? Why isn't he here?"

"I don't know. We'll find out once things calm down."

Please, Lord, let Jake be okay.

"Tell me what we have," someone, maybe Belinda, says. Kelley Hudson's also at the truck, so it may have been her.

"Doris has been shot in the right lower leg and the right side," Leo says. "The side wound seems to be a graze, with the bleeding well-controlled. The leg wound broke the bone and is showing as a compound fracture. It had good pressure on it. She's alert and oriented."

"Yes, I am. I'd sure like something for the pain. It hurts like crazy."

Belinda reaches for Doris's hand. "We'll see what we can do."

Leo continues, "Angela was shot in the back, buttocks, and back of her legs with a shotgun—most likely bird load. The pellets had a fair spread, with limited penetration for the most part. Of larger concern is blunt force trauma to the head from the butt of a rifle. She's been in and out of consciousness and has vomited several times, including when we moved her from Evan's truck to my truck."

Belinda turns to Angela as Leo finishes his report. "You're going to be okay, honey. We'll get you fixed up."

"Belinda, here's your kit," her mom says, handing up a first aid kit even larger than Leo's as she crawls into the bed of the truck.

Leo moves out of the way and starts to climb down when Belinda says, "Stay. I may need you."

"Belinda, how can I help?" Kelley asks.

"You can start with Doris. Have my mom help you. Do you have a med kit?"

"Yes, a small one in my car. Phil went to grab it. You have hand sanitizer?"

Belinda gives her hands a spritz of sanitizer, then hands it to her mom and Kelley.

"Angela, I'm going to clean my hands, then we'll take a look at you. Sounds like . . ." Belinda turns to Leo. "I'm sorry, I've forgotten your name."

After he gives his name, she nods. "Sounds like Leo did a thorough exam, but we'll take another look." Belinda turns away from Angela. "We're going to need beds for them. I'm thinking maybe my parents' house. Mom, Dad, is that okay? We could put them in the guest room with the twin beds."

"Yes, of course. That's a good idea," the mom says, while the dad shrugs.

"Okay, then. As soon as we do a basic assessment, we'll see about moving them."

She softens her voice. "Angela, I need to look at your eyes. Can you open them for me? What color are your eyes, Angela?"

"Her eyes are green," Malcolm says with a sob. "They're a really pretty green."

I hug Malcolm tight and decide, as much as I want to stay right here, I'd best take Malcolm somewhere else. As I turn to move away, I notice the rest of our rather large family unit standing next to me.

"Hey, Malcolm, how about you and I go sit on the lawn?" Roy says. "We'll let them take care of Angela and then maybe you'll be able to see her."

Through my tears, I give what I hope is something resembling a grateful smile to Roy as he starts toward the lawn. Deanne gives me a quick hug as she walks by, and Sheila pats my arm and gives me a small smile.

Lois and Keith walk over toward David Hammer. David is Mom and Jake's neighbor; he lives between their house and the Snyders' place, next to the creek.

"Excuse me," Lois says to David.

"Yes, ma'am?" he says, in a rather pronounced Texas drawl.

"Do you know where Tate and Jake are?"

"Oh, yes! I do. I'm so sorry. I plumb forgot y'all would be worrying about them. They're fine. The truck broke down and we need to go back for them. In fact, I need to get my truck and do that now."

Just then, Sarah pulls in driving Jake's truck.

"Dad! My dad's here," Malcolm yells.

Poor Malcolm. He's crushed and openly weeping when Sarah steps out.

David hears him crying and yells, "Your dad's okay. I'm going to go and get him."

Sarah, realizing something's going on at Leo's truck, runs over. She must have caught a glimpse of Angela. She cries out, "Angela! Angela! What's happened to her?"

I go over to Sarah and touch her arm. She spins around. "Where's Tate? And Jake?"

"David's going after them. He says they're fine, but the truck broke down."

"What happened?"

"I don't really know. Doris and Angela have been shot, and Angela was hit in the head with the butt of a gun."

Sarah gasps as Belinda says, "Okay, people. Let's take Doris and Angela to my parents' place. It's a sight bumpier on their driveway than the pavement they've been on so far. I'd like to try to make them a little more comfortable for the ride. Dad, I have a blanket in my car. Can you get it for me? Anyone else have blankets or pillows in their rig?"

My bug-out bag's still in Leo's truck. I rifle through it, finding the backpackers' blowup mattress and blowup pillow along with a sleeping bag.

"How about a blowup mattress?" I ask.

"That'd be great but takes too long."

"Not this kind. Pull it out, give it ten breaths, and it's inflated."

Leo looks at me and sees me also holding the sleeping bag. He whispers to Belinda, who turns and says, "Yes. Bring those. Someone start on the mattress. Someone else get that bag out of its sack."

Evan, who's been very quiet after announcing the injuries to Doris and Angela, takes the sleeping bag. I hand the pillow to Sarah to blow up. I work on the mattress. It takes me twelve breaths to inflate.

With the things from my bag, plus what other people offer, Belinda soon declares it should be much more comfortable.

Doris, looking quite white in the face, says, "I sure hope so. Just rearranging took it out of me. Still wondering about something for the pain."

"We'll do our best with that, Doris. It's not easy to have something strong enough in a civilian first aid kit."

Doris, now propped with her back against the cab in a cozy nest and the blowup pillow behind her head, lets out a sigh. "I figured as much. Evan, I think I still have painkillers leftover from my gall bladder operation. Could you go to our house and get them?"

"Good idea, Evan, but I'll want to check them out before you give her any," Belinda says. "Go to my parents' house when you have them. Bring a few things you think Doris might need also. A robe would be good. Also, if you have antibiotics, we'll need those. Where's Angela's family?"

Tim, who has also been very quiet, standing directly outside the truck bed next to Angela, says, "She's my wife."

Belinda nods. "You're Jake's son?"

"Son-in-law. Angela's his daughter."

"She'll need a few things too. A robe . . . anything else she might need. I also need bandages if either of you can bring those."

Tim steps onto the wheel of the truck to peer in the bed. "Angela . . . my Angel. I'll see you soon. You're going to be just fine." His voice cracks as he steps off the wheel.

"Okay, let's get going. TJ, honey, you stay here for a little bit and sit with Malcolm. As soon as we get them settled, I'll send Grandpa back for you." She looks to her dad. "I'll need your help at the house first."

Her dad gives an aloof shrug.

Belinda looks around the gathered group. "Who's driving?"

To my surprise, Leo says, "Katie is."

Sarah nods. "Good idea. I'll stay here until Tate and Jake get back. Tim, you and Evan take Jake's truck."

I look around. Malcolm's still with Roy on the lawn. Calley and Mike are standing near the truck. Calley's openly weeping but is very quiet about it. Keith, Lois, and Karen are behind them. I grab Calley into a fast hug, then hop in Leo's truck. I'm happy to see the keys already in the ignition.

"Slow and careful," Belinda says loud enough for me to hear. Then she gives me very basic directions to head west on the paved road and she'll tell me when to turn. Leo, Belinda, and her mom are all precariously perched in the bed. Doris is leaning against the cab. Angela's lying in the bed. From my position, I can only see from her waist down. She's lying somewhat on her side.

I heed Belinda's advice of "slow and careful" and keep my speed low, watching for any potholes along the way.

With a bang on the cab, Leo yells, "The driveway's the next left."

Turning off the main road on to the gravel drive, I slow way down so we're barely creeping. The road's in about as good of shape as Mom and Jake's, which translates to not very good at all. Thankfully, it's shorter and we're soon at the house. I get out and ask how I can help.

"Doris passed out from the pain," Leo says. "You want to unload her or Angela first?"

"Angela's still out too," Belinda says. "Let's take Doris first—might be a little easier on her if she's already out."

Kelley, Phil, and Belinda's dad are already here, having driven ahead of our slow-moving truck.

"What's the plan for getting them in?" Belinda's dad asks.

"Doris is on a roll-up stretcher I had as part of my first aid kit," Leo says. "We had her propped in the truck since she was complaining of feeling sick. We can carefully adjust her, take her in, and then bring the stretcher back for Angela."

"Should work fine," Belinda says.

"I'll go get things ready," Belinda's mom says. "Tom, you'd best help carry Doris."

Belinda's dad, Tom, nods and I think I catch a slight scowl. I wonder what that's about?

"Kelley, can you help my mom prepare the room?"

Kelley nods and heads for the house.

"Katie can stay with Angela," Leo says. "She'll keep an eye on her and yell if anything changes that she needs us for immediately. Katie, she's in the recovery position and has vomited several times. The brace is on her neck—I wouldn't rule out a neck or spinal cord injury. You know what to look for."

I dip my head. "I'll be fine."

After a few minutes of fussing, in which Doris almost comes around but then goes limp again, they have her ready to move.

"Nice and easy," Belinda says.

Even so, there's a jolt of some sort and Doris lets out a scream. She looks around wild-eyed for a second, screams again, and is out cold.

Tom puts a hand to his chest. "That about scared it out of me."

"Let's get her in," Leo says in a rush.

As soon as they have Doris out of the bed of the truck, I climb in and sit with Angela. She's a mess. Leo put a neck brace on her, there's a large bandage across her forehead trickling blood, and she's covered with an emergency blanket. I lift the blanket slightly and see her clothing has been cut open in places.

Leo said she'd been shot in the backside. It didn't sound like the shot was as big of a deal as the head wound. She's on her side, and I can see where some of the pellets have hit. Most look like angry pimples, but a few are obviously more serious. There are even a few angry streaks along her side, where the pellets left deep scratches as they whizzed by. I hold her hand while I pray. *Please, Lord—please help Angela.*

Leo and Tom are back in a few minutes with the stretcher. "Any change?" Leo asks.

I shake my head.

"Let's get her inside. Belinda, Kelley, and Tammy are getting Doris situated," Tom says.

"How can I help?" I ask.

"Just get out of our way and let us do it," Tom huffs.

Leo looks at Tom for a long minute, then quietly asks, "Is there a problem?"

"You better believe there's a problem. My daughter is in mourning. She shouldn't have to care for people right now. Especially someone she doesn't even know. Why didn't you just take them to the hospital in Billings?"

"Daddy!" Belinda yells from the doorway of the house. "I can't believe you'd say something like that. Of course I am going to do everything I can to help Angela and Doris. I'd be glad to help a stranger on the road, and I'm most certainly going to help Doris, whom I consider a friend.

"Angela may be new to this community, but her folks have been here a few years now. Not that it matters one whit to me whether I know her or not. If you had a problem with bringing them to your house, you should've said something at the community center. Now, they'll be staying here until Mom and I can get them well enough to

255

move. If you don't like it, you can go and stay at my place and take care of TJ."

Tom's face turns several shades of red. He opens his mouth to say something, then slams his lips closed and lets out a noisy sigh. "I'm sorry, pumpkin. I'm just worried about you. I know you're a mess with losing Terry."

"Whether I'm a mess or not, this is what I do. You encouraged me to become a nurse years ago, to follow in Mom's footsteps, remember? When I decided to get more training and become a nurse practitioner, you were my biggest fan. I assume you didn't hear Evan when he told me how they couldn't go to Billings—*but* it doesn't matter now. They're here. Now, do you want to help get Angela moved into the house or not?"

Tom nods.

Leo and I say nothing as we set things up to gently move Angela onto the stretcher. I'm already in the truck, so I do as Leo asks while we get her situated.

Belinda kisses her dad on the cheek, then says, "Bring her on in, but take your time. I don't want her jostled too much. I'm not sure of the extent of her injuries."

Tom takes the end of the stretcher from his position on the ground. Getting Angela out takes a few minutes, with me bracing the center as Leo makes his way from the bed of the truck. The two of them carry her in. I follow, not quite sure what's expected of me.

The house is a good-sized ranch style. We go in the front door, which opens into a large living room with a fireplace. Past the living room is a family room and dining room combination with the kitchen off to the right. We turn left down the hall and stop at the first door on the left.

This is a decent-sized bedroom, with two twin beds separated by a nightstand between them. Other than the beds, nightstand, and a straight-backed chair, the room is empty of furniture. It's very crisp and clean. Doris is in the bed closest to the closet; she already has an IV attached. The bed for Angela, nearest the door, has been turned back.

Belinda and Tammy help transfer Angela to her bed. She stirs slightly when they move her, emits a pain-filled groan, and then settles again.

Belinda bites her top lip. "Okay. That's step one. I certainly wish we could take them into Prospect for treatment. Part of me wonders if going to Pryor would be good, even without the surgical ward there. It'd likely be better than here."

"Maybe we should stabilize them and then decide," Tammy says.

"Yeah. That's what I'm thinking. Let's do this—start an IV on Angela. I really need to take a good look at Doris's leg so we know exactly what we're dealing with, but I'd like to wait until Evan returns with the painkillers. You have anything around here, Mom?"

"Local anesthesia in my kit, just like you. We'll want to use it, too, but schedule two or three would really help. I don't know why you never wrote a few prescriptions for us to keep these things on hand."

"Yes, you do, Mom."

Chapter 34

Belinda's tone speaks volumes. She and her mom share a long, hard look. I have no doubt there's quite the story here.

"I only have OTC meds in my car kit," Kelley says. "We have some stronger things at home. Phil will be bringing a second kit over shortly."

"Good, very helpful. Thanks, Kelley. Remind me . . . you were a psych nurse in the Navy?" Belinda asks.

"US Public Health Service Commissioned Corps attached to the Department of Defense when I retired. Before that I had a variety of duty stations, not only as psychiatric NP but also working in clinics and hospitals on base."

"Any ER experience?"

"I was an emergency room nurse, prior to joining USPHS. My first posting was with the Indian Health Services. We did it all there."

Belinda looks over Kelley and then nods, apparently accepting her as part of the medical team.

"Leo, you have anything in the med kit of yours we should know about?" she asks.

"Not really, ma'am. I have more bandages. I'll bring it in for you to use."

"What's your history?"

"Ma'am?"

"Are you a military medic?"

"I'm a Marine, not a Corpsman, but I had medical training in case we were stuck somewhere without one. I have EMT training post-military but didn't take my certification. I can assist with your guidance."

"That's good," Tammy says, nodding vigorously.

Belinda gives a single nod, then turns to me. "And you?"

"No. I don't know much. I took a couple of first aid classes."

"Katie has basic and advanced first aid and CPR. She's read through my EMT books and taken most of the practice quizzes in my workbook. She has plenty of book knowledge but no practical experience. She learns fast and is excellent at taking instruction. She'll be able to help. Won't you, Katie?"

I'm a little awed at his description of me. He sounds . . . proud.

"I'll do whatever is needed to help my sister and Doris."

"Okay. That'll have to do," Belinda says, sounding less than impressed with Leo's glowing recommendation.

There's a loud knock followed by, "Tim and I are here."

Tammy steps into the hall. "We're back here, Evan. What'd you find?"

Evan and Tim walk in. Tim's eyes fall on Angela, and he immediately rushes to her bed, gently touches her face, then puts his hand on her arm.

Evan looks like he'd like to do the same things to Doris, but instead, he says, "Three tablets of Percocet from her surgery last year, and some Tylenol 3 I had for a . . . thing . . . but it made me sick, so I didn't take but two of them—thirteen in the bottle. And here's a couple of Xanax Doris had from when she got a colonoscopy. She was supposed to take them before she left but forgot."

"Okay. These will be helpful. I'm going to wake her and medicate her. We'll wait twenty minutes or so, then take a look at her leg. I hope it's not too bad. I'm not really set up for anything resembling surgery here," Belinda says and excuses herself to wash her hands.

Surgery? I thought she was a nurse not a surgeon. I must have given Evan a quizzical look because he says, "She's a surgical nurse practitioner. She works—*worked*—with a physician in Prospect as his right hand. She sees her own patients and assists with surgeries. I've heard she's very good. I also heard her physician was one of the doctors killed at the hospital a few days ago. Losing her husband and also her business partner has been hard."

"I had no idea," Kelley says. "I knew she was a nurse but didn't realize she was a surgical NP. We're very fortunate to have her. Even though you say she assisted with surgeries, my guess is she did a lot more than just assist."

Belinda walks back in, saying it's time to bring Doris around. Smelling salts do the trick, and Doris comes to with a yelp of pain. Belinda medicates her and gets her settled, then says, "While we're waiting on those meds to get into your system, I'll take a look over Angela."

Belinda steps out to wash again, then gloves up when she returns to the room. She does what appears to be a thorough exam of an unconscious Angela. She talks calmly to my sister while she checks her out.

"Okay, Angela. Your pupils are slightly dilated—the left more than the right. You're going to have a whopper of a headache when you wake up."

Angela shifts slightly and softly moans.

"Mm-hmm. I guess you probably already do."

"Can you give her something for the pain?" Tim asks.

"Not yet. I need her to come around a bit before we give her any narcotics. Let's take a look under the bandage."

She carefully undoes the bandage. After a moment or two of inspection, she asks, "How many times was she hit?"

"Two, we think," Evan answers.

"We weren't there," Tim adds. "They were watching the truck when two guys ambushed them."

Doris, sounding slightly groggy and in pain, says, "That's what it was—an ambush. We were with the truck and trailer, standing at the front. All of a sudden, my right side stung and I heard a ping on metal. The repercussion was very slight. I'd guess it was a .22."

Evan agrees it was.

"I was kind of surprised to see blood on my side. Then Angela yelped. She had been sort of turned toward me when the shotgun blast caught her backside and around to her left a bit. Then the creep shot my leg out from under me, and I went down.

"We were both trying to scoot around for cover when one of them came out of nowhere. He grabbed Angela by the hair and started to pull her away. She managed to get her gun out and gut shot the dirtbag. Then the other one butt-stroked her—at least two times. I had my gun out by then, ready to shoot, but someone else beat me to it. Who was that? You, Evan?"

"Jake. He heard a commotion and hightailed it back. We were all behind him."

"Jake? Really? He killed him? Evan, is Jake okay?" Doris asks with alarm.

"Yes . . . he's fine for now. It'll probably be a good idea for Kelley to spend some time talking with him. The wounds were lethal. All three shots, center mass. The two shots Angela took on her guy had the same result—just took him longer to die. We'll need to be here for both of them."

Angela and Jake killed a couple of guys today. I don't know what to say or think about this. I have no doubt those guys planned bad things for Angela and Doris, which makes part of me happy they're dead.

The other part of me thinks Angela and Jake will be pretty messed up over this. Of course, maybe I'm wrong.

I know Jake is willing to do anything for our family. Jake's always been on the quiet side, but his devotion to all of us is apparent through his actions, if not his words.

"What happened to your truck?" I ask.

"The ladies were at the front of the truck when the shooting happened. Either the .22 or the bird shot pellets damaged the radiator and who knows what else. We repaired it a few times and made it pretty close to home until it gave up the ghost."

Tom crosses his arms. "And why didn't you take them to Billings where a proper hospital is, instead of bringing them here?"

"Daddy . . . " Belinda murmurs, a warning in her voice.

"We tried to. Seems Billings has gone to pot. Some people in the little community we were in were trying to help us with Doris and Angela. Someone suggested going to Billings, but someone else said there's a roadblock on the road before Laurel. No one is getting through. We could've gone around the long way, but that's a rough road and they'd heard some kind of gangs are going through there shooting at people and stealing their stuff. I don't know if it's true, but we couldn't risk it."

Evan turns to Belinda. "Belinda, I'm so sorry to call on you like this, but we really didn't see any other options. If you can get them stabilized well enough to travel, we can try to get them to Billings or find another hospital. The one in Red Lodge maybe, but the same people told us they weren't sure how the staffing is there. Of course, they do have facilities . . . "

"We'll see. Dad, do you think you can go and get TJ? I hate to leave him there any longer. Take him to my place, please. Maybe you could stay there with him tonight since I'll need to take care of my patients. Let Angela's family know we're looking her over, and once I know more, someone will go to their home."

Tom turns on his heel and storms off. Both Belinda and Tammy watch him leave.

With a sigh, Belinda turns to Leo. "Help me turn Angela. Leave the neck brace in place, and let's keep her aligned until I can be sure of her injuries." In her gentle nurse voice, she says, "Angela, we're going to turn you over a little more so I can look at your back. Don't help us. We'll do all the work. You just keep resting and getting well."

Again, Angela groans in response.

"Good girl. I like that you can acknowledge me."

"It's a good sign," Tammy tells Tim.

Belinda spends a few more minutes looking over Angela. "Mom, let's start her on a course of prophylactic antibiotics. Tim, is she allergic to anything?"

"No. Not that I know of. Katie?"

"No . . . I don't think so but can't remember her taking many medications."

"Let's give her an ampicillin IV, then we'll do a course of oral Keflex once she comes around. Doris will need antibiotics also. You allergic to anything, Doris?"

"Nope. Nothing."

"Good, that helps. Once we see what we're dealing with, we'll know better what to use." Belinda turns back to Angela. "You're going to be okay, Angela. Leo and I are going to roll you back onto your side. You just rest.

"Mom, you think you can work on removing the pellets closer to the surface? Use a local and don't be in a hurry. If it's not easy to access, leave it. It looks like the shooter was a considerable distance away, so the penetration was limited. We got lucky there. Wait until I have a plan with Doris before you start, in case one of us needs to move out of the room.

"There's a few slices on her side, which appear to have been grazing wounds, and a couple spots near her shoulder might be a little deeper. I don't think she has a spinal cord injury, but I want to leave the brace in place for now to be on the safe side. It may also help keep her from thrashing as she comes around."

After Belinda finishes with Angela, she steps out again, asking Kelley to join her. They aren't gone long before they return and glove up.

"Okay, Doris. Time to take look. I'm going to give you a local, then Leo and I are going to get a gander at your leg. We'll use Lidocaine and Marcaine in equal parts. That'll give us some time to see what we have and take care of fixing you up. You ready?"

"Sure. Why not?" Doris says, slightly slurring her words.

"You feeling the meds I gave you earlier?"

"Sure 'nuff. Much better. Still hurts but kind of faraway instead of up close and personal."

"Let's take a look, then."

Evan's standing next to Doris now, holding her hand. Leo, Kelley, and Belinda are all at the foot of the bed, with Kelley and Belinda on one side and Leo on the other.

Tammy brings a chair in so Tim can sit and hold Angela's hand. She motions me to step out with her.

"How are you holding up?" she asks as we head toward the kitchen.

"I'm okay. What can I do to help?"

"In a bit, after Doris is evaluated, I'll have you help me with Angela. Is your mom home yet?"

Not trusting my voice, I shake my head in response. I wish Mom was here. I think about Jake and wonder if David was able to get him home. I wish he was here too.

"I'm sorry." She rests a hand on my forearm.

I suspect she'd like to say more, like "she'll be home soon" or something else to placate me, but she knows, as well as I do, every day my mom doesn't return, her chances of ever making it home diminish.

"I'll help you," I say.

Tammy pats my arm and offers me a glass of water. My mind is swimming with the events of the day and what will happen next. I'm an artist, not a nurse. I think about the recent changes in my life, not just since we've arrived in Bakerville but the last few months.

I guess since the bug-out bag arrived. That backpack really altered my plans. No, not the backpack . . . my plans altered before. When I met Leo and we decided to move in together.

The backpack opened my eyes to being self-sufficient. And then I started making changes with learning self-defense, taking first aid classes, and keeping my eyes open to what was happening in our world. Moving in with Leo opened my eyes to living of the world.

Not exactly what I should be doing. I remember a song from youth group that talked about living *in* the world but not being *of* the world.

Such subtle difference in those words: in and of. *B*ut now, in these last few days, those differences make sense. Leo and I have made a decision to no longer live together. Even if the world went back to normal tomorrow, we wouldn't move back into the same apartment until we're married.

This has been quite a journey so far.

My thoughts are interrupted when Belinda comes into the kitchen.

"How is it?" Tammy asks.

"It's a mess," Belinda says quietly. "Let's step outside. I need some air."

I don't follow them out.

Belinda stops and looks at me. "You too. Your boyfriend and Kelley will be out in a minute also. Evan and Tim can have some time alone with their wives while we plan."

After Leo and Kelley join us, Belinda says, "The bullet hit at an angle which broke both the tibia and the fibula. The breaks weren't entirely clean, and ideally, she'd have surgery and hardware to put her back together." Belinda pauses and lets out a big sigh.

"With Prospect hospital out of commission and the danger they were told about for reaching Billings, those aren't options. And if Red Lodge doesn't have staff . . . I don't know. I could assist with the surgery, but we'd need an orthopedist—it's really beyond what I should do on my own.

"Not to mention, I don't have any hardware. I don't want to transport her unless we know there's an orthopedist there. The good news—the bullet went through. I'm not really sure how that happened. We're pretty fortunate those idiots were using a .22 and shotgun with bird load from a distance, otherwise . . ." She shakes her head.

"She lost a little blood, but they were able to get it stopped pretty well, so I'm not too worried about blood loss. I want to clean it a little more, bandage it to protect the entrance and exit wounds, lightly set it, and then put her in a full-length air cast. We'll give her an IV dose of antibiotics and forty-eight hours of prophylactic orals. Tomorrow, I'll drive to Red Lodge and see what I can find out about the hospital. Then we'll know better how to proceed."

"With all due respect, ma'am, it'd be best for someone else to go to the hospital," Leo says. "With your skills, we shouldn't risk your safety if we can avoid it."

Belinda begins to argue, then stops herself when Tammy says, "He's right, honey. You shouldn't go, neither should I and neither should Leo or Kelley. If Sandy Styles were home, I'd tell her the same thing." Tammy looks at Leo and me. "She's a nurse also."

"Okay," Belinda says. "You're probably right. Katie stays home, too, and she becomes our apprentice so she can learn what she needs to know. Provided she's as competent as Leo says, she'll learn quickly. Katie, you willing?"

I liked taking the first aid courses and reading the info in Leo's books, but I'm not a nurse. At one time, I wanted to be a doctor, but really only because they make good money. I'm an artist at heart. I decide to tell it like it is.

"I'm willing, but you should know, I'm an artist, a graphic design major. I'm not sure I have the aptitude for this. I'd appreciate your honesty if you notice I'm not cutting it, then you can find someone else before wasting too much time on me."

"Deal." Belinda offers me her hand. "Now, we need to find someone to go tomorrow, and get Doris and Angela set for tonight. Mom, are you ready to work on Angela?"

"Yes. And Katie's going to have her first lesson by helping me."

"Leo, I'll need your help with Doris. Red Lodge hospital is our best choice. Tomorrow, we'll find someone to go to Red Lodge and see if they're still functioning. Not Jake, Evan, or anyone else in the truck today. In fact, I'd like Kelley to talk with everyone in the truck for a mental health evaluation."

"Let's put Phil in charge of finding someone to go tomorrow," Tammy says.

Belinda taps a finger to her chin. "He's the best choice. Kelley, you okay with that?"

"Phil will do what's needed," Kelley says simply. "He should be back here shortly with more of my supplies."

"I need a few specific things. Do you think you have them?"

"Let me know what it is, and if I do, we can have Phil gather it."

Belinda and Kelley make a list of supplies. Instead of waiting for Phil, it's decided to send Evan and Tim to find him and bring the items back.

Inside, Belinda gives Evan and Tim the list and asks them to not only find Phil but also Jake and Tate and to bring them all here. She asks they not rush so the medical team has time to care for Doris and Angela.

Chapter 35

The guys return in about an hour, but it's almost another hour before we finish what we need to do with Angela and Doris. Belinda is pleased Doris's side wound cleaned up so well. Doris was talking through the procedure, feeling little pain with the narcotics and the local. The leg was irrigated, but little else was done.

Angela stirred a few times while we worked on her, including vomiting once. Kelley splits her time between monitoring Doris and monitoring Angela.

After Tammy declares we're finished with Angela, both Belinda and Kelley check our work. They agree the BBs left should stay and they may rise closer to the surface.

After we clean the room and wash up, Tammy stays with Angela and Doris while the rest of us go out to the living room where the five men are visiting with each other.

Jake wraps me in a hug, then Tate hugs me. Tim says he might as well hug me also since he didn't do it earlier.

Belinda speaks about Doris's and Angela's conditions first, saying she feels good about where things are at this moment—Angela should start coming around in a few hours, and we'll know more then. Doris is resting comfortably and asking for Evan.

Phil hands Kelley the kit he brought, announcing he was able to find everything on Belinda's list.

"Well done, Phil. I don't know if anyone mentioned this to you, but we'd like to check out Red Lodge hospital," Belinda says.

"Evan told me. I'm happy to go and find out."

"Good, thank you. I'll write a letter for you to take along. Give it to whoever they'll let you see that seems to be in charge. I'll detail their injuries and we can, hopefully, find out if they have the staff needed for their care. Can you go first thing in the morning?"

"You bet. With the trouble Evan and Jake ran into today, I'll need to find at least one person to go along, riding shotgun. Just like in the old days of the stagecoach guards." Phil shakes his head.

"Seems we'd be smart to go back to that," Evan agrees.

Kelley glances around the room. "Since you're all here, I'd like to meet with you each individually. Evan, let's start with you, then Tim, Tate, and Jake—you're last."

"Sounds like a good plan, Kelley." Belinda nods. "We don't need any . . . um . . . mental health breakdowns during this fiasco. Let's briefly talk about my plan for staffing. I want someone in the room with them pretty much continuously for the next forty-eight hours, or until we can transfer them to a real hospital."

"Yes, that'd be best," Kelley says.

"My mom is in with them now. Katie, you'll sit with them next from 10:00 until 2:00. I know you aren't experienced, but it'll be fine. Leo, make yourself a bed on the couch. You're staying over and will take over for Katie at 2:00 a.m. I'm going to sleep in the guest room, so we'll be here if you need us. After your shift, move to the couch to get some shut-eye. Mom and I will take over at 6:00 so you two can go home. Kelley, why don't you head home after visiting with the guys, then join us again tomorrow—say around 9:00 a.m."

"Sounds good," Kelley agrees.

"Kelley, I'm going to take off," Phil says. "We brought your car so you can get home." He kisses her goodbye and is out the door, while Evan and Kelley move to a back bedroom to have their mental health chat.

I think it's a little strange Kelley, who's a real nurse, is going home and I'm staying. What can I really do? I guess if it's just a matter of sitting and watching so someone who knows something can be called, I can handle it. Still . . . it's not what I'd do.

Leo and I sit down to chat with Jake, Tim, and Tate. Before I can even ask Jake how he's doing or express my concern over what happened, we're interrupted by the urgent blare of a horn.

Phil steps back inside. "Jake, I think this is one of your people . . . at least, it's your little blue car."

We start for the door as Belinda and Tammy come out and ask what's going on.

I answer, "Not sure," and keep going.

Calley jumps out of the passenger's side before the car is completely stopped and runs to Jake, yelling, "He took her! That guy took Olivia! And he hurt Sarah."

Mike, Calley's driver, is behind her. "We have Sarah and Lois in the backseat. He grazed Sarah with a bullet."

Mike isn't even finished speaking before Tate, followed by Belinda and Leo, are at the car.

"I'm okay. It's really just a scrape," Sarah says.

Tate is holding and hugging her when Belinda orders, "Let me take a look, just to be sure."

I hadn't noticed Tammy, but she's suddenly there with Leo's fold-up stretcher, asking if they need it.

"Sarah, let's put you on the stretcher, and I'll take you in and look at you."

"I don't need a stretcher. It's really not bad. I ran from where that Morse idiot carjacked us back to the house. I'm pretty sure I can walk from the car into your place."

Belinda lets out an exasperated sigh before offering Sarah her arm.

"What's this about Olivia?" Phil asks, as Belinda helps Sarah from the car.

"She wanted to have her car. She and I went to her place to get it. Grandma, Karen, and Lois watched her children while we walked over the hill. We figured we had just enough time to get there before dark. Neither of us wanted to be walking around in the dark, but in the light . . . we didn't worry much.

"It's so close to her place, overland, we were there in only about fifteen minutes. We spent a little time looking at the devastation and . . . well . . . she was pretty upset about it. She said she wanted to go back tomorrow and see if she could salvage anything.

"Anyway, we got her car and started heading back right at dark. We were driving by the reservoir, when there he was. He had his gun pointed right at us. I told Olivia to floor it and hit him, but instead, she stopped and tried to back up. He was on her so quick . . . he stuck the gun right in her face. This time he wasn't wearing a mask, so it was easy to see it was Dan Morse."

Tate mutters something under his breath, while Phil makes a tutting noise.

Sarah pauses while Leo opens the front door and Belinda tells her to mind the step.

She sends Belinda a nod. "He told me to get out. He had Olivia scoot over to the passenger side. He said something really strange: '*Now you can go see your sister.*' I didn't know what he meant but didn't like the way he said it. I jumped into the ditch as he shot.

Honestly, I wasn't even sure he shot me, thought maybe I scratched myself on the brush or somehow caught the fence.

"Then, he took off with Olivia in her car. As soon as he was gone, I climbed out of the ditch and ran to the house. Tate, I'm so glad you told me to keep a flashlight on me. It got dark fast and . . . " Sarah starts crying.

"We didn't know they'd left," Calley says. "When we saw Evan at the community center, he asked if we'd take care of his dog this evening, so we were letting him out and feeding him. We were just at the driveway when we caught Sarah in our headlights while cresting the hill. She waved her arm at us, and we drove over. She told us what happened. When we looked at her arm, Mike said he was pretty sure she'd been shot and the gray around the edge was from the gun powder."

Mike nods. "Yeah. Pretty sure it is."

Sarah, now sitting on a dining room chair while Belinda looks at her arm, gives a slight shrug. Evan and Kelley, prompted by the commotion, are standing in the hallway.

"I agree," Belinda says. "Good thing you were quick on your feet and got out of the way. What a strange thing for him to say . . . "

"Do you think he had something to do with Doris and Angela being attacked?" I ask.

"How could that be? Weren't you in Montana when it happened?" Tammy asks.

Evan and Jake look at each other.

"We were," Evan says. "But it's still possible. Doris had said she thought she caught a glimpse of Morse when we were in Red Lodge. She wasn't sure, and we couldn't find him when we tried to look."

Jake rubs the scruff on his chin. "Yeah. It's definitely possible he could've been behind it."

Tim looks like he's about to blow up. "Let's go find him. We'll get Olivia back and . . . and . . . take care of that . . . that . . . psycho."

Evan dips his chin. "I agree we need to find him and get Olivia back. But not you, Tim. And not me. I don't think Jake or anyone else who's been directly involved should go. We aren't vigilantes . . . though, I'd sure like to be. We need to talk with Deputy Fred. Did you guys hear, when the sheriff department sent him home from his duty as a jailer, they made him a full deputy? I think the theory was he'd be the law in Bakerville until things calm down. Phil, I suspect he'll need your help."

Phil tilts his head. "Belinda, are you okay with me finding someone to go to the hospital in Red Lodge tomorrow, and I'll help Fred get a group together to find Olivia?"

"Yes. Of course. As long as you pick someone you trust to get it done, that's fine."

"It'll get done. I'm going to find people tonight to start looking for Olivia. Belinda, Tammy—Tom would be a good one to go with us. I know he hates Morse because . . . well, we're not sure what all he's done, but Tom's an excellent tracker."

"Yes, he is," Tammy declares with pride, while Belinda says, "He should go. But I really don't want TJ here tonight. It'll be a long night caring for Angela and Doris."

"He can go to our place," Jake says. "Might be good to have him there to help distract Tony."

"Sure, Jake. Good idea. Sarah, I think you're going to be just fine. Doesn't even need stitches. I cleaned it and put a little ointment and a bandage on it. I want to see you again tomorrow. You can go home."

"Let's take off, then. We'll stop at your place and Jake can pick up TJ, provided your dad agrees to go along," Phil tells Belinda, as he motions those who are leaving to get going before pulling Kelley into a tight hug.

"Jake and Tate . . . I still want to talk with you. It can wait until tomorrow. Tim, you too. Right now, say goodnight to your wife. Evan, you also. I'm going to leave for tonight but will be back here tomorrow to help Belinda and Tammy. Show up after ten in the morning," Kelley says.

Everyone says their goodbyes. Leo and I stay behind for our overnight shifts.

"You think she'll be okay? Olivia?" I ask Leo.

He hesitates a fraction too long before answering, "They'll find her."

Tears well up in my eyes as I whisper, "But will they find her . . . alive?"

He pulls me into a tight hug. We stay that way for many minutes.

Tammy and Belinda both go in to check on the patients. A few minutes later, Belinda is back.

"They're fine. No changes. Let's get something to eat. I didn't feel much like eating at the reception thing, but now I do. Come into the kitchen."

She points to a blue cooler on the countertop. "Leo, there's some roast and cheese in there. Why don't you pull them out? Katie, grab a cutting board from the drawer there and slice things up."

"You have power?" I ask, after seeing ice in the cooler.

"At my house. We have a small wind system and a generator, which I'm using to keep the freezer going. I keep Mom and Dad supplied with ice. We have cornbread also. Mom made the cornbread by cooking it on the grill. One side was slightly burned, but otherwise, it's okay."

Within a few minutes, we're at the table enjoying our snack.

"The cornbread is delicious," I say.

"Yeah, turned out pretty good. I guess we're going to have to get used to alternative cooking. We're fortunate to have a few things set up here. Most people in the community aren't as fortunate."

As we're finishing, Tom comes in the front door. He looks like a wreck. Without preamble, he asks, "Where's your mom?"

"She's with Doris and Angela," Belinda says.

"I'm here, honey," Tammy says from the hall.

"I need to talk with you. C'mon outside for a minute."

Leo wipes his mouth on a napkin. "I'll stay with Doris and Angela for you."

Belinda and I tidy the kitchen. A few minutes later, her mom and dad come back in.

"Belinda," Tom says her name as more of a sigh. "I need to talk with you, pumpkin."

I start to leave, but Tom stops me. "You might as well stay. What I have to say will soon be public knowledge."

I look from Tom to Tammy—she's obviously been crying. She gives me a nod as Tom says, "Sit down, pumpkin."

"Dad? What's going on?"

"I'm sorry, sweetie. It wasn't Morse."

"What do you mean? Of course it was Morse. Katie's sister saw him take Olivia. He shot her in the process. Everyone knows he was the one who burned her house down, and he definitely had a thing for her."

"Not that. Morse took Olivia, but he . . . he didn't kill Terry. I did."

Belinda blinks several times and then puts a hand to the back of her neck. "What do you mean, you did?"

"I did it. I knew all about him stepping out on you and abusing you. And then, when he started on little TJ . . . I had it out with him a few months ago, and he said it would stop. But when I saw you the other day, I knew he was still doing it, just being sneakier about it and hitting you where it wouldn't show. And I knew he'd been using again."

Belinda opens her mouth to say something, but her dad raises his hand.

"Wait. Let me finish." Tom takes a deep breath. "The day he . . . died . . . I caught him coming out of Morse's house. The wife was right behind him, and they were making out on the front porch. They didn't see me. I caught up with him. He was drunk or high or something. He told me to stick it and mind my own business. I snapped. Next thing I knew, he was dead. I'm so sorry, pumpkin."

"You're sorry?" Belinda screams. "Sorry! You killed my husband, my son's father, and you're sorry?"

"I don't know what else to say. I'm going to tell the others. Whatever they want to do with me, I understand. I do hope they'll first let me help find Olivia like they asked. But I had to tell you and your mom before I left. I had to make sure you knew what I'd done. Morse isn't a very good guy, but he didn't kill Terry. I did."

With that, he turns and goes out the door. His old pickup starts. Belinda jumps out of her chair and runs out the door. "Daddy! Daddy! Wait."

I look out the window as his truck skids to a stop. Belinda is at the driver's side. I can't hear what they're saying, but she's reaching inside. At first, I think she's smacking him but can then tell she's trying to hug him. After a minute or so, she steps away and he drives off.

Belinda comes back in the house. Tammy wraps her in a hug and gently guides her to the sofa. They stay there for a long time, rocking and crying. I go in and sit with Leo. We speak quietly as I tell him what happened. He'd been able to hear most of the conversation, but I fill in a few blanks.

After about an hour, Doris is stirring and in pain. Leo asks me to stay while he goes to ask about meds for her. He returns with a medication order from Belinda. It takes twenty minutes or so for the pain pills to start working and for Doris to get back to sleep. It's now time for my 10:00 p.m. shift.

"Why don't you go out and check on Belinda and Tammy?" Leo asks. "See if any of the shift plans have been altered."

Belinda is still sitting in the front room. She jumps slightly when she sees me.

"Hey, Katie." Her voice drips with weariness. "Mom's gone to bed. I'm going shortly, so Leo can have the couch. When your shift ends, you can take the guest room. It's one door past the room Angela and Doris are using. I'll stay with mom."

"Sure, so I should just wake you if I have a problem?"

"Yeah, you know what to look for?"

"Anything out of the ordinary that concerns me?"

She sighs. "I guess that'll work." With that, she shuffles off to bed.

I replace Leo in the room. The time passes quickly, and Leo soon relieves me. Angela and Doris barely stirred.

The guest room is fine. I set the alarm on my phone for 6:00 a.m. I turn the phone to max battery conservation—even so, I'm going to need to charge it tomorrow. Thankfully, we have car chargers.

Chapter 36

Thursday, Day 8

The alarm startles me awake. After using the hall restroom and washing up, I go into Angela and Doris's room. Belinda's sitting next to Angela, softly talking to her. When I walk in, Angela turns her head slightly. She's awake!

I rush to her side as Belinda says, "She's coming around nicely. She has a massive headache, but that's to be expected."

"Hey, Angela."

"Hey. Is Gavin okay?"

"Of course. Grandma Dodie has been . . . well, doting on him."

"That sounds about right. And Tim? I know he was pretty upset."

"He was worried about you is all."

"Yeah. Would you ask Mom to come in?"

I'm not sure how to answer, and during my pause she says, "Is Gavin okay?"

I look at Belinda, who only nods at me, then says, "He's fine, Angela. Would you like to rest a little more?"

Angela closes her eyes and goes to sleep. This time it seems like an actual sleep and not out cold like before.

Belinda motions me to the door.

"She's doing well. It's normal to be confused and repeating herself after a blow to the head like she's had. She'll be more alert next time she wakes. Leo gave her some Tylenol last time she was awake. I don't want her to have anything stronger yet. She didn't vomit overnight, so that's a good thing."

"She asked about our mom. Does she think Mom's here?"

"Just part of the confusion. I didn't tell her your mom's still missing. No reason to mention it right now."

"Where's Leo? I thought he was on until six."

"I just relieved him about fifteen minutes ago. He said he was going to go outside for a bit. You hungry? Feel free to help yourself to the remains of the food we had last."

"I'm not hungry but could use some water. Can I bring you anything?"

"Nah, I'm fine for now. I might let you relieve me in a bit so I can eat. I don't want us eating in the room. I guess you guys will have to stay here until one of your crew shows up. I don't think they left you a vehicle."

"Yeah, I guess we didn't think of that last night. Too much going on."

I'm in the living room when Leo walks in the door. "Good morning, Katie. You sleep okay?"

"Sure, didn't seem like long enough, though. What were you doing?"

"Working out a bit. I was feeling pretty sluggish and thought it might help. We're going to need to make a point of staying in shape. Of course, with the farming, building, and everything else . . . I guess we'll be in shape with that."

"I guess, but I still want to take time to practice our Krav Maga. We might not need to bike ride and stuff—well, for fun anyway—but I don't want to lose the slight skills I've gained so far."

"True. Evan asked me about helping put together a security detail. With everything happening, it seems smart to have more . . . I guess, protection."

"Just our area? Or is he thinking the entire community?"

"Our neighborhood, at least for now."

"And you want to be a part of this detail?"

"Not just me, we're thinking pretty much everyone. We, at the very least, want everyone comfortable with shooting and some basic up close and personal self-defense methods."

"So, what . . . you're going to teach Krav Maga?"

"Not necessarily. Evan has self-defense training from his time on the job. Jake recently started martial arts training. I have what we've learned in Krav Maga but also during my time in the Corp. I think we're each a little partial to our own methods, but we'll probably put something together based on all of it."

"Hmm. I guess it makes sense."

"It does. So the loose plan right now is everyone learns tactical firearms and basic self-defense. And then, anyone who wants to be part of the . . . I don't know, we don't have a name for it yet, but the tactical team, has dedicated daily training. PT, shooting, hand-to-hand, all of it."

"So, what? You'll be fighting machines?"

"*We'll* be fighting machines, babe."

"We'll . . . you think I'd be part of that group? I think with the medical team and helping Jake on the farm, I'll be plenty busy."

"True, but keep in mind, the medical team won't be needed daily. You'll be more on call for them."

"But don't you think Belinda will have training also?"

"You'll be able to handle it."

I shake my head, not completely disagreeing but not really believing it could work out as he expects.

A few minutes later, Belinda pops her head into the hall and calls for one of us to give her a short food break. I go in.

Doris stretches an arm in the air, wincing from the movement. "Remind me not to do that again."

"I bet. Can I get you anything?"

"I wouldn't mind some food. I'm starting to get hungry."

"I saw in the notes Belinda left you can have liquids. When she returns, I'll see what I can find for you."

After preparing a meal of warm Jell-O and hot tea for Doris, Belinda tells me I'm free to go and am back on at eight this evening. Since I'm stuck here until Jake returns, I decide I'll take a walk along the river.

Tammy and Belinda both have riverfront property. In the midst of the hoopla last night, I noticed a dirt-packed path winding its way toward the water.

I take a quick look around for Leo. Not finding him, I head out on my own. The trail is obviously well used. I can imagine Belinda and her son, TJ, walking to the river. Maybe Tom takes TJ fishing using this path.

So much sadness in this family. I totally get Tom killing his son-in-law to protect his daughter and grandson. Some people would consider this noble. I also know that taking the law into his own hands wasn't the right thing to do. Maybe he thought, with the way our world has changed, he had nothing to lose.

The path opens up, and there's the river. Jake says they've had a lot of rain this spring after a heavy snow year. The runoff from the mountains has the river high and muddy. Not suitable for fishing right now. Jake has a special hot spot he takes Malcolm where a creek meets the river. They went fishing last week, before the attacks started, but haven't been since. Maybe a few of us should give it a try. Fresh fish is always nice.

I wonder, if things don't come back to normal soon, if fish will be one of the things we exist on. The stored food won't last forever. There's also a lot of game around Bakerville—elk, antelope, and the occasional moose. And lots and lots of deer; almost too many.

There's a problem with the deer, though, a sickness that's been going around. Mom told me about it, but I wasn't really listening, so I don't know the details. I know she's concerned, and they started having their deer tested last year. I think the elk can get the sickness, too, but it's not as common.

A loud rustle in the brush causes me to jump. Before I can turn and see what's there, I'm grabbed from behind, my arms pinned to my side—a bear hug, completely engulfing me.

I immediately bend my legs to lower my center of gravity. Hands in tight fists, I throw my arms straight up. This gives me just enough space to slide to the left and drive my right elbow into his sternum.

An *oomph* escapes from him as I elbow him again, then turn to confront him face on, to attack. He's close, too close. I raise my knee to his groin. One, two, three strikes, while simultaneously pummeling him with my elbow to the base of his neck, right where it meets his shoulder. As he starts to go down, my knee meets his chin. A crunch of bone.

I jump back, putting distance between us. A moan but no movement.

I turn-tail and run, harder and faster than I've ever ran before. I don't look back. How far did I walk? I'm not sure . . . a quarter mile maybe? Where's the trail? There.

My lungs burn as I race toward Tammy's house. Toward Leo. Toward safety. I'm a hundred yards from the house. I chance a glance behind me. No one.

I crash through the front door, slam it shut, and turn the deadbolt. With a ragged breath, I cry, "Leo? Leo?"

His response is immediate. "What happened?"

Where is he? There. Crouched low, handgun holstered but obviously at the ready, using the kitchen wall as cover as he peers around it.

"Get down and scoot over here," he commands.

I oblige, dropping to my hands and knees and crawling to him.

From the hallway, Belinda quietly and calmly says, "What's going on?"

"I was attacked. Some guy, he grabbed me from behind. I got away, but don't know . . . I don't know where he is."

"Belinda?" Leo asks.

"Go," Belinda says. "We'll secure the house."

"Where'd you last see him?"

"On the ground. Next to the river." Leo gives me a questioning look. "I took the path to the river. I walked upstream . . . maybe a quarter mile."

"I'll be right back. Stay inside and keep the doors locked," he says, as he quietly goes out the back door.

Belinda and her mom both appear. Tammy's holding a shotgun. Belinda has a rather large revolver. Both muzzles are pointed toward the ground.

"Are you injured?" Tammy asks.

"I don't think so. Shook up but not physically hurt." I want to fall apart. I want to cry and whimper over what has happened. I blink rapidly to chase away the tears. Somehow, I manage to keep it together.

Belinda gives me a curt nod.

A knock from the front door reverberates through the house.

"It's me, Leo."

I start for the door, as Belinda says, "Wait." She cautiously goes to the living room, sliding the curtain just enough to peek out. "Go ahead," she tells me, standing at the ready.

I let Leo in, then relock the door.

"I couldn't find him," he says. "I found the place where he grabbed you. Looks like you bloodied his nose or something."

"Probably." I nod.

"Did you know him?" Belinda asks me.

"No, he wasn't someone I recognized."

"Evan and Jake should be here shortly. Maybe, once they're here, you guys should go out again," Belinda says.

"Agreed." Leo gives a curt nod.

It's only a few minutes until Jake's and Evan's trucks pull in. Leo and Belinda go out to meet them, telling them what's going on. I stay inside, going into Angela's room. Doris is awake and I tell her what happened, crying through the entire story. I'm physically and emotionally drained.

Doris and I sit quietly for many minutes. I'm startled when Angela wakes up with a gasp. She glances around, asks about Gavin and Tim, then wants to know if Mom can come see her. She falls back to sleep almost instantly.

There's a slight knock on the door frame followed by Evan and Tim entering. "Heard what happened. You okay?" Tim asks.

I nod, not trusting my voice.

"We're going to make sure there's always a guard here," Evan says. "And no more walks alone."

"Yeah. I never even thought about it being dangerous. That was stupid on my part." Tears fill my eyes again. I blink rapidly. One escapes.

"Is Leo inside?" I ask.

"In the living room," Tim says.

I excuse myself so they can visit with their wives. Jake, also in the living room, along with Alvin and Leo, walks over to me and wraps me in a hug.

"You did well, Katie," Jake says. "I'm so glad you knew what to do—how to get away."

"It was . . . instinct almost. We've practice things like that. I never thought . . . " I start crying again as Jake comforts me.

When I finally pull myself together, Alvin says, "We followed the blood trail a little ways. You must have hit him pretty good. Left quite a puddle, but it petered out pretty quickly."

I release a loud breath. "What about Morse? Did they find him?"

"I haven't heard anything yet," Jake says. "They did find something last night, though."

"Oh?"

"Yeah, Phil went to Dan Morse's house. Found his wife dead."

My hand goes to my mouth. "What?"

"I know what you're thinking—it wasn't Tom. He told Phil about killing Terry, but he says he didn't kill the wife. Phil believes him, and the evidence leads to Morse. Morse killed his own dog too."

Chapter 37

"Morse killed his dog?" Leo shakes his head.

"Yeah. That doesn't bode well," Jake says.

"What do you mean?" I ask.

Leo gently says, "Lots of people kill their dog and then themselves."

"So you think he's on some kind of suicide mission? Grab Olivia and then he'll . . . what? Murder-suicide?"

Jake and Leo both shrug.

A shiver runs through me. "They're out now? Looking for him?"

Jake dips his head. "They planned to start at dawn. A guy Morse used to be friendly with thinks he might know where to find him. Morse took him to a few caves in the national forest before. Seems Morse even has them set up for . . . I don't know . . . entertaining or something. He has camping gear and food—the whole thing." Jake gives a shrug. "Maybe he set them up as bug-out locations."

Leo crosses his arms. "So they're looking there first?"

"He thinks it's likely they'll find them in one of the caves."

Evan sticks his head out from the sick room and asks Jake if he can join them for a minute. Alvin follows.

After they're gone, I turn to Leo. "I'm okay, kind of shook up, but okay. Do you think this was related to Dan taking Olivia?"

"If we find the guy, I plan to ask him."

"How could you find him? If the blood trail stopped, there's no way, right?"

"We found where he parked. There's a river access road. You weren't far from it. The spot has a view of Tammy's house. In fact, I think I saw a pickup there this morning. I didn't think anything of it. Now, I wonder if he was watching us."

"What? Why?"

"I don't know, but it makes sense. He could've watched you take the path, then hope you'd turn upstream. When you did . . . " Leo raises his eyebrows.

"Yeah, when I did, he grabbed me."

We're quiet for several minutes before I say, "You're not going out with the guys looking for Morse, right?"

"I can't. They've been out for hours, and I don't know where they went. I'm going back to your parents' house after I do a few things here . . . not looking for the guy who attacked you but organizing medical supplies. Then I plan to work on some of the homestead projects. Jake said Tate's making Sarah take it easy. He'll bring her over here after lunch for Belinda to check her wound. Mr. Hammer was able to get Evan's truck running well enough to limp it home. Evan said the Hammers' daughter and one of his sons, along with their families, made it here from Texas. They arrived around four this morning."

"Really? That's great. I bet David's relieved."

"For sure. I guess it was quite a journey. They started with four vehicles—each adult driving one in something like a convoy, bringing as much stuff as they could. They ended up arriving in a little economy car with just the five of them and a diaper bag for the baby. Did you know David's son has a little boy just younger than Gavin?"

"No . . . I don't think so. I've never met the ones living in Texas."

Leo nods. "Yeah. They have one more son they're hoping will get here. He lives back east somewhere, maybe in Pennsylvania . . . I can't remember exactly."

"That's not good."

"No, probably not," Leo agrees. "Yeah, well, from what Evan said, they're calling it a miracle his Texas family was even able to drive here. They saw some pretty bad stuff. They stayed off freeways as best they could but ran into trouble in various places."

"Do you think my mom's having the same kind of trouble? That's why she's not yet home?"

Leo looks at me with sad eyes. "I have no doubt your mom's doing her best to get here."

"Sure, I know she is, but that isn't what I asked."

"I don't know, Katie. It just depends on where she is. I suspect some places are pretty bad, but some aren't much different than normal. Most likely, she ran out of gas and couldn't get more. She bought a bike just in case that happened."

"True. She's not much of a bike rider, but she'll get the hang of it quickly." Wanting to change the subject, I ask, "What's happening today?"

"They brought Jake's truck and my truck. Tammy and I need to do a few things to set up and organize better, then I'll head to Jake's house. You'll go home with Jake as soon as he's ready. Belinda has you scheduled back on at eight, right?"

"Yes, that's what she said—eight to midnight. I can sleep here again after my shift."

"Good. I'm midnight to 5:00 a.m. I'll bring you over and I'll just crash on the couch until it's my turn."

"You know, I could drive myself."

"Really?" He puts his hand on my shoulder.

"I guess not."

"No one should drive, or walk, alone now."

I shrug and change the subject again. "So what are we doing at the house? You working on the greenhouse?"

"Probably. I haven't got very far on it yet, other than finalizing my plans to make it bigger than Jake and I originally talked. Jake found more supplies the last couple days, so we should be good for building the larger greenhouse and the three lean-tos for the trailers and motorhome."

"Nice. I assume they're done with their . . . uh, acquisition team?"

"Yes, we've put the kibosh on it."

"I'm glad. I'd be a nervous wreck every time someone went out."

Leo nods as Jake and Alvin walk back in the room.

"Angela looks pretty good," Jake says. "She came around a little. Tim's going to stay with her for a while. Evan's also staying to visit with Doris, and they'll ride back together. We're going to take off. Will you be following shortly?"

My eyes meet Leo's, pleading with him to be ready to leave. He tilts his head to the side.

"Yeah. I have a few things to do, won't take long. Then I'll check in with Belinda."

"Okay, good. You think you can give me a hand for a short while? I'd like to begin putting the new solar systems in place. I thought I'd start on the cabin. Also, I don't think Angela's going to be in any shape to climb the ladder in the Tiny House for some time, so we'll need to move her. Maybe they could move into the bunkhouse with Keith, Lois, and Karen."

"Good idea. The bedroom's large enough to add a bed and some sort of . . . something . . . for Gavin in the room," Leo says.

"She has a playpen we can use as his bed. How long do you think until she can climb the ladder?" I ask.

"Weeks, months. I'm not sure," Leo answers. "Mrs. Hudson will be here shortly to talk with people. Mr. Caldwell . . . Jake . . . were you planning to wait until she shows so you can talk with her?"

"She and I had a chat earlier, when we were over at their place catching up on the Morse situation. I'm doing okay. While I hate that I killed someone, in the same circumstances, I'd do it again. Angela— " Jake swallows hard.

"Angela is . . . well, she's amazing, the way she kept her wits about her and defended herself. Then the other guy coldcocking her—no way I'd let him hurt her any further. I just wish I'd been there a little quicker, then maybe she wouldn't have got her brains rattled."

"Jake, you can't think like that," I say.

He gives a slow nod. "Kelley said the same thing. Don't worry. I'll be okay."

"Leo, I'd like to go ahead and go with Jake and Grandpa Alvin. There's lots to do at home, and I'm not needed here. I also want to make some food to bring over when I return. Doris is only on liquids, and Angela isn't eating yet, but they will be soon."

"Stick with liquids and soft things for now," Leo responds.

"Jake, does Mom still keep bones in the freezer for broth?"

"Yep. Not sure what she has in there, but I can find some for you."

"That'd be good . . . and maybe pudding or Jell-O," Leo says.

"I'll do it. And maybe make a few things for Belinda and Tammy also. I'll see you back at the house." I touch his arm as I walk by.

He stops me and pulls me in tight for a hug. "Take care today. Stay close to the house."

"We're being cautious today," Jake says. "We've posted a sentry. Evan gave us some pointers earlier, and we have plans to expand our security."

Back at the homestead, after saying my hellos to everyone and accepting hugs and accolades pertaining to this morning's attack, I take a quick shower. Then I spend a few minutes catching up with everyone before starting my tasks. Tony, Lily, and TJ are doing better than I expected. Of course, TJ doesn't yet know what's going on with his grandpa. Gavin, Tony, and Lily each say they miss their moms.

Art is on sentry duty. Jake, Alvin, Roy, and Keith are beginning to work on the solar systems. They start with the cabin. They'll disconnect the power and then reconnect it to the Tiny House, giving the Tiny House its own small twelve-volt system.

Angela will be disappointed to give up the Tiny House. As much as she likes Tate's parents, having her own space—even if it's very small and has a compost toilet—was something she was happy about. Maybe she could sleep on the futon until she recovers enough to climb the stairs. I'll ask Leo what he thinks.

Calley and Sheila are in charge of lunch and dinner today. The three of us share the kitchen as I finish my food projects and they start the midday meal. Calley and Sheila aren't their usual, chatty selves. The tension between them is thick, and I do my best to focus on my tasks to complete them as quickly as possible.

At some point, we'll have to make amends. Living in close proximity and needing to work together isn't very conducive to a long-term disagreement. The more I think about how upset Sheila was, the less sense it makes. She was so angry at me. For what? Because I mentioned God?

"Did you know there's a community meeting planned for 5:00 p.m. instead of the later seven o'clock time?" Calley asks, jarring me from my thoughts.

"Really? Why earlier?"

"I'm not really sure. Maybe they liked the earlier time from yesterday? When we were waiting for Tate and Jake to return, someone suggested it. Many others agreed it sounded good. I have to admit, I was only half paying attention with Angela and Doris being hurt."

Leo arrives shortly after noon.

"Hey, Katie, sorry I'm so late. Belinda had Tammy and I sorting and organizing. There's a whole lot more medical supplies than I expected, which is why it took so long. Of course, it's also a finite amount."

"I think Mom and Jake have some supplies."

"Maybe, Jake left some things there this morning."

Leo runs a hand through his hair. "I'm heading to the shower. I have to tell you, I'm sure glad your folks have things set up so we still have hot water. Most people aren't so fortunate."

Leo's right. Today is Thursday, and the power went out Saturday. Most people haven't been able to shower for five days.

We're visiting and putting the finishing touches on lunch when Malcolm comes running in the house.

"Come quick. Dad says he needs you. Come now!"

Calley and I don't hesitate as we run out the door.

Sheila yells behind us, "I'll turn off the stove and be out."

Leo is just coming out of the bathroom. Hearing the commotion, he follows us out.

Jake and Sarah are jumping up and down. Alvin's doing something like . . . I don't know . . . a jig, maybe? Grandma Dodie, also roused by Malcolm, is moving quickly to the group with Gavin in her arms.

"She's okay! She's okay!" Jake is yelling. "We have to go and get her."

"What's going on?" I ask. "Olivia's okay?"

"Mollie! Your mom! I was on the roof and my texter noise thing went off. I had a bunch of texts. One was from your mom. She's on her way home. I know the route and where to find her."

"Mom?! She's coming home?"

"She's coming home." Jake squeezes me into a bear hug. "We're going after her. Leo, I could use your help with this. I know Belinda wants you to stick around here, but Mollie could be injured, and I need you on shotgun."

"Absolutely, sir."

I can barely see from the tears in my eyes. Sarah, Calley, Malcolm, and I keep hugging each other. Our mom is coming home.

"I think we need at least a third person, sir," Leo says.

"Yes, we do. Mike, you up for it?"

"You bet. I've been fine. No dizziness or double vision since the day before yesterday. I'd like to go."

"Okay, then. Roy, how about you?"

"Yep. If I can bring that shotgun of yours."

"It's yours to use," Jake says. "Okay, ten minutes to get everything together. Then we're going to bring Mollie home."

The adventure continues in Mollie's Quest: Havoc in Wyoming, Part 3.

Thank you for spending your time with the people of Bakerville, Wyoming.
If you have five minutes, you'd make this writer very happy if you could write a short Amazon review.

I appreciate you!

Join my reader's club!

Receive a complimentary copy of *Wyoming Refuge: A Havoc in Wyoming Prequel*. As part of my reader's club, you'll be the first to know about new releases and specials. I also share info on books I'm reading, preparedness tips, and more.

Please sign up on my website:

MillieCopper.com

Now Available

Havoc in Wyoming

Part 1: Caldwell's Homestead

Jake and Mollie Caldwell started their small farm and homestead to be able to provide for an uncertain future for their family, friends, and community. They have tried to plan for everything, but they never imagined this would happen.

Part 2: Katie's Journey

Katie loves living on her own while finishing up her college degree, working her part-time jobs, and building a relationship with her boyfriend, Leo. When disaster strikes, being away from family isn't quite so nice, and home is over a thousand miles away. Will she make it home before the United States falls apart?

Part 3: Mollie's Quest

Two or three times a year, Mollie Caldwell travels for business. Being away from her Wyoming farmstead is both a fun time and a challenge. They started their farm to be able to provide for an uncertain future for their family, friends, and community. The farm keeps the entire family busy, meaning extra work for her husband while she's away. This time, while on her business trip, terrorists attack. Her weeklong business trip becomes much longer as she tries to make her way home.

Part 4: Shields and Ramparts

The United States, and the community of Bakerville, face a new threat... a threat that could change America forever. As the neighbors

289

band together, all worry about friends and family members. Have they found safety from this latest danger?

Part 5: Fowler's Snare

Welcome to Bakerville, the sleepy Wyoming community Mollie and Jake Caldwell have chosen as their family retreat. At the edge of the wilderness, far away from the big city, they were so sure nothing bad could ever happen in such a protected place. They were wrong. Now, with the entire nation in peril, coming together as a community is the only way they can survive. But not everyone in the community has the people of Bakerville's best interest at heart.

Part 6: Pestilence in the Darkness

Surrounded by danger, they band together with the community of Bakerville to move to a new defensible location. But they weren't prepared to have to give up so much for the security they so desperately need. And they quickly learn trust must be earned, not freely given.

Part 7: My Refuge and Fortress

When Jake and a group of hunters return to Bakerville and find their former neighbors slaughtered, they realize there is a new, even more deadly threat. Will their reinforced location be secure enough? And what about the radio announcement from the president? Will his promise of help arrive in time?

Find these titles on Amazon:
www.amazon.com/author/milliecopper

Acknowledgments

Thanks to:

Ameryn Tucker, my editor, beta reader, and daughter wrapped in one. I had a story I wanted to tell, and Ameryn encouraged me and helped me bring it to life.

My youngest daughter, Kes, graphic artist extraordinaire, who pulled out the vision in my head and brought it to life to create an amazing cover.

My husband who gave me the time and space I needed to complete this dream and was very patient as I'd tell him the same plot ideas over and over and over.

Two more daughters and a young son who willingly listened to me drone on and on about story lines and ideas while encouraging me to "keep going."

Wayne Stinnett, author (WayneStinnett.com). A few years ago, I was looking for tips on moving my nonfiction PDF books to a new platform. I read Mr. Stinnett's book *Blue Collar to No Collar*, and while there were useful tips for nonfiction, what I really discovered was, I had a story I wanted to tell. As long as I can remember, I'd start creating narratives in my head and, occasionally, move them to paper. *Blue Collar to No Collar*, and specifically Wayne's story, inspired me to move forward. Imagine my thrill and surprise when an email to him received a response and tips on how to proceed in my own publishing. Thank you, Mr. Stinnett! I'm also a fan of his fiction works, *Jesse McDermitt Caribbean Adventure Series* and *Charity Styles Novel Caribbean Thriller Series*—very fun reads!

My amazing Beta Readers! An extra special thanks to Tim M. for his expertise in firearms and all things that go boom, Joe I. for reminding me to keep it simple, and Judy S. for always saying, "I can't wait to find out what happens next!"

And to you, my readers, for spending your time with the people of Bakerville, Wyoming. If you liked this book, please take a moment to leave a review. I appreciate you!

Notes on Katie's Journey

For the fictional Caldwells, preparedness is a lifestyle. Many times, a book like this will result in a wake-up to the need to become prepared. Or for those who are already preparedness-minded, the need to move on to the next level.

To help you with your "prepper" research, I've developed a Pinterest page full of information shared in Katie's Journey. Go to: https://www.pinterest.com/MillieCopper33/havoc-in-wyoming-part-2-katies-journey/

About the Author

Millie Copper, writer of Cozy Apocalyptic Fiction and preparedness mentor, was born in Nebraska but never lived there. Her parents fully embraced wanderlust and moved regularly, giving her an advantage of being from nowhere and everywhere.

Millie Copper lives in the wilds of Wyoming with her husband and young son, tending chickens and attempting a food forest on their small homestead. After living off the grid for several years, they've recently gone back on the grid. Four adult daughters, three sons-in-law, four grandchildren, and one more on the way round out the family.

Since 2009, Millie has authored articles on traditional foods, alternative health, homesteading, and preparedness-many times all within the same piece. Millie has penned seven nonfiction, traditional food focused books, sharing how, with a little creativity, anyone can transition to a real foods diet without overwhelming their food budget.

The twelve-installment *Havoc in Wyoming* Christian Post-Apocalyptic fiction series uses her homesteading, off-the-grid, and preparedness lifestyle as a guide. The adventure continues with the newly released *Montana Mayhem* series.

Find Millie at www.MillieCopper.com
Facebook: www.facebook.com/MillieCopperAuthor/
Amazon: www.amazon.com/author/milliecopper
BookBub: https://www.bookbub.com/authors/millie-copper

Made in the USA
Middletown, DE
26 September 2022